DEATH IN THE STARS

Yorkshire, 1927: Eclipse fever grips the nation, and when beloved theatre star Selina Fellini approaches trusted sleuth Kate Shackleton to accompany her to a viewing party at Giggleswick School Chapel, Kate suspects an ulterior motive. During the eclipse, Selina's friend and co-star Billy Moffatt disappears, and is later found dead in the chapel grounds. Kate soon learns that two other members of the theatre troupe died in similarly mysterious circumstances in the past year. With the help of Jim Sykes and Mrs Sugden, Kate sets about investigating whether there is a murderer in the company — and wonders just who will be next to pay the ultimate price for fame . . .

DEATH IN THE STARS

FRANCES BRODY

ISIS
LARGE
PRINT

First published in Great Britain 2017
by
Piatkus
an imprint of Little, Brown Book Group

First Isis Edition
published 2018
by arrangement with
Little, Brown Book Group
An Hachette UK Company

A catalogue record for this book is available from the British Library.

ISBN 978–1–78541–630–9 (hb)
ISBN 978–1–78541–636–1 (pb)

Published by
F. A. Thorpe (Publishing)
Anstey, Leicestershire

Set by Words & Graphics Ltd.
Anstey, Leicestershire
Printed and bound in Great Britain by
T. J. International Ltd., Padstow, Cornwall

This book is printed on acid-free paper

For Barry Strickland-Hodge,
Steven Dowd, Barbara Gent and the
British Astrological Association

CHAPTER
ONE

The Letter

Southampton
8 June 1927
(In transit — Off to New York!)

Mrs Kate Shackleton
Detective
Batswing Wood Lodge
Headingley
Leeds

Dear Mrs Shackleton
Please forgive this hasty and confidential courtesy note. We met in Wakefield while you were undertaking certain investigations of a delicate nature. I was performing there at the Theatre Royal during a nationwide Gilbert and Sullivan tour. Our company is about to set sail for America where we have many engagements. We hope to impress the Midwest and find a welcome there.
To the point — I hope you will not mind that I recommended you to a friend and gave her your card. My friend is in the same business as I, though her star

gleams far more brightly. Songbirds shush at the sound of her silver-sweet voice.

I told the lady that you are discreet and if ever she needs discretion and investigation, she could do worse than turn to you.

Expect her dulcet call.
With kindest regards,
Giuseppe Barnardini

CHAPTER
TWO

The Northern Star

A week after receiving Mr Barnardini's letter, I was sitting by the window in my drawing room, picking out a tune on the piano. It was a lazy blue sky and white clouds afternoon, the sort that artists like to paint. The garden looked at its best. A robin perched on the firethorn shrub. Bees and a tiger moth butterfly hovered over the buddleia blue chip.

I was playing a music hall song, "The Empress of Ice Cream", and realised that it was because the letter was at the back of my mind. Mr Barnardini had not named his friend but there was just one performer who fitted that bill: Selina Fellini, known as The Silver Songbird. "The Empress of Ice Cream" was one of the songs she had written herself and was a favourite with theatre audiences. I had also heard her sing it on the wireless.

As I played, I watched a Bentley glide by. At first I thought it must be heading for the big house at the top of my street. Mine is a modest dwelling, once the lodge house of the adjacent larger estate, sold when the previous owner's fortunes dwindled. However, a few moments later the car came by again, this time on my side. It stopped by the gate.

3

It was the kind of car that my housekeeper Mrs Sugden says "will get you in anywhere. It'd take you through the gates at Buckingham Palace."

A man, wearing a linen suit and Panama hat, stepped out of the driver's seat and came round to the passenger side. He opened the door.

Glad to have resisted Mrs Sugden's desire to put up net curtains, I stared, blinked and stared again, before deliberately turning my gaze back to the piano. In spite of her hat and veil, I recognised the woman in the linen costume. It was as if, by playing her signature tune, I had summoned the magnificent Selina Fellini. I have seen her perform twice, most recently last year at the Palladium. She is an artiste who crosses boundaries and yet, by all accounts, never forgets her humble beginnings.

She and the man in the linen suit looked at the house and exchanged a few words. The two of them walked up the path. Fortunately, they looked at the door, not the window and so did not catch me ogling. By his gesture, I saw that he would not come in, but that she would. Hastily, I withdrew, ready to answer the door.

I was already in the hall when the knocker tap-tapped. Miss Fellini was standing at a little distance from the step, the man a couple of paces behind. She apologised for calling unannounced, introduced herself and her linen-suited manager, Mr Trotter Brockett.

She is an impressive woman. The briefest way I can describe her is to say that she has a vivid presence. In a crowded room, she would be the one to turn heads.

4

Mr Brockett would not have been out of place on the Riviera. His shirt was the same bright blue as his eyes. He wore a striped navy silk bowtie and a navy handkerchief in his top pocket, a cigar tucked beside it.

I invited them in. Mr Brockett demurred. "Today I am the chauffeur. I shall take a short walk while you and Miss Fellini talk."

Somehow, and this never happens with other clients, we ended up in the kitchen, a pot of tea and a plate of Mrs Sugden's homemade biscuits between us.

As she lifted the veil from her hat, I noticed her wedding ring. Without a trace of make-up, Miss Fellini looked striking, and possibly beautiful, with dark eyebrows, high cheekbones and full lips. She wore her long dark hair in a chignon. A strand had come free and she began to twist it around her finger.

As I poured milk into a jug, she turned her head and looked through the window. "You have a wood. How exciting!"

"I call it Batswing Wood. It used to belong to the family who lived at the top of the street. They sold it to the city about the same time as we bought this lodge house."

"It's lovely here! We lived on Grimston Street when I was growing up. Our door opened straight onto the street. In the summer holidays, our little gang would go adventuring, wandering off to parks and woods. We'd pass houses with great long paths and drives. I always thought about the postman and what a long walk he had to push letters through the door, but your house is just right."

"Thank you! It suits me very well."

Everyone knew her story, the local girl born in a poor but respectable part of the city, daughter of the Fellini ice cream family, and her rise to fame and fortune.

Her twang is still local, as is her directness. "You're a widow, I believe, Mrs Shackleton?"

"Yes. I moved here with my husband before the war."

She sighed. "I admire you for staying put, and for setting up your own enquiry agency. Giuseppe spoke highly of you."

This surprised me just a little because the man hardly knew me. His name came up during an investigation a few years ago. We had spent a very short time chatting together, in a railway station waiting room.

"That's kind of him."

"He doesn't say much about it but I believe he credits you with bringing about his very happy marriage."

I smiled. "I never thought of myself as Cupid."

Matrimonial cases were something that I tried to avoid.

She sensed my wariness. "Don't worry. I'm not here to seek your services in the romance department. I have a husband. He did come back from the war, though much changed." A brief sigh gave away more than she intended about her marriage. "He is not the carefree fellow who marched away."

"Are you here in connection with your husband?"

She looked startled, as if I had asked a question too soon. "Oh no, not that." She busied herself taking another biscuit. Everything suited her. "These biscuits are very good."

For several minutes, we talked about biscuits. She explained the Fellini method of baking ice cream cones.

By way of encouraging her to say more about her reason for calling on me, I mentioned the letter. "Mr Barnadini didn't say why you might wish to see me."

"Ah, no, he wouldn't." She hesitated in a way that made me wonder whether she had changed her mind about confiding in me. Perhaps it was some delicate matter that at the last moment she could not bring herself to put into words.

Only after I poured another cup of tea did Miss Fellini begin.

"I do have a difficulty."

It was a difficulty that most people would give a week's wages to enjoy. At the invitation of the headmaster of Giggleswick School, the Astronomer Royal, Sir Frank Dyson, and his party would be setting up their cameras and measuring equipment there in order to view the eclipse from high ground near the school chapel. Giggleswick is close to the village of Langcliffe. While staying in Langcliffe, I had seen the chapel's shining dome from a distance. It is visible for miles across the dales.

With the Astronomer Royal's permission, the headmaster had also extended invitations to others, including Miss Fellini. The date of the eclipse was Wednesday, 29 June — just two weeks hence.

"Well that's wonderful."

"I should like you to come with me. So much could go wrong. There's the time the journey would take, and I have a show every night. There might be an accident on the road, or a train could be delayed. I've made no arrangements and we're just two weeks off."

"Let me look at my diary." Somewhat puzzled by what seemed exaggerated anxieties, I went into the dining room which doubles as an office, and picked up my diary. I had matters to attend to during the next two weeks, but the date of the eclipse was free.

Back in the kitchen, I told her that I would be available for that day, if she needed me to go with her.

She nodded. "I do. You see, I'm not sure why I've been invited, though I suppose it's something of an honour."

It was obvious to me why anyone would invite her. "The astronomers will be viewing the sun and the moon. They want to be sure of a star to add to the mix."

She laughed. "That could be one explanation and I would love to see the eclipse but I'm concerned about the journey."

She explained her worries. Everyone knew the roads would be clogged and the railways packed. Miss Fellini was in the middle of a tour and with performances every evening could not risk being caught up in heavy traffic. Both her manager and her dresser urged her to be home in time to take a nap before the show. It would probably be necessary to take a flight.

She asked would I arrange transport from her house near Roundhay Park, to ensure that she would not be delayed. If I were her companion for the event she would feel confident. Neither her manager nor her dresser, Beryl, would take to the air.

A streak in my nature takes pride in dealing with practicalities and finding solutions. "It's short notice, but I do know a couple of airmen who fly a de Havilland."

She gave me the smile that shines from posters, picture postcards and magazines. "That would be wonderful."

"It's a small plane."

"There would just be the three of us, Mrs Shackleton, you, me and Billy Moffatt. He's a friend and a very funny and delightful man."

"Yes, I have seen him perform." He was a comedian people loved, one who tapped into life's disappointments and distress. He turned worries into comedy and drew roars of laughter from misfortune.

"Miss Fellini, I'll happily telephone my friends — for three passengers?"

"Yes, you must come. Billy would be no good in an emergency. He claims his interest is in gathering material for a few jokes. And it's Selina. May I call you Kate?"

She could call me anything she liked in return for the opportunity to see the eclipse.

That word emergency should have alerted me, but it was said so lightly that I almost let it pass. Truth be told I was delighted to be in the company of such a wonderfully talented person with a reputation for kindness and generosity. Yet my usual caution was not entirely brushed away.

She must have other people who could organise the journey for her. I asked why she had come to me. Waving away my remarks, she said Giuseppe Barnardini had told her that I knew people who operated a small plane out of Croydon and that, unlike many of the barely qualified pilots who were offering jaunts for ten guineas a time, these airmen were highly respected, even in government circles.

"How did he know about my connection with Croydon aerodrome?"

"Oh, he has friends all over the place. He said you are the soul of discretion and utterly reliable. I know he has an old school chum in some government department."

That smile again. Such warmth and intimacy. It was easy to see why people spoke so well of her, and those who hardly knew her thought of her as a friend.

In the hall, I made the telephone call. It took me some time to be connected to Charlie, the pilot. He jumped at the chance of coming to Leeds for a short flight to Giggleswick and back.

"We're taking a photographer up there the night before and bringing him back the next day so I can easily squeeze you in."

"Thank you! Where will you land? Miss Fellini lives near Roundhay Park."

There was a slight pause, while his brain ticked. "As I remember, there's a field in Roundhay, Soldiers Field?"

"Yes. That's near Miss Fellini's house."

"Then that should be the place. I'll check for permission and let you know."

I went back into the kitchen to tell Selina the good news.

She was examining her perfect nails. She had heard my side of the conversation and beamed. "I must write to Giuseppe and thank him for putting me in touch with you."

Again, that niggle of doubt crept in. She must know scores of people who could arrange a flight. It was odd that she should ask an investigator to arrange transport.

"Giuseppe said that he recommended me in case you ever needed an investigator."

She picked up her gloves. "I was in a blue funk the day I spoke to him. I had a feeling that something bad might happen. If this eclipse passes off smoothly, I'll know everything will be all right and that I was worrying unnecessarily."

Trotter Brockett, the manager who drove the Bentley, had found his way into Batswing Wood at the back of my house. I spotted him through the kitchen window, and so did she.

"Thank you so much, Kate. I'm glad I came. Will you come to an eclipse party on the night of the 28th at my house?" She gave me her card. "Then we can go straight from the party to Giggleswick."

"Thank you. I'd like that."

She moved quickly, pushing back her chair, standing. She intended to avoid my questions.

11

I was not a slowcoach, nor too star-struck to push for an answer. "Selina, what really brought you here? There's something else."

She gave an exaggerated shrug. "It's too ridiculous. I've been overwrought."

"Can you tell me more?"

"Not really. It was my fevered imagination. We theatricals are good at drama."

We were walking along the hall towards the front door. Close up I could smell her perfume. It had a musky scent, the kind of scent that might mask fear. In one of those fleeting moments of insight, I wished I had suggested my assistant Jim Sykes go with her to Giggleswick. Perhaps what she needed was not a friendly female detective escort but a sturdy bodyguard. "You said, regarding the flight, that your friend Billy Moffatt would be no good in an emergency. Are you expecting some kind of emergency?"

"Did I say that? I suppose I'm just a little wary about flying. I'm glad you'll be there."

I opened the door.

The effusive Mr Brockett came along the path to gather up Selina. "What a wonderful little wood you have at the back, Mrs Shackleton. Splendid! Splendid!"

"Thank you." His warmth of manner and congratulations were such that he might be giving me credit for planting every tree.

He escorted Selina to the car and then came hurrying back. I glanced at the path to see whether he had dropped one of his kid gloves.

"Sorry, Mrs Shackleton. I know I'm a fusspot. Selina just told me that you'll accompany her to Giggleswick. I'll be most grateful if you will protect her. She's very precious to me, and too kind for her own good. Total strangers make demands on her and she is very bad at batting them off, if you take my meaning."

"I'll do my best, Mr Brockett."

"And do please make sure she returns in good time for a proper rest before her evening show."

"Yes of course."

He thanked me, and turned to wave from the gate. I felt an odd sense of foreboding as I watched the car draw away towards Headingley Lane. Perhaps Mr Brockett was wise in refusing to take to the skies and make for Giggleswick. Perhaps he knew something that I did not.

It was only later that it occurred to me that she had not mentioned her husband by name. I remembered reading his name once, in a magazine article. Jarrod Compton.

CHAPTER
THREE

Corridor of Darkness

It was such a privilege to be on the Giggleswick invitation list that I for one had memorised instructions. Over Britain, totality would take place shortly before 05.30 GMT when the altitude of the sun would be only about 12 degrees. We were asked to be present and correct by 4.00 a.m. in order to ensure an orderly procedure.

I felt excited at the prospect of flying in a chartered plane to such a unique event, as well as being a smidgen daunted to be wearing a mantle of responsibility. The immensely popular variety star Selina Fellini, dubbed The Silver Songbird, and her comedian chum Billy Moffatt had placed their trust in me.

Everyone else who was setting off for Richmond, for Settle, for Giggleswick or Barden Moor by road or rail had long gone. With numbers expected to be in the millions, and over seventy thousand people converging on the Yorkshire Dales, day trippers needed to allow plenty of time.

To be on the safe side, Selina, Billy and I left her house at 3.00 a.m., to meet the airmen.

The sky was dark and, as predicted, clouds hid the moon. Wet grass gave off a sharp fresh scent. Selina's house was set back, in a considerable acreage, but as we left it behind, I saw lights twinkling in other distant houses. Nearby, a group of unsteady partygoers, linking arms and singing, called a greeting. It was the kind of night when perfect strangers decided they had more in common than might ever have been imagined. A lone man, swaying his way home, whistled an old wartime tune. Billy Moffatt linked arms, with me on one side and Selina on the other. "This'll be the best part. Camaraderie. Expectation before disappointment. Make the most of it!" His voice carried across the night air as we took our shortcut across a field.

The whistling man on the nearby path recognised Billy's voice. He stopped his whistling and called the comedian's catchphrase. "It ain't funny! It's proper sad!"

Billy called back. "Well said, that man. It's sad and it'll get sadder." He lowered his voice. "Folk are easily amused. And they think I'm kidding." He shouted into the darkness. "I'm not kidding!"

The whistler laughed. "Wait till I tell the wife who I met in the dark."

Billy carried a flashlight, holding it steady, which surprised me given how much he had drunk. And it was not just drink. I understood only too well that injury and grief led men like Billy to relieve the pain of wartime wounds in whatever ways they could. The partygoers, out of respect for Selina's wishes, smoked their cigarettes on the terrace. A smoky atmosphere affected her voice. She had confided that on the occasions when they went for a drink after a show, she would seek out those public houses that catered to the needs of performers, such as the Wrens, which kept a bar free from smoke. Yet other indulging had been quite open during the party. Two of the dancers wore little gold boxes on chains around their necks.

Billy squeezed my arm. "As I was saying before I was so rudely interrupted by a member of the paying public, far be it from me to put a damper on proceedings but . . ." He stopped dead, raised the flashlight to his face, wiggling his ears, rolling his eyes and pursing his lips to a shush. Suddenly, he shifted the beam and picked out a young fox, its head turned towards us. Held in the glare, the animal did not move. We, too, froze to the spot. Billy lowered the beam. A cloud shifted, revealing the new moon which lit the tip of the fox's tail as it loped off towards Roundhay Park. Did animals sense what was to come, have some instinct that the world, or at least our part of it, would soon be trapped in a tunnel of darkness?

A mist wrapped itself around us. We had crossed the first field and our shoes now tapped the pavement. Billy's boots rang out, steel tips on paving stones. Perhaps it was the sound of our own strides that changed the mood.

We crossed the road towards the Soldiers Field, so called because that was where soldiers mustered during the last war, and probably other earlier wars.

My shiver was from a sense of excitement and anticipation, not due to the chill. Miss Fellini, or Selina as I am asked to call her, had wanted to help me into a fur coat, saying how cold it would be on the journey and during our wait in the school grounds. But the fur coat turned me into a brown bear. I stuck with my British wool.

We lapsed into silence. The ground here was a little soggy. A ferocious cricket match or hobnail boot races had churned up the grass. My feet sank a little into the earth.

There would not be another such day as this for seventy-two years, the scientists said. The world, strange as it seemed, would by then be going on without us; strange because Selina Fellini seemed larger than life itself with her dark hair and dramatic Italian beauty. Her voice enchanted, her patter left audiences in stitches. She could sing musical comedy and opera equally well. Unlike some performers on the new wireless programme from the British Broadcasting studio in Leeds, she sounded almost like her real self, warm and tuneful.

Seventy-two years hence, perhaps some echo of that sound on the airwaves might reverberate through the world. By then, Billy Moffatt's jokes would be long out of fashion. No one would remember his well-known catchphrases that audiences loved. "What's tickled your fancy, cos it ain't funny." "It's proper sad, that's what it is." At that evening's performance, at the City Varieties, he had made a joke about the eclipse, based on a weather forecast of the probability of cloud. "Probability? Probability? Are you daft? This is Yorkshire. We deal in certainties. Course there'll be cloud. I've put me hard-earned brass on it." The audience roared with appreciation.

So he must certainly be there for the eclipse. He already knew what tale he would tell when next on stage. It was rehearsed, he had confided in me, over a special Eclipse Cocktail. He would tell a tale of the tens of thousands flocking to vantage points across Wales and the North of England before dawn, optimists all. He would imitate the chug-chugging trains from north and south, the discomfort of charabanc passengers, the roar of motorcycles and the screaming frustration of being caught in a procession of cars on usually empty roads. Punters turning up to watch the one-night-only special duet of sun and moon, they all had too much hope and imagination. Well that ain't funny. Folk ought to choose their disappointments more carefully in future.

I smiled, though it wasn't really amusing to think all our efforts might be for nought. Perhaps it is the way he tells them on stage, with his actions and his expressions.

As we crossed the field, my eyes adjusted to a different kind of darkness. There had been some shift in the clouds. The small plane became visible, a strange and lonely shape waiting in the blackness. A mist rose. Two figures stood near the plane. The tip of a cigarette glowed. A strange feeling came over me, a familiarity with the scene, a memory or a dream.

It gave me an extraordinary feeling of confidence to know that Charlie and Joe, pilot and engineer, would be flying us to Giggleswick.

Billy saw them too. He was linking my arm and his grip became tighter, betraying a sudden tension that he covered with a joshing remark. "Nah then, Kate, tell me they'll have kettle on in Giggleswick, or might we expect champagne?"

"I've no idea what to expect. If there's to be champagne it'll be after the chaps from Greenwich have done their work, and the schoolboys been packed back indoors."

Selina laughed. "They'll need more than a kettle, the numbers that'll be there."

Billy came to a sudden halt unbalancing we two on either side. "Hang on a minute! Schoolkids?"

"Well Billy, it is a school." I wondered if what he sniffed, swallowed or injected impaired his concentration. Did he really think that pupils would be kept indoors on such a momentous occasion? "This will be educational! It's an experience the boys will remember for the rest of their lives. Sir Frank wants to bring in the young and spark their interest in science and astronomy."

Billy groaned. "You might have told me. Disappointed adults, that's one thing. Disappointed kids, that ain't funny."

Selina withdrew her arm from his and strode ahead a few yards. "We won't be disappointed, Billy. We're going to see the eclipse and there hasn't been one for over two hundred years. Can't you turn your story around that? The Astronomer Royal wouldn't have chosen that spot if he didn't believe we had the best chance there."

Billy took his time answering. "It ain't triumphs make a funny routine, Selina, it's disasters and humiliations, just like in real life." He sighed. "I suppose I could make a joke of the name. I couldn't have conjured a better name if I'd made it up. What sort of a place is Giggleswick anyway, when it's at home?"

He had asked me this before, earlier in the evening, but since then had slipped away to take whatever he takes, and so I explained again. "It's a village in the Dales, Billy, close to Settle."

"Aye well it must have no theatre or I'd have played there."

"Giggleswick School Chapel is on high ground. That's why the headmaster invited the Astronomer Royal to view the eclipse from that spot."

Selina had gone quiet. She was looking at the aeroplane, which loomed large now that we drew so close. Billy relaxed his hold on my arm. He said softly, "Never been up in the air."

Selina cleared her throat. "Neither have I."

Perhaps that was why I was with them, a kind of lucky charm, someone who had flown before. I knew Selina to be superstitious because although she had not yet made it clear why my services were needed, beyond booking Charlie, Joe and their aeroplane, she had said something slightly odd during this evening's party. She mentioned that during the past year there had been fatalities within the company. The deaths were ruled accidental. Her dreams were disjointed and troubling. She feared that "something might happen". Before I could press her on the matter, we were interrupted by tipsy dancers from the Daisy Chain troupe, pressing us to join a conga. The matter of non-accidental deaths hung in the air. I had no further opportunity to ask her what she feared.

The feeling that she was keeping something back had grown so slowly that it half seemed like my own invention.

The de Havilland 50, with its stylish slope, snootily pointed its nose in the air, as if it might just decide to take off alone if it felt like it. The plane had the kind of shape a schoolboy might draw, with wings having an extra shelf to them.

Billy sniffed the air. "Is it leaking?"

"It's Castrol engine oil," I answered as memories flooded back. Ever after, the smell of engine oil would also bring back the scent of Selina Fellini's perfume. I could not identify the underlying notes of that scent, but it was expensive. A dab would go a long way.

Billy whispered, "I won't mind for myself if the aeroplane drops from the sky. But I'd be sorry about you and Selina. She's my ally and my closest friend."

It had not occurred to me that the plane might drop from the sky. My father had called at the house yesterday while I was out. It was nothing important, he had told Mrs Sugden. He just happened to be in Leeds. They would see me on Sunday, as usual. I should have telephoned him.

The clouds parted. Lit by the moon, Charlie the pilot, the taller of the two, strode towards us, smiling a greeting. Joe the engineer followed.

I introduced them to Selina and Billy. Joe, a typical jovial airman, with the familiar small moustache, expressed his delight and for a moment I thought he would kiss Selina's hand. That would have been far too French.

Charlie explained how long the flight should take and that we were to land on the school cricket pitch which would be lit for us. "After that we're taking a newspaper reporter and photographer up into the line of totality so that they can describe the event from above the clouds and take pictures above cloud level. When the show's over, we'll be flying the *Evening News* photographer back to London, but we'll drop you off back here in the field, and see you safely home."

Joe looked from Selina to Billy. "Now, anyone not flown before?"

When he had asked that same question some years earlier, I was the one to put up my hand. This time it was Selina and Billy's turn to receive instructions and reassurance.

Moments later, I was climbing into the plane. A sudden sense of anxiety spread through my body ending somewhere around my heart, a kind of tightening. I tried to pinpoint the fear, to name it. My fear wasn't for the flight though I wondered how the pilot would find his way to a remote spot in the Yorkshire Dales in darkness. My thoughts were suddenly filled with "What ifs". A single stubborn cloud might spoil all the work of astronomers and scientists who had laboured long towards this extraordinary phenomenon. The countrywide fever of

22

expectation and excitement might turn into a big national failure, a waste of effort, a squandering of hope with damp and drizzle snuffing out nature's miracle. A theatrical flop.

Yet several astronomical camps had been set up by the men from Greenwich, crossing the line of totality that stretched from Cardigan Bay in Wales to Hartlepool in the North East. Someone must come through and successfully record what needed to be known for knowledge to move forward.

Within moments, the plane was revving for take-off. The engine began to hum. Selina crossed herself. She leaned in close to me and whispered, "I'm sorry, Kate. I shouldn't have put you in danger."

"We're not in danger. Charlie and Joe are the most experienced airmen. I'd trust them with my life."

For a fraction of a second, the moon lit her face. She bit her lip but did not speak.

Perhaps out of nervousness, Billy began to spout one of his catchphrases but the noise of the engine drowned his words.

I was sitting close to Selina and would have been aware had she given off waves of anxiety about this journey, but after crossing herself she sat quite calmly. If it was not the flight she regarded as putting me in danger, then what?

At that moment, Joe leaned in close. "We're entering what will be the corridor of darkness."

CHAPTER
FOUR

The Eclipse of Death

It was strange to look down through the darkness to the world below. Long rows of slowly moving traffic were heading towards vantage points. The yellow lights from car headlights glowed like the eyes of a crawling giant snake.

I could dimly make out the shapes of houses. Selina sat very still, hands clasped as if in prayer. Billy kept up a chirpy monologue, barely audible until he raised his voice above the sound of the engine to deliver punch lines. Although he is extremely entertaining, I wished he would be quiet.

Suddenly, he made a grab for my shoulder. "Look at that!" He pointed to the land beneath.

We were above open ground and there was a bonfire below. A group of people moved and swayed, dancing around the fire as if in some strange ritual.

Billy leaned close. "Wild runs the noble savage, beating his drums against the swallowing of the sun. Now peasants rage because the light of the world is to be extinguished."

The scene vanished from sight as the plane continued on its course. We were above the clouds now.

Billy became silent. For the rest of the journey no one spoke.

I hugged my arms close, glad to have brought a muff. Here we were in June and my feet felt like blocks of ice. Selina was wrapped in her furs. I thought of the fox we saw as we crossed the field, caught in the glow of Billy's torch, and of what was sacrificed so that we human beings might enjoy our present comforts. Selina had confided that men made her presents of furs. They expected nothing, only the knowledge that their gift might keep her warm. Sometimes she passed them on, to her dresser, to her family. Of course, she could afford to buy her own furs. It was said that she could command two hundred pounds a week. Yet her present tour of the Northern music halls was a benefit, for the support of those entertainers who had been less successful than herself.

A call from the pilot made me look down again. Lights had been spread, a runway created. We were above the grounds of Giggleswick School. That must be the cricket pitch. Everything had been thought of. Slowly, the plane came to meet the earth, its wheels juddering as we bumped across the field.

Charlie and Joe jumped out first, extending a hand to help first Selina, then me and then Billy from the plane. Charlie was talking to Selina, asking how she felt. Billy looked a little wobbly but was grinning, looking across at the boys in Officer Training Corps uniforms who formed a line along the perimeter of the cricket pitch.

A small party emerged from the gloom to greet us, led by a tall thin figure in dark suit and muffler. "That'll be him," Billy whispered. "I might make something of this, a man who spends his life staring at the stars." Billy moved to be close to Selina, for whom the gentleman was making a beeline. Part of Billy's act was to create characters and give them comic monologues. I wondered if we might soon expect an impersonation of the Astronomer Royal.

Of course it was not Sir Frank Dyson who stepped forward to greet us but, quite rightly, the headmaster of Giggleswick School, Mr Douglas, and his wife, along with the school's head boy, Alex McGregor, a lad of about eighteen, clad in the Officer Training Corps uniform.

After exchanging a few words, Mr Douglas led Charlie and Joe away, in search of the *Evening News* reporter and photographer whom they would be taking back to London in a few hours' time, once the official photograph had been developed.

Mrs Douglas ushered us to the cricket pavilion where we met Mrs Dyson, the Astronomer Royal's wife, and her young daughter, Ruth. The girl looked shy at being introduced to Selina. She was at that awkward age I remembered so well, her hat tilted at a jaunty angle. As she tugged at one of her knee-length stockings to pull out the wrinkles, I noticed that she was clutching an autograph book.

Finding seats for us at one of the smaller tables, Mrs Douglas, the headmaster's wife, drew Selina into conversation. Billy amused Mrs Dyson and Ruth with a few jokes from his performance of the night before. The head boy, Alex McGregor, brought a tray of tea and homemade biscuits. If we needed anything, we must ask him, he said, and later he would show us to our viewing point. Mrs Douglas urged Ruth not to be shy about asking for autographs. "Whose do you have so far, Ruth?"

"The prime minister's, all the chaps from Greenwich and the cameramen from two of the film companies, Gaumont and Pathé. I've still to find British Polychromide and one other whose name I forget." Buoyed up by her success so far, Ruth somewhat shyly asked Selina if she would sign her book. Selina graciously obliged, resting the book on the table and drawing a little picture with the caption *The Day the Sun Stood Still*.

A woman at a nearby table held a camera that had a clock drive attached, made from Meccano parts. I exchanged a few words with her, feeling a pang of envy and regret. People in my local photographic society had been exchanging advice and ideas about how to photograph the eclipse. Annie Maunder's book *Camera Work in the Eclipse* had been widely circulated and avidly read. Because I was here "on duty" with Miss Fellini, I would forego this once in a lifetime opportunity, though I had slipped a camera into my bag. It wouldn't do for the eclipse, but there might be some other moment worth capturing. I was already aware of the hundreds of people gathering just beyond the school walls, and I was keen to take a look about, though the light was poor.

Mrs Douglas had moved away from the table. I glanced at Selina. She smiled. "Mrs Douglas has gone to find two senior boys to show me round the school premises." There was a sigh in her voice and I felt a stab of guilt that perhaps this was just why I was here, to save her from extremes of hospitality.

Something was required of me. "Do you want me to come with you, or to get you out of it?"

"No it's all right, but I need to find Billy first. Will you wait here and I'll bring him back? He likes to stroll about earwigging and I do want us to be together for the big moment."

Young Ruth Dyson and I were left at the table together. "I'm glad Miss Fellini is bringing Mr Moffatt back. I'd be sorry to miss his autograph. We saw him once in Wembley. He was so funny."

"Yes he is, and good company, too."

"Is he well? Only I thought he looked a bit poorly earlier, just before he dashed off. Some people are really very nervous about today. Even I had a headache this morning."

"I'm sure he'll be fine."

As might be expected from the Astronomer Royal's daughter, Ruth was well-informed and began to give me details of the equipment and of the other spots across the country where Greenwich astronomers had set up camp. "We all went into the chapel early this morning for a service and to pray that the clouds would part if only for the crucial moment."

When Billy returned, looking more cheerful, he happily signed Ruth's book and included a catchphrase

28

and a stick-man drawing. We then went to explore, walking across the cricket pitch towards the domed chapel. The area in front of the chapel was dotted with tents and items of equipment. Pointing out a telescope, Ruth explained that the instruments had been stored in light huts, specially erected to protect them. "The sun's rays will be reflected into that telescope by means of a mirror that moves by clockwork as the sun moves. It has something called a seleostat. The men named it Joshua."

"Joshua?"

"They give everything names. Nothing to do with the Bible, they just love that song, you know the negro spiritual, 'Joshua Fit the Battle of Jericho'. Fit means fought. Mother said Daddy's men are the best kind of warriors, armed with knowledge." She pointed to another telescope. "That one has a prism in front of the glass to catch the light of the sun's crescent just as it is dispersing."

"My goodness, what's that?" Visitors were gathered round a very long structure and being asked to step back.

"That's a specially made camera, forty-five feet along. I believe that's the one that allows pictures to be taken as if the sun stands still. The photograph will be developed straightaway and the press photographers will copy it." She pointed out a man setting up some paraphernalia over by the chapel. "He's not with us. He's come with recording equipment from the BBC to test whether the eclipse will have an effect on radio waves."

"You've certainly found out such a lot."

"Yes. I came up early with Daddy. It's the second time I've been."

One of the masters called to the OTC boys who began to form a line across the area where the equipment stood. Arms outstretched, in a way that must make them ache, they stood on guard, preventing observers from coming too close. Alex, the head boy, was on the end and gave a little wave.

We inspected the monster camera and dutifully gathered round to stare but not touch. Miss Dyson gave a little speech of explanation. It was hoped that not only would there be still photographs of the eclipse but a cinematograph film would be created. That was why the film companies were here. She adopted an apologetic tone. "Daddy's chaps would be able to explain it all properly but they've too much on today."

"It's a mammoth operation, Ruth."

"I know, and it has been planned for so long. The Astronomer Royal previous to Daddy made the first plan, and Daddy came last year. The chaps have spent ages setting up equipment, taking measurements, making preparations. There are other Greenwich encampments across the line of totality, so somewhere there'll be success. I just hope it's here. Daddy feels lucky about it."

I glanced inside a tent where men were working by lamplight. Two huddled over a table. One held a millboard and pencil. An air of tense concentration spilled from inside the canvas. It reminded me of the feeling one gets if standing close to runners while they wait for the starting pistol. Three more men were just standing, smoking, waiting. One of them was the prime minister. Mother would be most upset if I did not make myself known to Mr Baldwin, or Stanley as she called him. They were on good terms, and my aunt was a close friend of his wife, Lucy. Nevertheless, I left Mr Baldwin to his own devices.

Mrs Douglas, the headmaster's wife, appeared at our shoulder. She glared at the men and all but tut-tutted. If they had been her husband's pupils I felt sure she would have told them to extinguish their cigarettes. "We've asked all the villagers and everyone in the surrounding area not to light fires until after 5.30 this morning. There is a good deal of smoke when a fire is first lit and it could impair the view." Ostensibly she spoke to me but her words were for the benefit of the smokers. The men, puffing away like steam trains, paid no heed.

Having arrived far too early because organisation demanded we should all be in place, there had been time for our blood to freeze and teeth to chatter hard enough to make jaws ache. Selina had been interviewed for her opinions and expectations, photographed by newspaper photographers and the cinematographic cameramen.

A wireless connection had been rigged up and the BBC's six-dot signals sounded at 5a.m. and 5.15. Silence fell as the time neared. We three stood side by side, Selina, Billy and I. In the early light, the sight all around the grounds and beyond was extraordinary.

Beyond the school, all along the hills, were thousands of people, a great mass of humanity. In spite of the line of OTC boys and the policeman on the gate, dozens of girls and young women had hitched themselves astride the surrounding dry stone walls.

Bitter cold travelled from the soles of my shoes and turned my feet and legs to blocks of ice. I pulled down my hat, having lost feeling in my gloved fingers even inside the muff. My cloche didn't prevent my ears from freezing sufficiently to drop off. My eyeballs turned to glass. Never had ground felt so cold. The goose bumps on my legs grew to the size of potatoes. I thought of the people we had seen by the bonfire as we had flown over the countryside. Was that how ancient man and woman kept fear at bay? We were one with those people of long-gone centuries, gathering according to some instinct that preservation or destruction depended on how they danced, sang or sacrificed. Whether we feared or welcomed nature's proceedings, joining in came from some deep impulse. The tens of thousands had gathered on the hilltops and hillsides like the sun worshippers of old. My brain seemed no longer to belong to me. I was part of something altogether bigger.

Someone from Sir Frank's party called out, "Five minutes!"

Amid the murmur that followed the announcement, Billy whispered, "It ain't funny." A deep silence descended.

Four minutes to go, and the sky was cloudy, as weather forecasters had predicted. It would be the most awful shame for all these men from Greenwich if their efforts were in vain and we saw nothing. We had all been supplied with goggles made of a single piece of cardboard with tiny eye screens. I reached in my pocket and brought out my goggles, ready to raise them.

"Three minutes," a voice called.

Yet for the birds that had started their dawn chorus in the usual fashion, this was a morning like any other, where even birdsong took on immense poignancy. After the three-minute call, a lark sang. The great invasion of their territory by humans onto their dawn doings did not worry the birds or stop their chorus.

We within the area of the school chapel were all quiet but such was the excitement beyond the school, all along the path by the wall that divided us, a collective whisper rose.

The sky remained cloudy. Billy would have his comic monologue of disappointment and wasted effort. We were in for a gigantic flop. At "two minutes", the whispering from beyond the dry stone wall faded. At "one minute" came a collective intake of breath and the rustle of sleeves as goggles were brought to the ready. The OTC boys were all standing together and as one they raised goggles to their eyes. In the dim light, the effect was extraordinary. The dark centres of their protective goggles turned their eyes to empty sockets, creating a platoon of boys with skeletons' heads.

Miraculously, the clouds parted at twenty-three minutes and thirty seconds after five o'clock.

The prayers of that morning had been answered. The clouds had parted just in time for us watchers to witness the eclipse. Sir Frank Dyson and his men were lucky indeed, and so were we.

As the moon began to blot the sun, shadow fell, deep and dark and bitter. The world turned utterly bleak and icy cold. Slowly, light abandoned us. Birds stopped singing. Stillness enveloped us. Now and forever silence and darkness would hold. We all knew it. The light of the world died. And then a voice grown hollow was counting aloud, counting the seconds.

From the deep grave of darkness came some stirring in the air, a hesitant light. Behind me, someone sighed. A circle of colour appeared, as if splattered from small brushes. An unseen crayon, pink and orange, outlined an oddly shaped black cloud as if mapping some new country in the sky. There was a sigh of relief as the light grew. We there on that dawn had witnessed the eclipse, watched earth snatched into the void, and then returned to us.

We could see again. The chapel, the ungainly instruments, the puny tents, the hills beyond, and each other, all came back to life.

The silence stretched and then suddenly a cheer went up and a great sense of relief swept through the crowd. There were hoorahs and applause and as hands clapped, two young men from the Greenwich party flung out their arms and in time with the clapping of their fellows began to dance a fandango.

Selina joined in, laughing and clapping and then humming and improvising a fandango tune, like some American jazz singer. One of the young men held out a hand and she began to dance with him. She whirled and twirled. The dance did not last long. Selina parted from the young man with a smile. He kissed her cheek and returned with his fellows to their instruments and measurements. The schoolboys from the Officer Training Corps began to speak to guests and escort people from the chapel grounds.

It would be a little while yet before Charlie and Joe returned from taking the reporter and photographer into the line of darkness. I turned to Selina, ready to speak, to ask would she come for refreshments. Even after our airmen returned, we might have a wait until the official photograph was developed, to be taken to London for the *Evening News*.

Selina's gaiety of a moment before had fled. She gulped. "Billy." She was looking about for Billy Moffatt. Only Billy wasn't there.

She then caught sight of the OTC lads, over by the chapel, taking their cue from the Greenwich scientists and dancing. A small crowd had gathered. "He'll be over there, showing off." She laughed with relief. "He'll be dancing the fandango."

We set off in the direction of the chapel, unaware that we had witnessed not just an eclipse, but the eclipse of death.

CHAPTER
FIVE

Missing

Watching such an extraordinary occurrence had left me slightly wobbly at the knees and queasy in the gut. Perhaps Billy had experienced a similar queasiness to mine and had gone to find the facilities because he was no longer among the OTC boys who had now been rounded up by a master and given some new task. Alex, the solicitous head boy, remained watchful and keen to be of service. He had clearly been appointed to take care of Selina.

"Where is Billy?" Selina asked. "We said we would stay together."

We looked about. Now that I could turn away from the heavens and return to earth, I was almost over-whelmed by the numbers of people. Women and girls were still sitting astride the dry stone wall, wondering how best to get down. Having clambered up there in darkness they realised that climbing down in the light challenged modesty and the preservation of stockings. There was much merriment as OTC lads began to help them down.

A few people went into the chapel, for reassurance or prayer. I guessed Billy would not be among that number. Most observers were now leaving, making their way to cars or to the railway station. The party from Greenwich were still about their business, checking their equipment, jotting down figures, comparing notes.

Alex stepped forward. "He can't be far away. If you want to get a cup of tea and warm up, I'll take a look for Mr Moffatt and let him know where you are. Mrs Douglas has made arrangements for you to take tea in the dining hall."

I thanked him.

"Don't mench!" He grinned and went off to find Billy.

Selina looked suddenly ghastly, stricken. I touched her hand. "It's over. We can relax. Let's go into the school and warm up. It's only a few minutes' walk down the path."

She shook her head. "I can't bear it if something has happened to Billy."

"What do you mean?"

"Something has happened. I had a feeling something bad would happen today but I told myself it was just anxiety. I thought if I were here, and if you were here, everything would be all right. I should have held his hand."

Billy was a little old to need his hand holding in public. My dealings with highly strung performers are strictly limited. Should I share Selina's concern, or reassure her?

"Billy's probably hurried to the front of the queue for tea and toast, or champagne." I spotted Miss

Dyson, still clutching her autograph book, and waved to her.

She came over beaming with pride. "Wasn't it wonderful? Daddy is such a lucky man. He's cock-a-hoop that the clouds parted."

"Yes, we're so fortunate. Now, have you seen Billy Moffatt?"

She shook her head. "Some people have gone to the pavilion." She glanced at Selina and picked up on the sense of urgency. "He's such a popular person. Someone will have swept him off. Shall I hurry ahead and see if he's there?"

I thanked her. "Yes, and we'll catch up."

Billy was clad in the uniform of dark mackintosh and trilby hat. Selina called Billy's name and a similarly clad man of the same height turned. He was not Billy. When the man turned to look at Selina he appeared singularly disappointed that he was not Billy.

"I'm making a fool of myself." She strode on, looking at her feet. "He's just thoughtless. He's so thoughtless."

It had become obvious during the hours in his company that Billy's old war wounds caused him pain. Usually, he hid the fact well. On stage, he performed odd little stretching and twisting contortions. Off stage he sometimes disappeared for ten minutes and reappeared looking better. I had seen him sniffing cocaine on the terrace the night before. It was likely that while Selina was fretting, he was relaxing in some hidden corner, but I did not say that. "He knows we'll be returning from here, and that Charlie and Joe will be back for us."

By the time we neared the cricket pavilion, Miss Dyson was already waiting. "I've looked and he's not here. Mrs Douglas is enquiring of the servers whether he was first in for a cuppa and has left." She smiled. "Everyone knows his face, and his jokes. Even people who don't go to the shows hear them from those who do."

A distant sound made me look up. The aeroplane was returning. The OTC boys heard it too. They formed a line around the cricket pitch. A master raised a megaphone and called for the pitch to be cleared. We stepped onto the porch of the pavilion to be out of the way.

Selina relaxed a little. "He'll hear the plane. He'll be back."

Mrs Douglas came from the pavilion and joined us. She shouted to make herself heard above the sound of the plane landing. "Young Miss Dyson will track down Mr Moffatt. You and the airmen must come to the dining hall. We have a private room ready for your refreshments. There'll be a bit of a crush for the scones in the main hall." She watched with a satisfied smile as the boys stood to attention around the pitch to keep the landing space clear. "This is very good training for the lads. They are loving every minute."

The plane slowly descended and bumped its way across the pitch. The school gardener and cricketers wouldn't be pleased at the indentations made by the wheels.

Mrs Douglas touched my arm gently. "Shall we set off? The airmen can follow. I know you need to take off again soon." When Selina didn't move, she added, "Please, come this way. We have the gardener's little buggy to transport you. It's such a clever piece of motoring engineering." She turned to Miss Dyson. "Will you direct the airmen, my dear?"

"Yes of course. I wanted their autographs anyway."

Lamblike, Selina and I were herded from the pavilion porch, edging our way around the pitch, heading for the opening that led to the lane. "That's where he'll be," Selina said quietly. "He'll have changed his mind and decided to look around the school. He went to a ragged school himself and he's always keen to see how the other half lives."

Mrs Douglas had sharp hearing. "I haven't seen your friend perform but I know he has a reputation as a cheeky chappie. I expect he'll be observing us all and stealing our little mannerisms for his next comic monologue, so that the world can laugh at how ridiculous we all are."

In the lane, an ancient man with a crinkled parchment face was seated on a metal contraption with a single bicycle seat for the driver and a plank for passengers behind. The three of us dutifully squeezed on and were bone-shaken along the winding lane. Several buildings came into view. Mrs Douglas pointed out dormitories and classrooms until the vehicle came to a stop outside the largest of the buildings.

"Thank you, Perkins. Now be a good chap and go back for the airmen." Mrs Douglas alighted and led us into part of the school that she called the Hostel, along a plain corridor with none of the usual awards, memorials or pictures of famous old boys.

We walked through the busy dining hall.

Though most people were too discreet to stare, a few heads turned to look at the star: Selina Fellini, Silver Songbird, everyone's darling. Aware of surreptitious glances and a few bold stares from small boys, Selina returned smiles and scanned the room for Billy. So did I, but to no avail.

We found ourselves in a small private room where a table was set with a white cloth, the best china tea service and tiered plates of sandwiches and scones.

Mrs Douglas poured tea and asked us to be sure to help ourselves. As if only just remembering who and where she was, Selina gave a professional smile. "Thank you. So kind."

"My husband would join you, Mrs Compton, but he has several matters to attend to."

When she had gone, Selina said, "Why does she think I want to see the headmaster? She's using my married name to remind me that my husband is an old boy and should have come with me."

"It's kind of her to give us a private room."

Selina glanced at me and then lowered her head like some unhappy child.

"Selina, what is it? What is it you're not telling me? I've had the feeling from the start that there was more to this than my being the right person to book an aeroplane for you. Half a dozen people could have done that."

She bit into a scone and finished chewing before she answered.

"This will sound ridiculous. When there's a new moon, or some change, or the planets . . . I don't know how to say this. That's why I wanted you by me. I confided in Giuseppe Barnardini, you see. We shared the same singing teacher aeons ago."

She did not finish. At that moment, Charlie burst in. "Giggs has changed a bit since I was a boy. We didn't have a gardener on a homemade tractor in those days."

I poured him a cup of tea. "Did you have a successful flight?"

"You'd have to ask the reporter and the photographer. I believe they were happy enough and sufficiently impressed, though I must say it was like Piccadilly Circus up there. Sightseers at ten guineas a go, newspapers competing for pictures, and an official flight on behalf of the Astronomer Royal in an Imperial Airways fourteen-seater, a coup for the *Daily Mail*." Charlie picked up a sandwich. "How about you, Miss Fellini? Has it been worth the jaunt?"

Selina paused. "It was amazing, to witness the eclipse and to dance a fandango with handsome chaps from Greenwich. Billy turned green with envy and disappeared. The OTC boys are searching him out now."

"So I heard. Joe is with them. Someone gave him a bottle of beer but being an old boy I daren't refuse the headmaster's wife when she ordered me here to take tea. You're not worried, are you?"

Selina shook her head. "Absolutely not. I expect he's eloped with one of the beauties who were sitting astride the wall. By the time they get to Settle, he'll remember he has a performance tonight and he'll turn back."

"Well for what it's worth, Joe thinks Billy turned green at the gills during the flight. He reckons our funny man isn't cut out for flying. I don't suppose he would set off for a train without telling you?"

"No he wouldn't."

Sensing something wrong, Charlie spoke with a confidence none of us felt. "Don't worry. We won't rush off without him. The official picture hasn't been developed yet. Once the *Evening News* photographer has his copy of that, we'll have to be airborne. Perhaps that's what Billy is waiting for so he can go home by train without losing face." He picked up another sandwich. "Have you heard that Giggs is being acclaimed as *the* place in the country for viewing the eclipse? It came over the wireless."

Selina made some reply and Charlie launched into an explanation of flying across the line of totality, above the clouds where there was a perfect view. Selina appeared to be listening but she was looking beyond Charlie to the door, waiting for news, dreading it too. With thousands of people on the move, it was no mystery that Billy might have been caught up in chatting to some of them, or taking a look around. For the first time, I wondered whether Selina's fears indicated some kind of distress or exhaustion. If so, she did not need me. She needed a doctor, and bedrest.

The door to our small room opened. Alex the head boy stepped into view, frowning. He was without his greatcoat. "Miss Fellini, Mrs Shackleton, we've found Mr Moffatt. He has been taken into the chapel. The doctor is sent for."

Charlie put down his cup. "Wait here. I'll go see what's happened."

But Selina and I were already on our feet.

CHAPTER
SIX

The Scent of Cedar Wood

With few words, except to say Billy was not himself, Alex led Selina, Charlie and me back to the chapel. In the short time since the eclipse, the sky had lightened.

As the building that dominates hill and dale loomed into view, I felt a sense of foreboding that quickened my breath. Coming closer, I saw that although the green dome suggested Eastern splendour, the chapel was as local as could be, made of millstone grit, sandstone and limestone.

Selina had turned deathly pale. Charlie took her arm. "You don't need to come in."

"Yes I do."

Alex tapped on the chapel door. It was unlocked from the other side. Another OTC lad held the door open until we stepped in and then locked it again.

"Mrs Douglas didn't want people barging in until the doctor comes," Alex explained.

We stepped inside and straightaway the sweetest scent created a feeling of calm. I looked about, half expecting some priestly figure to be swinging a censer, flooding the place with heady incense. I looked at Charlie. "What is that?"

He touched a bench. "Cedar wood." He spoke in a whisper. "We all loved the chapel."

I glanced about. Not seeing Billy or Mrs Douglas, I turned to see if they were at the back of the chapel. A beautiful stained-glass window showed the Creation, with the Heavens, Adam and Eve, beasts and fish and shells. A Creation window designed to delight little boys. But no Billy.

Selina came out of her dream. "Where is he? He's not here. Has the doctor been?"

"This way, Miss Fellini." Alex walked across the marbled floor, Selina behind him.

Charlie and I followed. Being here seemed unreal. Bathed in the scent of cedar wood, and in such a sanctified atmosphere nothing bad could, would or should happen. We caught up. Charlie stepped forward and put his arm around Selina. She had started to shake.

That was when Mrs Douglas appeared from the far side of the chapel. We walked across. She tried to block our way. "I've made the patient comfortable. He's here, by the organ."

Billy was lying on a too-narrow bench, still and pale, an OTC greatcoat under him and another covering him. That explained why Alex had worn no coat. Mrs Douglas tried to keep us at a distance. "He mustn't be moved again until the doctor comes. There are no bones broken but one can't be sure. I've tried to bring him back into consciousness."

Selina pushed past Mrs Douglas. She knelt beside Billy and took his hand. "Billy, Billy. Idiot! What did you do? Where did you go?" She turned to us. "He's breathing. He's all right."

Charlie hovered uncertainly by the pulpit.

Not knowing how long the doctor would be, I wondered whether I should examine Billy myself. Even though it is so long since I did nursing, one never forgets.

Mrs Douglas might have read my thoughts. "I've done what I could. He's unconscious and has a weak pulse." She retreated to the first pew, leaving Selina and Charlie standing by Billy. "I've had Red Cross training, Mrs Shackleton. As headmaster's wife one has responsibilities."

Glancing across at the door, I saw that Alex stood sentry, waiting for the doctor's knock.

"It won't hurt if I take a look." I tapped Charlie's shoulder, encouraging him to draw Selina away. "Let me take a look at Billy. I was a nurse in the war. Give him a little space and let him have air."

Charlie took the hint. He drew Selina towards a pew. "Come and sit down, Miss Fellini. Billy is in good hands."

Billy's breath was shallow, his pulse slow and his skin cold and with a yellowish tinge that I had not noticed that morning or the night before. But last night's party had been dimly lit, and the morning dark. There was a reddish mark on either cheek. Perhaps someone had slapped him, trying to wake him. I pulled back each eyelid. His eyes were like pinpoints. "What have you taken?" I asked the unconscious man. I looked through his pockets: wallet, comb, small spirits flask, tobacco, cigarette papers, matches, pencil stub and a piece of folded paper. I opened the paper. He had jotted a few words in a hasty scrawl.

Sun and Moon's Spectacular Variety Turn. Giggleswick?
You shoulda seen em! Goggles everywhere — change
name of village — Goggleswick.

At that moment, aware of someone behind me, I turned. It was Mrs Douglas.

She took something from her pocket, clenching it in her fist, speaking quietly. "Is this what you're looking for?" She turned her hand and opened her palm for me to view what she held. It was a pillbox. She spoke in an urgent whisper. "We've worked so hard to make today's event a celebration for the school, for British science, for the Astronomer Royal and his party. He's taken something, hasn't he?" She reached for my hand, palm uppermost, pressing the small box on me. "Something like this could tarnish the school's reputation and overshadow today's achievements."

I opened the pillbox. There was a coating of white powder on the inside, and several tablets. Brazen it out, I told myself. While sniffing cocaine might not raise an eyebrow in certain circles, a public school had its reputation to consider. "Mrs Douglas, it's just tablets. It could be aspirin."

"I'd rather not know what is in the tablet. It's enough to recognise the powder."

At that moment the door of the chapel opened, held by Alex. Two more boys came in, both coatless. The lads carried a stretcher. A small, round man in black overcoat, stethoscope dangling, stepped into the chapel behind them. But it was the boys who mesmerised me. They were about fifteen years old and yet carried the empty stretcher with the militaristic precision of seasoned soldiers. Would we forever train our little boys to be officers and to playact what might one day be real, tragic, and final?

Charlie had drawn Selina to a second-row pew, leaving space for the stretcher bearers. Mrs Douglas moved to assist the doctor. I waited and watched. As expected, the doctor shooed her aside.

I diverted Mrs Douglas. "Where will he be taken?"

"To Little Howson, it's our sickbay. If needs be, he'll be taken to hospital."

I watched the doctor carry out the same precise checks that I had. He also looked into Billy's mouth and felt his throat. After that, Billy was transferred to the stretcher, and the greatcoats replaced by blankets. Alex and another boy put their coats on again.

As if on late cue, two masters arrived, to take over the carrying of the stretcher. They, Mrs Douglas and the doctor put their heads together in confab.

The doctor asked, "Who is the patient's next of kin?"

Selina clutched her fur tightly around her. "Mr Moffatt is a widower with no parents or children. I can be contacted, Selina Fellini — Mrs Jarrod Compton, or our manager Trotter Brockett who is at the Queens Hotel in Leeds. Please spare no expense or trouble on Billy's behalf."

What followed felt strange in the extreme. We walked from the chapel, across the grounds to the gate where a policeman still stood. He held the gate. The notice on it read, "Astronomer Royal Only".

We walked the path that led to the school buildings. One of the masters strode ahead, clearing the way. Another master and a sturdy OTC lad carried the stretcher.

Mrs Douglas told me that we were taking Billy to Howson's San, the school sanatorium.

The countryside was still alive with herds of moving human beings who had scaled hills and swarmed through valleys. A cyclist had camped in the lee of the nearby dry stone wall and was now rolling up a groundsheet.

"Someone fainted," the lead schoolmaster said to any passer-by who showed the curiosity to ask. "Stay clear, please."

One insensitive wit called out that some people would do anything to push ahead and get to their motors before the roads clogged altogether.

We walked down a sloping yard to the school sickbay. Matron waited by the door. Everything after that happened so quickly and quietly that afterwards it barely felt real.

Billy was taken inside. Charlie and Selina followed. Mrs Douglas and I brought up the rear. Mrs Douglas spoke a few words to the matron. She then turned to me. "I'm so sorry but I believe there is little more I can do and no point in crowding the professionals. Mr Moffatt is in good hands with Matron and the doctor."

"Thank you. You've been most helpful."

"I wish Mr Moffatt well. I suppose he was a soldier and we know that the pain makes some men try anything. I'm sorry if I was abrupt earlier. It was the shock."

I suddenly felt sorry for her. For weeks, months, she and the school staff had prepared for this day. They had accommodated the scientists, drilled the boys, prayed for their moment of glory, and bore the intrusion of reporters and nosey parkers. No doubt the publicity would be good for the school in the long term, but now the strain showed.

She spoke kindly. "The ambulance will be here quickly. There are emergency ambulances on alert in the nearby fields where vehicles are parked. The police will ensure priority. Let me know if there is anything else we can do. I'm sure you'll understand that the school has a reputation to consider."

"Yes." How had she been aware that Billy had taken narcotics? In a way it surprised me that a woman cloistered in a public school would be so alert to drug-taking. Perhaps I should not have been surprised. The old boys who came back were no different in the ways they dealt with their pain than other returned soldiers, and the young will always want to experiment.

She hesitated, ready to speak again. "You are not a theatrical yourself?"

"No."

She nodded. "The headmaster, my husband, he . . . On this occasion I believe I can speak for him. Unfortunately there is no place at this school for Miss

Fellini's son. We are fully subscribed for the near future."

Now was not the time to say that I did not know Selina had a son.

Mrs Douglas waited as if for some assurance that I would pass on the message, and then she turned and walked away.

I found Charlie and Selina in the corridor of the sickbay, seated on straight-back chairs. Charlie stood. "I'll let Joe know that Mr Moffatt won't be returning with us. And I'm sorry, Miss Fellini, but we must be airborne as soon as the *Evening News* photographer is ready to go. We'll land on the same field as this morning and then fly on to London."

He looked uncomfortable, a man with a careful timetable whose reputation demanded that he keep to it.

Matron opened the door of the sickbay. We all looked at her. "Just a few details for the doctor. What is the patient's full name?"

Selina answered. "William James Moffatt."

"His date of birth?"

"Second of June, 1891."

"Thank you. The ambulance is on its way."

"Can't he come back with us to Leeds? I can take care of him, bring in a doctor and nurses."

"He is in no fit state to travel. Doctor has arranged for him to be taken to the infirmary at Castleberg which is close by."

Selina was not convinced. "Is it a good infirmary?"

"Oh yes. Believe me, that is the wisest course of action. The busy roads and railway between here and Settle and Skipton would make his journey intolerable."

Selina bit her lip. She nodded. "Then I'll come with him."

Charlie hovered, looking at me. I motioned for him to wait as I sat down beside Selina. Suddenly my reason for being here took shape. It was up to me to ensure that Selina returned home in time to rest before her evening performance.

"Selina, let me stay with Billy. We engaged the plane so that you would be home this morning and able to rest. Billy knows that. He'll expect you to go back with Charlie and Joe. When Billy regains consciousness, he'll be mortified if he thinks he has kept you here."

She put her head in her hands. "I can't abandon him." Her voice sounded suddenly choked. She put a hand to her throat. "I can feel it, my throat contracting."

"Is it possible to cancel tonight's performance?"

She shook her head. "We don't do that. We can't disappoint the audience."

"Then let me stay and you go. Billy will not want to think you'll croak like a frog and have people throwing rotten eggs at you."

She smiled at so preposterous a thought.

Charlie spoke gently. "You saw the roads from the air as we came. Traffic will be crawling. Trains will be packed, and all fully booked."

"You'd planned to rest," I reminded her. "Mr Brockett was adamant."

She made a dismissive gesture. "Adamant is Trotter Brockett's middle name. Others have to dance to his tune. I don't."

"You know what hospitals are like. You'd be barred from seeing Billy until visiting day. I know it's not the same, but if you're prepared to fly back, I'll stay here. I'll go with Billy and whatever changes the doctor reports, the least thing, I'll telephone. I was a nurse and so I'll know what they're talking about."

It had to be her decision. Billy looked very bad to me, like a man sunk into a coma.

"You're right. I'd be useless." She reached out and touched my arm. "If there's anything he wants, Kate, he must have it."

"Of course."

Charlie did just the right thing. He leaned towards her, offering both his hands to draw her from the chair. "Come on, Miss Fellini. I'll see you all the way home. Billy is in good hands with Mrs Shackleton. She's the person I'd like to have on stand-by if I took poorly."

It was the last two words that did the trick. Billy had taken poorly. The words diminished whatever torrent raged in the poor man's body and mind.

Selina let Charlie draw her from the chair. "And you'll telephone me, Kate?"

"I will, and Mr Brockett at the Queens Hotel."

"Thank you for thinking of that. I'll ask Beryl to let him know. He'll need to make arrangements for tonight, a substitute act for Billy." Just saying his name put her on the verge of changing her mind, but Charlie took her arm.

"He'll be . . ." he bit back words. I believe he intended to say, He'll be right as rain, or he'll be on his feet in no time. The arrival of the ambulance allowed him to say, "He'll be tucked in a hospital bed before we're airborne."

She looked from him to me. "I can't leave him to be bumped along in some ambulance to an old workhouse infirmary. That's what it'll be."

"I'll go with him. I'll make sure he's in good hands, or nurse him myself if I must."

"Will you?"

"If that's what you want me to do."

"Yes. I wish you would." She put her hand in her coat pocket and took out a wallet.

"Not now. I'm still working for you."

"How will you get back?"

"By train probably. I'll stay to make sure Billy is being properly taken care of and if necessary I'll stay overnight."

"That's very good of you."

"I need to write a note for my housekeeper. Will you be sure to have it delivered for me?"

"Of course. That's the least I can do."

There was a table at the end of the corridor. I took writing paper and an envelope from my satchel and sat at the table to scribble as much as I could about what had happened so far, and to ask Mrs Sugden to speak to my assistant, Mr Sykes, and to keep him informed.

Selina watched me. "There must be hospitals nearby if this one isn't suitable, if they can't help him here."

"Yes. When he is stable, and when the roads clear. There is a big hospital in Skipton, but being moved so far now won't do him any good." I did not add that perhaps nothing now would do him good.

She squeezed my arm. "I'm grateful, Kate. I never imagined this, just my fear that something would go wrong. It's as if I brought it on him myself."

I paused in my writing. "You said that two deaths in the company may not have been accidental. Something must have prompted you to believe that."

"I tried to tell you last night. It seems ridiculous. I'm not superstitious but this past year two friends died who shouldn't have died. Each time, it was when the moon is new. I talked to someone who knows about astrology and asked did she think that something malign in the stars was affecting us all. She said I must be careful."

"Can you explain a bit more?"

"Finish your writing and I'll tell you."

"Tell me now. I don't work alone. If there's something my assistant needs to know, let's not waste time."

She nodded. "I hoped I was wrong. First Dougie Doig was killed on the road this time last year."

"Dougie Doig?"

"Doig was his stage name. Douglas Dougan. He had a novelty animal act with his three performing dogs. People gossiped, but we were just good friends. Close friends. We were at York Theatre Royal. Dougie left the theatre after his act. Shortly after, he walked under a tram. An accident, it was said. In January you may have read about the Sunderland Empire closing during investigations after an accident on stage. That was Floyd Lloyd, a delightful old chap, and a clever ventriloquist. He was like an uncle to me. Floyd was horribly crushed to death when a sandbag dropped from the flies. We'd had such jolly times, he and I. His dummy was Manny Piccolo. Floyd always said that he was rather dense but that Manny Piccolo was a genius and would solve all our problems. He had a special moment in his act where members of the audience could ask Manny's advice. Everyone loved him." She loosened her coat. "It's so hot in here. You were right not to wear fur." She sighed. "And now Billy. I can't bear it. It's as if I put a jinx on anyone who comes close to me."

Hastily, I scribbled a rather long PS on my letter to Mrs Sugden, confident that she would be able to decipher my hand. I asked Mrs Sugden to find out the background to the deaths of Douglas Dougan and Floyd Lloyd, and for Sykes to come to the Varieties that evening. He knew less about the world of theatre than I. If we were to investigate accidental deaths on behalf of Miss Fellini, it would be helpful for him to know the company.

There was no point in telling Selina that she should have told me all this much sooner. I sincerely hoped that she was wrong and these events were unconnected. More than ever it seemed to me that Selina Fellini was a woman on the edge and that Billy's collapse would be taken to her heart and given the weight of some judgement from heaven.

"Selina, I work with a former policeman, Jim Sykes. I'm going to bring him in on this. Might you be able to arrange seats at the theatre for him this evening?"

"I'll have tickets left at the box office."

After adding this information, I sealed the envelope and gave it to Selina. "I don't believe Billy's indisposition is connected with the stars and the phases of the moon." I took the pillbox from my pocket. "Mrs Douglas handed me this pillbox. I believe that Billy is suffering from having taken too much of something. Do you know what the tablets are? I'll need to tell the doctor."

"The tablets are antacid. He doesn't have an addiction to drugs."

"Not even cocaine?"

"Well there is that, and he takes something for pain but it's his usual dose of morphine and it never varies."

"But this is his pillbox?"

It was distinctive and modern, picturing an elegant couple dancing. She stared at the pillbox and gave a slight gulp. "I suppose so."

Charlie called from the doorway. "Mrs Shackleton, you need to come now if you're going in the ambulance."

"I appreciate everything you're doing, really I do." She leaned and kissed my cheek. I could now identify the underlying notes of her perfume. It was the scent of cedar wood.

CHAPTER
SEVEN

Bouncing Back

By the time Charlie brought the aeroplane in to land on Soldiers Field, scattering three dog walkers and an elderly man taking his constitutional, a tinge of pink brightened the clouds. The day looked set fair. Perhaps the sky was pleased to have put on such a spectacular performance. Joe stayed with the plane and their additional passenger, the newspaper photographer. Charlie insisted on walking Miss Fellini the short distance to her home. Once there, he was as enchanted as every other visitor at the sight of the place, but he and Joe needed to make haste if the *Evening News* was to show the world the early morning picture of the darkened sun and its corona. Charlie reluctantly shook hands with Selina. He expressed the hope that Billy would soon recover.

"Oh, he will," she assured him. "He always bounces back."

Selina stepped inside her house, went directly up the stairs to her bedroom. She sat down, unclasped her clutch and took out the Oxford pencil tin that was just the right size to contain the injection needle.

She placed it at the back of her stocking drawer. Would Billy bounce back?

CHAPTER
EIGHT

It Ain't Funny

Our having come from last night's eclipse party direct to Giggleswick created the sense of night and day merging. I looked at my watch. It was just 7.00 a.m. as we journeyed to Castleberg in a kind of convoy. Two policemen on motorcycles rode at the head. The old doctor and I sat in the back of the ambulance with the still unconscious Billy Moffatt. Every inch of the cobbled way caused a shudder in the vehicle.

I should know better than to ask stupid questions but at that moment I was not the former VAD nurse, but the friend for such a short time and with responsibility to stand in for Selina, and whoever else loved Billy. "Do you think he can hear us, Doctor?"

The old man's thin lined face with its prominent nose and small eyes, along with his stooped shoulders and grey homburg and dark coat, gave him the look of a nicely rounded baby elephant. He looked at me as if the thought of whether Billy might hear us had never occurred to him. "You won't be able to sit and talk to him, if that's what you're thinking. He needs peace and quiet, and nursing care."

"I was a VAD nurse."

He perked up. "So was our infirmary sister. She went on to do further qualifications. Perhaps you met her. She was in Egypt."

"I didn't go to Egypt."

That ended our conversation.

I tried again a few moments later, taking the pillbox from my pocket. "This is Billy's. I believe he may have been taking something against the pain."

"Ah." He took the pillbox and sniffed. A few grains of white powder clung to the inside of the lid. He licked a finger, dabbed up a grain or two and put it to his nostril. "He was an old soldier, or young old soldier I should say?"

"Yes."

He put the pillbox in his pocket. "I'll see he gets it back."

His words cheered me. He expected Billy to pull through.

Selina was right. Castleberg was the local workhouse. Yet the infirmary appeared well-equipped and efficiently staffed. Billy was placed in the men's ward, with screens around his bed. As expected, I was not allowed to sit by him. Over an hour passed before the ward sister came into the corridor to talk to me.

A tall, gaunt woman with high cheekbones, olive skin and dark eyes, she blinked several times as if the reflection of her own starched white apron startled her.

The thought of staring and blinking made me wonder whether anyone, in spite of all the warnings, had stared into the sun this morning and damaged their eyes. There would be something in the late edition of the papers if that had happened. The thought worried me.

"You're here for Billy Moffatt?" It was a Birmingham accent. Who knew what brought her this far north.

"Yes."

"I can put a chair by the bed if you'd like a little time with him."

This was unprecedented. Stray visitors only got in the way of hospital routine. If she was offering me a chair by the bed, there could be only one reason.

My mouth opened but no words came.

She stood, waiting, and then said. "I'm sorry. How thoughtless of me. You were here for the eclipse. You mustn't have slept. Do you want to rest somewhere?" She smiled. "Doctor said you were VAD. You're welcome to come to the nurses' room."

I shook my head. "Thanks for the offer, but no. I take it that Billy hasn't regained consciousness."

"Come on." She beckoned me to follow her. We walked along the corridor to a door painted green and with a small pane of opaque glass. She opened the door. A younger nurse was reading a newspaper. At a nod from the sister, she poured me a cup of tea. The sister and I sat side by side in two battered chairs. "I'm sorry to tell you that Mr Moffatt is unlikely to regain consciousness. He is in a coma. We have made him comfortable."

I should have known, and part of me had known since that moment in the chapel when I looked at his pinprick eyes. I knew that he had taken too much of some narcotic. But why? Perhaps the icy cold of that morning had affected his old wounds and caused him a lot of pain. It must be that.

"Can nothing be done?"

"Doctor thinks not. He tried to reverse the symptoms."

"Of narcotic poisoning?"

"I can't confirm that, and while there's life and all that. The best of us can be wrong."

"I will take you up on the offer to let me to sit with him. I promised Miss Fellini I would."

She stood. "Come on. It won't hurt and who knows, he may be aware that there's someone by. I believe in miracles and prayer."

I followed her along the corridor. She touched her neck. "If you look at him here, you'll see where the needle entered. His collar is stained with a drop of blood. I assume he injected himself?"

With the screens around the bed, Billy Moffatt and I occupied a nook of never-never land where there was nothing to do but wait. When his lips were dry, I moistened them. With a damp flannel, I cooled his brow.

Selina's fears had seemed exaggerated. I recalled her words.

Something bad might happen . . . Douglas Dougan . . . walked under a tram . . . Floyd Lloyd . . . delightful . . . a clever ventriloquist . . . accident on stage . . . crushed to death . . . something malign in the stars.

Yet there was no malign force at work here, or was there? Had Billy brought about his own destruction? I could see quite clearly the needle mark on his neck. Selina seemed so sure that calamity was written in the stars; but placing a needle against flesh required a human hand. Would he be capable of reaching that awkward spot on his neck while holding a needle? I tried, holding an imaginary needle against my neck. Yes, that was certainly possible, awkward but possible.

The letter from Giuseppe Barnardini, telling me of his recommendation, had contained a strong hint of what was behind my engagement. He had told Selina that if ever she needed discretion and investigation, she could do worse than turn to me. If something was written in the stars, then no human intervention could prevent it. If some malicious person were wreaking foul play under the cover of the alignment of planets or phases of the moon, that was a different matter. But who might that person be? As far as I knew, no other acquaintance of Billy's was here. A total stranger would need to be mad to approach him and stick a needle in his neck. Billy would have struggled. He must have injected himself, and misjudged the dose.

As I watched with Billy, I again went over my first meeting with Selina, searching for something palpable.

I made myself go back to the beginning, to the day when Selina first called on me. Was there something I missed? Why had I been so foolish as to think this would be a simple assignment? Book an aeroplane flight, which anyone could have done for ten or twenty guineas; accompany her to Giggleswick, and return.

Returning in the aircraft was now off the list for me. I would be struggling to find a seat on a train, together with tens of thousands doing likewise.

What was it that should have set off louder alarm bells as she and I sat in my kitchen with a pot of tea and Mrs Sugden's biscuits?

She explained that an invitation had come out of the blue from the headmaster of Giggleswick School for her to view the eclipse from the Astronomer Royal's encampment. She was curious and yet had misgivings. No sooner had she voiced these misgivings, she dismissed them. It was simply a feeling something may go wrong. She had a show every night. There might be the possibility of an accident on the railway or delay on crowded roads. She had never yet let down her public.

Now that I thought back, it was clear that I should have pressed her more about those misgivings. Instead, I had simply listened and taken what she said at face value. She expressed concern about the time the journey would take.

That was when I crossed my fingers and assured her about the safety of flying.

We had both been right: she about the possibility of an accident; me about the safety of flying. Of course, there was more than one kind of flying. Who knows to what heights and wild regions Billy Moffatt's drug-taking had led him? The "accident" Selina feared had happened, and to Billy, although to me it appeared as a self-inflicted injury.

I took Billy's hand that was cold and unresponsive. He was far away, deep in his coma, but I spoke to him.

"You're safe Billy, safe from any more harm. And Billy, what did Selina mean when she talked about the possibility of an accident?"

Answer came there none from poor Billy, still deep inside his coma.

What pictures might be flitting through the shadows of his mind? I hoped they would be pleasant scenes, not mud, not the walls of a trench, not the scuttle of rats. If thoughts of his career on stage came to him now, I hoped it would be of triumphs, not of a hostile audience. And love, he must have loved as we all do. I had seen in his eyes that he loved Selina.

How I wished he could talk to me. I did not even know who found him and where. One of the OTC boys I presumed. He may have wandered off to inject himself, perhaps seeking a quiet corner of the chapel, which some people might regard as sacrilegious. Perhaps it was during the tension of the countdown, or when the world turned dark and cold.

I squeezed his hand, just in case. "Selina wanted to be here. I'm here in her place. She loves you, and so do all your admirers. Come on, Billy. Let's have a miracle. Let's say, God save Billy. If not, you know what they'll say when they hear about you. They'll all miss you. They'll say it ain't funny. Not one little bit. It ain't funny."

If Selina had been right to think that two accidental deaths in a year were more than coincidental, then Billy's collapse increased those suspicions.

The possibility of foul play loomed large. If that were the case, then those nearest to Douglas Dougan, Floyd

Lloyd and Billy Moffatt must come under suspicion. I thought back to the party, the eclipse party at Selina's fabulous house.

"Did I miss something, Billy? Was there someone at the party who might not be trusted?"

The cast of colourful characters who formed the background in the wonderful world of Selina Fellini and Billy Moffatt stepped before my mind's eye.

There was Selina, of course. She was the person close to Billy, and to the other two men. But a murderess would not call in a detective, would she?

CHAPTER
NINE

A Particular Interest in Obituaries

At nine o'clock, Mrs Sugden, Mrs Shackleton's housekeeper, was in the street with a bucket and shovel. She saw the messenger boy's bike at the gate. Durkin the coalman had passed that way and Mrs Sugden had gone out to pick up any gift his horse may have left on the road, before anyone else beat her to it. Mrs Sugden collected horse muck for her gardening friend Stanley's allotment. Stanley Belt was old and wizened as a weathered gnome but grew the sweetest carrots and cabbages known to man or beast.

Triumphant, she finished her shovelling and straightened up, ready to walk back and take her booty to the heap in the back garden. That was when she saw the skinny red-haired messenger lad at the door. He was pushing something through the letterbox.

Striding back along the street, she waved to him. A dignified figure with an air of natural authority, Mrs Sugden did not hurry but kept to her usual measured pace towards what she proudly regarded as her own front door. Strictly speaking, it was Mrs Shackleton's front door. Mrs Sugden's preference was to use her own entrance, to the annexe at the back of the house.

At the gate, the messenger stood by his bike. "I've already shoved it through."

"Who is it to?"

"Mrs Sugden."

"That's me." She set the bucket down. "Where is it from?"

"I fetched it from Roundhay from a big house set back and painted white." When she gave him a look, he added, "I was given it by a woman in a dark frock."

"Just a minute. I'll see if there's an answer." Mrs Sugden opened the door. She had expected Mrs Shackleton to be back by now and if she wasn't, why not, that was what she asked herself as she picked up the letter. And why a letter when Mrs Shackleton was over-fond of the telephone?

She opened the envelope, took out the sheet with the familiar handwriting and read it quickly. "Thank you. No answer."

The lad waited.

"Just a minute." She found her purse and gave him sixpence, which was over the odds but when a letter came from Roundhay sixpence seemed more suitable than a few coppers.

The lad thanked her, touched his cap and had mounted his bike before she picked up the bucket to take round to the back to the manure heap. She lifted off the tarpaulin cover, placed there when the weather turned warm on account of a recent glut of bluebottles.

When she had deposited her prize and replaced the cover, Mrs Sugden made a plan. She had thought all along it was a bit fishy that Selina Fellini, who everyone went crackers for, should be asking Mrs Shackleton to book a plane for her, and to stop out all night at one of those parties certain people held. After that they were to go to a posh school in the middle of nowhere to see the eclipse. What good would it do anyone to forego a night's sleep for half a minute of staring at the sun disappearing? The sun disappeared most of the time and no one thought anything of it.

She reread the letter. All this eclipse business hadn't done this comedian chap any good by the sound of things. It was just like Mrs Shackleton to have volunteered to sit with the poor fellow in hospital as if she still wore a nurse's uniform and was under orders.

Not that Mrs Sugden hadn't been a bit curious about the eclipse. She was awake early, let out Sookie the cat and followed her into the dark wood at the back as the sun came up. She'd put on her gloves and, not being one to waste time, gathered nettles. There was no fanfare for the eclipse in Batswing Wood, though Sookie went very still and didn't like it. Mrs Sugden saw the pattern appear on the ground as the moon blocked out the sun. A couple of the neighbours were there, including young Thomas with his mam. They exchanged a few words. Thomas seemed pleased enough. When it was all over, which was in no time at all, Thomas produced his pencil and sketchpad and straightaway began to sketch the pattern he had seen on the ground. While it was still in his mind's eye, he said.

Then it was back inside for a cup of tea and a slice of bread and butter.

Mrs Sugden once more read Mrs Shackleton's letter. Well this letter took the biscuit, it really did. She took a piece of scrap paper from the clip and made notes of what she must do.

Alert Mr Sykes

Look up the dates of the new moon for last June and this January

Call on Mr Duffield at newspaper library for information about the accidental deaths of two theatrical performers

a) Douglas Dougan (stage name Dougie Doig), dog trainer

b) Floyd Lloyd, ventriloquist

If this wasn't a rum do, she didn't know what was. It put paid to making nettle soup while the nettles were still fresh.

Still, hers not to reason why. Though just what she was supposed to "alert" Mr Sykes to she did not know. He could have the letter and work it out for himself. She began by going into the dining room, which served as an office, and taking down an almanac from the bookshelf.

She found the information quickly and wrote:

New moon, June 1926: 10 June

New moon, January 1927: 3 Jan.

She wondered which part of the country saw the new moon first. Probably that lot in London if they ever bothered to look up. She had never thought before that each month brought a new moon. It was something you took for granted. But what that had to do with people dying, she couldn't think. People are as likely to die when the moon is new as when it wanes. Phases of the moon did not seem to her to be a great starting point for investigating deaths, if that's what was going on. No ailing person Mrs Sugden ever knew had looked out of the window, spotted a new moon and thought, that's me done for then. Time's up.

As she returned the book to the shelf, she caught sight of herself in the sideboard mirror, in her muckment of old skirt and hessian pinafore.

In half an hour, she was spruced up and ready to set off. She took the shortcut through the wood along to Woodhouse.

Jim Sykes lived on Beulah Street and it suited Mrs Sugden to walk along there. It was the kind of street where normal people lived. Two women in pinnies and turbans exchanged words across the street. Children too young for school played on the pavement and tugged at the gas tar in the gutter. It was melting a bit in the warm weather but not enough for little fingers to tug it out. A little girl in a patched dress and sandals too big for her had chalked a shop on the pavement. Mrs Sugden stepped into the road to avoid trampling her wares, a roughly chalked shape, probably meant to be a loaf of bread, an apple or potato, several small shapes that might have been sweets and something with ears. "Do you want to buy summat, Missis?"

Mrs Sugden had a soft spot for children with a bit of imagination. She took a guess at the bread. "I'll take a loaf, please."

The girl spat on her hand and carefully rubbed out the loaf. "That'll be a farthing."

Mrs Sugden thought this could turn out to be an expensive day. She took out a penny. "What else can I have, to the value of a penny?"

"Do you want the rabbit?"

"Aye, go on then. I'll make a stew with it."

She waited until the child carefully erased the four-legged creature and its two ears, and then gave her the penny.

"Thank you, Missis." She rubbed out a tiny square. "You can have a free sweet for being a good customer."

"Thank you."

Mrs Sugden walked on.

Sykes's house was three more along, the door and window frames painted sage green, as were the two houses on either side, to show they all belonged to the same landlord. She tapped on the door but there was no answer. Jim Sykes would be out working. She had to hand it to him. He had a real knack for investigating for the insurance companies. It brought in a good income that kept them ticking over between other cases. He'd stuck at the last investigation until he proved that a claim for fire damage after a suspicious arson attack on the premises of a failing mill was at the instigation of the owner.

Mrs Sugden knocked but there was no answer. She had already added her own message on the outside of the envelope, just in case there was no one in at the Sykes's. All the same she waited a few minutes, in case Rosie was upstairs, and then pushed the envelope through the door.

As she retraced her steps, the little girl looked up again. Mrs Sugden was ready to say that she wouldn't buy anything else because she had no more room in her bag, but the girl just smiled and went on chalking, replenishing her provisions.

By the time she stepped off the tram in town, Mrs Sugden had gone through several versions of what she might say to Mr Duffield who kept the library at the newspaper offices. This gentleman had called at the house with his wife, who was friends with Mrs Shackleton's mother. The words married late in life might have been invented for Mr Duffield because that's what he had done. His appearance had improved as a result. He no longer looked like a shabby man at death's door. Now he was a smartly turned out man at death's door.

Mrs Sugden arrived. She did not take naturally to the telephone but now that she was here, facing the newspaper office porter, she wished she had picked up the wretched implement and telephoned to say she was coming. "I'm here to see Mr Duffield."

The porter looked up from his crossword puzzle. He saw a woman who looked as if she knew her own business, square of jaw with braided hair pinned up around her head and a smart hat. "Is he expecting you?"

"I'm Mrs Sugden here on behalf of Mrs Shackleton. He'll know who I am." And she saw from his eyes that he knew the name Shackleton. He picked up a telephone that appeared even more forbidding than the one that graced their hall. This one had several buttons attached.

He spoke into it, and then looked back at her. "Mr Duffield will come down to meet you."

"Thank you."

She waited, while turning her attention to the faded photographs on the wall, taken from old newspapers.

Somewhere far off, a lift rattled. Footsteps sounded along the nearby corridor. She turned to see Mr Duffield and was glad he was a few yards off and far away enough not to see her surprise that he had stopped dyeing his hair that dramatic black. It was now an almost clean white with just a touch of straw colour. It made his face appear less sepulchral.

With perfect manners, he greeted her as if all that morning he had waited for no one else.

A thrill at the newness of this experience lightened Mrs Sugden's step as she followed Mr Duffield through corridors to the clanging lift. She had a small notebook and a newly sharpened pencil in her bag. I could have worked in an office, she told herself. I could have filed documents and filled out ledgers. Still, it was better to be working for Mrs Shackleton as a housekeeper than someone who led a more mundane kind of life.

From the lift they crossed a landing and went into a large, high-ceilinged room with big windows that let in lots of light.

Seated at a heavy old table, Mrs Sugden explained Mrs Shackleton's odd request regarding the deaths of two performers sometime in January this year and June last year.

Mr Duffield, elbows on the table, brought his palms together and rested his chin on his hands.

"I have names." Mrs Sugden felt apologetic about this. "One is an odd name, Dougie Doig, real name Douglas Dougan. The other is Floyd Lloyd."

Mr Duffield nodded. "Very precise, as I would have expected from Mrs Shackleton, and from you, dear Mrs Sugden. Now will you have a cup of tea?" Not waiting for an answer, he waved to a junior who was filing index cards. "Raymond! A nice cup of tea and a digestive for our esteemed visitor, please." He handed Mrs Sugden that morning's paper. "A little read while you wait."

While Mrs Sugden sipped tea, Raymond went to assist Mr Duffield by climbing a ladder and taking down a large box. Mrs Sugden watched while Raymond placed the box on a long table. Mr Duffield removed several newspapers and shared them between himself and Raymond. They each looked through the papers, young Raymond with great rapidity. Mr Duffield turned pages more slowly, stopping when something caught his eye. Raymond drew Mr Duffield's attention to an item. It did not take Mr Duffield long to come back with the appropriate pieces.

He showed the pages to Mrs Sugden for her consideration.

She read quickly from each of the papers. "Those are the two accidental deaths."

In spite of allowing his hair to turn its natural colour, Mr Duffield sported coal-black eyebrows. He raised one, but had the tact to make no comment. Mrs Sugden read his look. It said that if Mrs Shackleton had decided to look into these matters, then perhaps inverted commas would be required around the word "accidental", and a big question mark over everything else.

He asked Raymond to type up the items. Mrs Sugden, something of a typist herself, envied the young man's speed.

In the time it might take for a lesser mortal to roll a sheet of paper around the platen, he presented her with a foolscap sheet of typed copy.

She thanked them both.

Mr Duffield escorted her back to the lift. "Give Mrs Shackleton my compliments and say I should be happy to look further into these distressing incidents, at coroner reports, for instance."

"That would be very helpful, Mr Duffield. Shall I come back tomorrow?"

"Yes, please do. I shall look up the obituaries. I take a particular interest in obituaries."

CHAPTER
TEN

A Probability of Cloud

As I kept watch at Billy Moffatt's bedside, it was strange to think that only hours earlier we had enjoyed a party to celebrate the coming eclipse.

Now Billy lay grey and still. His breathing was shallow and his pulse slow. I thought back to that party and to the people I had met. It puzzled me, as it had puzzled Selina, that this company of variety artistes were so unfortunate to have lost two of their number in such a short time. Unless some miracle ensued, Billy Moffatt would join them in their heavenly chorus.

The party to celebrate the coming eclipse was held in Selina's newly built house near Roundhay Park. It began late, after the theatres emptied. Her downstairs room, the size of a ballroom, glowed with gentle light from uplighter globes and lamps in etched glass, held aloft by elegant figurines. Being a gathering mainly of performers, artistes and entertainers there was no lack of pianists. In spite of the lateness of the hour, Jake, the human half of Jake and his performing pony, charmed notes from the ebony grand piano. Sandy Sechrest, the elegant memory woman who always wore black, turned the pages of the music, which had shifted towards slow and sentimental as the night wore on.

One of Selina's older brothers livened up proceedings with a rendition of "La donna è mobile". Her younger brother, Marco, played the accordion and sang "Has Anybody Seen My Gal?".

Marco's wife, Jess, told me that Marco had been a middleweight boxing champion but gave it up while still undefeated. Now he led the family's expanding ice cream business. He and Selina were each other's favourites. There was just fifteen months between them, and they had both "married out". Jess was Jewish, also from Grimston Street. Selina's family accepted Jess because Jews, like Catholics, "had heart" and you could put barely a wafer between them. Agnostic Jarrod Compton was welcomed for his charm and the glamour of a show business family. Jess stayed silent on her own family's reaction to the marriage. She did not see them these days. They had moved north.

On first coming into Selina's house, there had been so much to look at and admire that it was hard to focus on individuals, and to find something significant that might explain why Selina had been anxious enough to contact me.

Now, sitting by a hospital bed I found it difficult to concentrate. Not having slept all night was no help.

Impressions. That was what flitted through my mind. The impressions and images were so amorphous as to be useless in helping me to understand anything.

In my mind's eye, glamorous couples glided across the highly polished parquet floor to the tune of "Always".

Half a dozen sleepyheads lounged on the feather-cushioned casual sofas that were dotted about the room. The burr walnut table held dipped-into dishes of caviar and plates of crackers alongside sausage rolls, pork pies and pickled onions — an odd combination of the luxurious and the everyday that suited the gathering of show business people. The dancers seemed capable of eating for England. Pip Potter, strongman, also tucked in heartily. Sandy Sechrest, the memory woman, picked at a bread roll. She seemed alert to everything that went on around her, and solicitous of Selina. Perhaps it was the thought of flying but Selina seemed a little anxious. She disappeared for a while. I looked about for her husband but did not see him. Later, someone said that he had set off alone on his motorcycle, heading for Richmond.

Billy Moffatt stirred uneasily. For a moment I thought he might be regaining consciousness. His lips were dry. The sister had left a piece of lint and a glass of water. I moistened his mouth.

How close were Selina Fellini and Billy Moffatt? I knew so little about them.

Selina hadn't said much about her husband Jarrod, except that war had changed him. A husband need not be so very greatly changed to become jealous of a successful wife who became good friends with the men around her.

A waiter, hired for the occasion, replenished dishes. As the evening wore on, the party thinned. Several musicians and five of the dancers had left early for the railway station. The Powolskis, sister and brother acrobats, and a dour-looking chap called Maurice Montague, master of music, whose act consisted of playing twenty-nine instruments in quick succession, had roared into the night on a motorcycle with sidecar.

Members of the Fellini family, chattering and calling to each other in a mixture of English and Italian, had set off in Selina's chauffeur-driven car and two taxis, heading for Barden Moor.

Over the previous days and weeks, maps in the newspapers had been carefully studied and observation points argued over. The band of totality, about twenty-eight miles wide, extended across North Wales, Lancashire and Yorkshire.

Perhaps Selina's husband had gone to secure his place early. Why had she not invited him? Or perhaps she had. Selina's stories of two accidental deaths set my thoughts racing. Say those deaths were not accidental. She had been close to the two men who died. Billy Moffatt was the chosen friend for this visit to Giggleswick, the person she wanted with her on the morning of this special day.

What had triggered his collapse? Perhaps he had some underlying condition that was exacerbated by the flight and standing for so long in the bitter cold. Yes he had been sniffing cocaine at last night's party, but so had some of the dancers, elegantly fingering the tiny gold containers hung at their throats on slender chains. Yes he had probably dosed himself with morphine, but that was no great surprise in a man whose war injuries would always plague him.

What else might I remember that would be of value? Someone had set an alarm clock on top of the piano, so that they would all be sure to go outside and look at the sky at the appointed time, more in hope than expectation.

For a time I had sat on the terrace with Jake the animal trainer. He had come to the company as a replacement for Dougie Doig's performing dog act. Jake would not be parted from his highly prized miniature pony at such a crucial time. The animal, a sensitive creature presently bedded down in the porch, might take fright.

None of these recollections helped me, or the poor man lying in the bed. I touched the needle mark on his neck, a recent mark. "What happened, Billy? Did someone do this to you?"

Unsurprisingly, the dying man did not answer.

I wondered whether someone at the party, some enemy of Billy's, had left early and come out here. In spite of the policeman on the gate it would not have been difficult for a determined person to find their way into the grounds of Giggleswick School.

Not everyone at the party wanted to observe the eclipse from a vantage point on a chilly hillside. My housekeeper, Mrs Sugden, preferred to stay at home with the cat. Selina's linen-suited manager, Trotter Brockett, claimed he needed his beauty sleep, but he hovered making some of his performers nervous by his presence, and urging Selina and Billy to be careful and warning them not to look directly at the sun. He left the party moments before we did, saying he would wait to see photographs of the eclipse in the early editions.

At the start of the party, I had the pleasure of chatting with Sandy Sechrest, and so I went across to the piano to say goodnight to her and Jake for whom she was turning the pages of sheet music. Facts were Miss Sechrest's stock in trade. It was not necessary, she had explained with great solemnity, for her to see the eclipse as long as she had all the necessary information. Nevertheless, the plan of this living archive, this walking encyclopaedia as she was sometimes called, was to follow the advice reportedly given by the Astronomer Royal to the boys of Bradford Grammar school. If they were unable to find a vantage point, they should go to a wooded area and stand beneath trees. By looking at the ground, they would see the eclipse through the shadow pattern of foliage. Miss Sechrest had consulted a map and felt confident of making her way from Selina's house in Roundhay to Gledhow Valley Woods. She disliked crowds and hoped to find a solitary spot, avoiding the throng.

She had reassured Jake that all would be well. He was upset because Mr Brockett had been very short with him when he mentioned that the steep rake of the City Varieties stage made it difficult for his pony, Pinto, to dance backwards. Beryl Lister, Miss Fellini's dresser, said she would keep an eye on the house. At the break of day she would wake those left behind so they could see what they could see, from the highest point in the park, though it was her opinion that hangers-on from the party preferred the newly created Eclipse Cocktail to the real thing. I took the impression that Selina Fellini relied on Beryl a great deal. She had a round, pleasant, unlined face with gap teeth, was ample in figure and wore her fair hair centre-parted and pulled back into a bun. Beryl's concession to party attire was to wear a long-sleeved sage green dress buttoned down the front. She would brook no nonsense from those she called "hangers-on" and had already presented Jake with a carrot to feed to his sensitive miniature pony "on the way home".

Jake had taken the carrot. "But Beryl, Selina sweetly said I could share Maurice's room, and Pinto can bed down in the garage."

"It's Mrs Lister and Miss Fellini to you and I'll thank you not to trade on Miss Fellini's good nature. I happen to know you and Pinto have digs in Chapeltown, so off you go. That pony needs his sleep."

I admired Beryl's sternness. As we were about to leave, she fixed me with her candid stare. "You'll make sure Miss Fellini isn't kept in Giggleswick till all hours by her admirers. She needs her rest for tomorrow night's performance, or tonight's I should say since we're already in Wednesday."

"She'll be back in good time. The airmen have another assignment so will keep to their timetable."

"Good. I hope the trip will be worth it. You know there's cloud forecast?"

A cynical few dared say that this being England, and the weather damp and cold, there would be no miraculous sighting. Bookmakers' odds were three to one against. Weather forecasters all agreed on a probability of cloud.

A probability of cloud was what Billy Moffatt had hoped for.

It was time to stop considering any possibilities the party might throw up and think only of Billy.

I risked looking at my watch. The time was passing so slowly, as if in honour of this funny man, allowing him those extra minutes on this miraculous earth.

Time, understanding my appreciation, stood still.

There were footsteps in the ward. A nurse put her head round the screen, and then withdrew. Somewhere nearby there was an exchange of words between the nurse and a patient. A man coughed. A trolley squeaked along the corridor.

I squeezed Billy's hand. "What have I missed, Billy? What might you tell me?"

But in that moment, a terrible shudder and a gasp shook poor Billy, and then he was still. Billy would speak no more. Uselessly, I touched his throat for a pulse. There are not enough people in the world who make us laugh. I'd come to like Billy Moffatt in that short time we were acquainted. I told myself that if he had recovered he might never have been the same again. I hardly knew him. He was a grown man who made his own choices and yet his flight from this life felt like my own personal failure.

A voice in my head whispered, someone is guilty.

Stop it, I told myself as I walked quietly from the bedside and around the screens placed there for privacy. These are variety performers, not the Borgias.

There will be simple explanations. There are always simple explanations.

A man in the bed opposite was sitting up, watching. The man next to him began a coughing fit. I left the ward quietly.

Cleaners had been hard at work. There was a strong smell of Vim as I walked along the corridor to find Sister. Yet even the normal atmosphere of the hospital did not dispel my imaginings.

Someone may have tampered with Billy's morphine dosage. Or, and here was a horrific speculation, what if Billy himself had wanted the other two friends out of the way so that he might be Selina's favourite? If Billy had a hand in Douglas Dougan's and Floyd Lloyd's demise, his own death may be heaven-sent retribution, or a revenge killing.

Sister was in her small office. I tapped on the door. She took one look at me and knew. But still I said the words. "Billy died a few moments ago." He had clung to life for just four hours after being found by the chapel.

She glanced at her watch. "I'm so sorry. Come and sit down, Mrs Shackleton. You look done in."

"He didn't regain consciousness."

"Poor man, and what a loss. I saw him once, just after the war. It was his contortions as much as what he said kept us all in stitches." She straightened her apron. "I'll contact the doctor. Did the other patients realise, do you think?"

"I'm not sure. The man in the bed opposite was quite alert."

"He's reliable. He won't upset the others."

I must give no hint of my mad suspicions. Normality was called for. Since I barely knew the man, there was the sadness one feels at any passing but not that deep distress when it is someone well known and loved. "Regarding the formalities . . ."

"Yes?"

"May I use the telephone? Miss Fellini asked me to let her know and so I must break the news to her and to Billy's manager who is staying at the Queens Hotel."

"Go speak to the porter. Say I give permission for you to make the telephone calls." She stood. "And what will you do now? Can I get you anything?"

"No, thank you. After I've made the telephone calls, I'll walk to the railway station and catch the next train back."

"Very well. I'll inform the school. Headmaster and Matron will want to hear." She straightened her cuff.

"Something occurred to me, regarding the injection mark in his neck." She paused. "I know that you gave Mr Moffatt's pillbox to the doctor, but I'm wondering was there a needle?"

"Ah, that's a good question. No there wasn't."

She frowned. "I hope he didn't leave a needle lying about in the school grounds."

There are some telephone calls that make me wish that what Mrs Sugden calls the infernal contraption had never been invented.

Selina's telephone was answered by Beryl Lister, and I admit to feeling relieved that there might be an intermediary to break the news, someone who knew Selina better than I did, and was protective of her. "Mrs Lister, Kate Shackleton here, calling from the hospital in Giggleswick."

"Ah."

"Are you sitting down?"

"I wasn't. But give me two shakes and I will."

"Are you sitting down now?"

"I am."

"I'm sorry to say that it's bad news. Is Miss Fellini able to come to the telephone?"

"I ran a bath for her and her masseuse has arrived. If it's all the same to you . . ."

"Yes?"

The line went quiet. Finally, she said, "I'm inclined to let her have her massage and a sleep. She has a tablet she might take."

"She did ask me to let her know straightaway."

She sighed. "If this telephone call had come half an hour later, she would be asleep by now."

"And that would be good."

"It would."

"Then I leave the news to your discretion, Mrs Lister. Please say that I'll come to the theatre this evening. I'm sure there'll be questions she wants to ask me."

Though at present I could not think what her questions might be or how I would answer them. Billy collapsed. He died. That was as much as I could say.

The hospital porter sat on a stool close by, having relinquished his chair to me. He was a stout, elderly man whose perfectly groomed walrus moustache gave him an air of melancholy. Without commenting on the conversation, he simply came to my aid. "Let me get the next number for you, madam. Who is it you'd like to speak to?"

"Thank you. I need to speak to a Mr Brockett. He's staying at the Queens Hotel in Leeds."

I could easily have done this myself, but my mouth had turned dry and the top of my head felt as if it might start to spin.

It took some time for Mr Brockett to be located. Eventually, the kindly porter handed me the receiver.

"Brockett speaking!"

"Mr Brockett, Mrs Shackleton, calling from Giggleswick."

"Ah, Mrs Shackleton, glad to hear from you. Thanks for ensuring Selina came home safely, but something's wrong I hear. Beryl telephoned me a couple of hours ago. She tells me Billy took a funny turn."

"I'm sorry to say that it was rather more serious than that, Mr Brockett."

"Was it now, well I'm just seeing one or two people about filling in for him tonight so you can tell him not to worry. If you'll find out visiting hours, I'll come and see him."

"Mr Brockett, are you sitting down?"

CHAPTER
ELEVEN

The Cigar

At the hospital gates, I realised that I did not know which direction to take for the railway station. I looked about for someone to ask, just as one of the boys from the school came towards me. It was Alex, the head boy who had placed his OTC coat over Billy. Now he was back in school uniform.

"Hello. You look a bit lost, Mrs Shackleton. Is it what I think?"

"Mr Moffatt just died."

"Oh." His face crumpled. The poor boy thought he had saved him. He was too young to have had news broken so abruptly. "I'm sorry. You and the other lads did your best."

We stood for a moment. He waved at the entrance to the hospital. "I enquired. The porter said someone was sitting with him. I thought it might be Miss Fellini."

With the makings of a proper gentleman, he hid his disappointment well. Having hovered about waiting for the country's biggest variety star, he got me.

"Miss Fellini had to go back to Leeds. She has a performance tonight."

90

"Yes I know. I'm hoping I might get to the Saturday matinée."

"She sends her thanks to you and the other boys who helped find Billy."

"I only wish we'd found him sooner."

"It's good that you found him as quickly as you did." He was too young to be holding himself responsible. "If it's any consolation, finding him sooner would not have made a difference."

"Thank you for saying that. I'll tell the others. They're all busy up at the school, a bit of a do going on for the remaining guests." He looked towards the hospital entrance. "I suppose I should ask in the hospital if they want me to take a note to the head."

"The ward sister or the doctor will telephone. The sister may want to consult with the doctor first but they'll certainly let the school know very soon."

He nodded. "Are you going back to the station?"

"I am."

"Shall I walk you?"

"I wish you would. I'm likely to walk in circles."

We set off. Alex was frowning. I felt sorry that such an important day for him and his fellows had taken this desperately sad turn.

A villager wished us good day. Alex had to shake himself into answering, but it broke his silence. "I wish Mr Moffatt had stayed with us, when he came over to have a word."

"Where were you?"

"We were by the chapel."

"I wondered where Billy disappeared to. One moment we were all together, Miss Fellini, Mr Moffatt and I, and the next moment he was gone. Did he go into the chapel?"

"No. Four of us OTC chaps were near the front of the chapel. When everyone got so excited after seeing the eclipse, we were larking about, trying to dance the fandango. Mr Moffatt joined in for about thirty seconds and then he just laughed. He took out a cigar, lit it and walked off."

That made sense. He knew how sensitive Selina was regarding her throat and her aversion to a smoky atmosphere. He would not have stood beside her with his cigar. What I didn't understand was why he had just walked off without a word. Had he already injected himself? If so, when and where did he take out his needle and put it to his neck? Mrs Douglas thought that he had taken drugs. I wondered what made her think that. Perhaps she had looked into his eyes and knew the signs.

"Alex, will you please show me where you found Billy?"

"Yes. He was behind the chapel, sitting on the ground with his back to the wall, slumped over."

He must have been so cold, so very cold, and tired too, if he had sat down on the ground. We turned around, retracing our steps, walking back from the village towards the school grounds.

Alex pushed open the small gate that still held the sign "Astronomer Royal Only". "What do you think

92

caused his death, Mrs Shackleton? Only something struck me as odd. He had an odd look about him."

"What kind of look?"

"I'm not sure how to describe it, as if he'd swallowed a lemon. Sorry to seem cold-hearted but I'm interested because my father and uncle are doctors and that's what I'll be too."

The area that earlier had been so crowded with people was now deserted. The astronomers' equipment had been cleared away.

He was such a sensible and intelligent young man who clearly thought that it would be fair of me to share my thoughts, and yet that would be wrong. "I don't know the cause of death. I wondered that myself. We'll wait to hear from the doctor."

He gave a scoffing laugh that sounded too cynical to have come from such a young person. "Between you and me, Mrs Shackleton, if it's Doctor Davison, he'll say heart attack. He nearly always says heart attack or heart failure, or cardiac arrest, which I suppose can never be far from the mark."

"You think differently, Alex?"

"It looked to me as if he'd taken something. We had a boy last year expelled for that sort of thing. He'd managed to gather his own little stash of opium."

"You are very observant."

"I've read up on it. Have you done any such thing as nursing?"

"I have."

"I watched you in the chapel and I guessed as much."

"Yes." This was far too grown-up a conversation to be having with a boy, but he must be seventeen or eighteen, almost a man.

"I haven't said anything to anyone of course, Mrs Shackleton."

"That's the best course under the circumstances." We were back in the area surrounding the chapel. All the equipment had been removed. The area was well trampled, with here and there a few tent pegs left from where temporary shelters had covered equipment. There were tab ends and a few sweet wrappers. If Billy wanted to inject himself he would have needed to find a less public place than this.

"This way!" Alex walked around the side of the chapel. There was an area of brushwood and a stunted tree.

He came to a stop. "Mr Moffatt was here, by the wall, as if he'd leaned against it and slid down."

He illustrated by putting his back to the wall, sliding into a sitting position and then leaning forwards, his head lolling in a way that made me shiver. Just as quickly, he jumped up.

I walked back and forth, looking at the ground. There was no needle. Near to where Alex said Billy had sat was a discarded cigar.

"You say he lit a cigar?"

"Yes. That must be it."

So Billy had strolled round the side of the chapel to smoke, to be alone and lick his wounds. The success of the eclipse put paid to his routine.

He was unlikely to have injected himself with so many people close by. Besides, having lit a cigar, he wouldn't easily be able to handle a needle.

I took a hanky from my pocket, bent down and picked up the remains of the cigar. Either he had stubbed it out quickly or it died shortly after lighting. I folded it into the hanky.

"May I?"

I opened the hanky and let Alex take a look at the cigar. He sniffed it. "Interesting."

Alex returned it to me. I put it in my satchel.

"I read a story, ages ago." He spoke lightly as though making conversation at a dinner table. "It was by William Le Queux. Have you read any of his?"

"No. My father reads them though."

"In this particular story, someone was poisoned by a cigar."

I then felt slightly ridiculous for having picked up the dead cigar, like some tramp searching gutters for tab ends. "I'm not sure why I picked this up. Perhaps because it was the last thing Billy did — smoked."

"Mrs Shackleton, why did Mr Moffatt come over here to light up rather than stay with his friends?"

"Miss Fellini is very sensitive about her throat. Her livelihood depends on her voice and she has a performance this evening."

"I see."

I felt reluctant to walk away from the spot where Billy sat down, where he lost consciousness, almost as if doing so was a betrayal.

Alex also stood like a mourner at a funeral. "We're both wondering about his death, aren't we, Mrs Shackleton? And because I know the doctor, I can say with certainty that it will be heart failure. You can't go wrong with that."

"Alex, as a doctor's son you'll know that there will need to be a post mortem in the case of an unexpected death."

He looked disappointed. "Yes I suppose that's true. I wish it could be me carrying it out."

"That's ghoulish."

"No. It's medicine."

It was time for me to go back to the station. I had no timetable and didn't know how long I might have to wait for a train. "Well, thank you for bringing me here. I'd better be off now."

"What will you do with the cigar?"

That was a good question. It crossed my mind that Billy not only sniffed his drugs but smoked them too. I should like to satisfy my curiosity. Alex was looking at me with such intensity, his eyes alight with intelligence. He reminded me of the very first boy I took tea with, when we were both too shy to speak. This wasn't true of Alex.

It would be ridiculous to say that I picked it up as a memento. "I might just take it to a friendly chemist, out of interest."

Quick as a flash he was on the alert. "We have a laboratory here. No one will be taking any notice what we do at this time of the day. I'm a bit of a whiz in the lab, and I know there won't be a train from Giggleswick for at least another hour."

I hesitated.

He pushed his case. "You see, some materials evaporate pretty quickly. By the time you got home there might be nothing to find."

"There probably isn't anything to find now." But his words gave me pause for thought. Chemistry was never my strong suit and this chap, young as he was, did indeed seem a bit of a whiz. If he was right and the cigar had been tampered with, and the substance might evaporate, then it would be negligent not to try and find out. To return home and visit my chemist friend with a chewed cigar was not an enticing prospect, and would probably waste his time. Of course the simple thing would be to take it back to the infirmary, but it might lie around there the whole day.

Alex tilted his head. "We won't know if we don't try."

"Are you sure we can do it without getting you into trouble?"

"I'm sure. I'm head boy to keep me out of bother and I'm expert in keeping my nose clean."

With a somewhat stealthy air, we set off for the school laboratory, in possession of the cigar.

"If anyone spots us, we'll say I'm showing you round the school."

We were climbing the stairs to the second floor and so far had not met a soul, boys and masters having been given the rest of the day off to make up for their early start that morning.

The metal sign on the door read Chemistry Laboratory.

Alex glanced both ways along the corridor before taking a key from his pocket. He unlocked the door and swung it open for me.

"You've done this before, Alex."

"Once or twice. It's useful to be trusted." He followed me in, closing the door behind him.

The lab, permeated with a faint smell of sulphur and ammonia, was a large classroom with high windows. No passer-by shorter than fourteen feet would see in.

The impression was of dark wood and gleaming glass bottles. Eight benches stood in two rows of four along the centre of the room. Each had cupboards below and shelves attached above. The shelves held a myriad of bottles and dishes in various shapes and sizes. The names came back to me from my schoolgirl flirtation with chemistry. Erlenmeyer flask, beakers, round-bottom flask, reagent bottle, Bunsen burner, evaporating dishes.

Down either side of the room were scrubbed tables, sinks and contraptions with rubber tubes.

Alex waited for me to give him the cigar. "I have an idea about this, from the smell of it. It's a weird smell."

"You're right, but I have a summer cold. I'm not the best judge today."

In spite of the care I had taken to wrap the cigar in my handkerchief, strands of tobacco had loosened and lay nest-like against the white cotton. "Before you do that, because this might be quicker though I don't know . . ." I reached into my pocket. Prior to giving the pillbox to the doctor I had extracted one of the tablets. "Billy had these in his pocket. I don't know what they are." I handed him the tablet.

He sniffed. "Not much of a smell."

He picked up a small dish, took it to the sink and turned on the cold water tap. I stood beside him while he broke the tablet and dropped half into the water. It fizzed. He dipped in his finger and tasted.

"Be careful!"

"It's all right, just an antacid tablet. It's turned the water alkaline. See for yourself."

I tasted. So Selina had known what tablets Billy carried. Poor Billy, not only an old soldier with painful wounds but an acidic stomach, too. Mrs Douglas had thought the pillbox contained drugs, though of course she was right that it had originally held cocaine.

We both froze at the same moment as footsteps sounded along the corridor, and someone paused by the door. I hoped that no conscientious science master decided to come in and plan a lesson. It was one thing to have the excuse of being shown around the school, quite another to be in a locked laboratory with the head boy, watching him conduct a poison test on a cigar.

False alarm. Whoever it was continued along the corridor.

Alex cleaned the small dish, rinsed the remains of the tablet down the sink and wiped it down. "Now for the cigar. I have an idea that this isn't just tobacco. I'm going to do a hydrosulphate test."

"What's that?"

"It's a test for metals. I create a little concoction and add iron sulphate. You can watch if you like."

"No, you do it. I don't want to put you off." This no longer seemed like a good idea. I blamed my sudden feeling of exhaustion. I had not slept for almost thirty hours.

I sat down on one of the benches while he gathered up a dish and bottles from one of the cupboards. "I'll do the sodium fusion test first." He had his back to me as he worked but gave a commentary. "I've added ferrous sulphate and now . . ." He picked up a bottle. "I shall add hydrochloric acid and that should . . ." He stared at his concoction, and then raised his arms like a champion boxer and leapt in the air. "I'm right! Look!"

I stared into the flask. "What am I looking at?"

"The colour!"

"It's blue."

"It's Prussian blue. That's a positive result for cyanide."

"But how did you know what to look for?"

"The smell, when I said the cigar had an odd smell, it was bitter almonds."

"So Billy smoked a cigar laced with cyanide?"

It was too much to take in. Billy had been poisoned. I walked to the window and looked across at the house opposite, but then stepped back in case someone across the way had the same idea and saw me. What on earth must I do now? After the initial elation of his discovery, Alex was also nonplussed. "No civilised cigar maker would create something like this. He'd kill all his customers." He stared at me. "Someone has been reading William Le Queux."

"Not I."

"Mr Moffatt himself? Is that why he wanted to be alone?"

"Alex, you're not having me on, are you? This seems absurd."

"Yes, doesn't it?"

"Are you absolutely sure?"

"Completely sure. The fact that cyanide was in the cigar means that the heat will have made it work rapidly. Mr Moffatt didn't have a chance. He must be strong, and have flung it down quickly, to live for as long as he did."

"Then I'll need to take this cigar to the authorities, and soon. I'd have to give reasons for my suspicions."

"It's a simple enough test. Do you want me to repeat it, step by step?"

"Absolutely not." I did not want to waste time. This made no sense. If Billy had intended to kill himself, why do it so publicly? It was hard to believe that no thought of Selina and her reaction had crossed his mind. He was so fond of her, anyone could see that. It was horrible to think of his doing something that would distress if not destroy those left behind. If someone else had tampered with his cigar, surely they would have left some mark or indication that Billy may have seen before he put the cigar to his lips. Of course it was still dark and he would have lit up without paying too much attention. If it had been given to him, he might have decided against smoking, passed it on and killed someone else. The thought horrified me. Billy would have had no compunction about giving a cigar to a boy if he didn't fancy smoking it.

"What are you thinking, Mrs Shackleton?"

"I'm thinking someone else must have given him the cigar, because where would Billy get hold of cyanide?"

"It's alarmingly easy to produce if you know how."

"Wouldn't Billy have tasted something odd, or smelled something, as you did?"

"He may have had a cold, or a poor sense of smell. And there is one thing that puzzles me, if he was responsible for his own death."

"What's that?"

"If he knew enough to be able to create cyanide, he would have known that cyanide salts react at a higher level with stomach acidity. He wouldn't have bothered to bring his antacid tablets if he planned to light up that cigar."

Late afternoon sun streamed through the lab windows. The vertical mullions cast stripes of shadows across the room. Patches of sunshine made visible motes of dust in the air. My boy genius companion stood by the sink, pouring away the solution he had created. He turned on the tap. "What do you want to do, Mrs Shackleton?"

I was finding it difficult to gather my thoughts. What did I want to do? If the headmaster's wife was so protective of the school's reputation that she worried about a pillbox of tablets and a sprinkling of cocaine, then what might lie in store for the head boy if he was

102

found to have brought me into the laboratory and conducted a test for cyanide?

To whom should I hand the evidence — if evidence it was — the local police, the hospital? And evidence of what, that was the difficulty. Was it suicide, or murder?

Alex was waiting for me to answer.

Footsteps once more sounded along the corridor. This time, they began to slow and came to a stop by the door.

Alex's eyes opened wide in alarm. He pulled the key from his pocket and indicated a door at the end of the room. In his haste to reach the connecting door, he was speeding off without the vital evidence. I rewrapped the cigar and quickly followed him into the next classroom just as the door to the lab opened. We tiptoed from an adjoining laboratory and in a moment, after he unlocked and relocked another door, we were back in the corridor.

"It's all the same key," he whispered. "The masters are terribly strict with us and awfully lax generally."

"Alex, let's get out of here. I don't want to land you in trouble."

We made our way to the front door without being seen.

"I'll catch you up on the path, Mrs Shackleton. I must just cancel a game of chess."

As I walked back through the school grounds in the direction of the village, I thought about what to do. Having given the pillbox of antacid tablets to the doctor, I ought immediately to take the remains of the cigar straight to the hospital. Alex had used the lab unauthorised, but that paled into insignificance beside the need to establish the true cause of death. Establishing the cause would not help in finding out whether Billy's act was self-inflicted. It might have been, or some malevolent person had given him the poisoned cigar.

As far as I knew, people intent on self-destruction would think not only about the means but time and place. Had Billy really boarded the aeroplane this morning intending to take his life? Surely not.

Given the bond between Billy and Selina, it seemed impossible that he would simply have walked away, without a kiss on the cheek, without a goodbye.

CHAPTER
TWELVE

The Long Way Home

I walked slowly back towards the village, needing a plan. Taking the partly smoked and distinctly chewed poisoned cigar to the hospital would be one course of action. It would involve explaining that I picked up the cigar from the ground. I might deliver it into the hospital sister's hands and ask that it be passed to the doctor for analysis. Soon. I could not rely on the evidence of a schoolboy. There needed to be an expert scientific analysis.

Another course of action would be to follow my original idea of going to my friendly chemist and asking him to analyse it. His report, and a statement from Alex, could be presented to the coroner's officer.

There was no time to lose.

Perhaps I would be able to find out whether Billy was in the habit of smoking cigars and, if so, where he got them. Somehow I doubted that he knew much about chemistry, or creating cyanide. Selina had remarked that Billy attended a ragged school. Ragged schools, while keen on the three Rs of reading, writing and 'rithmetic, were not renowned for teaching urchins chemistry, or any other subjects that would unsettle them, make them ambitious beyond their station and critical of a world that kept them firmly in their allotted place. Of course Billy could have picked up knowledge of cyanide while in the army. Men returned from war with a vast array of murderous skills.

By the time I had obtained a second, and professional, analysis of the cigar, a post mortem may have taken place. Perhaps something significant would come from that.

Alex had been longer in catching me up than I expected. I looked round to see if he was in sight. Not yet.

The walk gave me time to think. This was what I must do. Go straight from the train to my chemist friend. If the analysis revealed poison, I must report the findings to the coroner's officer. The chemist would do that in any case. By acting in that way, there would be no need to bring Alex McGregor into the picture, except to say that I had asked him to show me where Billy was found. I would explain that because Alex and his friends saw Billy smoking a cigar, I picked up what remained of that cigar, which was rather a lot, just out of interest.

All Alex would need to do was confirm that he took me to the spot where Billy was found. I now regretted that dash to the lab. It could be thought that the cigar had been exposed to some other chemical while in my and Alex's possession.

It also raised the question about where the cigar came from. Would I act differently if I knew for certain Billy had intended suicide? Perhaps before taking the evidence to a chemist, I might find out whether Billy had left a note somewhere.

It seemed to me unlikely that he would have gone to Giggleswick, taking his first ride in a plane, acting jolly, with the thought in the back of his mind that Wednesday, 29 June, day of the eclipse, would be the last day of his life. On the other hand, what a way and what a day to die, an extraordinary day and a dreadful death.

"Mrs Shackleton!" Alex caught up with me. He had been running. "I thought you must have come this way when I didn't see you on the hill."

"This is the road to Giggleswick station, isn't it?"

"To Giggleswick station, yes. You'll be better going from Settle. There's a sooner train and it's a pleasant walk."

"Then lead on, Alex."

He gave a rueful smile. "This way you won't need to pass Castleberg and the infirmary."

We turned back. At that moment, I did not care whether the walk was pleasant or otherwise, but he was right in thinking that I would prefer not to see Castleberg again.

We walked in silence as far as a beck, colonised by a flock of sedate ducks. There we paused. There is something soothing about gently flowing water. Alex quoted Spenser. "Sweet Thames, run softly, till I end my song."

"What a peaceful little stretch of water."

"It's called Tems Beck," Alex explained, "spelled T.e.m.s, pronounced Thames. When first years write home, they like to say they have walked by the Tems. A correction of their geography and spelling comes back pretty quickly, and then they explain. I meant to tell that to Mr Moffatt, in case he fancied the idea for his routine."

"Yes, he might have."

"It's probably not funny. I'm hopeless at jokes."

One of the ducks suddenly executed a graceful dive towards something we could not see. Sunlight created sparkling dots of light on the water, adding to the sense of unreality, yet the world about us appeared oddly normal. We passed a big house, where someone was cleaning the windows, a national school where children played in the yard, laughing and calling to each other.

Alex had gone to some trouble to take me the scenic way to the station and so I commented on the fine church.

"It's St Alkelda's. No one outside a few square miles of Yorkshire has heard of her. Do you want to go in?"

"No. I best get on, what with my little cargo of cigar, and that people will have questions for me."

He nodded. "Only I don't suppose you will ever want to come back here, after today."

"Perhaps not."

Outside the Black Horse, a drayman, helped by a barman, manoeuvred a barrel of beer from the cart while the horse waited patiently. On Belle Hill, a woman came from her house carrying a shopping basket. She wished us good morning.

Was it still morning? I felt as if a century flew by since the aeroplane landed on the cricket pitch, and that nothing would ever again be real.

★ ★ ★

We arrived at the station with half an hour to spare before the Leeds train arrived.

"Alex, we're going into the buffet, and this will be my treat. It's been a terrible day for all of us, after starting out so well."

The poor boy was rather subdued. He had been so good and helpful, and for all I knew was missing a meal because of me.

There was a single waitress behind the counter. An elderly couple sat by the window.

"What will you have, Alex?"

The woman behind the counter wiped her hands on the teacloth. "I've run out of just about everything. They came in like locusts this morning. I baked more scones but they've all gone as well. Had to send out for more milk, cheese and eggs."

I felt the need to eat something. "Will there be time for me to have a cup of tea and a bite of anything at all before the Leeds train arrives? And whatever this young man would like to order."

"Oh aye, there's time. I'll fry you an egg, madam. Won't be a jiffy." She looked at Alex.

"I'll have welsh rarebit and a pot of tea, please."

"You're Giggleswick School head boy, aren't you?"

Alex came to life, remembering his exalted position. "Yes."

"You must all be very pleased with yourselves up at the school."

He nodded. "We are. Thank you."

Five minutes later, we had a pot of tea on the table, and two cups. I stirred, poured, and explained my plan to Alex, finishing with the words, "So you see, I shall keep you out of it entirely, except as the person who showed me where Billy died and walked me to the railway station. I'll present the evidence to the chemist without saying the cigar has already been tested for . . ." Not wanting to say the word cyanide in public, I lowered my voice. "Tested and found positive. There'll be a post mortem and that will reveal the cause of death."

Alex ran his hands through his hair. "Not sure about that."

"Why not?"

He raised his cup and spoke to it rather than to me. "It would have taken one tiny whiff to kill Mr Moffatt. In the William Le Queux story the substance was discovered because the cigar was examined quickly. That's how it works in the stories. It's found in the tea, or the stout, or the champagne. Cyanide disappears from the body after a very short time and it might already have done so."

"I'll have to take a chance on that, Alex. Writers take liberties. Poetic licence. William Le Queux and his fellow scribblers may not be the most reliable sources."

"I hadn't thought about that. I'll need to read up a bit more." Alex sighed. "Not that I suppose I'll need that kind of information when I go into practice in Dundee, but you never know."

"How true."

"Mrs Shackleton, if I don't hear from any other quarter, may I get in touch with you to ask what happened? I'd like to know how this business turns out, and I'll be very discreet."

I smiled. "I'm sure that coming from a family of doctors, discretion is bred in the bone. Thank you for your help." I gave him my card.

Just half a dozen of us stood on the platform waiting for the train, but only one of us carried an item that may have been laced with a lethal poison.

My earlier concerns about crowds and the difficulty of a return journey were unfounded. It was one o'clock and people had departed Giggleswick quickly, anxious to be home and catch some sleep. Given how early the sun and moon had put on their performance, it was likely that many people had already returned to work in shops and offices. It would have been possible after all for Selina to have let the plane go without her. She would have made it back on time before the performance. But all in all I was glad that she had not waited, given how ghastly she looked earlier. At least now she would have rested before Beryl Lister broke the news of Billy's death.

The station master came from his office and stepped onto the platform, flag and whistle in hand, a sign that our train was due.

Moments later, in a swirl of smoke and steam, slowing as it neared the station, the train trundled into view and shuddered to a halt.

Although I felt tired and my brain fit to burst, I was glad to have just two silent fellow travellers in the compartment as I tried to think about everything that had happened and make some sense of the day's events.

But I couldn't think clearly, my brain being too scrambled for anything but that swirling indefinite mishmash of uncertainty. It was now that I remembered something Billy had said during the party. It was the kind of ridiculous remark one did not take notice of at the time. Billy was telling everyone what a flop the eclipse would be and that if by some remote chance the clouds parted and the sun came out, he would have to change his routine and it was such a good routine that he would rather top himself. The memory of his words made me shudder.

I felt sure that Billy hadn't tampered with his own cigar. So, who had? In a sudden burst of generosity, he might have handed the cigar to one of the astronomers, even the Astronomer Royal. One of the cleverest men in the country might have been done in through a comedian's magnanimous gesture.

I closed my eyes for the rest of the journey, aware that I was simply going round and round in circles. Leeds was our final destination so there was no fear of my being carried on along the rail lines beyond my station. In spite of shutting my eyes, sleep did not come.

I stepped out onto the platform, conscious of the precious cargo in my pocket, having wrapped the handkerchief in a page from my notebook and put it inside an envelope.

Not expecting to be met, or for anyone to know of my arrival, I strode towards the barrier. It was a surprise to hear someone call my name.

The man placed himself directly in front of me and said again, "Mrs Shackleton!"

It was Selina's manager, Trotter Brockett, not a man or a name one would easily forget.

"Mr Brockett, hello."

"At your service, Mrs Shackleton."

He looked beyond me and I thought he must be waiting for someone else.

When it was clear everyone from my train had gone through, he took a breath. "This isn't funny."

"What?"

"Did he put you up to it, one of his pranks?"

"What do you mean?" And then I knew what he meant. He did not believe that Billy had died.

"Mr Brockett, I wouldn't dream of playing such a nasty trick. I'm so sorry. My call from the hospital was genuine."

"Oh." He deflated like a collapsing Yorkshire pudding. "No."

I took his arm. "Come on, I'll walk you back to your hotel."

"Not Billy, not Billy."

"I'm afraid so." I thought back to my telephone call to him. When Mr Brockett had received the dreadful information about Billy with barely a comment, I thought that was due to shock. He and Billy must have had an odd sort of friendship if he thought that Billy would ask me to pretend something so, well — fatal.

Mr Brockett could barely put one foot in front of the other. "He liked to play jokes on me. And sometimes, he wouldn't want to go on stage any more, when he was down. He once sent a message — tell Brockett I've died and gone to heaven. I thought he'd put you up to giving me a punch line, a punch, a punch."

I practically held him upright, helping him back to the hotel. He was winded. His breath came in gasps. "Pranksters. We were merry pranksters, we two. I was thinking of some way to pay him back. I knew he wasn't well when I heard from Beryl that Selina had come back without him. I've arranged a replacement. That call, couldn't believe your call. It had to be one of his cruel jokes."

Surely no one would joke about something so serious.

Mr Brockett stopped and looked round. "He's going to jump out, isn't he? That quip of his, he's still joking. This isn't true."

"I am sorry. What a dreadful shock for you, Mr Trotter."

"I was going to feign surprise. Say I'd cancelled the performance."

In the grubby smoke-ridden station, passengers hurrying to and from their trains turned to steal a quick glance at us. Even at his most sober and distraught, Trotter Brockett looked healthy, tanned, and distinctly un-English. He was once more dressed in a pristine linen suit, this time with a mourning band on his arm. Presumably he had donned this band as a response to the "joke". His shirt was the palest blue and he wore a black tie. The attempt at sobriety had not detracted from his naturally jaunty manner when I spotted him first. Now that jauntiness had fled.

114

We left the station and stepped into the bright light of day. The sun shone on young women in gay cotton dresses and a clerk in his shirt sleeves, jacket draped over his arm. A delivery boy on a bike sped past a horse and cart, the blinkered horse sweating in the afternoon sun.

Across on City Square, a young couple lingered by the statue of a nymph.

After a few more moments, I thought Mr Brockett steady enough that I could release his arm. He took mine. "Come to the hotel. I'll order coffee. You must tell me . . . tell me what happened."

"Coffee would help." It would fortify me for the visit to my friendly chemist. But if Alex was right and the poison might evaporate, I must lose no time. We reached the entrance to his hotel. "Mr Brockett, I'll see you in and settled with a brandy. I'll be back in less than ten minutes. There's something I must do that won't take long."

He gave me the look of an abandoned child.

The commissionaire quickly noticed that something was wrong. He glanced at me.

"Mr Brockett is feeling unwell. I'll be back very shortly. Would you kindly find us a quiet table?"

The waiter led us to a table by the wall. He pulled out the chairs.

Mr Brockett sat in a kind of trance. I waited until brandy was brought and he had taken a few sips. "Don't move. I'll be back."

I left the hotel and hurried along Boar Lane, still wondering why on earth Mr Brockett thought I would

115

ring him from the hospital and pretend that Billy had died. He must have convinced himself that it could not possibly be true — an extreme case of refusing to acknowledge a horrible truth. I of all people ought to understand that. I tried to remember precisely what I had said to him.

The voice startled me. "Mrs Shackleton, hello! You're off to the Grand Pygmalion. Snap!"

At first I could not place the man and then realised that it was Maurice Montague, master of music, player of twenty-nine musical instruments. He is a middle-aged man with greying hair, an air of sorrow and a well-brushed shabby suit.

"Mr Montague, hello. No I'm not shopping."

The Grand Pygmalion is a much prized and enchanting department store, but today I had other priorities.

Mr Montague assumed a jaunty air, as if practising for a time when pleasantries would be required. "I see from the papers that you were lucky in Giggleswick."

Lucky in Giggleswick. It would be a good title for a bad poem. "We saw the eclipse, and it was extraordinary. Unforgettable."

"I'm so glad. Now can't stand here chatting." He tapped the side of his nose. "Man to see about a dog, or rather a piano. But lovely to have seen you."

"You too, Mr Montague." I hurried on. What a charmer, to make it sound as though I had attempted to waylay him. It was a relief that he had not tarried, nor asked me about Selina and Billy.

116

Feeling guilty at having abandoned the distraught Mr Brockett, I hurried towards my favourite chemist's shop, Brownlaws. Bright young Mr Ernest Brownlaw mixes his potions in the rear of the premises.

Fortunately, I arrived at a quiet time. Ernest Brownlaw's face lit with pleasure when he saw me. He somehow divined that I had not come for a packet of aspirin.

"Mrs Shackleton, good afternoon."

"Good afternoon, Mr Brownlaw."

"What can I do for you today?"

I lowered my voice. "This is an odd request."

"I would expect no less of you."

"Would you please test this cigar for poison?"

"Ah." He cleared his throat. "Yes. I can do that."

I passed the envelope containing the handkerchief-wrapped cigar across the counter.

"Is there any indication of what I am looking for?"

"Cyanide."

To his credit, he did not blink an eye. "Right-i-ho. Will you take a seat?"

I chose the spindly chair by the cabinet that held eyewashes, eyebaths and bottles of iodine and Indian brandy.

Penny Scott, the fair-headed assistant, was showing an anxious-looking woman two different sorts of shampoo guaranteed to cure dandruff.

When the customer had made her purchase and left, I took the opportunity to buy some rather luxurious rose-scented soap flakes. By the time my soap was wrapped, Mr Brownlaw beckoned me to the counter.

"Would you mind leaving this item with me? I have your telephone number and I will give you a call about it. Only I have just remembered old Mr Ponsonby will be in for his prescription on the dot and he hates to be kept waiting."

I hesitated. I would have liked to know straightaway, and would have sat it out. But I remembered the distraught Mr Brockett and my promise to return.

He sensed my hesitation. "Honestly, if it turns out that you've captured a poisoned cigar I won't keep you waiting." Mr Brownlaw looked rather cheerful at having been asked to conduct the test. "Did you ever read that spy story, Mrs Shackleton, by — oh what's his name? — William something."

"William Le Queux, and no I didn't, but I've heard of it. Are you able to tell me anything about the cigar?"

"Oh yes, I can do that all right. It's what they call a puro, that's to say the filler, binder and wrapper are made of the same leaf. That means it's a good quality. It's Cuban and it has a distinctive scent that I must say has been somewhat diminished by being carted around in a hanky. It might be a Bolivar but don't quote me. A friend's father smokes them and they're not to my taste."

"Thank you, Mr Brownlaw. I'll wait to hear from you."

"Might I look forward to sending some dabbler in cyanide to the gallows?"

I made light of my curiosity. "Oh, it's just something that came up."

118

"Something that would come up only for you, Mrs Shackleton!"

"But you will give it early attention?"

"Of course. This isn't something to dawdle over. If it's a positive, you'll hear soon enough."

CHAPTER
THIRTEEN

Over The Moon

What I really wanted to do after leaving Brownlaws chemist's shop was to catch the next tram home and soak in the bath. Ass's milk and rose petals might do the trick or, failing that, warm water and Brownlaws rose-scented soap flakes.

But I set off walking back along Boar Lane to the Queens Hotel, hoping that a glass of brandy had done Mr Brockett at least a tiny bit of good. Retracing my steps, I reached the entrance to the Grand Pygmalion just as Maurice Montague was stepping out. And he really was stepping out, like a man with springs under his soles, making me think of the cow that jumped over the moon. He was grinning, and nodding, as if some invisible person had just palmed him a brand new five pound note. He was not looking at this street, these people, this world, but into a rosy future. I know it's a good shop, but just what had he found in there to tickle his fancy?

"You look chirpy, Mr Montague."

"We meet again, and so soon!" Brightness lit his eyes. He rocked on his heels. "Not following me, are you?"

"Certainly not! I'd do a better job."

"Glee is the word, Mrs Shackleton. And if I don't tell someone I shall burst. May I rely on your utter discretion?"

That word again. I should adopt it as a trade mark. "Of course you may."

"You are looking at a man with a job, a proper job, a day job, with certain hours — just now agreed. I am a man who has leapt over the moon."

"Really? What about your theatre work?"

"I shall fulfil my commitments until the end of the tour. Our other engagements are all within reach. For a man whose work stops at a civilised hour catching a train to Huddersfield or Halifax will present no impediment."

I congratulated him. "May a discreet person ask the nature of this new job?"

"I am to play the piano in the music department of the Grand Pygmalion and offer advice to customers on choosing the correct musical instrument." He put a finger to his lips. "But not a word! I shall break the news myself at the right moment." He looked about, to make sure we were not overheard. "A certain person has his golden boys and girls and if you are not among them then future prospects are dim, regardless of talent and the public's esteem."

I understood him to mean the "certain person" who was at that very moment waiting for me to return to the Queens Hotel. "I wish you well, Mr Montague, and you can rely on me."

He raised his hat. "In life a person must know when it is time to go. People must jump before they are pushed."

We parted company, his cheeriness leaving me fortified for the difficult task of facing Trotter Brockett.

It had taken me less than half an hour to go to the chemist and to exchange words with Maurice Montague. The hotel commissionaire was looking out for me. He opened the door. "I told the waiter you were coming back. He'll bring your drinks and sandwiches. Poor Mr Brockett looks shocking."

"Thank you."

I found Mr Brockett in exactly the same position as I left him, shoulders slumped, his face a mask. The Riviera tan had turned the colour of mustard. He looked at me with a puzzled air.

"Sorry I had to leave you." His brandy glass was empty. "The doorman tells me we'll be served soon."

He gave the slightest of nods.

"I'm sorry if I wasn't clear enough on the telephone. It must have been a terrible shock for you."

How much clearer might I have been other than to say that Billy was dead?

He wet his lips with his tongue. "My fault, my stupid fault for believing Billy to be invincible."

I sat down beside him, unsure what to say that would not be platitudinous.

He reached out and patted my hand. "Not your fault. I was a bit of an ass on the telephone. It was good of you to ring. You caught me at a moment when I was with a chap who is going to stand in for Billy tonight. He'd just let loose a torrent of jokes and so . . . I was laughing at the jokes and then . . ." He sighed.

122

"How did you know to meet me at the station, Mr Brockett?"

"When I realised that you had kindly stayed with Billy so that Selina could go home and rest, I thought the least I could do was meet your train. You see, I expected Billy to be with you — oh, not fit and ready for duty, something of the wounded soldier, but I thought he might be coming back with you. I have always regarded him as indestructible. Such plans I had for him, for him and Selina."

The waiter brought tea and sandwiches. I poured and stirred sugar into his tea. "Do have some sweet tea. It will help you get over the shock."

"Yes, that's what they say, isn't it?"

"And eat something. You have difficult times ahead."

He gave a small smile. "Something must have kept you in Giggleswick. I met two previous trains, one from there and one from Settle."

"I'm sorry you had the inconvenience."

"Not at all." He shook his head. "And I'm forgetting my manners. No one has helped you off with your coat. I daresay it was chilly enough when you set off in the early hours."

"It was, but I'll keep it on thank you."

"You've had the most appalling time, Mrs Shackleton. I am grateful to you for taking care of Selina. I only wish I had been there to shoulder the burden."

"I'm glad that she came back on the aeroplane. I wasn't sure at first that I'd done the right thing, with she and Billy being so close."

"An artiste needs her rest. Beryl will take good care of her."

"She is very much more than Miss Fellini's dresser then."

"She is indeed. Selina relies on her a great deal. Selina is too kind for her own good. Beryl shoos away the hangers-on and scroungers."

Tiredness ought to have dulled my senses. Yet Billy's untimely death sharpened my every thought. Billy was a man who pulled his weight. But what about the two other deaths Selina had mentioned, the second-rank animal act performer and ventriloquist? Might they be hangers-on to be shooed away? Was Beryl the real power behind this empire of entertainment?

I wondered whether my estimate of Billy was correct. He was a damaged man, a drug taker, a survivor. "Had Selina and Billy worked together long?"

"Oh yes. They go way back, personally and professionally." He sighed. "I had plans for them both. This is confidential. We were still in the talking stage but quite far on."

"Planning for a new show?"

"In the West End, pairing the two of them. He has a good singing voice, you see, and they are the most popular entertainers in the land. It would have been . . ."

It was my turn to pat his hand.

"My golden girl and my golden boy. Ahh! I'm old enough to call them both young."

"What will you do now?"

"Keep on keeping on. I shall be my usual self at the theatre tonight, and pull everyone together. I still have Selina to think about. People imagine she has reached the top of the tree, but just wait, just watch. She is on her way up in the world. This will be a terrible blow to her, but it will show her why she needs support such as yours, and not just when life is difficult."

"Really, I did very little. Anyone would have done the same."

"You are too modest. Now tell me, what did the doctor say?"

"Nothing to me. Billy's death was so very unexpected, and sudden."

I explained the way in which Billy had simply vanished by the time the light returned after the eclipse and how he was searched for and found by senior boys.

"How extraordinary. And no one had any idea what might have come over him?"

"I believe there was a suspicion that he may have taken something, for pain."

Brockett shook his head sadly. "That is a distinct possibility. He was badly wounded, poor chap. He told me once that a surgeon had said a good cure would be to lie in the sun on a Mediterranean beach for six months. He made a bit of a monologue of that, as you might expect."

I smiled. "That sounds right up his street."

"But you see, it could have happened if my plans for them had come to fruition. He could have spent months every year on the Isle of Capri."

"Such a loss."

"What else can you tell me, Mrs Shackleton?"

I shook my head. "I'm sorry not to be more informative. The doctor wasn't there when I left, but I believe there will be a post mortem." My hat felt suddenly tight. I adjusted the pin. "Selina asked me to give the hospital your details, which I did."

"I shall go in person, to see the doctor and poor Billy, for the last time. I'll need to make arrangements, collect a death certificate and so on."

Mr Brockett picked up a biscuit. "I am very glad you were with Selina. Have you known her from her early days?"

Not knowing what Selina may have said to him. I did not answer directly. "As you probably know, she came to me because I was able to arrange for two very good airmen to take us to Giggleswick." I shifted the topic, telling him how they had gone on to London with a photograph of the eclipse for today's paper. This reminded me that I must buy a copy. "It was the first time Billy had flown. I believe he was quite nervous though tried not to show it."

Mr Brockett stared into his coffee. "I will miss him, not just professionally but personally. I loved Billy. He was a ray of sunshine on his good days and a dark cloud when the black dog stalked him down. I admired his courage. On the days when he hid away barely able to speak to people, he still came up trumps on stage and made everyone laugh."

"I didn't realise he suffered in that way, or at least not to that extent."

126

"Like many comics, he was a sensitive soul. I pray that he has found peace."

When we had nothing left to say, Mr Brockett offered to call for a taxi to take me home. I thanked him for his offer but said that was not necessary.

"Mrs Shackleton, as I hinted a moment ago, and since there are just the two of us, let me put a thought in your head. Selina's star is on the rise. Between us, Beryl and I take good care of her. But Beryl can't do everything. She makes costumes, extremely talented. Someone of Selina's stature needs intelligent and practical support from someone like you, and so do I want that for her. There! I've put the idea in your head."

How had Selina explained me to him? It would be surprising if this very well-connected man had not made enquiries of his own regarding the person his star performer had recruited.

CHAPTER FOURTEEN

The Elusive Mr Brownlaw

It was half past three when I arrived home. Mrs Sugden was in the corner of the front garden she gives over to dandelions for dandelion wine, which she loves and I loathe. She was stooped over, gathering leaves. "I'm making a nettle soup and I thought I'd add a touch of variety."

"Oh, good. My favourite." It was not my favourite but I like to humour her occasionally, especially when I have asked her to do something beyond the call of duty. "Did Miss Fellini send on my note?"

"She did and I've done as you asked. Door's open. I'll come through and tell you."

My black cat Sookie lay on the path, sunning herself. I paused to stroke Sookie's ears, noticing that the poor thing was expecting again.

Inside, I hung up my coat and kicked off my shoes.

Mrs Sugden followed. "Do you want to eat?"

"No, thank you. What I really want is a bath, but first to know how you got on this morning."

"I'll come to that, when I fish out my notes. I was out early on, in the wood at the appointed time for the eclipse. All we witnessed was the shadow. Young

Thomas was out there with his pencil and paper to make a drawing, and record the exact time. But how did you get on? I saw from the stop press that Giggleswick was a success for the Astronomer Royal, and that he chose well."

"He did indeed, only it didn't go well for everyone."

I told her about Billy's collapse and death.

"Good heavens. What happened? The world turned shocking cold in that brief time. It gave me a funny turn. You could feel the change in the air."

We gravitated towards the kitchen.

She let out her breath in a deep sigh. "I knew summat had gone amiss when I got your letter. He was a popular comic."

"Yes."

"I saw him a couple of times, years ago. I was never that keen myself because he made his humour out of misery, but I'm sorry he's dead."

"It was terrible."

She is quick on the uptake. "Collapsed you say?"

I nodded. "Best not to say more just now. Miss Fellini had feared something might happen."

"I see. And that's why you wanted to know about the other two deaths."

"Yes."

"Well I went to the newspaper offices, just as you asked. And I passed your letter on to Mr Sykes. He sent word that he'll be at the Varieties for tonight's performance. I'll fetch my notes. They're in the office."

There was a time when Mrs Sugden disliked the dining room being called an office. Now that she was more than just a housekeeper and helped with investigations, she was happy enough to change the name of the room as and when it suited her.

She came back a moment later with a sheet of foolscap. "Mr Duffield is looking a lot smarter these days." She straightened the sheet of typing. "He had his young clerk tap this out for me. He says he'll look into it more if you want him to."

I took the typed sheet from her. The typewriter ribbon was overused and the words pale on the page, but readable.

York Gazette, 11 June 1926
Death of a Fine Performer
A tragic accident occurred on the Haxby Road tram route late yesterday evening. Douglas Dougan (53), better known by his stage name Dougie Doig, was knocked down and killed by a tramcar on St Leonards Place. Mr Dougan had been appearing at the Theatre Royal in impresario Mr Trotter Brockett's touring show. Having completed his popular act, "Dougie Doig and his Daring Dogs", the veteran entertainer left the theatre at the interval.

The distraught tram driver stopped the vehicle as quickly as he could but too late. Police issued an appeal for witnesses to come forward.

Silver Songbird Miss Selina Fellini, overcome with emotion, spared a few words for your reporter. "The company is heartbroken at the loss of Dougie."

Visibly shaken, impresario Mr Trotter Brockett said, "I am truly devastated. Variety theatre can ill afford the loss of such a talented performer. The public has lost a great favourite." Asked about the fate of the three performing "Daring Doig Dogs", Mr Brockett assured this reporter that the clever canines are safe and well, but pining.

The company continues its tour, opening at Bradford Hippodrome next Saturday.

Sunderland Echo, 4 January 1927
An enquiry is taking place into the circumstances surrounding the tragic death of much loved ventriloquist Mr Floyd Lloyd. Mr Lloyd, 72, appearing in *Aladdin* at the Sunderland Empire, was on stage alone rehearsing a new act when a sandbag fell from the flies striking him where he sat centre stage with his lifelike doll Manny Piccolo.

The theatre management issued a statement saying that it is cooperating fully with the Sunderland Watch Committee. An inquest will be held on Tuesday.

So these were the two deaths that Selina thought might not be accidental. That made three deaths, all fellow performers, all men, all close to her.

"Thanks, Mrs Sugden. Do we have anything on a coroner's verdict for either death?"

"We do. I followed up on that. Both deaths were put down as accidental. The tram driver afterwards said he thought he saw another person close to Douglas Dougan but no one came forward. The stage manager at the Sunderland Empire was exonerated. The Watch

Committee ordered immediate closure and the ropes and everything were checked. There was no satisfactory explanation for the sandbag falling when it did."

"How extraordinary."

"So, what happens now?"

"I'm not sure."

"Did you get any sleep last night, Mrs Shackleton?"

"Not a wink. We went straight from the party to Giggleswick."

"Think of yourself for a change. Have that bath, why don't you? I'll go run it now. You'll be no good to anyone if you don't have your rest."

"You're right. I need to talk to Miss Fellini. Will you telephone her dresser, Beryl Lister, and say that I'll come to the theatre tonight?"

"Will you see the show?"

"I hope so."

"What will you wear?"

"The green, I haven't worn that for ages."

"You'll freeze. There's no back to it."

"Perhaps I'll attract some warm glances." I looked again at the typed sheet Mrs Sugden had presented me with. "I want to know why Miss Fellini suspects these deaths aren't accidental. They appear to be and, as you say, the coroners thought so."

"Mr Duffield is seeing what else he can find out. I'm off to see him again. He came after me into the street and said I should speak to the paper's theatre correspondent. He knows all there is to know about performers and their doings."

"Really?"

"I've arranged to call in at the paper again, before he sets off to see a show."

"Good." I took the new soap from my bag. "Take a sniff of this."

"Very nice. I'll run that bath for you."

She called back as she reached the top of the stairs. "I'm not sure I'm all that keen on this Silver Songbird of yours. She left you to hold the poor man's hand and see him into eternity, and from all accounts she's told half a tale."

"How do you come to that conclusion?"

"She should have told you before that people were dying like flies around her."

"Not exactly like flies." I was about to defend Selina, but the thought occurred to me, now that I looked back, that she had become anxious too quickly, almost as if she expected Billy to die. They had been in each other's company since the previous evening, and she was ideally placed to have given him a cigar, or to have tampered with what was his very last injection.

I looked at the telephone, willing Mr Ernest Brownlaw to ring with the results of his test.

At the top of the stairs, Mrs Sugden emerged from the bathroom. "Them bubbles should float you to dreamland."

"Thank you. If Mr Brownlaw rings with the results of a test, would you say I'll ring straight back? Or he might just say positive or negative."

"And if he doesn't ring?"

"Give it two hours and then you ring him, or I will if I'm still awake."

★ ★ ★

Before changing for the theatre, I sat at the kitchen table, with a plate of ham salad and a slice of bread and butter. "Any news from Mr Brownlaw?"

Mrs Sugden opened the bun tin. "He'd gone out. I left a message."

How annoying of him. I'd expected him to operate with the same speed as young Alex in the school laboratory. "I'll try once more."

"Eat your tea or that dress'll fall off you!"

"It won't take a minute. I need to know."

"Stay put. I'll get the number for you."

I gave her a moment and then followed her into the hall. It might be best if I asked for him.

She handed me the telephone. An assistant picked up and announced the name.

"Brownlaws Chemist."

"Hello, it's Mrs Shackleton here. Is Mr Brownlaw available?"

"Who did you say is calling?"

"Mrs Shackleton."

"I'm sorry but he's not here. He said to tell you that he had an emergency."

"Did he leave any other message?"

One word would do, positive or negative.

"Only what I said, that he had an emergency."

Something was not right. I had known Ernest Brownlaw for a long time. Delay and prevarication were not his style. Unless something had gone seriously wrong for him, he would have been in touch. At the very least, he would have left me a proper message.

134

CHAPTER
FIFTEEN

New Moon

Jim Sykes and his wife Rosie dressed in their best for this unexpected trip to the City Varieties. Sykes wasn't surprised that something else had arisen as a result of Mrs Shackleton arranging a flight to take Miss Selina Fellini and her friend to Giggleswick. Both he and Mrs Shackleton had a feeling there was more to Miss Fellini's sudden visit than met the eye. In Sykes's view, theatricals saw themselves as a race apart. He knew from experience that they referred to the rest of the world as "civilians", as though every performer from the biggest star in the firmament to the lowliest warm-up man considered themselves enlisted in some exalted service. Well perhaps they were. If so, it was an exalted service with the first commandment Thou Shalt Dissemble.

Sykes hadn't told Rosie that this outing was connected with work. Nor did he mention that Mrs Sugden had made the telephone call to confirm tickets. It didn't hurt to let Rosie believe that he had come up with the good idea of a night at the Varieties.

Rosie brushed the felt navy cloche that she had retrimmed with a length of pale blue petersham. "What does this hat look like?" She put it on for inspection.

He was not sure how to compliment a hat. He calculated that it was probably not the hat that needed reassurance. "It suits you to a T. You look grand."

"Oh, give over. I look presentable."

He kissed her cheek. "Presentable to the king and queen, love. Now if we don't put a spurt on we'll be late."

She looked at the clock on the mantelpiece. "We've bags of time."

"There could be a crush and we've to pick up our tickets. We were lucky to get cancellations. That's what happens, see, when you call from a telephone."

Rosie said nothing regarding the telephone. She knew very well that if one was installed they would be the calling point for everyone in the street who had an emergency, or a brother in Harehills that they needed to speak to as a matter of life and death.

As it turned out, and as Rosie predicted, they arrived early. No sooner had Sykes announced his name to the woman at the box office counter than an effusive man with a halo of white hair and good nature appeared. He was short, with a sun-struck complexion and a theatrical moustache carefully curled at the ends. His eyes were the brightest blue, giving him the appearance of someone who had stepped into his blue shirt and linen suit to disguise the fact that here was no ordinary mortal but a man from the planet sunshine, arriving on earth to bring cheer to the world.

"Mr Sykes, my great pleasure to meet you. Trotter Brockett at your service, Miss Fellini's manager." He shook hands with Sykes. "Mrs Sykes, good evening and welcome. So glad you could come."

What on earth sort of yarn had Mrs Sugden spun when she rang for tickets? Or perhaps they had already been arranged through Mrs Shackleton. Sykes had hoped to be the anonymous observer and here he and Rosie were being treated as honoured guests. Who does he think we are? Sykes wondered. Rosie had cottoned on too. She gave Jim that look, having caught him out. This was work, and she knew it.

Mr Brockett had still not finished his welcome. "Please accompany me to the bar. A cocktail is called for and I shall show you to your box in due course. We kept the royal box free."

"Please don't on our account." Sykes stubbed his cigarette in the giant ashtray. "If it's all the same to you I'd prefer to sit in the stalls." He felt rather than saw Rosie's cringe of dismay.

"Of course, of course, wherever you please. We do have a sell-out performance but always keep a couple of reserve seats for the press so we're happy to oblige."

The penny dropped. Mrs Sugden must have said he was a journalist, or a theatre critic. She might have alerted him as to who he was supposed to be. Either that or this fussy man meant that although the seats were for the press, they were being reallocated to him and Rosie.

Mr Brockett spoke to the box office attendant. "Elaine, tickets for Mr and Mrs Sykes, in the front stalls?"

Elaine managed a smile and smoothed her brown hair. She fingered a narrow wooden box stuffed with tickets and brought out two. "Here we are."

Mr Brockett was supplied with two tickets which he passed to Sykes. "Now do please come with me to the bar for drinks on the house." He led them to the stairs. "Have you seen Miss Fellini perform before?"

"Years ago," Rosie said. "She was wonderful then, long before she had such a big name for herself."

Mr Brockett continued to speak in a pleasant intimate way, as if they were his oldest friends. "So you saw Miss Fellini in the old days. Happy days, eh? Delightful family, the Fellinis. They thought it best to shorten their name to Fell, you know, so as to fit in I suppose. I insisted that Selina remain Fellini, much more appropriate for a lady who tops the bill. Talented, the whole family. They make the best ice cream, but of course you know that. It's sold here in the theatre. The father grows grapes. Who else in this benighted county could find a way to grow grapes in a glasshouse in the back garden? Mr Fell is an artist too, etches on metal, pictures from nursery stories, and he paints flowers on glass. The whole family is so proud of Selina, so proud."

Sykes and Rosie followed him up the broad staircase into the softly lit bar with its dark wood, plush seats and carpeting now somewhat worn, and the highly polished bar with brass fittings. Sykes asked for a pint and Rosie for a glass of sweet sherry. Brockett ordered an Eclipse Cocktail. "I developed a taste for this last night at Miss Fellini's party. Just dropped in, you know. I leave it to the youngsters to keep late nights."

They went to sit at one of the small round tables with cast-iron legs. Rosie and Sykes sat on the plush seat against the wall. Brockett perched on a stool as if he never sat anywhere for very long. The waiter brought their drinks in double-quick time.

Brockett sipped his cocktail and chatted about the show and about the theatre, without really saying very much at all. Sykes guessed that he was used to being pleasant to any person who might be remotely useful. He had made a fine art of it.

"I'm most grateful that Mrs Shackleton accompanied my star on her aeroplane journey this morning. It had me worried, I can tell you. I'm an ocean-going fellow myself when it comes to travel. Miss Fellini did a brief but highly successful tour of the eastern seaboard of the United States and we could have flown from New York to Boston but preferred to travel by rail."

It annoyed Sykes to be at a disadvantage. Mrs Shackleton had mentioned that Miss Fellini was driven to Headingley by her manager, and that was all she had told him about the chap. Then it dawned on Sykes that Trotter Brockett simply had the knack of knowing how to be a person's intimate chum within moments. Well, two could play that game. Sykes, after confiding that he also preferred ocean travel but that he wouldn't mind taking a turn in the air, asked questions about New York and Boston, based on items read in the Sunday papers.

Rosie, sipping her sherry, was glad to think of a question. "Have you been a performer yourself, Mr Brockett?"

"Oh no, not I. Born into the business of course but always behind the scenes and out of the limelight, organising, bringing on talent, that is my forte."

We're here for a reason, Sykes told himself, and he wished he knew what that reason was. If he did he would be able to guide the conversation. Mrs Sugden had sent him a copy of the information about the accidental death of two performers from Mr Brockett's company but the whole idea struck Sykes as entirely spurious.

Why would anyone kill Douglas Dougan, a man who worked with hoops and leaping dogs? As for Floyd Lloyd, had the professional holder of conversations with a dummy made mortal enemies while moonlighting as a gangster? Perhaps the dummy was a secret copper's nark.

No coroner worth his salt would miss the stench of foul play in those situations.

As it was, Sykes could do worse than let Mr Brockett talk, and go on talking. He asked him about his background, and what it was like to be born into the business of theatre.

Trotter Brockett hinted at but brushed over hardships. He dropped the names of famous performers at a rate of ten a minute. Vesta Tilley. Little Tich. Nellie Wallace. Charlie Chaplin. Tom Major. Jenny Hill. John Bottle. Beryl Cooper.

He had interests in two theatres and immediately this tour ended another tour was planned. He glanced

140

about the bar. "I don't let this be generally known. We keep much under wraps in this business, but since you are admirers of Miss Fellini I'll let you into the secret. There is to be a new musical show, specially written for her."

Mr Brockett finished his cocktail, waylaid an usher, took a programme and presented it to Rosie. He then excused himself and with smiles and nods in several directions made his way to the stairs.

"Rum chap," Sykes observed as Brockett slipped out of sight. "I wonder how many people he tells his 'secret' to in order to stir up excitement about some future musical extravaganza?"

"He's rum? What about you? I wished the floor would open and swallow me up when you refused to sit in the royal box. What an honour. It's where the Prince of Wales used to sit when he came to see Lillie Langtry. Why do you think there's a coat of arms above the stage?"

Sykes drained his pint. "Aye well, if you sit in a box you've a door behind you and you don't know who might come in or why. I'd rather sit with my back to the wall or with people who are harmless looking at the top of my head."

"You're mad. You take it all to the extremes."

"Perhaps I do. But I can't change now."

The call came for people to take their seats.

"Come on, our lass." Sykes stood, glad that Rosie had not taken him to task over his slight deception regarding their evening out. Not yet anyway.

They followed the crowd, looking at the letters and numbers on the rows for guidance. Just too late they watched a family of four take the seats at the end of the row. They had to excuse themselves and tramp past, stepping over a handbag and squeezing by a large pair of knees.

The place had a smell all its own, the luxury of plush combined with the whiff of camphor, orange peel and cigarette and pipe smoke.

Sykes was on alert though he did not know for what. Roundabout him, people were chatting, leaning in close to each other, keeping their voices to that low level of intimacy that sometimes precedes a performance and is drowned by the rustle of paper bags as suckers of sweets and chewers on toffee make sure they have their necessaries handy.

Sykes looked up at the royal box. It was empty. He thought that it did not give the very best view of the stage and yet good enough. What's more, someone sitting in there might tuck him or herself a little way to the side and be able to see the door opening. Perhaps Rosie was right and he was a bit mad, though he liked to think of his little habits as cautiousness.

The house lights lowered. An air of expectancy filled the auditorium as members of the orchestra tuned their instruments and the conductor took his place.

Mr Trotter Brockett stepped from the wings and walked to centre stage in front of the safety curtain. He welcomed the audience as if every single one of them was his very best and oldest friend. He assured them that Miss Fellini was delighted to be once more appearing in her home town, treading the boards where she had first appeared as a child. His voice became sombre as he told them that he had an announcement to make. "I very much regret that our splendid and much-loved comedian Billy Moffatt will not be with us this evening." As he spoke, the safety curtain behind him was slowly raised. Mr Brockett waited for the collective "aww" of disappointment at his announcement regarding Billy Moffatt's non-appearance. He raised his voice, intimating great things as he said, "Billy's place will be filled this evening, at very short notice, by that popular and brilliantly funny local man who promises to have you all in stitches: Mr Jimmy Diamond!" To a low level of applause, the velvet curtains swished gently open.

Rosie whispered to Jim, "Wasn't it Billy Moffatt who went with them in the aeroplane?"

"Shh," was Sykes's reply. All he knew was gleaned from the hastily scrawled letter that Mrs Sugden had put through the door, saying Moffatt had been taken to hospital and that Miss Fellini had concerns about two accidental deaths at the time of the new moon, this January and last June. When Sykes had gone round to see Mrs Sugden, she was not much wiser than he was and had nothing to add.

The sound of the orchestra grew, as more instruments came into play. Mr Brockett had to raise his voice to be heard above the music, but heard he was. "Ladies and gentlemen, please put your hands together for our very own whirling twirling darlings, the Daisy Chain Dancing Troupe!"

The stage lights went up, revealing a tableau of glamorous creatures, their costumes sparkling with sequins and decorated with coloured feathers. As the overture began the dancers sprang into vivid life, spinning and high kicking, swaying and tapping.

"What legs!" Rosie took out the toffees. "And did you ever see such kicking?"

But Sykes had once more glanced towards the royal box. The door of the box opened. A tall figure dressed in black, with a white muffler, stood there for a few seconds, closed the door and left. It was as if he were checking that the box was empty.

Sykes experienced an odd shiver. Rosie hadn't noticed the man and Sykes was glad. He hoped that regardless of Trotter Brockett's babbling, his wife would regard this evening as an unexpected treat and would forget the tenuous link it had with his work.

A moment later, Sykes glanced up at the box again. Once more the door opened. This time Mr Brockett ushered in another person. It was Mrs Shackleton. Sykes was not usually given to moments of foreboding but as Mr Brockett closed the door on the box, Sykes experienced a distinct feeling of unease.

Half a dozen dancers twirled off while the remainder tap danced at the front of the stage. The ones who had twirled off then danced back. They each carried two musical instruments that they placed on a table at the back of the stage. They repeated this until the table overflowed with instruments, banjo, accordion, bagpipes, flute, violin, cello, guitar, trumpet and some Sykes did not recognise. A tall man, dressed in a green and red

144

satin coat and a skull cap with tassel, cartwheeled onto the stage, stood upright, swaying to a dance of his own invention with wild movements like a creature made of bendy rubber, craning his neck this way and that. The dancers took a bow to much applause for them and the eccentric dancer musician.

Rosie glanced at the programme. "He's Maurice Montague, master of music."

"Well he looks a right shower."

"He's playing the fool. Red and green should not be seen except on fools."

Maurice Montague made an elaborate inspection of his instruments. He turned to the audience and gave a loud "phew" of relief. "There they are. I thought they'd been half-inched again." He picked up a fiddle and began to play and sing "The Fiddle is My Sweetheart". With every chorus he picked up a different instrument. By the time he reached the wind instruments, he had the audience singing along with him. Even Sykes sang a few words. It was always best to appear part of the scene, not the one who watches and whose attention and suspicions are everywhere, particularly on that royal box and Mrs Shackleton sitting there all alone. Once more, Maurice Montague picked up the fiddle. He played it as he took his bow and the dancers appeared and carried off the instruments.

A prancing pony trotted onto the stage accompanied by a slight young man dressed in a velvet suit with gold braid that matched the pony's trimmings.

"God bless the poor pony," Rosie whispered. "That stage is on a terrible slope."

But the pony danced, leapt through a giant hoop and let its master ride bareback while juggling with six batons.

When the magician took centre stage, Rosie nudged her husband. "The kids'll have to see this show. I'll get tickets for them in the gods."

Pip Potter, strongman, tore a London street directory in half. He lifted dumbbells that Sykes felt sure weren't as heavy as the man made out. But when a BSA motorcycle was wheeled on and Pip Potter raised it with one hand, even Sykes felt obliged to applaud. Two much-spangled young acrobats, obviously sister and brother, stepped onto the bike. The brother held his sister aloft. When the strongman once more raised the bike, this time with two hands to balance the young acrobats, the audience went wild. The pair leaped from the bike as Pip Potter took his bow.

Rosie consulted her programme. "They're the Powolski twins."

The pair performed such daring high-wire feats as to leave the audience gasping.

When the lights went up, Rosie made a dash for the door, expecting a queue in the ladies' room. Sykes stayed put. He glanced up at the royal box, trying a bit of telepathy to make Mrs Shackleton look in his direction. Eventually, she did, or he thought she did.

After the interval, a singer bounced onto the stage singing "Clap Hands! Here Comes Charley!" followed by half a dozen popular songs. Sykes knew a good voice when he heard one and this chap was good, though French and making the most of his accent in the romantic songs. He was handsome too and knew it, winking, smiling and charming the ladies with his chatter between songs and his sentimental nonsense.

It was all a little disappointing really. Sykes remembered the old days, when he was a lad. You could always rely on a bit of pelting with rotten fruit. Perhaps the replacement comic, Jimmy Diamond, would be a flop and attract a few boos and hisses. Sykes wondered about this replacement. Mrs Shackleton's note had said Billy Moffatt was taken to hospital. The whole business seemed to Sykes a bit of a rum do. It would test his skills.

What he liked about investigating insurance fraud was that you knew where you were with that kind of business. There were the insurers who made their brass from charging people for lots of events that might never happen and a few that did — including death. Then there were the cheats and twisters who made their brass from making something happen that shouldn't have happened and following it up with a claim.

He somehow knew that his dealing with show business people would not be quite so clear-cut and might edge towards the intricate.

The replacement comic told a story of standing on Woodhouse Moor that morning with hopes of seeing the eclipse and staring at banks of grey clouds. He had his audience in stitches giving an account of his friend who set off in his car at midnight to find a good spot from which to observe, and then closing his eyes for a bit of shut eye. "He said it was the best eclipse he ever slept through."

Sykes, who had heard Billy Moffatt on the wireless, knew that if Billy had been there, he would have taken off his hat to the man, or hated him, or both.

Next came Sandy Sechrest, the memory woman. Sandy Sechrest wore a dramatic black dress with bat-like wings, a choker of jet beads at her throat. She opened her arms to the audience. "Ask me anything, as long as it is connected with knowledge and your wish for enlightenment. I answer no questions about my personal history or by what blessing I came to have the most remarkable memory in the world."

His curiosity about the memory woman increased. Now that she made a point of drawing a veil over her background, he very much wanted to know all about her. The first thing he wanted to know was this: is she a fraud?

Sykes had seen a rather solemn memory man once, and knew that he had suffered some dreadful illness as a child. As a consequence, he passed his childhood years lying in bed, reading encyclopaedias. But this was the first time he had seen the memory woman.

She won't match up, Sykes thought. No woman would. It's brave of her to try. Of course, the audience would be dotted with stooges, all primed to ask certain questions to which she knew the answers. It occurred to him that this was his opportunity to test the water. If there was some unease in the company regarding sudden deaths, as Mrs Shackleton's hastily written PS had hinted, he could, in an anonymous fashion, ask a few questions.

Hands shot up. Questions were called as she pointed. "The man in the third row." "The woman on the first row of the upper circle."

There were questions about football teams, about which general commanded in some particular battle, and about the changes of names of capital cities in those Balkan countries and in remote parts of the empire. On each occasion, the memory woman repeated the question for the benefit of those who had their back to the questioner and may not have heard.

The memory woman stretched out a long pale hand. "The man on the fifth row."

Sykes cleared his throat. Rosie sank a little lower in her seat.

CHAPTER
SIXTEEN

The Empress of Ice Cream

I was a few minutes late being shown into my seat in the royal box at the Varieties, having taken time to send up a note for Miss Fellini, telling her that I would come to her dressing room after the show.

I glanced down at the stalls where people chatted quietly while marvelling at Madam Sechrest, the amazing memory woman. A few people had brought their supper, treating me to the aroma of sausage sandwiches. Cigarette smoke curled towards the ornate ceiling. I thought of Selina and her worries about her throat. Having had my rose-scented bath and, miraculously, two hours' sleep, I felt ready for the fray.

Selina would have questions about Billy. It might be a comfort to her to know that he had not appeared to suffer. It might even be helpful to learn that he had popped off to smoke a cigar after witnessing the eclipse. Of course, I should have to omit the fact that he may have inhaled a bellyful of cyanide. That little gem of a possibility would have to wait, until I heard from Mr Brownlaw.

I had spotted Sykes and Rosie in the fifth row of the stalls. The only drawback about telling the story of the cigar was that my admission would give him an opportunity to be superior. Allowing a schoolboy to become involved — however intelligent and helpful, and however many doctors that boy boasted in his family — had not been a good idea. It could be construed as tampering with evidence. Why hadn't Brownlaw telephoned?

Pay attention, I told myself as someone asked the memory woman which team knocked Accrington Stanley out of the FA Cup in the 1906–1907 season.

She answered in a clear confident voice. "Bradford City beat Accrington Stanley in February 1907. Bradford City one, Accrington Stanley nil."

The questioner must be a plant, and the solitary audience member clapping loudly enough to break his wrists must be a Bradfordian.

Madam Sechrest was not perturbed. "Am I correct?" she asked her questioner.

"You are that, lass."

Quelling the audience's merriment, the memory woman asked for another question. Hands shot up.

Mr Sykes came to his feet. What was he thinking of? It was not like him to draw attention to himself while "on duty". Either he had some obscure question about the Battle of Trafalgar, or he had somehow hit on an idea that might shed light on our investigation.

Leaning against the brass rail of the royal box, I waited.

Sykes spoke with his usual confidence. "Miss Sechrest, not counting today, when was the last total

151

solar eclipse visible in England, and when will the next occur?"

It was not a difficult question as the newspapers had been full of such information in recent weeks.

Sandy Sechrest repeated the question. Perhaps this habit of repeating the question gave her time to gather information from the filing cabinet of her brain. She answered quickly. "The last total solar eclipse was on 22 May 1724. On 24 January 1925 an eclipse of short duration could be seen not from land but from north of the Hebrides. The next total eclipse will be in the year 1999."

There was a gasp from a few in the audience who hadn't kept up with the newspapers, and a sigh from those who now realised they had missed their once in a lifetime opportunity. Miss Sechrest paused and then spoke again with a mixture of challenge and humility in her voice. She had picked up a little phrase from her counterpart, the Memory Man. His phrase was, "Am I right, sir?" She paraphrased. "Am I correct, sir?"

Having spoken once, Sykes's confidence swelled. "You are, madam. And I have a supplementary question along similar lines if you'll permit."

She made a gracious gesture. "Ask your question, sir."

"Madam, are you able to tell me the dates of the new moons over the past eighteen months?"

For the first time, she hesitated, and the pause stretched. And then she answered. "The calculation is based on local time in London." She reeled off a list of days and dates starting with 10 January last year and continuing to the present month.

"Am I correct, sir?"

Sykes answered quickly. "You are, madam. Thank you."

There was a round of applause. Madam Sechrest took a bow.

At first I could not fathom the thinking behind Sykes's questions regarding new moons. Then it occurred to me that he was trying to stir things up a little. This was his attempt to find out whether anyone else in the company shared Selina's concerns, or nonsense, about deaths at the time of a new moon.

Madam Sechrest had hesitated for a little longer on this question. That seemed to me natural enough. Even a woman with miraculous powers of memory would take a moment before she could reel off eighteen dates. It was an astonishing feat.

If I were to continue this investigation on behalf of Selina, I must talk to Sandy Sechrest. Someone with a brain such as hers must have noticed incidents, events, exchanges that others may have missed.

The measure of my task suddenly became utterly daunting. If Selina was right and the three deaths were not accidental, what was the link? True, each death had occurred at the time of a new moon, but given three deaths over eighteen months that meant there were fifteen new moons when no suspicious deaths occurred in Selina Fellini's world.

I had no more time to ponder this riddle because at that moment the theatre erupted as Selina herself swept on stage, looking radiant in a low-cut purple gown, a feather boa around her shoulders and with feathers in her hair that would not disgrace the chief of some gallant tribe.

And at that moment, the door to my box opened.

I looked round, half expecting to see Mr Brockett who had ushered me in here not long after curtain up. It was not Mr Brockett but a tall figure dressed in black. I did not see his face as he instantly turned away on seeing me. He closed the door gently behind him. It was the briefest of moments before I guessed he might be some person from the gallery whose restricted view made him think the box was empty and he might risk taking a better seat for the last part of the show.

Having no objections to sharing the box I left my seat and opened the door, to call him back. The corridor was empty. I opened a door that led to the backstage area, but saw no one on the other side. Much as I wanted to see Selina, I was on duty and it intrigued me that an intruder could appear and disappear so quickly. I turned round and followed the horseshoe path to the other side of the theatre. No one. Perhaps that edgy feeling that alerted me to impending trouble was imagined because of the strangeness of the last twenty-four hours. I found a spot in the dress circle from where I could see both the audience and Selina's performance.

It would take a better pen than mine to describe the feelings of love and admiration that rose from the auditorium and all corners of the theatre as Selina Fellini sang. Her range is enormous but she is best

154

known for her songs that give comic and tragic accounts of the lives of girls and women from the poor end of life, which she knows so well. Her songs can be sentimental, comic or full of sly digs and innuendo.

Everyone knows Fellini's ice cream and there were whoops of delight when she began to sing "The Empress of Ice Cream".

I'm the girl from Grimston Street
Old wellington boots on my feet
I make the ice cream of which you dream
I'm the girl from Grimston Street
Give us a lick, the boys all say
And I surely wish I could
But without the penny they're not having any
I'm the girl from Grimston Street.

In between songs, Selina talked to her audience and at the edge of her words, just for a few seconds, I caught a sense of her vulnerability but perhaps only because I knew of her fears. All that fled as she sang. When she sang, her confidence filled the theatre, drawing the audience to her heart. With warmth in her voice and ease in her movements she sang, swayed and did a jolly little dance. At last, she talked to the audience as if she were sitting in their kitchen as she had sat in mine. She told them about flying across their world in the middle of the night and seeing the dark towns, patchwork fields and strangers dancing around a bonfire calling on the sun not to abandon us. It was almost as if she spoke a eulogy for Billy Moffatt, and for everything that was ever lost.

She sang one more song about a lass and her soldier boy who pulled the wool over her eyes until she got wise and did the same to him. As the song ended, she stepped to the edge of the stage, smiled down at the orchestra and then into the audience. Her change of demeanour from gay to grave prompted a similar response. "I have something to tell you all and it is most painful for me to do this but you have a right to know."

An odd hum of sounds came from the stalls below and the circle above. People did not know whether this was a prelude to a funny story or, what might be, from the sound of her voice, something bad. They did not come here to hear bad things. There was enough of that at home and at work.

"Before curtain up, Mr Trotter Brockett announced that Mr Billy Moffatt would not be performing tonight."

The murmur increased. There was an air of expectancy, almost tangible.

"Billy and I were together this morning to see the eclipse. He of course expected a probability of cloud. Those of you who know Billy's humour won't be surprised at that. He dealt in making the funny sad and the sad funny. I would rather you hear this from me than from tomorrow's papers. Our funny, delightful, annoying and wonderful Billy collapsed and died today. I cannot say more, except to ask that we remember him now, with a moment's silence and a private prayer for

156

the soul of Billy Moffatt, William James Moffatt who turned thirty-six years old this month. After that silence, I will ask our friends in the orchestra to play Billy's tune, and for you all to join me in singing Billy's very special song, 'It Ain't Funny'."

That moment of utter silence, followed by singing and weeping, would never be forgotten by any person who was in the City Varieties theatre that night.

The national anthem followed. People stood in silence. They did not have the king or God's saving of him on their mind. All thoughts were of true royalty, the prince of comedy, Mr Billy Moffatt.

CHAPTER
SEVENTEEN

Dressing Room One

As the national anthem reached the final verse, Mr Brockett came and stood beside me in a companionable way until the last note of "God Save the King".

From the stage, Selina looked up at us and round the whole theatre as she took her final curtsey.

Mr Brockett gave a rueful smile. "She was wonderful. They love her, simply love her."

"What a beautiful eulogy for Billy."

He nodded. "She has a sense of occasion, an instinct for what's required. Some of the audience will have seen her when she entertained the troops. People don't forget. They say, 'She's one of us'." He held the door for me. "You changed seats."

"Yes."

We walked back the way I had come, went through a door and across a bridge to the backstage area. "Was the box comfortable? I have asked the management about reupholstering the seats."

"It was very comfortable. I fancied a change of viewpoint."

"I do that myself, often where I can listen to what people think, hear their approvals and disapprovals."

"I thought I might have had company at one point, a tall chap opened the door for a look-see during Selina's song."

"I'm sorry you were disturbed. There's always someone from the gods who sees an empty space below and tries their luck."

"That's what I thought. He disappeared quite quickly once he saw me."

"More fool him," Brockett quipped and then suddenly remembered himself and said, "I do beg your pardon. You must be on edge after such a long and difficult day."

I waited for him to lead the way along the corridor.

In a sudden change of tone, he politely quizzed me for a response to the performance. Having missed the opening moments and being somewhat preoccupied, I felt unqualified to do much more than offer praise, and especially of Selina.

"She is very precious to me. I want to be sure she has her rest, especially after such a shock. Everyone wants a little bit of her magic. I do my best to protect her. It was good of you to arrange the flight to Giggleswick, although I confess that I did not feel easy until I knew she and her two feet were back on terra firma."

We entered a black painted door marked "Private". The passageway beyond was narrow and smelled of mops and buckets.

I waited for Brockett to continue, but he came to a stop, and took a noisy breath before speaking. "You must be tired after your ordeal. Do say if you wish me to call you a taxi. It's been a trying day for all of us,

159

though Selina was magnificent. She touched just the right note."

"Her tribute to Mr Moffatt was very moving."

"She loved him, we all did. He needed a lot of support lately, having been losing confidence for some time. Selina stood by him, always stands by her friends. His loss is a terrible blow."

"Yes, and such a shock."

"She will need all our support, and so if she does make you some offer to . . . continue with her . . ."

"That wasn't our arrangement, Mr Brockett."

"No, no of course not."

"I arranged the flight. That is all."

"Yes of course, but Selina likes to have people around her who are efficient and protective."

Several dancers flashed by, chatting to each other, throwing us a hello and making a dash for a dressing room.

We stood with our backs to the wall to allow more performers to pass. "I'm glad you're here to guide the way, Mr Brockett. It always surprises me that even the smallest theatres could compete with Hampton Court maze for twists and turns."

He was not to be deflected in his praise of me. "Your arrangement for that aeroplane flight was a stroke of genius because she was so determined to be at Giggleswick today. You must know many people, lots of contacts, to have pulled that off at short notice."

"Don't we all, Mr Brockett? You must be acquainted with far more people than I ever hope to know."

"Yes, yes. I suppose that to be true. You meet all sorts in this business."

We reached a door bearing the painted name "Dressing Room 1". On it was pinned a large gold star whose points curled at the edges.

Mr Brockett rat-a-tatted on the door. Selina's familiar voice called for us to come in.

Brockett patted my shoulder. "I'll leave you to it and will come back shortly. She's bound to ask questions and I have no answers. I told her that I would go to Giggleswick tomorrow and make arrangements, but the hospital say it's too soon."

Selina was seated at her dressing table in front of a gilt-framed looking-glass edged by small bright bulbs. She wore a robe and had taken the pins from her hair. Through the mirror, she gave a wan smile and asked me to come and sit down. Beryl was by the far wall hanging the purple costume on a rail.

It was not a large room but had a sumptuous feeling, given off by the plum-coloured velvet throws and cushions covering an Empire couch on one side of the room and a small armchair to Selina's left. As I sank into the plush battered armchair, a wave of tiredness swept through me. Lit by a gas fire, the room was warm. A large cut-glass vase tightly packed with roses and lilies sat on a spindly table and gave off a sweet, almost cloying scent. The table was draped with a silk tasselled shawl. Next to the vase was a bottle of Shalimar. Beside the clothes rail, where Beryl straightened dresses, was a corner washbasin. Above it, shelves were crammed with pots of make-up and more

161

flowers. The smell of greasepaint, freshly ironed clothes and Selina's familiar cedar wood scent, which would ever after transport me to Giggleswick Chapel, mingled with the aroma of flowers.

She paused in the act of taking off her make-up, and then began again, wiping the colour from her face in easy, practised movements. Only then did she turn to me.

"I can't believe it. Beryl told me. I almost didn't say Billy's name on stage tonight thinking that when Kate comes, she'll tell me it was a mistake."

Beryl crossed the room from the clothes rail and drew up a stool. I brought my chair forward. The three of us sat in a small tight circle.

Beryl bit her lip. "They probably thought me a queer old bird when I rang the hospital again during the interval. Just to be sure. First the news from Mrs Shackleton, and then Mr Brockett rang back to make sure and then me. Billy was so well, you see."

Why hadn't I already decided what to say? In danger of being induced into a stupor, I took in the drapes of velvet and silk. It struck me that theatre people are particularly partial to buying glamour by the yard, the glamour that must sometimes seem in short supply when the curtain goes down and theatre lights dim. Yet all the silk and velvet in the world would not soften the harsh reality of Billy's death.

"I wish it were wrong, or a mistake. But I sat with him. He didn't regain consciousness."

Selina closed her eyes and crossed herself, as if now she finally believed the truth. I have seen before what happens to a person as bad news slowly sinks in. Something invisible detaches and floats away. Whatever it is can't be seen. The person sits in almost the same way, moves in almost the same way but breathes a little differently and is somehow diminished.

The air felt sucked from the room. Ceiling and walls moved closer. The dark red silk and velvet throws cried blood.

Selina's breathing was suddenly a kind of rasp, a chasing after air. Beryl poured her a cup of black tea from a flask. It smelled of lemon and honey.

Selina pressed her hands on the dressing table. "I should have stayed with him."

I said nothing. How strongly had I dissuaded her from staying? Too strongly perhaps, but at that moment the events of the morning became a blur. The image blotting out all else was of Billy, lying forever still.

Beryl chipped in. "By all accounts there's nothing you could have done. Billy wouldn't want you to upset yourself."

Selina shrugged off Beryl's remark. "How do you know what Billy would have wanted? How do any of us know?"

Beryl stood. "There'll be a crowd out there. I'll send them packing."

"Don't! They also loved Billy."

Beryl spoke somewhat sharply. "They think they do. They didn't know him, no more than they know you." She picked up some autograph books, checked that they had been signed, and moved to go.

"Don't send them away."

"It's started to rain."

"They won't mind the rain."

Mr Brockett chose that moment to knock and come in. "Are you ready, Selina? Shall I fetch the car?"

"Trotter, let me alone for now. Let me talk to Mrs Shackleton."

"Of course! I'll leave you two ladies together." He closed the door gently as he followed Beryl into the corridor.

Selina looked down at the spilled powder on her dressing table. "Now I've upset Beryl. She's known Billy as long as I have." She then turned to me. "I don't understand. What happened? How could he just die?"

I chose my words carefully. "I don't know. There'll be a post mortem." I did not want to share my suspicions. She should give me a clue, a hint as to how much she wanted to know at this moment. "He was made comfortable. The ward sister let me sit by his bed. That was unusual. It was kind and I appreciated it."

"Did he know you were there?"

"I like to think he did. I held his hand, spoke of you, said you cared for him."

"I should have been with him."

"You couldn't. He would have known that."

"Did he respond? Did he know you were holding his hand?"

"I'm sure even in the depths of unconsciousness a person can be aware of not being alone. He showed no distress."

"I don't understand."

164

Taking off my hat, I rubbed my fingers through my hair. The action might bring my brain back to life.

She repeated her words. "I don't understand. Trotter arranged for Jimmy Diamond to stand in. Did he know about Billy before I did?"

"I believe he arranged for a replacement when he knew Billy had been taken into hospital. I expect Beryl telephoned Mr Brockett when you arrived back from Giggleswick alone this morning. I suppose that's when he made the arrangement with Jimmy Diamond."

I avoided saying what time I had given news of Billy's death to Beryl. Beryl had used her judgement and let Selina sleep before she told her.

"Trotter makes sure that everything and everyone works to the show's advantage." She picked up a hairbrush and put it down again. "I can't believe it. I knew when I saw him on that stretcher that he wouldn't be performing just yet, perhaps for a long while, but he's a bouncer-back. I told the airmen that. Billy bounces back. I felt sure he'd be on his feet again."

Not having known Billy, except recently, I wondered how right she was. He had struck me as one of those people who are high as the sky or in the dumps and what helped him to fly high might be what caused his downfall.

Selina closed her eyes. "Billy, poor Billy. He came through the war, and there was never a day when he was without pain, but he would have kept on keeping on. I know that." With closed eyes, she leaned forward, holding her jaw. "What happened? It couldn't have been whatever was in that damn pillbox, could it?"

165

"No. You were right that it contained antacid tablets. The doctor will issue a death certificate. Before that we'll be just guessing."

"Did you have to stay to make some arrangements?"

"Not arrangements, no. It's too soon for that."

"What then?" She looked at me, full of sympathy. "You'd been up all night and then sat with him. Did you go home and rest?"

She was calculating the time, and remembering that I had encouraged her to go back in the aeroplane.

"We're both tired. Shall we talk about this tomorrow?"

"I'm sorry. You haven't slept. Was it difficult to get back, the trains and so on?"

"Not very."

"Then there's something else, something you're not telling me. You're a nurse. You were with him, talked to the doctor. What is it? What are you keeping back from me?"

It was bad enough that her friend had died, and annoying that Ernest Brownlaw had not been in touch about having tested the cigar.

"I asked the head boy to show me the spot where he and his friends found Billy, that's all."

"And did he?"

"He said that Billy joined in for a few minutes when they were dancing a fandango, and then he took out a cigar and went round the side of the chapel."

"That explains why he walked away. He knows I hate cigar smoke."

166

She pressed her face in her hands. Either she had forgotten that she had taken off her make-up, or had not done it to her own satisfaction. She picked up a piece of cotton wool and wiped her mascara. "You know I have my suspicions about Dougie Dougan's and Floyd's deaths. Am I going mad or is there something suspicious here too?"

"When you called on me, you only asked me to arrange the flight. You were very vague when you said that something bad might happen."

"Yes I know."

"It was only later that you mentioned suspicions regarding other deaths. I'll look into everything if that is what you wish. When and if there is something to tell you, I won't hold back. But please don't ask me to say more now."

"But I must, at least about Billy. He took morphine for the pain. Might it have been that?"

"There will be a post mortem."

"You said that. But I have to know. You see, he would ask me to inject him sometimes. He did on that morning. We found a spot in the school where we weren't seen."

"You made the injection in the neck."

"How do you know?"

"There was a mark."

"But it was his usual injection, nothing more, nothing less."

It was not up to me to advise her to keep quiet about the fact that she injected him. Instead, I said, "If you had not, he would have done it himself, wouldn't he?"

"Yes."

It was sometimes difficult to be precise in measuring, or the morphine may have been stronger than usual but I kept those thoughts to myself. If she was asked to speak about the events of that morning in a coroner's court, that would be the time to admit to administering morphine.

"If he asked you to do it, and that was what he usually took, then don't reproach yourself."

"I can't help thinking I could have killed him. But we all stood around for ages after that, shivering and waiting for the clouds to part. Why did he just walk away? He could have said he was going for a smoke. Perhaps he felt ill then."

"We can't know."

"I knew he had a cigar in his pocket. He was going to light up as a celebration when the sky stayed cloudy and everyone else was disappointed. But he had nothing to celebrate. He hoped for failure, because that would be sad funny."

"Did he often smoke cigars?"

"No, he was a gaspers man. He stuck to the cigs he'd always smoked, but never near me."

"I wonder where he picked up a cigar?"

"Who knows? Trotter dishes them out occasionally."

Later there might be a way of finding out. If I asked now, my question would screech suspicion.

Now that I thought about it, away from Giggleswick and the excitement, horror and exhaustion of the day, I realised that it would be a difficult matter to explain my actions to a coroner's officer.

All the worst possible outcomes flitted through my mind. I would be an interfering female, tampering with evidence, or a crank. In the event of even a cursory investigation, there would be a no-smoke-without-fire scandal for Giggleswick School, the disciplining of the head boy if our laboratory capers came to light, and a shadow cast on the day's achievements.

She sighed. A look of enormous sadness and pity came into her eyes. "I didn't think it would be Billy."

"What do you mean?"

"It's not right. Something isn't right and I can't say what."

"Selina, that's why I'm here. But I can't help unless you talk to me."

"Jarrod will have to know about Billy."

"Jarrod, your husband?"

"Yes."

"Where is Jarrod?"

"I don't know. But he was here, in the theatre. He left something for me." She slid several sheets of folded paper from under a box of powder and pushed them towards me.

At that moment, Beryl came back into the room. She took her coat from the hanger. "Trotter has brought the car round." She turned off the gas fire. She unplugged the iron before walking round the room, picking up a scarf and a shawl which she placed on hangers. Selina had dropped a piece of cotton wool. Beryl put it in the waste basket. "I'll be downstairs."

"We'll be down in a minute, Beryl." Selina turned to me. "Come back to the house with me, Kate. There's something I've been meaning to tell you."

CHAPTER
EIGHTEEN

Shadows in Limelight

I agreed to go back to Selina's house. Apart from being intrigued by whatever she wanted to tell me, and needing to know just what was going on, my car was still on her drive from the evening before when I had driven to her eclipse party.

While Selina changed, I picked up the pages that she had pushed towards me and that were folded and refolded until the whole was a tight little square. I unfolded the sheets of paper slowly, in the way you might release a cut-out newspaper doll if you suspected you had snipped in the wrong place.

She fastened her dress. "Only he would fold something so small, as if trying to make it disappear, as if pretending it almost didn't matter."

I smoothed the pages on the dressing table, blowing away the dusting of face powder. "Read it, Kate. Tell me what kind of person would write that."

It was written on graph paper such as a mathematician might use. The writing was tiny, fitting into the squares, forming a neat pattern. At the top of the page were drawn little scenes, matchstick men, women and children, street lamps, an ice cream cart.

The pictures followed on from each other, comic strip style. There was a title, *Shadows in Limelight*.

The opening was in the form of a verse.

From shadows into light
Brightness follows night
You slide from me collide with me
Never ever to let me be, let me be

There were more verses. Though cramped writing made them difficult to read, I was drawn in by the language and the images. It was a story of love and loss. I turned the pages, trying to get the gist of the piece. More poems followed, numbered but out of order, as if they were meant to fit somewhere. A boy meets girl narrative unfolded. The lovers lose each other, not when he goes to war but when he returns. One needed a magnifying glass for this. I began simply to look at the headings of paragraphs. Hardship. Separation. War. Injury. Reconciliation.

Selina, now dressed and ready to go, was watching me.

I handed the papers back to her. "You asked me what kind of person wrote it, but since it was left by your husband it must be by him. Is he a poet? An author?"

"They are songs. Jarrod writes the music and lyrics of all my songs, the ones that are credited to me."

The penny dropped. She was known for songs about working-class girls and women and their lives and sang these with great conviction because she knew the

172

struggles and the laughs at first hand. She could cross over from romantic to vulgar with a toss of her head. Everyone thought she wrote the songs herself.

"Then this is a play with music?"

"Yes. He has already written the music. He told me so last night."

"When?"

"At the party. Oh, he didn't come in to meet people, not wanting to talk to strangers. He was staying the night, tucking himself away in my sitting room to write a clean copy and leave this one for me."

"The songs are wonderful and the story is a classic. Even though I only looked at it quickly, I could see it coming to life before my eyes. It's just that it's presented in this very odd way in such tiny writing on graph paper."

"It will all make perfect sense." She gave a slightly scoffing sound. "His writing and his compositions will make sense. Nothing else will."

She need not have shown me this material now, not unless there was some connection between this and her distress at Billy's death.

"Is this a musical play?" I wondered whether it was the piece that Trotter Brockett hoped to bring to the London stage, with Billy starring opposite Selina.

"Shall we go? I'll tell you about it at the house."

I picked up my coat.

She switched off the lights as we left. "I wonder if Jarrod knows about Billy, or if he knew that Billy was going to die?"

"How could he have known?"

We walked along the dimly lit corridor. "He and Billy were great friends from a young age. They served together in the Leeds Pals regiment. Billy was best man at our wedding."

My brain ticked over slowly. Either she believed Billy had confided that he would commit suicide and make it look accidental, or she believed that Jarrod had a hand in Billy's death. Or she simply thought Jarrod needed to know.

She walked ahead of me down the flight of stairs. "Are you still willing to help me?"

"Yes."

"Jarrod was badly hurt in the war. He was disfigured and left with a lot of pain. He has had very good treatment and kept his humour all the way through. Recently, he's changed, changed utterly. It's almost a Jekyll and Hyde thing where some other angry, vicious creature inhabits his soul, and then departs."

Trotter Brockett and Beryl were waiting in the stage door area. Brockett embraced Selina and kissed her cheek. He escorted her to where her fans waited by the Swan Street door. Beryl and I followed in the slipstream of her glory. With practised professionalism she exchanged words and accepted condolences on Billy's loss.

"Does Billy leave a family behind?" someone asked.

Selina sighed. "No, and that is both a sadness and a blessing."

With that, she was ushered by Beryl into the Bentley.

A silent figure in black appeared from the shadows and climbed into the front seat beside the driver. It was Sandy Sechrest.

Mr Brockett wished us goodnight and set off to walk to his hotel.

Selina slid across the wide back seat to make room for me. Beryl went round to the other door and climbed in, she and I sitting on either side of Selina.

Having had only two hours' sleep and a most exhausting day, I felt like a person slapped around the head with a wet kipper. Concentrate, I told myself. Meeting so many performers and friends of Selina's in so short a time, I tried to make connections between what was happening now and the deaths of Dougie Doig and Floyd Lloyd.

Everything that had happened felt too close, too deeply unsettling, and inconclusive. Some pause was needed, to gain perspective, recoup and gather my wits. I would be glad when I could talk about the day's events to Jim Sykes.

And I must pin Selina down. There was a slippery quality about her, and always that sense that she was holding back.

Selina whispered, "I wish I knew where Jarrod has gone."

"Did he give a hint? You said he stayed at your house to make a clean copy of his manuscript. What did he intend to do with it?"

"He was a little evasive, but he mentioned he might type it."

"Perhaps you're worrying too much and he'll be at your house when you arrive home."

"He isn't there. I telephoned. We're here at the Varieties until Saturday. What other damnable blows will fall between now and then?"

Beryl answered, "Give over! Nothing else can happen. Bad things come in threes and we've had our share."

The Bentley pulled onto Selina's drive, followed by a taxi containing three other members of the company, the Powolskis and Maurice Montague. During the journey, Beryl told me that Selina, having a house of many rooms, was providing hospitality to other company members. The young acrobats, the Powolski brother and sister, who were hard up, had been given a room. Maurice Montague, master of music, down on his luck, was also staying at Selina's house after unspecified setbacks. Unspecified except that Jake's performing pony had chewed the smaller of Maurice's accordions and that Maurice's rail journeys cost more than anyone else's due to the charges for transporting his twenty-nine musical instruments.

Beryl seemed somewhat peevish about Maurice and I felt glad for him that he had his new job at the Grand Pygmalion.

The young acrobats Powolski and Maurice climbed out of the taxi. The fleet-footed young Powolskis were first into the house, with Maurice close behind.

There had been a note of scepticism in Beryl's voice when she told the tale of the Powolskis' poverty and

Maurice Montague's setbacks, but of approval when she spoke to Sandy Sechrest, as if feeling the necessity to exclude Sandy from any suggestion of exploiting Selina's good nature.

"What are your digs like, Sandy?"

"Passable thank you, Beryl."

Selina said, "You'll come in for a bite of supper, Sandy?"

"Thank you, I will."

Sandy, Maurice and the Powolskis made a beeline for the kitchen. Selina and I went upstairs to where she had her bedroom, bathroom and sitting room. Beryl called from the bottom of the stairs, "We'll bring you some food!"

While Selina changed into nightwear, I went into the bathroom. I have stayed in grand houses in London and in the country but they were centuries old, full of draughts, creaks and groans and usually with a shortage of toileting facilities. This bathroom was a picture of black and white tiles, shining chrome mirror tiles above the wash basin and a geometrical pattern on the black and white linoleum. Faucets and towel rails were decorated with an Egyptian motif. I washed my face and hands, combed my hair, and felt glad to have a few moments to myself. I don't spend a lot of time thinking about my own house. It's up-to-date as such houses go. But if I could have picked up Selina's bathroom and taken it home, I would have been a happy woman. A happy woman who would spend an awfully long time in the bath tub.

I went back into the sitting room. Selina was seated in one of the chairs by the fire, tying the belt of her silk robe that was patterned with peacocks. The room was decorated in the palest green with low tables set beside the chairs on either side of the hearth. Coals blazed in the grate of the green-tiled fireplace. An elegant dancing figure graced the mantelpiece, along with a brass, chrome and Bakelite circus strongman, a female acrobat on a tray in his hand. The acrobat, adorned in links of chain, held a curved bar decorated with dumbbells.

She saw me admiring the little ornament. "Touch it. The acrobat spins and turns but never loses her balance."

I tapped the acrobat's arm. She wobbled a little, spun and slowly returned to her original position. Lucky little acrobat.

Before we had time to begin our conversation, Beryl and Sandy came into the room, each carrying a tray with a bowl of soup, bread and butter, ham and cheese, waving away our thanks and leaving us to it. Trays perched on our laps, we tackled the soup.

Selina kicked off a pair of flimsy slippers. "You must think I'm unbalanced, or psychic. I feared something bad would happen today, and it did, almost as if I had wished it."

"What made you fearful?"

"A feeling, an instinct."

"Was it because you knew of Billy's addiction?"

"I'm not sure that he does have, did have, an addiction. It's true he occasionally sniffs cocaine. I've told him that's such a dirty habit. But no one would blame an old soldier for taking morphine. It's prescribed. It's medicinal."

To my knowledge I don't have a maiden aunt but I felt like one as I pointed out that Billy's narcotics were unlikely to have been prescribed, or medicinal, and could be dangerous.

She stretched her toes towards the fire like some modern-day Cinderella, staring into the flames.

"Selina, smoke signals up the chimney won't help. We're both tired. It's been a terrible day, but you came to me for help. You feared something bad might happen and it has. I've begun investigations into how your friends Dougie Dougan and Floyd Lloyd died, but if you have any suspicions that Billy's death was anything other than accidental, say so now and tell me why."

She poked the fire. "You're very hard."

"Tell me what you are thinking."

If she had nothing more to say, then I would leave. The weariness of the long party, the flight and the extraordinary experience of watching the eclipse left me feeling that there had been a shift in reality. The world, always out of kilter, had undergone some new spin. I would not have been surprised to hear an alarm clock and wake up. Something deep inside me hoped that might happen. I wanted a real alarm to wake me, to quell the alarm I felt inside. She had stitched past deaths to the image of the new moon and pinned on fresh fears.

Here we were, sitting in this delightful house, this monument to style and light, on the point of entering a new darkness.

The eclipse seemed to have created a different feeling about the world. We all go about our business feeling we have a modicum of control, making choices about the smallest things as if they are of earth-shattering importance. But a chill had entered my soul when the world turned dark. I envied those who, however briefly, danced the fandango when the light returned. She had danced, and so had Billy. I was the one on the side lines, watching, asking the difficult questions.

Selina's words ricocheted around my brain. Something bad is going to happen. An uncanny sensation almost overwhelmed me. We humans have such a short time on earth, the snap of a finger, the blink of an eye. Our paths cross with so many people and sometimes I think back to the days when I was eighteen, nineteen and into my twenties and wish I had done something differently, been less diffident, more ready to recognise an overture of friendship. The opposite was true now. Never before had I felt such a strong instinct to turn away.

"Selina, do you think Billy found some way of ending his own life today?"

"No! He was looking forward to something. Trotter had a show in mind for us, to open in the autumn."

"Were you looking forward to that?"

"Yes and no. You see, Jarrod also had plans. Plans for me — that manuscript — Jarrod hopes and dreams that it will be a moving picture."

"Did Billy know?"

"I'm not sure. He knew that Jarrod was writing something for me."

"Was there a part for Billy in the moving picture script?"

She shook her head.

"So there was a conflict of interest between the plans that Trotter Brockett had for you and Billy, and what Jarrod hopes will happen."

She stood and twirled the little acrobat on the mantelshelf. "I don't see it that way."

I would go soon. Before I left, should I pass on Mrs Douglas's message that Selina's son would not be welcome at Giggleswick School? That was none of my business.

"Miss Fellini . . ."

"Selina."

"Selina, you've asked me to investigate but I have a feeling that you don't want answers."

She talks like she sings, with warmth in her voice and, on stage, always seems spontaneous.

"Kate, the reason I came to you is because my friend Giuseppe said you take a logical approach and go about with your eyes and ears open and that you do not judge harshly."

She paused, but I made no response. It was a bit late to be going over my testimonials. What I wanted to know was this: what comes next?

The best thing I could do was to concentrate on the here and now and try and find out more from Selina. "Was Billy staying here?"

"Yes. In the end bedroom along the landing."

"Let's take a look."

"Why?"

"That's what we should do."

"You think he took something, and that he may have left a note?"

"Let's see."

CHAPTER
NINETEEN

Billy's Room

We walked along the landing. The house was silent. If the others were still having supper downstairs they were quiet about it.

Selina opened the door and flicked on the light. The room was plain with white walls and a blind at the window. The furniture was fumed oak: dressing table with mirror, wardrobe, a single bed made up with a plain white counterpane, bedside table, lamp and rattan chair.

The sheet and pillow were of heavy cotton and on the pillow was a single long black hair. Selina picked it up and wound it around her finger.

On the wall was a painting in the style of Atkinson Grimshaw, a solitary figure walking along a moonlit path through trees. Perhaps it was an Atkinson Grimshaw.

On the dressing table stood a bottle of hair oil and a leather case containing shaving brush, soap and razor along with hairbrush, comb and clothes brush. She removed the cork from the hair oil and dabbed a touch on her wrist.

I picked up a notebook from the bedside table and looked through the pages.

"That's his workbook, for his sketches and ideas."

There were headings, characters and lines of dialogue. I flicked through but saw no indication of anything personal. The most recent entries concerned "Unfortunate Little Man goes snow shifting — no coat", "Old soldier breaks into brewery" and "Works outing".

Selina opened the wardrobe. There was an everyday wool suit, worn at the cuffs.

She stroked the sleeve of the jacket, and put her hands in the pockets. "Nothing in the pockets but matches, tobacco and a stubby pencil."

I went to look, just in case that tobacco was the same as the cigar. I took a sniff at the few strands that were mixed with the kind of grit and dust that lines the bottom of some pockets. This was tobacco from a cheap cigarette, a gasper.

She opened drawers which contained a few items of clothing, a pack of playing cards and some profession-ally produced postcards with Billy's likeness. She raised a photo card to her lips. "He travelled light. He always said he didn't like to have much stuff, didn't see the point."

His battered, empty suitcase was under the bed.

She sat on the edge of the bed and picked up a cowboy novel from the bedside table. Nothing fell out of the pages except a Woodbine packet that marked his place. She examined it, in case there was a word.

"Might he have left anything at the theatre?" I asked.

"Only his costume. On stage he wore baggy trousers, workman's shirt, a pair of braces and big boots with no socks. He shared a dressing room so there wasn't much space."

I sat down on the nearby wicker chair. "Let me ask you one or two questions because I'm so in the dark here."

"I know. I haven't been very clear, but I'm not sure how to be. Everything kind of merges together. I knew something bad might happen but I never thought it would be Billy."

"You say that as if you expected someone else to die. Who did you think it might be?"

"I don't know. Jarrod and Billy have always got on. Even last night, at the party, although Jarrod didn't want to talk to anyone, he spoke to Billy. They were outside together, under the trees."

"You said that Jarrod has been acting strangely."

"Yes, for months. It's a kind of madness. Sometimes he is his normal self and at other times he looks at me as if he doesn't know who I am, and I think about Iago whispering to Othello. Jarrod looks at me as though I've betrayed him. Last night he was cheerful, and then I don't see him, like today, when he just left something for me and disappeared."

"Was he acting strangely when Dougie Doig had his accident?"

"That was a year ago and no, he was himself then. He did come to Sunderland to see the show. He brought Reggie one Saturday."

"Reggie?"

"Reggie's our son, named for Jarrod's father. He's at boarding school."

It suddenly made sense that she was reluctant to say very much about Jarrod. The best outcome for her would be reassurance that those other deaths really were accidents, but I must keep an open mind. A third death in such a small company did seem more than coincidence.

"Can you put a date on the first time you were aware of Jarrod behaving strangely?"

She shook her head.

"When the invitation came to you to view the eclipse, was it just to you, or to you and Billy?"

"It was to me and Jarrod, addressed to Mr and Mrs Jarrod Compton, but Jarrod wouldn't come. I told him that people would love to see him at his old school but he said no."

"Why do you think he said no?"

"He knows himself that something is wrong and that he might . . . make a spectacle."

"Does he live here when you are touring?"

"No. He has a place in Bridlington. He loves the sea and has a flat on the seafront. He was in a sanatorium there while recovering from surgery and he decided to stay out of a liking for the place and the East Riding landscape, and because he goes back to the sanatorium for treatment."

"How does he get about, does he drive?"

"Yes. He has a motorcycle. He sometimes turns up at a theatre and slips into one of the boxes or stands at the back where he isn't noticed. I told you he writes my songs. He still loves me but in his own strange way. And I love him."

186

I thought of the person who had stepped into the box and gone out again. "Does he wear a white silk muffler around his face?"

She looked surprised. "How do you know?"

"I believe he may have come into the box where Mr Brockett put me. When he saw it was occupied, he went out again."

"Trotter sometimes arranges to have a box kept empty for him, just in case. Only this evening I suppose he didn't expect him. Everyone knows him, you see, and Harry the doorkeeper or the front of house staff would say, 'Oh, Mr Compton is here'."

"I went to try and speak to him, having no objection to someone else sharing the box."

"And did you see him, where he went?"

"No. By the time I opened the door and looked, there was no sign of him."

She put her head in her hands. "This breaks my dream."

"What dream?"

"I dreamed of a man on the stairs of the theatre, a man who wasn't there but was. You know, like the poem, meeting a man on the stair who wasn't there. In the dream, it's a winding staircase, somewhere like the Palladium. In my dream, the man is turning somersaults all the way down the stairs. And it was Jarrod, only it couldn't have been."

"I know that feeling when dreams and the people in them are two things at the same time. Is there some significance about the stairs and acrobatics?"

187

"Did you ever wonder why there are so few acrobats and high-wire men in the theatre now, and hardly any jugglers, except for youngsters like the Powolskis?"

I hadn't thought about it, but now that she mentioned it, the truth came home. "You mean those who came back from war were no longer able to perform?"

She nodded. "Jarrod and I met as child performers in this very theatre. I sang and danced. Jarrod did acrobatic tricks, and he juggled." She smiled. "You'd have thought him made of rubber in those days."

"He was a performer, too?"

"Not really. This was when we were kids. I can't remember all the details but the theatre put on auditions for children, and then a show. I expect it was a wheeze to bring in a good audience of lots of parents and aunties and uncles. It was the summertime. Jarrod was home from Giggleswick School and I was helping out at home with the ice cream making. We weren't paid to be in the show so it was a bit difficult for me as I was meant to be pulling my weight for the family. It was different, later on, when I was a child in the panto and paid each week."

"Who taught you?"

"I always danced and sang but it's thanks to Beryl's parents that I had some training. She and I started in the infants' class together at St Charles's. We lived on Grimston Street, ten kids in our family. She lived on Valley Street and was an only child. We were always back and forth. I could find my way to her house blindfolded, along the ginnel onto Cherry Row, over

Green Road and up through the streets. Her dad was an engineer, so they were well off. Her mam and dad sent her to singing and dancing lessons, only she wouldn't go alone. She said she would go if I did too. Her dad paid for us both."

"And you were the one who succeeded."

"Beryl didn't mind. She never was all that keen. It was her parents' idea that she should learn tap and ballet and singing, to brighten her up a bit they said. I suppose it was to make up for her being an only child."

"So she never took to the stage?"

"Oh, the odd time, when we were kids, that's all."

"And what about Jarrod? Were you and he childhood sweethearts?"

"Nothing like that. We weren't in touch for a few years. When I was nineteen I was very lucky and landed a principal boy role in panto." She smiled. "It was thanks to my singing and my legs rather than acting talent. Jarrod was just seventeen and writing reviews. He came along to review the show, and remembered me. He was waiting at the stage door on opening night."

"Selina, I have to ask you something."

"I know. You have to ask me if Billy and I were lovers."

"Were you?"

"No, but there were rumours that we were and we never bothered to deny it. Rumours don't deserve denial."

"If Jarrod heard these rumours, who would have been the Iago who whispered them?"

189

"I don't know. Perhaps I'm wrong. I don't know what goes on in his head any more. It was one thing when he wanted to keep out of sight because of being self-conscious. His face is disfigured, on the left side. Half a mask was made for him, a very good mask but he doesn't like to wear it. It's hot and itchy. Even so he was on a more even keel than Billy in lots of ways, funny, enjoying his writing, saying writing was what he was meant to do and that with half his face gone he had a good excuse not to socialise.

"A few months ago everything changed. He became angry and irrational. He'd have sudden outbursts of temper and make accusations, being horrible to people, pushing passers-by off the pavement if they came too close. Staff at the sanatorium became concerned about him. He stopped going there, for his massages and everything that made his life bearable. He had moments of being the old Jarrod, when he was writing, or when some sort of calmness came over him. I don't know how closely you read what he left for me, but one of those songs was about a man who could only live underground, in tunnels because he fears he is affected by the moon."

"Did Jarrod know that you asked Billy to take his place and come to Giggleswick today?"

"I suppose he knew I would take someone else and Billy would be the obvious choice."

"Because?"

"Because we are such old friends."

We had left the door open. Beryl came in. "What on earth are you doing in here, sitting in the cold when there's a nice little fire burning in the grate in your room?"

I stood. "It's my fault. I was interested in seeing round, and taking a look at Billy's room."

"Well you've looked, so frame yourselves and come where you'll be comfortable. I've brought you drinks."

"We'll be along in a minute, Beryl." Selina turned to me. "Give me a few moments, to say goodbye to Billy."

I nodded and left the room, following Beryl back down the landing, leaving Selina to remember Billy, and to say goodbye to her lover. She was doing the right thing, denying her and Billy's affair. The only way to hug a secret close is never to tell a soul. If one other person knows, then there is no secret.

Beryl looked back along the landing for Selina.

Until now, I had thought Beryl older than Selina because of the way she sometimes behaved like a mother hen. Mother hens could be extraordinarily protective of their chicks.

CHAPTER
TWENTY

The Mystery Man

When we went back into Selina's room, Beryl began to gather up the dishes and plates.

I helped and took the tray, so she was not able to hurry away. "It was a good supper, Beryl, my compliments to the chef."

"That would be young Babs Powolski. She made the soup this morning."

"Do you have a minute, Beryl?"

"I have lots of minutes."

"I believe I saw Jarrod tonight. He came to the door of the royal box."

Beryl picked up a spoon that we had missed. "Jarrod's become our mystery man. No one sees him come or go, through the actors' door or through the main entrance, even though he isn't easy to miss."

I didn't want any more mystery than already existed. "If he is self-conscious about his appearance, isn't it understandable that he should slip in to see the show, unnoticed?"

Beryl agreed. "Completely understandable. Why shouldn't he come to see the show and hear his own songs? Only Harry said he didn't come in at the stage door. Front of house manager swears one of his people would have noticed Mr Compton."

"Does Jarrod usually come in person to bring songs to Selina?"

She thought for a moment. "Not usually. He has been known to send a song through the post. He sometimes waits until she visits him."

There was no subtle way of asking the next question, but I wanted to ask before Selina returned. "This may sound odd, but the last thing Billy was seen to do was to light a cigar. I'm wondering whether it was for some special occasion, or whether he usually smoked a cigar."

She looked at me blankly. "He wouldn't normally, not unless someone gave it to him."

"I suppose someone might have, at the party."

"It's possible. Selina doesn't let people smoke indoors because of her sensitive throat, but there was a box of cigars on the veranda."

"Yes. That could be it." I imagined a box of cigars, with at least one laced with poison and sincerely hoped that was not it.

"Do you think it upset Jarrod that Selina invited Billy to come to Giggleswick?"

"I shouldn't think so. Jarrod knows that Billy liked to gather material for his act."

"Would you have gone, given the opportunity?"

She brushed away the question. "I wasn't asked. Selina always likes a male escort."

Her answer intrigued me. I wanted to know who else might in the past have played the role of escort, perhaps Douglas Dougan or Floyd Lloyd.

At that moment, Selina returned. She stood in the doorway and stretched, rolling her head, making cracking sounds in her joints. "I wonder if Jarrod was in the theatre to hear me tell people about Billy? They were so close, together through most of the war."

Beryl shut her eyes as if the thought of Jarrod hearing about Billy in a public announcement didn't bear thinking about. "If he did, where has the poor lad gone? It could turn his mind altogether to hear such news."

Selina did that thing people sometimes do of talking as if this is a continuing conversation rather than something that has been going round and round in their own head. Speaking as if the other person already knows what they are thinking. "I don't believe he'll harm me. These dreams I've had." She stopped abruptly.

"What dreams?" Beryl asked.

"Beryl, don't go yet. I'll show Kate the cuttings." Selina opened the top drawer of a bureau. "I've kept these cuttings because I had a feeling, an instinct. I don't know what else to call it. Two horrible things happened and I knew there would be another, and that it might never end."

She handed me the newspaper cuttings with the information that Mrs Sugden had discovered at the newspaper library. By now I was beginning to feel dead on my feet and overloaded with information. I sat down and read the pieces. Douglas Dougan, knocked down by a tram. Floyd Lloyd killed on stage when a sandbag dropped from the flies.

The items had been cut out of newspapers, but with no title for the newspaper and no date. They were less informative than the transcripts Mrs Sugden had shown me earlier.

"They're distressing incidents. Is there any reason to regard them as other than accidents?"

"Dougie wouldn't walk under a tram. And why, if a sandbag dropped from the flies, would it be precisely where Floyd was rehearsing?"

Beryl set down the trays she had been about to whisk away. She drew up a small chair and sat down. "It's a rum business."

I felt sure Selina and Beryl had discussed this already and so asked, "What do you make of it, Beryl? Do you also think Mr Dougan's and Mr Lloyd's deaths weren't accidents?"

She tucked her hands into her cardigan sleeves. "I did wonder with Dougie that it might have been drink. It was after the interval."

Selina disagreed. "A person doesn't walk under a tram just because he's had a drink. If that were true we'd lose the entire male population over three Saturday nights."

"You have instincts, Selina, but you know my opinion. I can't see that either of those deaths was anything other than a bad accident. Dougie liked a drink and I wouldn't put it past him to have misjudged crossing the road or been so caught up with his own thoughts that he didn't see the tram coming."

"What about Floyd, who never touched a drop? He signed the temperance pledge as a boy. All he did was seat himself in his usual place on stage to rehearse his new routine with Manny Piccolo."

"Ah, now that's another matter. If you ask me they shouldn't have let that theatre open its doors again after that. Something was amiss. Probably some stage hand who'd had one too many and then realised there was a frayed rope or some such and managed to rectify it before the investigation began. Drink'll be at the back of it, mark my words."

I did mark her words. If her explanation for both accidents was alcohol, she could be right, or she could be completely wrong.

Beryl looked from Selina to me. "Selina has instincts, uncanny instincts, and so I'm prepared to give her opinions weight, but I don't share them."

Instinct is a marvellous thing. It cannot be explained and yet it cannot be ignored.

Selina put the cuttings back in the envelope and placed it on the table by my chair.

"Were those deaths really accidents?" she asked, as if questioning a well-informed coroner.

I decided against mentioning that Mrs Sugden and Mr Sykes were already on the case. "If you want me to find out more, I will try to do so."

"Yes, that's exactly what I want you to do."

"Can you think of any connections between Floyd Lloyd and Douglas Dougan, or any explanation of circumstances? Did they have enemies in common?"

"Neither man had an enemy in the world. They both started young in the business. We all played together a number of times in the early days. Their acts stayed the same over the years but the public changed. Neither was as popular as he once was but that's true for lots of the performers in our business." She crossed her arms over her bosom and hugged herself.

Beryl picked up a shawl and put it around Selina's shoulders. "There's nothing you can do about that. Hard times, it's hard times all round. No one resents your success. There's others would turn their backs on old timers and falling stars." Beryl shot me an appealing glance. "Selina is doing this tour out of the goodness of her heart. She doesn't need to tour the old music halls. She has offers, big offers, but her generosity gets the better of her."

Selina squeezed her dresser's hand. "I can't turn my back on the audience that made me, or the people I looked up to when I was a kid."

It struck me that if she took up the offer of Trotter Brockett's London show, or her husband's plans for the silver screen, then she would be bound to move on.

Beryl gave an impatient tut. "Your audience will follow you wherever you go. Your friends will urge you on. God gave you talents. You've done enough with your charity. Leave the good works to the Salvation Army."

She picked up the trays and I went to open the door for her. When I came back to the hearth, Selina was tapping the little acrobat, making her twirl.

"Selina, am I right in thinking that you suspect your husband of some kind of mania?"

She lowered her head. "I want to be sure . . . I can't say this. You see, Jarrod's wounds, the physical wounds are obvious. I want to know that he's not . . . that he wouldn't be capable of murder." The little acrobat slowed, and then was still. "Jarrod and I married young. What we had was so different, so unforgettable that there's still this unbroken thread. He's in my dreams and I'm in his. I believe the balance of his mind is disturbed and that he'd somehow imagined things about me and Billy and was jealous of Billy."

"And the other two performers, Douglas Dougan and Floyd Lloyd, were you close to them? Might Jarrod have imagined things about them?"

"Not in the same way, for heaven's sake. Dougie was a good friend. We spent a lot of time together. Floyd was like an uncle, always looking out for me, full of advice." She smiled. "Not always good advice. I took very little notice of him. He didn't realise that the theatre has changed. We all got tipsy together often enough. There was nothing romantic between me and Dougie or me and Floyd."

"Would that friendship be enough to make Jarrod jealous?"

"If something in Jarrod's head has turned him peculiar, then who knows how he thinks or what he might do?"

"With Jarrod in Bridlington and you touring, you must see each other so rarely."

"He has his motorcycle. I have my car, and the trains. We always managed to see each other until recently. Every August we go away with Reggie, somewhere remote where we can be ourselves. Reggie has never minded that his father is disfigured. He

198

knows he was a soldier. But I don't know what we'll do this year, now that Jarrod can turn at a moment's notice. I wouldn't want Reggie to see him like that."

Part of me knew that she only wanted one answer: that she was wrong. But what if she was right? What if she was more than right and yet was avoiding the harsh truth, that her jealous and angry husband was a murderer?

"You want me to investigate your husband, and his links to the deaths."

"I'll pay you well, Kate. I'm wealthier than I ever dreamed, but I have just one condition."

"And that is?"

"If you find out that my worst fears are true, come to me first. Don't go to the police."

I hesitated. Even if it were me alone, I couldn't agree to that condition, but Jim Sykes is a former policeman with a policeman's way of looking at the world. If he arrived at the truth first, it would be impossible to rein him in. "I would like to say yes but circumstances may make that difficult."

"What circumstances?"

"Another life might be at stake, your life."

She gave a dismissive gesture. "If it's my life then I might take the chance, or I would if not for my son. I want to see him grow up. If it's another's life then that would be different. But will you agree to that condition as far as possible?"

"I will."

Now that she had mentioned her son, this was the moment for me to pass on the message: that

Giggleswick School would have no place for him. The fact that she had considered sending Reggie to Giggleswick School now explained why she had gained an invitation. I had thought it was because of her fame, fortune, and reputation for generosity.

She took a cheque book from her bag and reached for the pen that had signed so many autographs.

"What age is Reggie?"

"He's eight."

"And where does he go to school?"

"He boards at Ampleforth and I believe he's happy there. Jarrod's not Catholic but he took instruction and agreed to have Reginald brought up in the faith."

So she was not the person who had enquired about a place at Giggleswick School for Reggie.

She passed me a cheque for two hundred pounds.

"This is too much."

"Bring me peace of mind and it will be more than worth it to me. Now where will you start?"

That was a good question, with no single answer. "We need to follow up the two accidental deaths and to find out the post mortem results on Billy."

"What will you do first?"

"I told you about Mr Sykes. Between us, we'll see whether there's more information to be had."

"He won't go to the police?"

"He'll come to me first. If the deaths truly were accidental then your fears are unfounded."

"Not the police. I don't want the police involved, just in case." A look of great sadness came over her. "I doubt now that Jarrod and I will ever be together again,

200

after these horrible episodes of his. But we'll always be married. There's an unbreakable web between us, and that's not just to do with me being Catholic. We don't mate for life, but we marry that way. There's a reason for that term wedlock."

Now was not a good time to discuss the metaphysics of mating. "Since we know he is in Leeds, I want to speak to Jarrod. Would he stay overnight, or go back to Bridlington?"

"I hope he won't drive back in the dark. He's reckless on that motorcycle." She smiled. "I've ridden it myself and toppled off."

"If he does stay here, where might he go?"

"I've thought about this, and the fact that he said he would type his script. There's a typewriter at his mother's. I'll give you her address." I took out my notebook, turned a page and handed it to her.

She wrote Mrs Compton's address. "Oh, and I'd better tell you, she loathes and despises me. I don't want to give her the satisfaction of telephoning to see if he's there."

"You should. Not give her the satisfaction, but telephone. It would save time."

"She'll be in bed and won't thank me for ringing. And if he isn't there, she'll worry."

There was a tap and the door opened. "I'm sorry. I didn't realise you had company." It was Sandy Sechrest, the amazing memory woman, still dressed in black.

"It's all right, Sandy. Do come in."

Sandy glided towards Selina, hugged her and kissed her cheek. "I can't believe it. That's why I didn't say anything in the car. What a dreadful shock, especially for you, to set off with Billy and come back alone. You must feel so bereft, darling. None of us can believe it."

Selina squeezed her hand. "I know."

"I'm here for you. You know that, don't you?"

"Yes. And Sandy, Kate Shackleton is going to look into all the deaths, Dougie's, Floyd's and Billy's. They may be accidental but they may not. May I count on your discretion and to help Kate, and the man who works with her, what was his name, Kate?"

"Mr Sykes. Jim Sykes."

"Of course, though I don't know how I can help."

Selina began to cry. She took a dainty lace-edged hanky from her clutch bag and blew into it with a good deal of energy. "First Dougie, then Floyd and now Billy. It's too much to bear."

Sandy spoke soothingly. "You've turned the corner, Selina, believe me. I've cast you a new horoscope and I can assure you that from now on everything will be all right. There'll be no more deaths of those near and dear to you, not for many years."

The mysterious memory woman gave a small bow and left.

How did she know everything would be all right, unless she was the one responsible for the deaths?

It was my turn to take my leave, without the bow, but first I had to find a way of asking Selina a question.

As if we were still having the conversation about young Reginald, I asked, "And are you and Jarrod happy with Reggie's school?"

"Oh yes. He's doing very well there. We have high hopes for him, and neither of us wants him to go into the business."

Perhaps Jarrod was not as happy with Selina's arrangements for her own and Reggie's life as Selina had thought.

"When you took out your pen to sign Ruth Dyson's autograph book, you had a pencil tin in your clutch bag. Was that Reggie's? Children often like a new pencil case."

She gave a small gulp. "I see now why you were recommended. That was Billy's. I carried it about for him."

"To hold a cigar?"

"Not a cigar, no." She bit her lip. "He put me in charge of his morphine. You believe I gave him an overdose when I injected him."

"No. If you had, there would have been a reaction earlier."

We were at the front door. Selina did not open it. "You know you are welcome to stay."

"I need to be home."

She would have come out with me but I stopped her. "Don't get cold. You stay indoors. As soon as I have something for you, I'll be in touch."

I hesitated.

"What?" she asked. "Have you thought of something?"

"Do you mind if I ask the Powolskis and Maurice Montague whether they can shed any light?"

"They'll be in the kitchen still." She kissed my cheek. "Thank you for everything. Come back to me soon."

"I will. As soon as I have something to tell you, I'll be in touch."

The Powolski siblings were sitting on opposite sides of the kitchen table, smoking and drinking black tea. Maurice Montague sat along from the brother, an evening paper in front of him. He was asking them questions from a quiz in the paper.

I had met them at the party and now apologised for interrupting their quiz.

Babs spoke first. "Please do to interrupt. Maurice asks questions to which only he knows the answers." She smiled.

We all shook hands. "You were all wonderful tonight. It was a great treat."

They accepted my compliment and looked interested in what I might say next, all except for Maurice who said that he felt there might be a curse hanging over this company.

Not only had Dougie Dougan and Floyd met with terrible accidents but the railway company had damaged Maurice's mandolin and Jake's pony had taken a bite out of his accordion.

Adam Powolski must have heard these stories before but he was patient towards his fellow performer. "I check our wires every evening now. You cannot trust any living human being with your life or your instruments."

I sympathised. "Billy's death must have come as a great shock to you all."

Babs nodded. "He was such a funny man. I have learned all his jokes."

"You know him so much better than I do. Did he seem in any way unwell last night?"

They all said that he did not.

"The last thing he did was to light a cigar. I thought it might be a comfort to the person who gave it to him if I could tell them that he had a moment in which to enjoy it."

I was pleased with this devious way of asking my question.

Unfortunately, no one had any idea of who might have given Billy a cigar, though they agreed he would not have bought it himself.

I left them to their newspaper quiz and tea, and wished them goodnight.

Maurice Montague caught up with me. "I'll walk you to your car."

The moon shone brightly as we left the house. Globes of electric light on the drive competed with moonbeams. My Jowett car looked like a miniature of a motor set alongside Selina's Bentley.

"I'm obliged to you for keeping my confidence, Mrs Shackleton. I was that pleased with setting the seal on my arrangement with the Grand Pygmalion today that I let myself run on."

"Think no more about it. I'm glad for you."

"I'll be sorry to part with my instruments but it will be a relief to be settled."

He did not sound entirely certain. "It will be lovely to be in such surroundings and I'm sure that the customers will greatly appreciate your playing. I'll come in myself."

"I hope you will. I'll keep my fiddle, but the rest can go so if you know of anyone who wants an item, let me know. Everything's in tip-top condition except the chewed accordion."

"May I ask you a question, Mr Montague?"

"Ask away, and call me Maurice."

"Maurice, earlier you said that a person must know when it is time to go, must jump before they are pushed."

"Did I say that?"

"Were you thinking about others in the company who were pushed?"

He gulped. "I was speaking generally."

"Pardon my curiosity but I'm interested in your profession, or what will soon be your former profession. It's so glamorous from the outside, yet it must be hard, and hard to let go."

"I haven't promised myself that I'll let go entirely. An artiste is always on the lookout."

"Who were you thinking of, who was pushed before they jumped?"

"People whose time was up."

"And who decides when that moment comes?"

"Who do you think? You wouldn't have to be around too long to see Beryl snipe at me and the young Powolskis, just because Selina is kind to them. And the public is fickle. Some acts lose their appeal. Perhaps mine is one of them."

"You were wonderful. Everyone loved you. I'm always sorry that I never saw Dougie Doig and his dogs. Was his an act that lost its appeal?"

"I did wonder whether he was preoccupied that night of the accident. Dougie was in his prime, but two of his dogs were old." Maurice took the last cigarette from a packet of five. The struck match lit his tired face. "You're thinking someone had it in for him."

"The thought crossed my mind."

He tossed the spent match across the grass. "You could be right."

"You mentioned Beryl?"

"She resents it when people come too close to her Selina."

At that moment, Sandy Sechrest swept out of the house, pulling a dark cloak around her. She stopped by the car. "You off, Sandy?"

"Yes. I'll see you tomorrow."

My moment had passed. Maurice turned to go. "I'll turn in myself now. Goodnight, Mrs Shackleton. Goodnight, Sandy."

We wished him goodnight.

"May I offer you a lift, Miss Sechrest?"

"Thank you but no. I like to walk."

That was as much information as I would gather tonight. I climbed into the car and started the engine.

As I was about to move off the drive, a motorcycle sped along the road, its rider clad in black and with a white muffler wound around the lower part of his face and trailing out behind him.

CHAPTER
TWENTY-ONE

Losing The Way

The journey home from Selina's house in Roundhay unnerved me. Street lights had dimmed. Darkness made the way hard to follow. The moon hid its face. I did not know the area well enough to be familiar with landmarks. The direction was south a little way, towards the town, and then veering west. Streets twisted and turned. Where I expected there to be a junction there was none. When I thought the road should be straight, it forked. For twenty minutes or more I drove blindly, feeling utterly lost, wishing I had driven back into town and out again. All the while some inner voice whispered to me of a dark, deep current of events. To be lost in this way was a warning. If I found my way home, before running out of petrol and before bumping into some obstacle in the dark, I should give up this task, return Selina's cheque and advise her to go to the police.

At last, a familiar landmark came into view, the dark moor, soon followed by Hyde Park public house, in darkness but with its own unmistakeable shape.

I expected that Mrs Sugden would have gone to bed. If so, she had obligingly left on a light in the hall.

Leaving the car by the kerb, I walked to the door, fishing for my keys. It opened. There was Mrs Sugden, still fully dressed.

"Where have you been? We were that worried about you."

"I had to go home with our client and find out just where we stand."

"And did you?"

"I went home with her. As to where we stand, I'm not entirely sure."

"Well Mr Sykes is here. He wasn't prepared to leave till we had word of you. Come through and warm up. I can feel the cold coming off you like icicles."

Sykes was sitting at the kitchen table with a mug of tea. He poured one for me. "That was such a moving tribute Selina Fellini paid to Billy Moffatt. I was telling Mrs Sugden."

"Yes it was." I circled the mug with my hands, trying to bring life back into my frozen fingers.

"How did he die? She didn't say."

"That's a good question. He collapsed. I believe there'll be a post mortem. He'd taken drugs for years. The last thing he did was smoke a cigar. I've asked Ernest Brownlaw to test it but he hasn't come back to me. It's probably nothing." There might be a moment when they needed a fuller story of that but for now I wanted to hear what my trusty assistants had to say.

It being the warmest room in the house, the three of us stayed put in the kitchen. The foolscap sheet on which Mr Duffield's assistant had typed the articles regarding the deaths of Douglas Dougan and Floyd

Lloyd lay on the table by the sugar basin. Mrs Sugden added water to the teapot. She could barely keep the outrage from her voice. "I consider it a diabolical liberty that after the night and day you've had, nobody fetched you straight home from that there theatre, and you half dead on your feet."

"I couldn't refuse to go back with Miss Fellini but I did turn down an invitation to stay the night."

"Any normal person would need her own bed." Mrs Sugden pushed a plate of sandwiches towards me.

Sykes had treated himself to a small bottle of whisky and poured a finger in my tea. I took a drink, and picked up a sandwich. "Potted meat?"

"Bone marrow and cucumber. Do you the world of good after the night and day you've had."

I related Selina's fears and her story, the estrangement from her husband and the oddness of Jarrod having entered and left the theatre without being seen by the doorkeeper or front of house staff who all knew him. "I do believe he was the person who opened the door of the royal box after the interval." I also told them about the motorcycle speeding off into the night as I left Selina's house. We agreed that could have been anyone.

"I saw him," Sykes said. "A tall fellow put in an appearance standing in the royal box, dressed in black and with a white muffler. Maybe it's one of these cases where she regards herself as estranged and he doesn't. If he has suspicions of a rival, that could explain his appearance. Might he have found his way into the same viewing area as you for the eclipse?"

"It was admission by ticket. Anything's possible but from how Selina described him, tall, disfigured, she or Billy would have noticed him."

Sykes took a sandwich. "What did you think of my little experiment in the theatre tonight?"

"I wondered what you were up to."

Mrs Sugden looked at him. "You didn't tell me about that."

"I raised my hand during the memory woman's act. That odd remark in Mrs Shackleton's letter about the deaths of two performers at the time of a new moon set me wondering. I asked Miss Sechrest the memory woman for the dates of new moons over the past eighteen months, just to see if she was in the least rattled or made a connection."

"And did she?"

"She answered coolly enough as you saw, giving her usual 'Am I correct?' knowing full well that she was correct. I wanted to see whether Miss Fellini's fears were hers alone or had pervaded the company."

I thought back to that moment. "She hesitated. She does that for effect, but that hesitation, after your question, seemed to me to be different, more genuine. Sitting in the stalls, you were closer to her. What did you think?"

"There was barely a change in Sechrest's demeanour, just the tiniest hesitation, a break in her icy concentration. She's impressive. I can imagine her being broadcast on the cat's whiskers, being quizzed by a panel of boffins."

"You should suggest it at the Woodhouse Lane studio. I'm sure the broadcasters would love to have an unusual programme."

"Would they capture the atmosphere, though? The tension, the audience holding its breath as they did when she was ready to spout her answer. She showed no change of demeanour for any other questions people asked, only that one, about the new moons."

I thought back to Sandy Sechrest's remark to Selina, about casting a horoscope. "I believe Miss Sechrest is interested in astrology. Perhaps you set her thinking along some other lines."

Mrs Sugden had listened patiently to this exchange but it was clear she had something to say. She produced her notes. "You were right about Mr Duffield at the newspaper offices. He's a man who knows his onions. Not only did he look up those two deaths, the dog trainer and the ventriloquist, but he mentioned the paper's theatre correspondent. He and I caught up with each other later in the Central Library. I didn't go into this earlier, Mrs Shackleton, because I thought you had enough on your plate, but the theatre correspondent takes a special interest in the demise of performers — not out of suspicions or to be morbid but because he likes to know what happens to old music hall performers now that the writing is on the wall."

Sykes interrupted. "What does he mean by the writing is on the wall?"

"Their days are numbered, according to the theatre man. People want a different kind of entertainment, the moving pictures, the cat's whiskers, gramophone records. He calls it the end of an era."

"And did he have any specific information about the performers we're interested in?"

"He did." Mrs Sugden passed a sheet of paper across the table. "There's the address of the ventriloquist's widow, and here's the name of the unfortunate tram driver who ran over Mr Dougan and left his three dogs without a master. It's all right Miss Fellini having feelings about deaths not being accidental but she isn't the horse's mouth, is she? The widow would be a better source of knowledge and the tram driver ought to have an idea whether Mr Dougan fell, jumped or was pushed."

Mr Sykes glanced at Mrs Sugden with admiration. "You've done well there."

"Nothing to do with me," Mrs Sugden said modestly. "It's the newspaper men to thank for what I managed to come home with. And something else."

"What?" Sykes and I asked in unison.

"Well if you'll look closely, there are more deaths in that profession than might be expected. It's the saddest of times for them. You and I might not notice if some performers slip out of view but for them it's a terrible thing not to be able to entertain the public as they once did. Some know nothing else, you see." She consulted her notes. "There have been suicides, drowning, shooting, gassing and all for what you and I might think as no reason whatsoever. One poor chap who liked to mingle with the audience after the show heard himself called a falling star. He went home and shot himself.

Another poor fellow, comic, didn't raise a chuckle, copped for a few rotten tomatoes, went off and drowned himself in the river."

"Well that's tragic." Sykes drained his cup. "But it's not pertinent."

"Pertinent enough to me." Mrs Sugden pursed her lips. "You see, here's a profession, and this is according to the theatre correspondent who writes for more than one newspaper and is in the process of planning a book . . ." she paused to let the weight of her words settle. "Here's a profession where a way of life is dying."

Sykes let out a groan. "You wouldn't have said that if you'd been in the City Varieties tonight. The audience went crackers for the whole lot of them, especially Miss Fellini."

"Well I wasn't sitting in the Varieties. I was keeping a helpful old gentleman away from his work by being very thorough in my researches. After that I was up in the library, making notes of the coroners' reports."

She handed me her notes on the coroners' verdicts. A passenger on the tram had spoken up for the driver, saying he didn't have a chance to stop. The man just tumbled onto the line. It was thought someone had tried to save him but did not stay around to help afterwards. In the case of the accident on stage, one of the stage hands was dismissed but there was not sufficient evidence of neglect to bring charges. The dismissed stage hand had complained bitterly and was said to have previously been considered an exemplary worker.

214

Mrs Sugden was rightly pleased with her efforts. "The theatre critic told me that the stage hand was given another job a few weeks later at the Newcastle Empire."

She was still clinging to her theory that the deaths were part of a wider pattern of a way of life coming to an end and leaving a trail of casualties in its wake. "Just because tonight's was a good performance — and how could it not be when Selina Fellini was on stage? — that doesn't mean anything. We all know about the energy behind death throes."

"Do we?" I asked, trying to think of an example.

"Aye, we do. A big proportion of people in that profession are dead but they won't lie down."

Sykes looked to me to change the direction of proceedings. When I did not, he said, "So do you want me to go see the unfortunate tram driver? If anyone knows whether Dougie Dougan's death was an accident, surely he will."

"Yes. Do that tomorrow, see if you can find him at his place of work. I'm going to see Selina's mother-in-law to see if her son Jarrod spent the night in his old bed."

Mrs Sugden cleared her throat. "The company moves on from the City Varieties after Saturday."

"They do," I agreed.

"So there isn't a lot of time if you don't want to be chasing Miss Fellini round every theatre in the north of England."

"I hope it won't come to that, but if it does I believe there are just two more weeks, in Huddersfield and Halifax."

"Then let me go visit the ventriloquist's widow. If we all do our bit, it will save time."

We had our work cut out for tomorrow. Before Sykes went home, and Mrs Sugden put the porridge in the pan for morning, I gave them a blow-by-blow account of the party, and the journey to Giggleswick, and all that Billy had said and done — just in case I had missed anything.

CHAPTER
TWENTY-TWO

An Unexpected Visitor

My main plan for the day was to visit Selina's mother-in-law, Mrs Compton, in the hope of finding her son Jarrod at home.

I checked my watch. It niggled that I had not yet heard from Ernest Brownlaw. Yesterday, Alex McGregor carried out his test for cyanide so very quickly. It was surprising that Ernest Brownlaw was not equally prompt in his professional analysis. Something was amiss. I tried to think of a plausible explanation. Perhaps he saw no urgency in contacting me regarding a negative outcome. Some emergency had arisen. His wife or child was sick. He had mislaid my telephone number. None of the explanations sufficed.

On the dot of nine, I telephoned his shop.

Penny Scott answered. "Brownlaws Chemist."

"Miss Scott, Mrs Shackleton here. I was in yesterday."

"Yes of course. I hope you liked the soap flakes."

"I did, very much. Now is Mr Brownlaw there?"

She hesitated. "I'll just see. He might have popped out."

It is not an enormous shop. At this time in the morning, I would have expected her to know whether he was in or out.

She came back quickly. "I'm so sorry, Mrs Shackleton, you've just missed him."

"Miss Scott, I really would like to speak with him."

"Yes of course. I'll ask him to call you the moment he returns."

"Did he leave a message for me?"

"Just a mo, I'll check."

One word was all I needed.

I heard a voice in the background. There was a noisy shuffling of papers.

"I'm sorry but I don't see any message on the pad or in Mr Brownlaw's diary."

We ended the conversation. Short of calling her a liar, or going to the shop and searching the back room, there was little I could do. I might just buy my rose-scented soap flakes elsewhere in future. But why was he avoiding me?

Mrs Sugden picked up the morning's post from the mat behind the front door.

"Ernest Brownlaw is avoiding me, Mrs Sugden."

"Oh no, not Mr Brownlaw, he has a soft spot for you."

"Soft spot or not, that's what he's doing."

I had one more telephone call to make. My parents live in Wakefield. Since my father's call at the house when I was out, I had not managed to speak to him. Reluctant to disturb him at police headquarters, I asked the operator to connect me to the home number. My mother would still be in bed, drinking tea and reading, but I could leave a message with Pamela, giving a hint that I was on a case and saying that if I could not come on Sunday, I would telephone.

The house phone rang, and rang. As I listened and waited, I pictured the scene in the hall at my parents' house, the house where I had grown up. There would be flowers on the hall table, the umbrella stand with a couple of walking sticks, kept for occasional hikes, and several brollies, including the green one with the broken spoke.

I hung up.

To break the spell of unlucky tries, I put in a call to my father at his office.

He was away from his desk.

So far, this was not my day for telephone calls.

I turned my attention to the next task: introducing myself to Mrs Compton. Selina's mother-in-law lived in Gledhow Lodge. She was listed in the directory under her late husband's initial, R. Compton. I decided against telephoning in advance. This call might best be made in the old-fashioned way, in person. I would present my card and hope that surprise and curiosity might do the trick of opening her door.

Intrigued as I was at the prospect of meeting the woman who, according to Selina, loathed and despised her, the person I really wanted to meet was her son, Jarrod. Selina had described her husband's changed nature; his Jekyll and Hyde personality may or may not mark him as a murderer. I hoped he had stayed the night with his mother, tapping away on his typewriter. I would be able to judge for myself whether he struck me as a man to rival Othello in his capacity for jealousy of his wife, her late lover, her men friends, and her astonishing success.

Unnerved by the mystery tour route I had created for myself the night before, I spread the road map on the dining room table, pinpointed Gledhow Lodge, and looked for the most direct route. It appeared to be along Grove Land in the direction of Potternewton. Usually lodge houses are easily visible from the road, so fingers crossed that I would find my way with no trouble.

Mrs Sugden hovered, as she invariably does as I am about to leave the house. "She'll be a bit of a toff, this Mrs Compton, living at such an address."

"We're in a lodge house, Mrs Sugden. Hers may be a modest place too."

Mrs Sugden shook her head. "You haven't heard then. Gledhow Lodge is the house where a chief constable lived years ago. They don't stint."

"I'll let you know."

"Do you have your calling cards?"

"I do. I have everything, including an umbrella in case it rains." Mrs Sugden is so determined to be helpful that I refrain from unkind remarks and never remind her that she delays my every journey and frequently makes me forget something.

"Would you like a bottle of water in case you get lost?"

"No thank you."

"Do you want me to come with you and read the map?" She was diverted by the sound of the doorbell, left the room and strode along the hall. The door opened.

"Hello! What are you doing here?"

That was not normally how Mrs Sugden answered the door.

At any other time, the cheerful answering voice would have gladdened my heart. "Hello, Mrs Sugden. I'm here to see my auntie Kate."

"You better go through."

Harriet was already through, almost before I had time to hide my dismay. "Harriet, what a surprise."

She deposited a carpet bag on the floor. "Aren't you glad to see me either?"

"Of course!"

"You're not. I can tell. And Mam said you'd be just as glad to see me as she was to see the back of me."

"It's just that I wasn't expecting you."

"I know, but I couldn't wait to get out and Mam couldn't wait to be rid of me. She said, 'Go and live with your auntie Kate since you're always on about her. See how she likes having you moping about the place'."

That sounded like Mary Jane, the sister I had come to know and love. I was adopted at birth and met her for the first time when she had a crisis, a few years ago.

"Of course you can stay, but why didn't you or your mother think to telephone?"

"I didn't because it was too late last night and too early this morning. Mam won't call you because she's crafty and she wouldn't want you to have the chance to say no."

She looked at the map spread on the table. "You're on a case."

"Yes, as it happens."

"Oh good! I can help you." She took a closer look at the map. "I'm good at maps. I came top in Geography."

She looked so eager, and certain of her welcome.

"What did you and your mam fall out about?"

"I'm so fed up. Everything's always the same. I'm supposed to help in the post office. I'm supposed to mind the little one. Honestly, anyone would think I was a maid of all work instead of number one and only daughter."

"But you like helping in the post office."

"And now I'm being squeezed out of that. Auntie Barbara May turned up. You know she leaves her husband every couple of years?"

"I didn't know that."

"Well she does."

"Why?"

"Just to show him, show him that she can. Only she's sharing my bed and she snores and kicks and I'm fed up of it."

"Apart from that, how is everyone?"

"Mam and Uncle Bob are better without me I should think. I like him but I won't call him Dad you know, even to keep up appearances."

"How's Austin?"

"Oh, being a boy it's different for him. He's never asked to mind the little one. The one time he did, he let the baby play with the poker so he wasn't asked again.

222

Boys can be so crafty. Is it all right if I make a cheese sandwich? I'm starving. I'll make one for you."

"I've just had breakfast, and I'm going out soon. There's some porridge left in the pan."

Her sheer energy was exhausting when I was trying to order my thoughts. It was like being stuck in sand as the tide washed in.

"How did you get here this early?"

"Caught an early train before they all got up and it was so s-l-o-w." She took off her coat. "So can I then?"

"What?"

"Be your assistant. I need to earn my keep if I'm staying here."

"You know the spare room is there for you . . ."

She grabbed me and planted a kiss on my cheek. "Thank you! I knew you'd say that."

"But I have an assistant, Mr Sykes, and there's Mrs Sugden who likes to expand her duties."

Harriet glanced about to see if Mrs Sugden was within hearing, but Mrs Sugden had tactfully made herself scarce. "There must be times when you need someone young and keen. I'll be ever so good and useful. I've been taking jujitsu lessons."

"Come through to the kitchen. Let's see how much porridge is left and you can heat some milk. Later, we'll have a chat."

She followed me through, carrying a folded newspaper which she placed on the table.

"I've thought about what to do next."

"Apart from being my assistant?" I poured a drop of milk into the pan, to make the porridge edible.

"If you're in the middle of a case, I understand why I can't join in."

"It's not just that. You're . . ."

". . . you're going to say I'm too young, which I'm really not."

I lit the gas under the pan. "If you're to have a job, you must have a proper employer, not your auntie. At present I'm at a delicate stage with a case, so you see . . ."

"Oh, I do see. I'll be here for when you need me. And I can teach you jujitsu as well. But in case you don't want me to start right away, I've picked out a job from the newspaper."

"Oh?"

"I'll stir the porridge. You look at this, Auntie." She handed me the newspaper. A job advertisement had been circled.

Wanted — Young Person to assist in General Duties. Hours by arrangement.

Apply in writing to General Manager, City Varieties Music Hall, Leeds.

"Well?" She took a dish from the cupboard.

"Absolutely not."

"Why?"

"No, no, no!"

"Why not?"

"It's not a suitable workplace for a child."

224

"I'm not a child. I'm fifteen. Mam started work at thirteen, so did all my other aunties, and Uncle Bob." She spooned porridge into her dish.

"Yes, I know you are almost grown up and you found your way here. What would you have done if there was no one in?"

"Waited, or climbed through a window."

I considered telephoning Mary Jane, but the thought of a long conversation and hearing a list of complaints against Harriet and Barbara May made me think better of it. "I'm going out soon and when I go, telephone your mother and tell her you've arrived safely."

"Yes I'll telephone. She won't care whether I've arrived safely or not."

"Of course she will."

She pulled a face. "This porridge is a bit lumpy. I make good porridge."

"So does Mrs Sugden. This has been made a long while. She gets up early."

"Mrs Sugden took typing lessons, didn't she?"

"Yes."

"I could do that."

Mrs Sugden chose that moment to return to the kitchen, glancing at the stove to see whether Harriet had made a mess of it.

"Harriet's going to stay for a while, Mrs Sugden. I've advised her against applying for a job at the City Varieties."

Mrs Sugden looked at the advertisement. "Your auntie's right. They'd have you doing nothing but tear tickets and waiting behind to put up all the seats when

225

everyone's gone. You don't want to be coming back up from the town late at night. You'd miss the last tram."

"I don't care."

"There'll be something more suitable."

Harriet added a spoonful of treacle to her porridge. "Well I want to find something soon and pay my way." She sat down to eat her porridge.

"You don't have to find work immediately. Perhaps you'd like to visit your gran in Wakefield. And you've never met my parents."

She stirred the treacly porridge. "Yes I have. My gran is your mam and my granddad who died when you were a baby was your dad."

"But you know that I was adopted, and I didn't meet your gran or my sisters until your mam came to find me."

"I know that."

"So when I say you never met my parents, I mean Mr and Mrs Hood who brought me up. They live in Wakefield, too, like your gran. Your gran will be pleased to see you."

"I don't want to go today. I've just arrived."

"Well, we'll see." As far as this case was concerned, I could see no end in sight.

By unspoken agreement, Mrs Sugden and I went into the front room, out of hearing.

"What am I going to do with her, Mrs Sugden? She wants to help. She'll be rummaging through the filing cabinet the minute I'm gone, thinking she'll come up with the solution to some great mystery that has eluded us."

"The filing cabinet is locked. I'll put the key round my neck."

"She wants a job."

"She wants money more like. I know someone who might let her earn a few bob today and tomorrow."

"Who?"

"Miss Merton. She's organising a garden party for tomorrow afternoon. It's for some of the academics and their wives, and administrative staff, and foreign students."

Miss Merton is still our neighbour, though not quite so close by. When her brother became university vice chancellor, they moved into a rather impressive residence not very far away. "How do you know Miss Merton would want Harriet's help?"

"She asked me to help and I had to say no. If I take Harriet round there she'll be snapped up. She's willing and she's handy. There's baking, jellies to make, and lemonade. I'll find her a pinafore."

I was still not entirely happy about having Harriet in the house. By now, most of the variety performers I had chatted to had asked where I live. And somebody from that company was a killer.

CHAPTER
TWENTY-THREE

Mother-in-Law to the Star

Gledhow Lodge was easily discovered. From the front, the solid two-storey house boasted five windows downstairs and five upstairs, including two large bay windows. Like my own house, it stood close to a wood. A low wall surrounded the property, as well as a privet hedge and a tree at either end of the garden, one taller than the house. I parked the car and stepped out onto the pavement. Although I had intended to think of an opening gambit, I was suddenly unsure how to begin. According to Selina, it would be an understatement to say that there was no love lost between her and her mother-in-law. What they did have in common was concern about Jarrod and, presumably, love for young Reggie.

I opened the low wooden gate, walked to the front door, rang the bell and waited, calling card in gloved hand. First impressions count. I straightened my hat.

A maid answered. Gone are the days when such a maid would wear cap and apron. This was a shy, pretty girl of about fifteen with bobbed hair and her fair share of spots. She stared first at me and then at my car.

"Hello. Will you present my compliments to Mrs Compton and ask if she will see me?"

She took the card and was about to say yes when she remembered instructions. "I'll have a look." She hesitated, unsure whether to ask me in. It was my guess that not many visitors called at Gledhow Lodge these days. She compromised, leaving the door ajar with me standing by the doorstep.

Moments later, she was back. "Mrs Compton asks, 'What is the nature of your call?'"

"I'm here regarding Billy Moffatt."

She knew the name and smiled. "I'm sure she will see you in her sitting room. Come this way please." At the sound of her own voice, the young woman straightened up, as if proud at having passed a test. She closed the door behind me and I followed her along the hall's attractively tiled floor.

She opened the second door. Mrs Compton looked younger than I imagined. She must be in her fifties but she had aged well. Her skin was smooth and when she stood to greet me, she stepped forward gracefully, moving like a dancer. "Please come in."

"Thank you for seeing me."

It was a pleasant airy room with William Morris wallpaper, a parquet floor, an Aubusson rug and a low fire burning in the grate of the marble fireplace, more for cheer than warmth I thought. There was a piano, sheet music open on the stand. I felt a pang of envy, guessing that she was probably a really good pianist. From Selina's description I had expected something of

229

a harridan but she graciously waved me to a small sofa and sat down opposite. "Will you have coffee?"

"Thank you, yes."

Why be so hospitable to a stranger, I wondered. The maid had forgotten to mention Billy. Mrs Compton must have excellent hearing to have heard me say his name. And then the answer came, from the stillness of the room. She was lonely.

Perhaps the hospitality would evaporate the instant I had given her news of Billy's death, and when she knew I was here as Selina's emissary.

Suddenly suspicions about the deaths of Douglas Dougan and Floyd Lloyd having a sinister slant seemed ludicrous in this oh so civilised room. Selina was uneasy and full of doubts. Fame, success and an overweening sense of responsibility had frayed her nerve ends. I had allowed myself to take the story of an over-anxious woman at face value, or had I? Yet it was I, not Selina, who was on tenterhooks while waiting for information about a damned cigar.

"Mrs Compton, I'm here at the request of your daughter-in-law, Selina."

There was the slightest tightening of her jaw. She waited.

"I was in Giggleswick yesterday, with Selina, to witness the eclipse, in the company of Billy Moffatt. I'm here so early in the morning because Selina did not want you to read news about Billy in the paper."

"I've already seen the paper. There is no mention of him." She reached for her newspaper. "I saw that Selina was at Giggleswick. There's an article." She turned the pages. "Here it is. 'Even stellar star Selina Fellini didn't eclipse the eclipse.' She must be disappointed that there is slightly less about her than the event itself." She said this without a hint of irony, as if simply observing a fact of life. "And Jarrod, was he invited?"

"Yes, but chose not to go."

"Who invited Selina?"

"The headmaster I believe."

"Was she shown around the school?"

"One of the older boys gave her a guided tour."

"Jarrod ought to have been there. What is the point of one parent being shown around the school?"

Suddenly the words of the headmaster's wife made sense. Jarrod's mother had enquired about sending young Reginald to Giggleswick. But why, when Selina said he was settled at Ampleforth? Perhaps Mrs Compton wanted her grandson nearer home, and away from Roman Catholics.

I pushed those thoughts of family tugs of war to the back of my mind. She was all but dismissing my attempt to tell her about Billy. I pressed on. "The edition is too early to have the news about Billy Moffatt. I'm sorry to tell you that he died yesterday morning, after collapsing in the school grounds."

She suddenly became rigidly still, staring at me as if believing I had come specially to torment her. Her mouth opened but for the longest moment no words came.

"Billy dead? How? What do you mean, collapsed? He was thirty-six years old."

"I'm sorry. It must come as a shock, and to hear the news from a stranger. I believe he and your son were close."

She stared at me. "Who are you?" She looked at the card. "I mean, I know your name, but why are you here? Couldn't Selina telephone me?"

"She asked me to act for her."

"Act for her? Are you a solicitor?"

"No. I arranged the flight to Giggleswick."

"You are some sort of tour guide, or travel agent."

That job, or being a solicitor, seemed suddenly rather attractive.

"Selina contacted me through a mutual acquaintance."

"Well I'm sorry to hear about Billy. We loved that boy once. My husband spotted Billy when he was a kid entertaining a theatre queue. He gave him his first chance. But if I were a religious woman, I might say it was God's judgement."

"Oh?"

"Selina sent you because she would have been embarrassed to tell me herself. Billy was Jarrod's best friend but recently he has been . . . well I don't believe I need say what Billy has been to Selina."

Remembering Selina's denial that she and Billy were lovers, I wondered who had gossiped to Mrs Compton and whether that same person had told tales to Jarrod. "I know nothing of that, Mrs Compton."

"I was in the business myself. I hear things, though it surprises me to know that Billy was in Selina's company at Jarrod's old school. I'd call that bad form."

This was not going well. Yes I was here to break the news, but also to find Jarrod.

"Is Jarrod here?"

"No he is not. He lives in Bridlington."

"He was in the theatre yesterday and left some songs for Selina in her dressing room. She thought he might be here."

"Perhaps he sent the songs via someone else."

Under her cool exterior, she was practically bristling with distress and rage. I could understand why. It was ridiculous that a total stranger should come and tell her that her son and daughter-in-law's friend was dead, and in the same breath enquire about her son. "I'll tell Selina that Jarrod isn't here and that I've passed on the news about Mr Moffatt. I'm sorry to have disturbed you."

She was suddenly reluctant to release me. "Stay and have coffee. Violet takes so long to make it that the least you can do is drink a cup."

Mrs Compton crossed the room to a table that held a cigarette box. She offered it to me. I shook my head.

"My daughter-in-law likes to twist people around her little finger and keep a coterie of followers, usually male. From the cut of your jib, I'd say you wouldn't fall for that." She lit her cigarette. "So Jarrod left her more songs. At least she acknowledges privately that he writes them."

"He writes wonderful songs. What he left for her read like something of a musical play." I wanted to know what plans Jarrod had for Selina, and whether these conflicted with those of her manager Trotter Brockett, putting the two men at odds.

My praise of Jarrod's songs loosened Mrs Compton's tongue. "He was always talented, even as a little boy he would write stories and put on plays with his toy animals."

"He was a performer too I believe."

"As a child, yes. His father and I weren't sorry when he decided not to follow a life on stage. He might have gone into theatre management if not for the war, and my husband Reginald's death."

"He's still young, who knows what the future holds?" I made polite conversation, hoping she might give some clue as to where Jarrod may have gone. "Was theatre management your husband's line of work?"

"It was." She frowned. "Did Selina telephone, to see if Jarrod arrived safely back in Bridlington?"

"Not that I know of, not yesterday evening anyway. She returned home rather late."

"Then she hasn't telephoned Bridlington, just as she did not contact me." She looked at her watch. "She'll still be sleeping, as she does."

Mrs Compton stood. "Excuse me."

She went into the hall, leaving the door ajar. The telephone must have been on a party line because she exchanged a few words with someone straightaway, apologising and saying she had an urgent call to make.

A moment later, she was giving the operator a telephone number. She hung up the receiver but did not come back into the room. The telephone rang. She picked it up. "Yes, please let it continue to ring." After a minute, she spoke again, giving the operator a different number. She was connected quickly and spoke quietly. I did not catch all the words, except "Mrs Compton here", and "something has come up". She asked for Jarrod.

Several minutes passed.

"Yes I'm still here." She listened for a long time. "Thank you for telling me. Yes I'll look into that." She paused again. "Of course. Will you please ring me when my son returns?" During the few steps from the hall into the room, her walk had lost its spring.

"That was the caretaker's wife at Jarrod's block of flats. Apparently he went off on his motorcycle two days ago. He intended to view the eclipse."

"Did they know from where?"

She shook her head. "Reggie and his classmates were being taken somewhere, perhaps Richmond. There are so many places across the line of totality that I just don't know where Jarrod would have gone." She sat down. "Mrs Shackleton, unless your imagination is non-existent, don't let any son of yours ride a motorcycle. Not if you want to keep your sanity."

"What type of motorcycle does Jarrod have?"

"A Scott Flying Squirrel that he goes mad on. It terrifies me."

"They're very solid and he'll know all the roads."

"So I tell myself." She lit another cigarette. "I can't get over Billy Moffatt's death. Did the doctor give an explanation?"

"Not yet. Mr Brockett is in touch with the hospital."

"What is Trotter going to do?"

So she was on first name terms with Mr Brockett. "I don't know. He was devastated by the news. He did manage to find a replacement for yesterday evening's performance."

"Who?"

"Jimmy Diamond."

"Oh yes, he'll pass muster, but he doesn't have the range or the intelligence."

She clearly knew everyone and so I tested the water regarding Selina's suspicions.

"They have been a very unlucky company over the past year, with the loss of the animal novelty act gentleman and the ventriloquist. I read about their deaths in the papers."

I watched her. Might she also believe, as Selina did, that there was something suspicious about those deaths?

Her face was impassive. She would be good at poker. "Yes. I knew them both and was sad to hear. But that was months ago." Her face changed. She gave me a shrewd, assessing look. "Were you there when Billy collapsed?"

"No. He wandered off on his own, probably just as the eclipse ended. He was found unconscious by the chapel."

"I don't suppose Selina stayed with Billy?"

"No. The pilot couldn't wait so I stayed."

She sniffed as if this was exactly what she would have expected from her daughter-in-law. "Did Billy come round, say anything?"

"No."

She seemed relieved to hear that. What might Billy have said, I wondered. Perhaps she suspected Billy may have pointed a finger of blame at Jarrod.

"Jarrod will be upset. They were such good friends, so close. And I don't believe he knew about Selina and Billy. Any other man would have guessed, been angry, but my son isn't like that."

She went to the piano, picked up a framed photograph and brought it across to me. "Here's Jarrod, in uniform."

He was young, handsome, standing proud. "What a lovely man."

"Little more than a boy when he volunteered, but not too young to marry." She left off the word "unfortunately", but it was in her tone. "Anyone else would have gone on living with him, loving him, but not her. She won't give up on her sparkling career." She took back the photograph. "And does my daughter-in-law believe that Jarrod has murdered Billy, his comrade and old pal?"

The truthful answer would be that I did not know, or that I believed she held suspicions she dare not speak. "I'm sure she believes no such thing. But what makes you think Billy was murdered?"

"I don't think that, but it's what Selina might allow into her head. She plays comedy to perfection but she would relish the role of tragic queen."

You're jealous of her, I thought. Mrs Compton had given up her own career and now played the piano to the four walls of this room.

"Mrs Compton, I really am here because Selina is concerned about Jarrod. She thought he may have come to see you, and to type up his play."

"Ah, that's it. She's after a copy of his script. Everything must be on her terms. She likes to be in control. Jarrod doesn't need her money so she cooks up a benefit tour so that money for the Bridlington sanatorium doesn't seem to come directly from her."

"I understood that the tour was more broadly conceived, to support performers who are down on their luck."

"That too. If my daughter-in-law were honoured with a damehood, she would take the title Lady Bountiful. Being a wife and mother is far too commonplace for her."

At that moment, the young maid returned, pushing open the door with her foot and carrying her tray to the low coffee table that sat between us.

"Thank you, Violet." Mrs Compton poured. She mustered a great deal of self-control simply to keep the coffee pot steady. She was about to hand me a cup but as she reached for the saucer her hand trembled. That smallest of actions was excruciating to watch. In spite of her calm exterior, news that her son had come back to Leeds and not visited her was upsetting.

"Perhaps you think I'm being harsh towards Selina, and that when talent and loyalty to a husband are weighed on the scales, talent must tip the balance."

"I have no view, Mrs Compton, except that Selina's talent is undeniable."

"And so was mine. I gave up my career when I married and had children." She said that without a trace of regret and I thought she must have been happy with her husband and family. "I didn't want my children to go into show business though perhaps it was inevitable. Jarrod was so young, but such musical ability. From being a tiny boy, he wanted to fly. He terrified me when he was small, trying to cartwheel down the stairs."

I wished I could tell her that Selina dreamed of him doing just that. There was so much more in common between Mrs Compton and her daughter-in-law than either woman acknowledged.

"Will he come here, do you think?"

A note of bitterness entered her voice. "To use his father's old Remington typing machine? Perhaps."

"I'm sorry to press you, but have you any notion of where he may have spent the night?"

For some reason those were the words that touched her emotions. She sniffed and reached for a lace hanky. "Who knows where he may have spent last night? He might have hidden until the theatre closed and slept there. During the last few months, Jarrod hasn't been himself."

"Selina said as much."

"He finds it hard to be around people. He becomes angry and aggressive. He won't see the doctor and he's stopped going for his treatments at the sanatorium." She blinked away tears. "Last time he turned up here, a month ago, he wouldn't sleep in the house. He stayed overnight in the shed, in an army issue sleeping bag, with the wheelbarrow propped behind the door. There is not enough room in the shed for him to have stretched out." She interlocked her fingers and squeezed her hands. "There's something the matter with him. It wouldn't be safe for you to go on looking for him alone. Selina shouldn't have asked you."

Perhaps that was why Jarrod had stayed in the garden on the night of the party. He did not trust himself to be with people in case his strange and aggressive mood overcame him.

In my experience, brute strength rarely subdued a person who was distressed. "During the war, I nursed men who were badly injured. Mostly they were gentle, and kind, and embarrassingly grateful, but others were difficult. I wouldn't be afraid to come face to face with Jarrod."

"He no longer has any care or thought for his own comfort. He might have slept under a bridge or in a doorway."

"I'm so sorry to hear that, when he could be here with you."

"He makes trouble, sees offence where there is none. When the gardener arrives, he asks if Jarrod is here. He will only start work if I say no, he is not here. I go through that humiliating interrogation every time."

"Perhaps you and I might find him together, Mrs Compton."

She smiled. "You would take that risk?"

"I would. I like the sound of Jarrod. One of his songs, I glanced at it so briefly but it was touching. About a man who feels safe living underground."

"Did Selina enquire whether anyone had seen him come and go from the theatre?"

"She did. The front of house staff hadn't seen him and according to the doorkeeper, he didn't come in by the stage door."

"He won't come and go through foyers, or stage doors in a world where he no longer belongs."

"What then?"

"I'm surprised Selina doesn't know. There are passages between the theatres, and tunnels under the city. One passage connects with the Empire Palace. He knows that well enough and could have found his way underground to the Varieties. Perhaps that's where he slept last night, or in some dressing room after the theatres emptied."

It made me shudder to think of the poor man alone, finding some spot to lay his head.

Mrs Compton warmed to her idea that Jarrod would be somewhere near the theatre. "His father owned several theatres. I sold them long since, to give my children a start. They have all gravitated towards entertainment. Rodney, my youngest, is in California in the moving picture business. Eliza followed in my footsteps and danced in Paris. She married well, a charming Frenchman. They visit me. That's why I keep on this big house. I had hoped that Selina and Jarrod might come here with little Reggie. We're out of the way here. Jarrod could walk in the woods unnoticed, unregarded."

We sat in silence for a moment. It was difficult to imagine Selina settling to a life in this solid house.

"You must be proud to have produced such talented children."

She smiled. "Yes, even though their talent takes them away from me."

"It's good that Jarrod writes songs."

"It would be better if the singer loved him enough to care."

"I believe she does, and worries, as you do."

"Perhaps for a different reason."

"What reason would that be?"

"Selina is from a big Italian family. They have no great place in the world but once she had some success, they expected her to sing at La Scala, to tour the opera houses of the world. Instead she married into my family and came into show business at the seedy end as they would see it. Perhaps they might see it as an advantage to be rid of my son. Look to them if Selina is uneasy. I heard they brought over some musical director from Venice, hoping she might be persuaded to go there. As far as they are concerned, she married the wrong man. Italian Catholics don't subscribe to divorce. I wouldn't put anything past them. They might do for Jarrod what the war didn't, just so that she would feel free to start a new life."

"Are you telling me that you believe Jarrod's life is in danger?"

"There was one evening some months ago when he arrived here bruised and battered and not able to say what happened. And yes, he is in danger. I feel it in my bones. You're not a mother, are you?"

"No."

242

"If ever you become a mother you'll understand." She picked up the photograph she had showed me and walked back to the piano. Looking out of the window, she saw my car. "You drive?"

"Yes."

"It's something I always promised myself I might do. If I had a car, I'd set off now to look for Jarrod."

"Where would you look?"

She shook her head. "It's best that you don't know."

"I believe you would look below ground, along the passages that you talked about."

"Did you mean what you said, that you would help me look for him?"

"I did and I do. Shall we go now?"

She ran her tongue across her lips. "I'm afraid."

"Afraid of what you will find, or of going underground?"

"Both."

I have long been curious about the world below the city. Everyone has heard stories of tunnels and passageways there. They are said to have been used by the monks at Kirkstall Abbey. Generations of builders have layered up their constructions and the story goes that in places old streets intersect beneath our feet. There are reports of a complete hotel building with gates intact left over from I don't know when. How strange it would be if Jarrod Compton was living in a hotel inhabited by ghosts.

Mrs Compton climbed into the car. She wore stout shoes and a hand-knitted coat that looked warm enough to withstand the cold of underground tunnels. "Here," she handed me a shawl. "You might need an extra layer."

Her shopping bag contained a lethal weapon-size flashlight.

"Briggate. That's where we'll find our way into the underground passage." Mrs Compton pulled on motoring gloves. "Are we mad to do this?"

"Probably."

CHAPTER
TWENTY-FOUR

Uneasy Feelings

Jim Sykes wouldn't deny that he had enjoyed the show at the Varieties last night, but he wouldn't go out of his way to see another, not unless Rosie insisted. His own preference was for a pint and the odd game of dominoes. Listening to the tales of old fellers in the Chemic on a Friday night suited him to a T. A few years ago, he found it convenient to pretend he liked fishing. It surprised him to discover that he really did like it, the silence of it and the contemplation, the clearing of his mind as he waited for a bite. Sykes could be very patient.

Something about this job for Miss Selina Fellini gave him the willies. True, the pay was to be through the roof but there was something not right. He had a feeling they would come a cropper on this one. The whole notion was based on the imaginings of a highly strung performer. Not that Selina Fellini, The Silver Songbird, wasn't impressive. She was, when on stage. But all this business about new moons and accidental deaths not being accidental, that was the product of a fevered imagination. When their investigations uncovered nothing, the woman might well renege on her promised fee of fabulous proportions. People had put a stop on cheques before today.

Sykes was on the train to York, the name and address of the tram driver tucked in his top pocket. He didn't expect the man to be at home. If not, Sykes would make his way to the tram depot and make enquiries there. Surprise. That was the weapon of choice for Jim Sykes. So many months after a death, the driver would not expect to be asked again about the fatal incident.

Sykes had a liking for York. He had just about mastered the intricacies of the higgledy-piggledy streets, having come here several times in connection with the bread and butter work of fraud investigations, visiting insurance offices on Parliament Street and Goodramgate. It was an odd twisty town, with more churches than pubs and the extravagance of two rivers, the Ouse and the Foss. Little wonder the Romans and the Vikings had taken a fancy to the place. He went the way he knew best, leaving the station and walking by the river to the Ouse Bridge. From there he made his way along Fossgate. There might be a better way but if there was he would discover it on the way back. For now he followed the road, looking out for Barbican Road that would lead him into Cemetery Road.

The tram driver's house was across the road from the cemetery. The step and windowsill were scoured and the street neat and clean but the house needed a new door. This one was rotting away from the bottom. The mark of yet another landlord who didn't care. He knocked. A dog barked. From the corner of his eye,

Sykes watched the net curtain to see if it would be twitched. The dog barked again.

The curtain twitched. Sykes pretended not to notice the unshaven face and tousled hair of the man who looked from the window. The curtain dropped back in place.

Sykes hoped he did not look like a debt collector.

The door opened. What line should he take? That would depend on the man, Mr Alfred Packer. They looked at each other across the threshold. Something about the man sparked a kind of pity in Sykes. He had the look of a soldier just back from battle, puzzled, shocked and awestruck. He had also just woken and rubbed sleep from his eyes.

"I'm sorry to disturb you. Mr Alfred Packer?"

"Aye, that's me. Who's asking?"

"My name's Sykes. I've come across from Leeds." For once he decided that the truth would best serve. "And I'm sorry to disturb you." The term picture of misery could well be applied to Alfred Packer. Must be turning soft, Sykes told himself. I've half a mind to leave the poor fellow to his devices, and his misery.

"What is it you want?"

"Can I come in?"

The man hesitated. "It's not a good time, and there's the dog. I've to walk the dog now."

He hadn't asked what Sykes wanted. It was as if he knew and dreaded opening up an old wound.

"You're guessing correctly that it's about the accident. I'm here on behalf of someone who knew the deceased and simply wants to offer you sympathy for something that couldn't be helped, and to know whether you might answer a question."

The man did not speak. For the longest time, they looked at each other. Finally he said, "You've caught me in a mess, but I suppose you better come in. The wife and girls are at work." He opened the door.

Sykes stepped into a neat clean room where a collie dog wagged its tail and offered to lick his ankles. Sykes patted the dog.

The Packers were not a family on their uppers. There was a miniature grandmother clock on the mantelpiece, a mirror and pot dogs. A glass-fronted china cabinet stood by the far wall.

Mr Packer rubbed his chin. "I was just about to shave."

Sykes's day stretched ahead. With Mrs Sugden jumping in and wanting to do this and that for the investigation, Sykes wasn't sure what else he would do next. It was too early to chase after Sandy Sechrest. "Look, I've called unannounced and I'll be grateful for a chat but how about I leave you to have your shave? I see there's a pub by the cemetery."

"Aye, the Tavern."

"Let's meet at the Tavern in half an hour and I'll buy you a pint." Half an hour was long enough for a splash and a shave. It wouldn't do to give Alf Packer too much thinking time.

"What is it you want to know, Mr Sykes?"

"Douglas Dougan had a friend, and she's a big star though I won't name names. All she knows about his death was from the papers. She understands no blame lies with you, but there was something she wanted to know. If she could have answers, then she would sleep at night."

A sound something between a laugh and a cry came from Alfred Packer. "Then good for her, because I don't sleep, not any more."

Sykes did something unprecedented for him. He reached out, placed his hand on the man's shoulder. "I'll be in the Tavern. Spare me half an hour if you can."

Their eyes met. He would come, Sykes knew it. Meanwhile, there would be time for him to have a pint and a scotch egg.

Alfred Packer walked him to the door. "I'm not going in the Tavern. I'd be ashamed to be seen in there at this time of day, like a man with no work to go to. I'll see you by the cemetery gates."

"There he lies." Sykes stood beside the forlorn Alfred Packer, tram driver, looking down at a simple gravestone engraved with Douglas Dougan's name and the dates of his birth and death. Alfred let out a sigh. "I'm glad they didn't put that he was run down by a tram, by my tram, or what was my tram."

Sykes took off his hat. "Terribly sad, for him and for you."

Someone had planted flowers. Sykes recognised only geraniums and poppies but there were little blue flowers and white ones too. He wondered if this represented the red, white and blue of the union flag. "Who planted the flowers, Mr Packer?"

"My wife and daughters. They thought it might make me feel better, but it doesn't. I can't get it out of my mind. The company was good. They put me on a clerical job because I couldn't drive the tram no more."

"How did the accident happen?"

"That's what I was asked at the inquest. I said he must have just stepped out with no warning. My superintendent spoke up for me, having never had an accident. My conductor spoke up for me, but he didn't see it. One of the passengers spoke up, that the line was clear and then it wasn't."

"And afterwards, you've had time to think about it, what do you say now?"

"I couldn't say. I couldn't speak afterwards. They took me to hospital and kept me in overnight. Shock. They said shock. Everything went from my mind. I was a blank, and that's what was accepted, that he stepped out. But now I don't know. Should I have seen him? I see him in my dream."

Sykes took out cigarettes. They made their way to a bench and sat down, the dog sitting beside his master. Alfred put a hand on the dog's head. "And Dougie Doig, Mr Dougan, he had dogs himself. Three performing dogs he had. I don't know what happened to them, the poor creatures. We'd seen his show. They were such clever animals, jumping through hoops, performing somersaults, playing dead."

Sykes was glad to be able to offer a crumb of comfort. "The dogs have gone to a good home. One of his theatrical friends saw to that."

"I'm glad. But they won't get over it. They'll go on pining. Did you hear that at the instant of his death, all three dogs howled so loud they could be heard in the auditorium?"

"No, I hadn't heard that."

"I wish I could see them, but of course you can't explain to dumb animals. They only go by your tone of voice. This one, he likes to hear me say, 'Oh, you poor old feller, what a hard life'. He loves me to say that."

The dog thumped its tail in appreciation of the sentiments.

"Mr Packer . . ."

"Alf, call me Alf."

"Alf, you said you dream about that incident. What is it that you dream?"

He took a drag on his cigarette. "I dream that I see someone coming up close to him, and in the dream I'm sure they are going to pull him back. I can't brake in time, you see. But they don't pull him back, they push him. Push him in front of the tramcar."

"Have you told anyone about this dream?"

"I went back to the police. But it's all done and dusted and the coroner's report filed away. It's only a dream, that's what they said."

"Do you see this person, what they look like?"

"Just a figure, a figure, dressed in black. I don't see a face."

"Did you tell anyone else?"

"The works doctor. He said I needed a rest, that being the anniversary it'd all come flooding back. He give me a week off. That's why you find me at home."

"And is it to do with the anniversary that you feel so bad?"

"No. It's the sound of the trams. It's everything. It's what's in my head."

"And no witnesses came forward?"

"Not a single one. There was a call for them in the paper. It was a shocking night, see, cloud, rain. You wouldn't credit it in June, would you? People heard, they stopped. Afterwards some came round to see — gawpers. Then they all melted away. No one came forward as a witness." He scratched his neck under the muffler. "We was at the funeral, me and the wife and the superintendent from the depot, and my conductor — as was. There were theatricals, a lot of theatricals paying their respects. I was dreading meeting his family and being held to account, but no family came. Did he have anyone, do you know?"

"I don't believe he did."

Sykes had gambled his answer would make Alf feel better. Wrong.

"Poor man. That's even worse. No one to mourn him."

Sykes rarely told lies. He preferred silence. He was there to listen, not to talk. But in a case shadowed by phases of moon, dreams, a cigar and, if Mrs Sugden was to be believed, performers who jumped in the river if someone didn't laugh at a joke, perhaps a kind lie to a distressed man would not go amiss.

"There's something else, Alf. This wasn't public knowledge, you understand, but Mr Dougan did not have long to live. He had been diagnosed with a fatal illness. So if he did wander onto the tracks, then perhaps it was because of his distracted state of mind and a mercy that he died so quickly."

"Is that true? You're not just saying it?"

Sykes felt slightly annoyed. He was not a practised liar but thought he could do it as well as the next man. "If it is any consolation to you, in the eyes of God and man this accident could be seen as a blessed release from far worse."

The slightest of changes in Alf's demeanour assured Sykes that his kind lie had hit home. The two men walked through the graveyard, saying little. The dog trotted sedately behind, as if understanding the seriousness of this visit.

Sykes had a feeling that Alf might begin to recover in the not too far off future, and when he did there might be something else that he would remember. As they returned to the cemetery gates, Sykes handed his business card to Alf. "If any more details of that dream come to you, will you let me know? The mind can play strange tricks."

Alf became suddenly animated. "That's what I think. And see, it doesn't help me to be in that tram depot day after day." They crossed the street. "Superintendent put me in the office, working out timetables based on when each route is busiest."

"How does that work?"

"From ticketing information."

"Sounds like a complicated job."

"It suits me. Only . . ."

"Only what?"

"I overheard one of the lads. He said, 'All you've got to do in this place is kill a pedestrian and they promote you'."

"That's a terrible thing to say."

"They laughed. Some of them laughed."

"Fellers at work laugh at anything. I ought to know. I was a copper. Pay them no heed."

"Easier said than done."

"Tell you what, if you're not rushing back inside, will you walk me to the station? Once I'm on the wrong side of the city walls I'm liable to walk in circles."

Another lie, but Alf swallowed it. The two men and the dog walked back along Cemetery Road. Sykes began to think there was something in this theory about the death not being an accident. A man mindful enough to avoid treading on graves, who avoided cracks in the pavement, and so attentive as to be given the responsibility of timetabling the corporation's trams, was too careful not to have seen a strolling pedestrian.

The man needed a different job and a change of scene.

Once within the city walls, Sykes took a pause. "Will you do a bit of a detour with me, Alf? There's someone I'd like you to meet."

"Oh aye, who's that then?"

"A man who offered me a job in his insurance office yesterday, only I couldn't take it."

The detour took them towards Goodramgate. They strolled in companionable silence. When they were almost at the offices of the Jorvik Insurance Company,

Sykes asked, "Tell me, Alf, how tall was Douglas Dougan?"

"I'd say about five feet ten."

"And in your dream, the figure in black, can you say anything about him or her?"

Alf slowed his step. "Funny you should say him or her."

"Why?"

"Because in the dream the creature in black is not as tall, maybe five feet five. The first time I had the dream, I woke with an odd thought."

"And what was that thought?"

"No wonder that person couldn't save him. Douglas Dougan was a big fellow and the smaller creature, the demon, couldn't pull him out of the way."

"The demon?"

"Well, only because it's my own demon, isn't it? The wife knows a bit about dreams. She and our lasses work at Rowntree's Chocolates. They're all for interpreting dreams over the conveyor belt."

They walked in silence, Sykes still thinking of the demon in Alf's dream. A little demon might not be able to save a man from tripping under a tram, but that demon would be capable of giving a person a good shove.

They arrived at the branch office of the Jorvik Insurance Company.

"Here we are, Alf. You wait here two minutes while I pop inside. If the manager still needs a clerk, I'll mind the dog while you go in and have a word."

CHAPTER
TWENTY-FIVE

The Dark Depths

Before I had driven a mile from Gledhow Lodge towards the town centre, Mrs Compton's misgivings about our mission to go below the city streets grew.

"I don't like rats, and there'll be rats."

She was right. There are stories of an army of rats, led by a rat general, taking control of the upper streets at night. This rodent platoon has been seen leaving the market at two o'clock in the morning and marching twenty abreast and fifty or a hundred deep along Briggate, heading in an easterly direction towards the graveyard of St John's Church. I had no more desire to enter underground tunnels, passageways and hidden places during daylight hours than to meet General Rat and his platoon by night.

I spoke confidently. "Rats will be more afraid of us than we are of them."

"Do you think so?"

We were on Roundhay Road. I pulled in. "Would you rather we find someone else to do this? We could report your fears to the police. I'm sure they'd instigate a search."

"That would knock Jarrod's confidence entirely. The last thing he would want would be to have the police pick him up." She interlocked her gloved fingers and wiggled her thumbs. "We can do this."

"Good." I set off again.

I needed to find Jarrod and speak to him. Might I be able to judge whether he was a man capable of murdering Billy Moffatt, his best friend and best man who, according to Mrs Compton's information, became his wife's lover? Jealousy and revenge would be a powerful motive. Jarrod seemed able to come and go at will, thanks to his motorcycle and knowledge of both the theatre and his old school. He was clever. He had spoken to Billy during the party. As an old boy of Giggleswick School, creating a poison would not present a difficulty.

Roundhay Road was quiet, apart from the tram and a delivery boy on a bicycle. On the pavement, three women, baskets in hand, stood talking but turned to look as the car passed. Such stares always made me feel a little bit like royalty. I resisted the urge to give a gracious wave. My passenger sat very alert as we drove towards town. She looked straight ahead, absorbed in her own thoughts, perhaps preparing to come face to face with her errant former soldier son.

Now that I had quelled Mrs Compton's misgivings, I felt a slight concern. Selina's cheque for two hundred pounds lay on my dining room table. If I was wrong about the wisdom of this excursion, perhaps I might never cash it. Turning to Mrs Compton, I gave her a reassuring smile, while considering how best to go about this adventure.

Aware of my look, Mrs Compton glanced back. "When he was little, I could kiss him better."

Jarrod Compton had been damaged in combat. For that reason alone, I felt duty bound to help his mother search for him. Yet Mrs Compton was a smart, intelligent woman who might not want me to find Jarrod for Selina. Perhaps she, too, suspected him of murder. If so, the person who ended up in the deep dark passages under the city might be me.

If we did find a way to descend into this abandoned other world, which one of us should lead the way? If I led the way, that would give her courage. But if I did lead the way and bumped into Jarrod, he might overreact.

We neared the town centre. At the petrol station at the bottom of Eastgate, I bought fuel. Mrs Compton took out her purse and offered to pay for the petrol. I thanked her but refused.

I thought it a good thing that the petrol attendant saw us together and would remember my car. If we disappeared into the netherworld, he would be a witness.

I turned left into Briggate. Swan Street, home of the City Varieties Music Hall, was on my right. "Keep going," she said. "I know the way to the tunnel through the Empire Palace."

I stopped the car outside the splendid Empire Palace Theatre with its twin globes and statue aloft. As I looked about the busy thoroughfare, and saw so many people going about their business, taking not a jot of notice of anyone else, it struck me as absurd that Jarrod would go below ground to avoid being stared at. People were used to men who trembled, were missing a limb, had faces burned and scarred. What could be so terrible about his injuries that he could not get over them, and that he wanted to hide?

Mrs Compton climbed out of the car. She looked longingly at the Empire Palace Theatre. "I danced here. It was one of our troupe's first engagements back in '89. I was just eighteen."

"That must have been grand."

"It was. If Selina had any class about her, this is where she'd be playing now. You can't beat a Frank Matcham theatre. He knew what he was doing. He had vision, not like architects these days. Have you seen the monstrosity of a house Selina had thrown up in Roundhay?"

"I have, and I think it's marvellous."

She gave a scoffing snort. "No accounting for tastes. Shall we go in and make a start?"

"You said that you know an entrance. Where is it?"

"We find our way into the Empire and down into the basement. That's where we'll find the tunnel that runs to the Varieties, if it hasn't been blocked up."

"Are you really sure that's the way Jarrod would have gone?"

"Jarrod is well known by everyone at the Verts."

The Verts! I smiled. In spite of her expressed preference for the Empire Palace, she had given the City Varieties Music Hall its affectionate nickname.

She looked along the road in the direction of the Music Hall. "If it's true that no one saw him arrive or leave, this is all I can think of. And from the state of mind he has been in these past few months, it would fit. He would be determined to deliver his songs to Selina, and fearful of getting into some scrape along the way."

We were blocking the pavement. A young chap carrying a document case stepped round us.

"Mrs Compton, I want to do just a little more preparation. We have your torch, and that's all." I glanced across the road at the Kardomah Café. "Come on. We're going to have a coffee and make a plan, see what else we might need."

She was about to answer. Now that she had mustered her courage, she wanted to jump straight in. Without waiting for a reply, I crossed. Reluctantly, she followed.

We stepped through the doors of the Kardomah and breathed in the aroma of coffee. An assistant was grinding beans for a waiting customer. A waitress led us to a small round table at the back. Not knowing how long we might be below ground, I ordered a sandwich and so did she. We would share a pot of coffee.

"How did you come to know about the way into the tunnels from the Empire Palace?" I asked.

Mrs Compton took off her gloves and slipped them into her bag. "You'll have heard of Sir Oswald Stoll?"

"The theatre man?"

"That hardly describes him. He is the most gifted and remarkable man in the history of music halls and theatre. The Empire Palace is one of his, part of the Moss and Stoll empire."

"Yes, I've read about them."

"During and after the war, Oswald Stoll gave a huge amount to charity. And you wouldn't know that either because he was not a man to let his good deeds be known, unlike some I could mention. It was he who put up the money for the rehabilitation centre in Bridlington."

"How do you know him?"

"My husband had a small chain of theatres. After Reginald died, Sir Oswald bought the theatres from me. Most have gone now. Two burned down. Two became picture houses. One stands empty. At the time, none of us knew what was coming. I was glad not to have the responsibility. Moss and Stoll were expanding. It was all done through solicitors but it's a measure of the man that he came up to see us. Jarrod was ten. Sir Oswald gave us a tour of the Empire, right from the gods to the cellars, to see the tunnels. Afterwards we saw a show. He and Vesta Tilley took us to supper. Back in the eighties or nineties Oswald wrote songs for Vesta. He was heartbroken when she married Walter de Frece. Of course then Walter wrote songs for her. Jarrod never forgot it. He was always enchanted with the idea that Vesta Tilley's songs were written specially for her by her husband."

The waitress, an elderly woman with swollen legs, placed our order on the table. I waited until she walked away.

"Tell me something, Mrs Compton."

"What?"

"You've never actually been down there, have you, below the theatre, into those tunnels?"

"Well no, but Sir Oswald took Jarrod and Jarrod described them to me."

"How well did he describe them?"

"Why, that it was dark and that he was scared when the lantern flickered. The floor was bumpy in places. He saw a staircase that led nowhere, and corridors and bare brick arches."

"What else did he say?"

"That it was silent, except at one point they heard a kind of whooshing and Sir Oswald said it would have been the sewer but that it was far off. He'd have looked at the plans, you see, and the foundations. He and Mr Moss were very careful in their purchases."

"Did Jarrod say that it led to the City Varieties?"

"Yes."

"You're not sure."

"I am quite sure. He also said someone had been sleeping down there. He saw a blanket and a tin mug. Someone had tapped a nail in the wall and a pair of boots hung there by the laces."

"Your son went down there once, when he was ten years old." Now it was my turn to have second thoughts but I did not let that show. "How many years ago is that?"

"Twenty-three. But I know he has been down there since, with his friends before the war for a dare."

Mrs Compton and Selina had much in common. Both went on hunches and instinct. I respected that because often those sorts of feelings are exactly right and based on a mass of knowledge and years of noticing tiny incidents and noting casual remarks. "Tell me what little things make you know that he's down there."

"Jarrod used to talk about it being a good place for someone to live if they had nowhere else to go."

"That's the kind of thing a boy might say."

"When he came back from the war, he wanted to be where no one could see him and where he only came out at night. He talked about it then, living underground. Between us Selina and I persuaded him to go to the sanatorium in Bridlington." She closed her eyes. "He is below our feet now. I can feel it, instinctively. I have to find my son and bring him into the light of day."

"You're right, Mrs Compton. We must look but we need to be well prepared." I drank down my coffee. "Give me twenty minutes."

"To do what?"

"I'll tell you when I come back."

"Let me come with you." She sipped her coffee.

"Have you ever been a Girl Guide, Mrs Compton?"

"Heavens, no! That was after my time and I would have been too busy dancing for that kind of malarkey."

"Well, I was a Girl Guide, briefly. I know the value of being prepared. Will you have another cup of coffee? As well as pacing out, I'm going to the market. I'll be back soon."

She picked up the pot and poured. "Why are you going to the market?"

"Explorers need to be properly equipped."

Four balls of string, a compass, two bottles of ginger beer, two bars of chocolate and an extra torch in the smallest haversack I could find, that was what I bought from the market stalls. The haversack was much-used and came with a slightly greasy smell and stains. Someone wearing hair oil had used it as a pillow.

I went back into the Kardomah. Mrs Compton looked up, so eager to be off that she stood straightaway. "You were a long time. I thought you'd changed your mind."

"I've taken a compass reading. We'll be walking north and west and it's about 150 yards."

She allowed a look of grudging admiration. "How do you know it's 150 yards?"

"I paced the distance. It's not far but we don't know whether it will be safe down there or whether there'll be twists and turns. We must stay together. If I say we leave, we leave."

"Well, I wouldn't want to stay down there on my own. I don't have a good sense of direction."

We left the coffee house, and waited for a break in the traffic.

Once across the road, Mrs Compton led us along King Edward Street. From there we turned right, passing the stage door, and arriving at a pair of enormous double doors.

"This is where scenery is brought in," Mrs Compton explained.

The big doors were shut and locked but the wicket door opened at a push. I followed Mrs Compton into an enormous, high-ceilinged space so silent that the thud of the door closing behind me was startling. There was no one in sight.

She looked about. "We've come on the right day. If there was a changeover of shows it would be all hands on deck making room and shifting scenery."

"Lead on, Mrs Compton."

Lead on she did, to a door at the far end of the cavernous cathedral, passing backdrops, scenery and props.

"Let me." I held the door open for her. Fortunately, modernity had put in an appearance and there was an electric light switch at the top of the stairs. She switched it on and banished the darkness.

There was a smell of hops as we walked down the stairs. At the bottom of the stairs, she turned right. We passed through a corridor into a cellar room where beer barrels connected to pipes. I had not yet begun counting my footsteps. "How do you know where to go?"

"I went with Sir Oswald and Jarrod to the entrance-way. It's not something one forgets. Also, I remembered passing the beer barrels, and the smell."

Already, I was losing my bearings. Above ground, I had counted my footsteps from the front entrance to the theatre. Below ground, where should I begin? Mrs Compton went to another door on our right. "I think this is it." There was a key in the lock. She turned it.

"Bring the key with us." I did not want some efficient person to lock the door after we had gone through it.

She slid the key in her coat pocket. When she opened the door, there was no electric light switch. Setting down her shopping bag at the top of the stairs, Mrs Compton produced her torch. I took out my newly bought flashlight from the haversack, switched it on and led the way down the stairs. Behind me, Mrs Compton's heels tapped on the steps which were old and worn. I sensed that she moved cautiously, one hand on the wall, sticking so close to me that if she slipped we would both tumble down.

"Wait! I need my shopping bag. I'd just forgotten, we're not coming back this way. We'll be coming out in the Verts."

I continued down the steps and then waited while she went back for the shopping bag. To have left it there would have been a marker, in case anyone missed the key, saw the bag and looked for its owner in the deep dark depths.

At the bottom of the stairs, I took out the compass and set it. "We should be walking north and west."

There was a touch of admiration in her voice. "That's very clever. We could easily lose our bearings. I'm glad you were a Girl Guide."

"Hold the compass while I do something with this string." I took out the first ball.

"What's that for?"

"I would have left a trail of breadcrumbs but something might eat them."

Shining the flashlight about the walls, ceiling and floor was not a good idea. The space seemed cavernous and black as the deepest pit. The floor was not just uneven but bumpy and strewn with odd bits of masonry that had crumbled away from the walls and roof.

266

A half brick should do the trick to hold the string firm. I would just have to be sure not to tug at it in panic somewhere along the line or we would be forever lost. Mrs Compton shone a light while I fastened an end of the string around the half brick and added a couple of pieces of rubble.

When I had finished, we set off walking. I switched off my flashlight and led the way, counting my footsteps, not my best ever idea. I would be almost certain to lose count and we would surely walk more slowly through this gloom than above ground.

Mrs Compton also switched on her flashlight.

"You should save your beam, Mrs Compton, so that we have your flashlight in reserve." Something about this place made me speak quietly, though no one could hear.

She whispered, "It's so horrible to have darkness behind me."

"Do you want to walk ahead of me?"

"No!"

After what seemed an age, I switched on to check my watch. We had been walking only three minutes in a northerly direction.

When I spoke my voice sounded strange and hollow. "That story about performers using this tunnel as a shortcut to the Varieties, I don't believe it. No one would willingly come down here."

"Perhaps they come in at a different entry point."

I stopped so suddenly that she bumped into me. "There's a turn to the left." I moved the beam around the walls, revealing an arch, neatly bricked.

"Wait!" My first ball of string had run out. I took a second ball and knotted the ends.

"How many did you buy?"

"Four."

"It won't be enough."

"I know."

We continued a few more steps. I shone the torch towards an alcove. "Shine another light, Mrs Compton." There was something on the floor, like a pile of rags. I bent for a closer look. It was a sleeping bag.

"He was here!" She reached for the sleeping bag. "It stinks! He wouldn't have slept in this. This isn't my Jarrod's."

"Then whose is it?"

We took in the thought that there was someone else here. And why wouldn't there be? Tramps, old soldiers, drunks, people who might be moved on from sleeping in doorways. But why so far along the tunnel?

She spoke quietly, as if whoever had been here might still be here, and listening. "If I were reduced to sleeping in such a place, I'd be near a way out."

"Not if you knew it well enough, and wanted not to be seen."

She directed the beam away from the alcove. "Do you think there's someone nearby?"

"I don't know. That sleeping bag could have been here for years. It doesn't mean there's someone round the corner. Do you feel brave enough to call out Jarrod's name? He'll know your voice."

Her voice came out in a hoarse whisper. "I can't, I'm afraid."

We paused just twice, to attach the third and then the fourth ball of string. "When this runs out, we have to turn back."

She gasped, and for a moment I thought she must have tripped over the body of the sleeping bag's owner. My torch was trained on the ground. She had once more switched on her flashlight and directed it higher. I did the same, and then saw what blocked our way. It was a high iron gate. Beyond it was an ancient building, two storeys high and completely intact and yet with arches several feet above it that must support the road overhead. As we listened to the silence I heard, or imagined I heard, the faint rumble of a tramcar.

Rooted to the spot, we stared. There was no turning to the left or the right. Neither of us made a move to open those gates. The stillness and bleak emptiness set me shivering. What ghosts or other unworldly beings might dwell behind the old door that hung from its hinges, and behind those gaping windows that looked like empty eye sockets?

I lowered the beam of the torch. A thousand small pink eyes looked out at us.

Without looking at each other, we knew what to do. Hang onto the string. Turn round. Go back.

Instead, I led the way forwards.

Behind me, Mrs Compton gave an anxious cry so loud that it might have imploded the tunnel. "Jarrod! Where are you? And what have you done?"

I stopped dead. "Did you see him?"

"No. I was calling just in case he is somewhere nearby. Perhaps he's in that dreadful place? It looks haunted and about to collapse."

"Look, we've come this far. If you're right and there is a way between the two theatres, let's not panic. Shine your torch about and I'll shine mine."

And then we saw it, a narrower passageway. We could continue and pretend we never saw that awful sight of a long-abandoned hotel.

"How much string have we got?" she asked.

"Not a lot, but we must be almost there. Let's press on just a few moments longer."

We did. The fourth ball of string came to its end.

"Mrs Compton, we have to turn back. I'm out of string."

"Wait! I have an idea. Shine a light."

I shone my torch and watched her pick at the hem of her coat. "This will get us there." She pulled at a strand of wool.

"It's too fine. It'll break."

"No it won't. It's a bulky Aran." She took off her coat and held it over her arm. "Safer this way, it might snag otherwise."

I knotted the wool to the string.

We began to walk again. Movement helped. While standing still, tying the string, I had felt like a sitting duck. The tunnel being narrower helped too. No one would hang their boots in this small space.

I had lost all sense of time. Our footsteps gained an echo at a certain point as the chamber rose in height, and then suddenly my torch picked out a set of stone steps.

"Go carefully, Mrs Compton. There's sheen to these steps, and we don't want to slip at what might be the last hurdle."

I climbed slowly. Once there had been a wooden rail but it had fallen away. At the top was a heavy door, with no knob. I pushed at the door.

"This might be it, Mrs Compton, but if so I don't know how anyone would get in or out."

"Bang on it."

It is always easier for the person who gives instructions than for the one who has to carry them out. I knocked on the door.

"Thump the bloody thing, Mrs Shackleton. Do it as if you mean it!"

I banged on the door with the end of my torch.

Nothing happened.

I banged again though a terrible image filled my brain, from some old moving picture or Walter Scott novel. The door would open. I would step into a void.

There was a clatter of footsteps on the other side, and then of a bolt being shot back, and another.

Slowly, the door opened.

CHAPTER
TWENTY-SIX

Little Manny Piccolo

First, cut through the wood to Woodhouse, veer off and keep going. Mrs Sugden kept her eye on the skyline, looking through city smoke for the gasometer. The gasometer proved as good a guide for leading Mrs Sugden to Sheepscar as yonder star for the three kings.

Floyd Lloyd's widow, Rita Lloyd, lived at 14 Back Barrack Street, Sheepscar. Mrs Shackleton had the address from Miss Fellini who had visited Mrs Lloyd after her husband's death. Only one aspect of this business bothered Mrs Sugden and that was the thought of mithering the poor woman, asking intrusive questions to which she would have no answers, and raking up the upset of her husband's death all over again. True, she would be arriving with two crisp five pound notes in an envelope, supposedly from the charity set up for the relief of distressed performers and their relatives. But what could she possibly learn that hadn't been said already? That was the rub.

She knew all the shortcuts. That was a source of pride. Put a person in a motorcar and they forget their knowledge of back streets, cut-throughs and ginnels. Mrs Sugden knew her way around Sheepscar, having once upon a time gone regularly to Sheepscar Library to change books for an old lady who attended the Congregational Chapel.

She felt confident that she would do this little job better than either Mrs Shackleton or Mr Sykes. It never hurt to have a proper division of labour. Jim Sykes had gone to interview the working man in York, the tram driver who knocked down Douglas Dougan. Later he'd be talking to Miss Clever Clogs, she with the amazing memory. Mrs Shackleton had set off to talk to the woman who lived in the house of the former chief constable, mother-in-law of the variety star.

Mrs Sugden had a feeling for Sheepscar. She knew the kind of house the ventriloquist's widow lived in. The woman might be an attender at the chapel and borrow books from the library. If so, that would provide the opening of a conversation. She would tell her of knowing a neighbour of hers, Mrs Crisp, who kept her marbles till the end. The old lady liked to read romance as long as it wasn't too soppy, crime if it wasn't too silly, but nothing about war or cowboys and nothing that included whales and sea captains.

Mrs Sugden turned into Back Barrack Street. She found number 14 and went into the yard. The curtains were clean enough, cream lace which wouldn't need as much washing as the white. She knocked. There was a bit of shuffling about inside. The door opened. A girl of about fourteen stood in the doorway, her round face pale as the moon, with big brown eyes and her hair in pigtails. She looked Mrs Sugden up and down. The girl had a very childish air about her, wore a check frock, white socks and black plimsolls.

"Is Mrs Lloyd in?" Even as she asked, Mrs Sugden spied a woman in her sixties seated at a table, busy at something.

"Gran, it's someone to see you."

"Tell her to come in."

"Come in."

Mrs Sugden stepped inside, shutting the door behind her. The girl went back to the table where there was a pile of stockings. The old lady, her gnarled hands moving rapidly, folded a pair of stockings. The girl took the stockings and wrapped them in tissue paper. There were boxes on the floor full of the wrapped items.

"Have they sent you?" Mrs Lloyd looked her visitor up and down. "Only we're not finished and won't be for an hour."

"Oh no. I've come from seeing Miss Fellini who asked me to call on you." That was a simpler explanation than involving Mrs Shackleton and the detective agency.

"Oh well then, come and sit." She turned to the child. "Move the boxes, pull out the stool for yourself and give this lady the chair."

The child did so. Mrs Sugden sat down.

"Keep on with wrapping," the grandma said to the girl. "You're doing a grand job, but shut your little lugs, this will be grown-up talk."

Mrs Sugden put the envelope on the table. "Miss Fellini sends her regards and this envelope from the . . ." She hesitated to say charity. That word rankled with many poor people. "From the group she founded and represents."

274

Mrs Lloyd nodded. "You won't mind if we keep on folding and wrapping?"

"Don't let me stop you."

She eyed the envelope, picked it up and put it in her pocket without opening. "Tell her we appreciate it and it's come at a right time. We're just on the lookout for a new lodger."

With some regret, Mrs Sugden decided against chatting about the old lady, long gone now, and her choice of library books. However, not all her knowledge of Sheepscar went to waste. "Have you thought of enquiring at the library, whether they know of anyone looking for digs? Librarians know everything and everyone. Or you might try the chapel."

"I might just do that. I've only spoken at the post office and at Appleyards — you know, the motor firm."

"You have it all covered then."

"You have to have your wits about you. Will you have a cup of tea?"

"No, thank you. I just had one, and I don't want to get in the way of your work. But I wouldn't mind a rest for my legs and a chinwag if that doesn't trouble you."

"Feel free. We've little enough company, eh Lorna?"

"That's a nice name."

The girl smiled. She did not look up from wrapping the stockings, which were of a fine material. Both of them were taking great care with the work.

"She was named by her granddad, weren't you, love? He thought she might follow him onto the stage and be Lorna Lloyd. It has a nice ring to it."

"It does. You must miss him."

The girl slowed down a little in her folding. "He was a good granddad. He left me his doll, Manny Piccolo."

"That was nice.

Mrs Lloyd sighed. "Poor love. He'd paid tuppence a week for his burial, and his friends chipped in. And he left us his dummy. It was allus the dummy with him, his little Manny Piccolo." She looked suddenly hopeful. "Did Miss Fellini say whether she found anyone who'd like to have the dummy?"

"She didn't mention it. Are you hoping some other ventriloquist will take it?"

"I did hope someone would make an offer but they all have their own favourites, and Lorna would be loath to part with him, eh, sweet pea?"

"I would, Gran. He keeps me company. I hope you won't send him away."

"Chance would be a fine thing, though he's well-made and was popular. No one else could give him the same voice."

"I could," the little girl said. "When Granddad was here we all talked together, Granddad, Manny and me. Then I talked to Manny on my own and Manny talked to me. He does still. If I sit quiet with him and talk to him, he'll tell me all sorts."

"He loved that dummy."

"He's not a dummy, Gran! He's Little Manny Piccolo." Lorna placed a pile of wrapped stockings into the carton on the floor.

"Bless him, Floyd did his best. He was always on the verge of a big success."

276

Mrs Sugden nodded sagely. "Aye. It's hope that keeps us all going."

Mrs Lloyd handed a pile of folded stockings to Lorna. "This time it might have happened. A gentleman from the broadcasting company took Floyd to the studios and gave him a try-out on the wireless. There was talk of a programme, a variety programme."

"That'd be a nice change from listening to orchestras and the news and them annoying pip pips on the hour, forever reminding a person of the passing of time."

"You have a wireless, do you?"

"Not one of my own, but I have harked to it now and again."

"Aye well, it came to nothing, that wireless business. It was thought it might go ahead, even after Dougie died."

"Dougie? Do you mean Mr Douglas Dougan who had the performing dogs?"

"Yes, Dougie Doig was his stage name."

"So he was part of the plan for a wireless broadcast?"

"Aye, him and his dogs."

"What would performing dogs do on the wireless?"

"Oh, didn't you ever see them? Tell her, Lorna."

The girl smiled. "They could sing 'Nellie Dean' in barking language. They could stand on their back legs and bark 'God Save the King'."

"That all sounds wonderful. I'm sorry that never came over on the cat's whiskers. Would it have been a regular thing?"

"They talked about it being on every week. I can tell you, we wouldn't be here folding stockings if that had come to fruition."

"No, you would not. But we never know what's round the corner." And Mrs Sugden wondered about this coincidence, that the two men who would have startled the world with their talents had each met a sticky end. Perhaps there was something in it after all and that Silver Songbird Selina Fellini was onto something. "Was anyone else to have taken part in this programme?"

"Miss Fellini of course. She would have been the big draw, and the memory woman, Miss Sechrest."

Mrs Sugden felt a bit of a chill. Two out of four. Who might be next. "Anyone else?"

"There might have been if the business had got further along."

Lorna stopped folding. "I could have done it. Granddad said I could have joined in."

Mrs Lloyd reached across and stroked her granddaughter's hair. "Bless you, little one, we don't know what you'll grow into but it'll be good."

"I'm not little. And Manny talks to me."

"Oh aye? What does he say?"

Lorna jumped from her chair and ran upstairs. She returned moments later with a doll dressed in white trousers, red blazer and straw boater. She moved her stool to the corner of the room by the empty fire grate and sat the doll on her lap. "What do you have to say for yourself, Mr Manny Piccolo?"

The doll's head tilted. His mouth opened and in an uncannily high voice, he said, "Hello, hello, hello, who have we here?"

"I'm Mrs Sugden, Mr Piccolo, and very pleased to meet you."

"Likewise I'm sure. Give me a pair of stockings for my sweetheart."

Lorna answered, "You don't have a sweetheart."

"Oh yes I do. I met a very nice girl."

Mrs Lloyd laughed. "Tell him that's enough out of him."

"Did you hear that, Manny? Anything else to say for yourself before you go back upstairs?"

The doll's head moved from side to side and up and down. "Not much. Only your granddad Mr Lloyd tells me I have to cry murder, bloody murder!"

Mrs Lloyd stopped folding. She parted her dry lips and gulped. "Why did you make him say that?"

"I didn't. He says what he likes, don't you, Manny?" The dummy nodded. "I do that. I please meself, me."

"Shall I ask him something else?"

The grandmother shook her head. "Put him back, put him back and get on with the stockings."

Mrs Sugden felt responsible for the change in Mrs Lloyd's mood. In an attempt to make amends and leave discussion of the ventriloquist on a happier note she asked, "Did Mr Lloyd enjoy all his travelling?"

"He loved that life, he did. We never saw as much of him as we'd have liked but our loss was others' gain. Floyd had a second family with his theatre friends. He was like an uncle to the young ones. He told me that if the broadcast business had come off, he would have changed the name of his act to Uncle Floyd and his little Manny Piccolo."

Mrs Sugden sighed her regrets on behalf of the widow and child. She set her bag on the floor, picked up a pair of stockings and began to help with the folding.

Three pairs of hands made light work. They had almost finished when Mrs Sugden asked, "This wireless idea, when they were all going to do a show, who put the kibosh on it?"

Mrs Lloyd shook her head. "I've no idea. Floyd was too upset to talk about it."

Lorna looked as if she might say something but then coloured up and kept her lips tight shut until all the stockings were in the box.

"Mrs Sugden, would you like to see me and Manny have another little chat?"

"I would indeed, if your gran doesn't mind."

Mrs Lloyd took a five pound note from the envelope Mrs Sugden had brought. She stood. "You must stay for a cup of tea then. I'll see about getting three buns."

"That's kind."

"Least I can do for your help and your visit."

When Mrs Lloyd had left, Lorna took her stool to a spot by the window. She sat Manny Piccolo on her knee. "Manny, this lady has a question for you."

Astonishingly, the dummy appeared to perk up. Mrs Sugden wondered what string the child had pulled.

The dummy spoke. "Ask away, lady, ask to your heart's content."

"Manny Piccolo, who put the kibosh on your life as a smart boy on the wireless?"

CHAPTER
TWENTY-SEVEN

Sykes Meets His Match

As Sykes drove to Roundhay Park, he felt satisfied with himself over this morning's visit to the tram driver. It was the first time he had ever turned up to interview a person and directed that person towards a new job. Perhaps Alf would turn the corner and the heavy weight of blame he carried for Douglas Dougan's death would lessen enough to allow him to go on living his life in a useful way.

Sykes had asked Alf to let him know if that dream of his ever gave him the face of the person in black, who may or may not have pushed Dougan under the tram, or tried to save him. It was entirely likely that the deaths of Douglas Dougan and Floyd Lloyd were unconnected and that both deaths were, as described by the respective coroners, accidental. Yet he had a feeling that there was something dodgy about this oh-so-friendly and talented group of performers. Which one of them would he cast as villain?

In spite of the tragic consequences, this whole business struck Sykes as having the elements of a party game rather than a serious investigation. What's more, it was a party game where no one knew the rules. He needed to narrow down the scope of the enquiry. To do that, it was imperative to find out who was in the vicinity at the time the accidents had befallen Douglas Dougan and Floyd Lloyd.

He liked this part of the job, where he followed up possibilities and kept an open mind. There was usually some person who floated to the top and refused to sink.

On this fine warm afternoon, it was good to have the excuse of visiting Roundhay Park and taking a walk around the lake. This was where the memory woman took her daily constitutional when in the city. She was regular as clockwork in her habits. That much he had learned from Mrs Shackleton who had made it her business to find out. He thought of what Miss Sechrest's life was like as she toured the country, keeping herself apart from the usual theatrical digs. In every place they played, she made sure of knowing the nearest wood or park and finding her lodgings nearby. She was a planner and a thinker, just the kind of person to get away with murder.

He had high expectations of Sandy Sechrest. Others might waffle and waver. She was the one person in that company of performers with a powerful memory and the sense to provide a necessary shortcut or two.

Madam Sechrest knew the dates of new moons but he had an inkling that she was too wise to wrap that knowledge in webs of superstition. Truth to tell, he felt a little in awe of the woman and wished there had been some unobtrusive way of making an appointment. There would be no point in pretending that he had just bumped into her. She would see through that wheeze.

Unless she was in the habit of taking a detour, all he had to do was walk the perimeter of the lake and he would meet her.

Who might have been able to slip unseen from the theatre and push Douglas Dougan under a tramcar? Which performer was in the theatre prior to Floyd Lloyd coming to rehearse his new routine, in his usual spot on stage? It would need to be someone sufficiently agile to climb up into the flies, tamper with the fixings and let loose a sandbag.

That would be his first big question mark. Who had the opportunity? Followed by the second big question, what was the motive? It could be personal or professional jealousy, or some ridiculous quarrel that was allowed to fester.

Beryl, the dresser, had supplied the programme for each of the theatres. This gave the names of those performing and the order of performance, which was, annoyingly, subject to change.

As Sykes walked around the lake, now stepping aside to avoid a puddle, now pausing to watch a child push out a small boat, he thought about the woman he hoped to bump into. The Woman Who Remembers Everything. That struck him as being more curse than blessing. Imagine wading through life able to recall how many peers sat in the House of Lords in 1910 and which team knocked Accrington Stanley out of the FA Cup in the 1906–1907 season.

It was rare for Sykes to feel that the business of following his chosen occupation might be intrusive. But what if the memory woman was even now, as she walked, committing to memory some new sack of facts? She would not welcome his intrusion.

He must think of something, some believable reason for waylaying her.

And here she came. Offstage as on, she wore black, a black skirt, stockings, cardigan and floating scarf. From her sleek black hair, decorated with an ebony comb, to her soft much-polished ankle boots, Sandy Sechrest eschewed colour. She stepped carefully, now looking at the ground, now looking ahead. The effect was of a certain dramatic glamour. Sykes did not often imagine the people he met inhabiting other worlds but it struck him that Sandy Sechrest would not have been out of place in Paris, sitting in a café by the Seine, as French people are said to do, listening to intellectual conversations. He imagined her listening rather than speaking because she would gather in others' thoughts and knowledge, select what was of interest and toss away the rest. She would judge and find others wanting. On the rare occasions when she did speak to this imagined group of artists, writers and Bohemians, those about her would listen, and not be disappointed.

From the auditorium he had thought her pale and interesting. As she came closer, he saw that her habit of brisk walks lent a pink glow to her cheeks; windburn not sunburn.

"Miss Sechrest, excuse me."

She stopped and stared at him.

"My name is Sykes. I am the person who asked you a question in the theatre."

"You asked two questions. I recognise your voice. You work with Mrs Shackleton. What do you want?"

She continued walking. He fell into step with her, feeling ill-at-ease. If some fellow did this to Rosie while she was out walking, he would deal with him pretty sharply.

"I am sorry to disturb your walk but I hope to talk to you, either now or at a convenient time."

"What about?"

"Earlier today I spoke to the York tram driver who knocked down your colleague, Mr Douglas Dougan. The driver cannot get over the tragedy. It threatens to ruin his life."

"I'm sorry to hear that but I don't see why you have come to talk to me about it."

"I wonder whether there is anything you could tell me about that evening, about Mr Dougan's state of mind? Perhaps he was distracted, or had been drinking?"

"As to distraction, I cannot answer. As to drink, not according to the post mortem."

"Was there anything at all that struck you as odd about his actions that night?"

"He did not take his dogs with him. If he had been going to an off licence, which would be cheaper than buying a drink in the theatre, he would have taken his dogs for the outing. Had he been going to a public house, he would have taken his dogs in order to be bought a drink by other patrons. I don't know where he was going. I assume he would have been back in time for curtain call if he had not collided with the tramcar."

"Did you say this at the time, the oddity of his not taking the dogs, I mean?"

"I was not asked." She turned and looked at him with big liquid eyes that had soaked up tomes of knowledge and reams of facts. "Did Miss Fellini suggest that you speak to me?"

"Not directly."

"Ah. I believe I understand. Selina did not ask you directly but she is behind this enquiry."

"What makes you say that?"

"If I am right, you are a policeman, or a former policeman. You attended the theatre with your wife, who did not know the true purpose of your visit and was embarrassed that you made a show of yourself in public by asking what she thought of as ridiculous questions. Those questions were intended to determine whether I made a connection between the phases of the moon and the deaths of my fellow performers. From these deductions, I take it that you are an investigator. Selina always suspected, or came to suspect, that Dougie's death, and Floyd's death, were suspicious. Am I correct?"

Sykes sighed his defeat. "You are correct, Miss Sechrest."

"There is nothing innately strange about the fact that those two deaths occurred near or in a theatre. That was the place of work for both men. All work and workplaces have their particular hazards. However, if there was foul play, then the likelihood was that another performer either had information or was the guilty party."

286

"That is a possibility."

"To add to that mix of possibilities is the tragic death yesterday of everybody's good chum Billy Moffatt, whose moods were like the light and dark side of the moon."

I am outclassed, Sykes thought. She definitely belongs in Paris. He wondered had she studied philosophy. He would love to hear the story of her life from the moment of her birth, and beyond into past generations of clever Sechrests.

They came to a bench. She stopped. "Let us sit down. You may wish to take out your notebook."

"Thank you."

"Don't thank me. I do this for Selina."

Sykes took out his notebook and pencil. "You were part of the company in York when Douglas Dougan was run over by the tram."

"Yes."

With this woman, he would need to speak plainly. He thought of Alf, the tram driver, the dark night, Alf's subsequent dreams of a man dressed in black, or was it a man? "I wish either to eliminate the possibility of foul play in connection with Mr Dougan's death, or find evidence to the contrary."

"Your question?"

"Mr Dougan was knocked down by a tram at 8.20p.m. To be blunt, was there any fellow performer who may have had the opportunity to leave the theatre and to push him under the tram?"

"Put me at the top of the list. I was on stage at 8.35p.m. I am quick on my feet."

"Thank you. Anyone else?"

"Twelve dancers from the Daisy Chain troupe. Do you want their names now?"

"Not if they are the names listed in the current programme."

"Delete Maria Bowker and Lizzie Haworth. Add Jenny Crawford and Tilly O'Hara." She waited until he had finished writing. "Others for your list of suspects would be Floyd Lloyd, ventriloquist; Billy Moffatt, comedian; Maurice Montague, master of music; Pip Potter, strongman; Charles de Beauvoir, singer; the Powolski twins, acrobats; Selina Fellini; Beryl Lister and Trotter Brockett. I cannot answer for the stage hands."

Sykes prided himself on writing quickly but he struggled to keep up. It would have been simpler to ask her who might be in the clear.

She waited for him to finish writing. "Any one of them might have left the theatre and slipped out behind Dougie."

"Were people in the habit of going out of the theatre when not on stage?"

"If you saw the size of our dressing rooms you would not need to ask. Do you wish to know the order in which they appeared on stage?"

"That won't be necessary, but you remember the exact times?"

"There would be no reason for me to commit that information to memory but there is an order, a pecking order you might say. Dougie and his dogs would have been off the stage by ten past eight."

288

"Mr Dougan did not waste much time before going out. I wonder where he was going? Perhaps for a bottle of beer."

She stared at him as if he had spoken in Japanese. Sykes realised that no one usually asked her to speculate.

"Is there anything else you wish to ask me?"

"Regarding the accident at the Sunderland Empire, were you present?"

"I was not present in the theatre when Floyd Lloyd was rehearsing his new routine with Manny Piccolo. It was afternoon. We had no matinée that day. Anyone could have gone in. There was a police investigation. My fellow performers were deeply disturbed by the event. The thought was that the accident might have happened to any one of us."

A duck waddled towards them from the lake, examined the ground, looked to see whether they were eating and then retreated.

"So at least twenty-three people would have had the opportunity to leave the theatre and push Douglas Dougan under Alfred Packer's tram."

"Yes."

Sykes hesitated before his next question, because it involved speculation rather than facts. "And regarding motive?"

"Loyalty to Selina would be a motive and so leave my name on your list of suspects. Both Dougie and Floyd exploited Selina's good nature. They ate up her time and sympathy, borrowed money, told sob stories that she believed. In addition, Dougie was demented

289

and deluded. He used to say his dogs kept him sane but I never believed that. If he had not died under that tram, insanity would have caught up with him."

"Did others in the company feel as you did about the two men?"

"You would have to ask them. There was a feeling in the company that they let the side down, both of them. They should have retired years ago but you see most of us cannot retire."

"Because you are devoted to the work?"

"Because we would die of starvation."

Sykes looked at her, and then lowered his head. It was a sign of the times that we had come to this pretty pass with thousands struggling to stay on the breadline. "One more question, if I may." She waited. "Did you see Billy Moffatt with a cigar, or taking a cigar, or being given a cigar?"

"That is three questions, Mr Sykes."

CHAPTER
TWENTY-EIGHT

A Smell of Gas

Our walk through the underground passageways had given me serious shivers. I stood on the top step, Mrs Compton so close behind me that if I leaned back an inch she would topple down the stone steps. Having knocked as hard as I could on the dilapidated door that barred our way, a feeling of dread enveloped me. Perhaps there would be no one on the other side. Worse still, there might be the steep drop of my imagination and a demon killer waiting patiently for innocent callers, so as to have the pleasure of watching them tumble to a dark cold death. Had I worn hiking boots I should have tried to kick down the door rather than return to the tunnel and see the ghostly deserted hotel on the way back to the Empire Palace.

The sound of footsteps was reassuring. Coming face to face with a fiend from hell would be a more attractive prospect than retracing our steps. I whispered to Mrs Compton, "Be ready! Have your torch handy as a weapon."

At last, the door opened. In the dim light, I looked up at a figure in black trousers and jacket, a white silk muffler around his neck.

"Hello," he said. "Good thing this door opens inwards or I might have sent you flying."

"Jarrod!"

There was not room for two of us on the top step and Mrs Compton would have toppled me but her son opened the door wider and held out his hand. A moment later, I was standing in a cellar with flagged floor. The cellar was bitterly cold, but after the tunnel it felt like a haven of normality.

He helped Mrs Compton in and closed the door. "Mother? What are you doing here?"

"Looking for you, you great idiot."

We must have been an odd sight emerging from the narrow and crumbling stone steps, me in summer dress and motoring coat, Mrs Compton in her skirt and blouse, carrying a disintegrating woollen coat.

What ghosts, vagabonds or misfits inhabited that awful place from whence we came? If that was where Jarrod Compton had rested his head, I felt pity — and disgust. But this cellar looked cosily done out. It was lit by a single gas mantle.

"Mrs Shackleton, this is my son, Jarrod. Jarrod, meet Mrs Shackleton who has kindly helped me along the way."

"How do you do, Jarrod? I'm relieved to find you here."

"How do you do, and how did you get here?" He stared from one to the other of us.

Now that we had reached a place of relative safety, Mrs Compton assumed a winning air of nonchalance. "Oh you know, from the Empire Palace. We were just in the Kardomah opposite, having a coffee, and I thought we might find you here. Mrs Shackleton was intrigued by the thought of tunnels under the city and I've always wanted to take a gander myself."

I looked beyond him, at battered furniture, chairs and table, a small cupboard placed against the bare brick wall. This was only partly to assess the place. I wanted to avoid staring at his face. One side was quite perfect, handsome even. The other side of his face was a taut reminder of what it once was. Tight and scarred skin covered a hollowed out cheek. A closed lid marked where his eye had been. Whatever surgeon had operated should be congratulated. It was not a face any man would have chosen, but Selina's description had prepared me. I could not stop the thought that came on an instant. At least he came back.

He ushered us to two deep chairs. Patting an arm of the nearest chair, he sent up a cloud of dust. Nearby, a saucepan bubbled on a primus stove. "I was just heating some beans. I could eat them cold but it's more cheering to see the flame and smell the Primus. Are you hungry?"

I took my cue from Mrs Compton who told him of our snack in the Kardomah. Act naturally. "Not for me, thank you."

"You won't mind if I carry on?"

"Please do."

He emptied his beans onto a tin plate, carried the pan to a sink in the corner and filled it with water. He rinsed a spoon. Now that he was not watching me, I could watch him. His movements were very precise. He pulled out an old straw plaited chair and put his plate on the table.

Mrs Compton began to tell him of the letters she had received from his brother Rodney in California, and his sister Eliza in Paris. "Eliza will be coming over at Christmas."

"Good. And did Rodney say anything about the picture we hope to make, starring Selina?"

"He did mention it. I don't quite see how a singer will be a suitable star for a moving picture."

He tapped the side of his nose. "You will. Wait and see."

When he had finished eating, he took his tin plate and spoon to the sink and rinsed them carefully. "I can make a pot of tea."

We both thanked him but refused. "I'll float if I drink any more," Mrs Compton assured him.

He brought his chair closer, and saw the state of his mother's coat. "Isn't that the cardigan Beryl knitted for you?"

"Yes."

"What happened to it?"

"I wasn't entirely sure of the way through from the Empire. Mrs Shackleton bought four little balls of string to mark the way."

It was my turn. "It was our trail for getting back, but we ran out. Your mother had the idea of unravelling her coat."

Mrs Compton turned to me. "If you'd bought five balls of string I'd still have my coat."

Jarrod scratched his head. "You could have come in from Swan Street, or by the alley from the Headrow."

Mrs Compton sniffed. "We were curious about the passageways from the Empire."

"You thought I was sleeping down there?"

"It was a possibility."

In spite of the shawl, which she had given to me and I had given back to her, Mrs Compton was shivering. She put on the unravelling coat.

Jarrod stood. "I'll gather up your wool for you." He went to the door.

Mrs Compton was on her feet in an instant. "Don't go down there."

"I can see the end of the strand there on the second step. I'll have it for you in a jiffy, and your string too if you want it."

He was gone.

Mrs Compton groaned. "What if he doesn't come back?"

"Surely he won't leave us here?"

"No. No, of course he won't. He always liked me in that cardigan coat."

I looked about the room. There was a door on the wall opposite the one we had entered. "I hope that takes us into the theatre."

"I never came at it from this end."

We sat in silence for long enough for me to become concerned. Mrs Compton, too. She stood, went to the door that led to the tunnel, and listened. "He seemed calm, like his old self, but something comes over him.

That's when he bolts. He makes a dash for it like a frightened horse."

But Jarrod was as good as his word. He returned with a small ball of wool and a single large ball of recovered string. "I expect you'll want to be off home, now you've seen me."

"Won't you come back with us?" Mrs Compton tried to keep her voice light but the tone of pleading came through.

"I might do that. I might follow you up on the bike."

Two "mights" in two sentences did not bode well. A nudge would not hurt. "Selina mentioned you wanted to type up some work. I have a feeling she is keen to see a typed copy."

He turned and looked at me with renewed interest. "What did Selina say about the songs?"

"She loved them."

He brought his chair round and faced me and his mother. "I might do that then. I might come and do some typing, if people will leave me alone."

Mrs Compton spoke softly. "Or you could rest. You look so tired."

"I am tired. It takes everything. No one knows how much energy it takes. But I'm nearly done, nearly finished."

"If it takes too much out of you, don't do it, son. Let her sing the old songs. You don't look well."

His laugh sounded almost merry. "One doesn't look well with a goodly portion of face ground to dust, but writing makes me feel better. It's something I can do for Selina. I've nothing else to give."

296

Had there been another room, I would have left the two of them together.

Mrs Compton leaned forward. "She should make a home for you and Reggie."

He shook his head. "She tried. I can't do it. I can't live in that glass box she built. It's like a specimen case."

So many words came into my head, but there was nothing to be said. The note of helplessness in his voice was so sharp that as I stood to go I felt unsteady. I gripped the back of the chair.

"Go with her, Mother. I will come. My bike's close by." He stood and walked to the door, opening it for us.

Mrs Compton rose. She put the balls of wool and string in her bag, and clutched her cardigan. "Beryl might reknit this for me."

It is an understatement to say I was relieved to be back on ground-floor level, feeling safe from ghosts and rodents, but hating to leave Jarrod Compton in that cellar.

The doorkeeper was away from his post when we emerged into his stage door haven. He appeared a moment later. I hoped he would assume that we had come through the street door in the usual way, but something in his look told me that he knew. He noticed Mrs Compton's frayed woollen coat. He produced a clothes brush for me. "You seem to have picked up a few cobwebs."

While he was putting the kettle on, Mrs Compton brushed cobwebs from my back. "Did you notice that Harry looks guilty?"

"I thought he was just concerned at the look of us."
There was a mirror on the wall. I took advantage of it
to comb my hair.

She borrowed my comb. "Harry shouldn't leave the
stage door unattended."

"He hasn't. We're here."

"Now we are, but where was he when we came in?"

"Well where do people go when they drink lots of
tea?"

Harry returned, carrying cups. "It's nice to have a bit
of company. Will you join me in a cup of tea?"

It seemed churlish to refuse.

Mrs Compton gave him a hard stare. "Harry, look at
me!"

He looked.

"Now, look into my eyes and tell the truth. Did
Jarrod come into the theatre yesterday by that
underground route?"

"He did, Mrs Compton."

I admired her approach and made a mental note to
try it myself sometime.

"Don't look away, Harry! Keep looking at my eyes."

"Yes, Mrs Compton."

"Why did you tell Selina, Trotter and Beryl that
Jarrod was not here?"

"Young Mr Compton asked me not to say anything.
I did not say he wasn't here. I said he did not come
through from Swan Street and there was no motorcycle
in the alley. That was true."

"Then why are you telling me now?"

"Because you're his mam and you've spoiled your good coat because you've been down there, and now you're making me look into your eyes."

"Who is in the theatre now?"

"Usual staff, Mr Waterhouse the manager going over the accounts with Mr Brockett, the publicity man, and Mrs Kelly taking round the tea."

"What about the company?"

"Beryl is in the dressing room doing a bit of sewing. None of the players are here."

"Thank you. We'll go up."

Mrs Compton led the way. As we came closer to the dressing room, I caught a faint whiff of gas. It grew stronger. We turned to each other, exchanged a look and began to hurry to the dressing room.

"Cover your face, Mrs Compton!"

I took off my hat and covered my nose and mouth. She pulled the shawl from her shoulders and did the same.

In the dressing room, I went straight to the gas fire and turned it off. Luckily, Beryl had been sewing, not ironing which might have caused a spark and an explosion. The electric iron was unplugged from the light fitting.

Mrs Compton was shaking Beryl who appeared lifeless. She was seated on a stool and slouched over the dressing table, a costume under her hands. The small window above was closed.

Between us, we pulled Beryl from the room, shut the door and dragged her along the corridor. Somehow we managed to carry her down the stairs, me taking her feet and walking backwards, Mrs Compton holding her under the arms.

It took an age to negotiate the steps, turning corners, not daring to stop when my arms threatened to part from their sockets with the strain. As we neared the ground floor, I began to call for Harry. Beryl's head lolled like a floppy doll's, but she was breathing.

Once on ground level, Harry hurried to help.

Mrs Compton and I were shouting orders at the same time.

"Open the door, let's have some air! She's still breathing."

"Telephone for an ambulance and the police!"

Mercifully, the ambulance arrived quickly. Beryl was given oxygen and placed on a stretcher. She had opened her eyes, and closed them again.

Mrs Compton and I stood in Swan Street, watching as Beryl was put into the back of the ambulance. She looked at me. "One of us should go with her."

The driver called from his cab. "Sorry madam, that's not allowed. She'll be taken to the infirmary. You can enquire after her patient number and look on the board to see how she is."

Someone came up behind me. A familiar voice said, "Why is it not a surprise to find you here, Mrs Shackleton?"

I turned to see Detective Inspector Wallis of Leeds City Police, accompanied by Sergeant Ashworth. It surprised me that an inspector would turn up for an incident involving a gas fire. He wore his usual worsted suit, with an olive green tie. We eyed each other. I wondered what it was he found noticeable about me. I always tried not to look too closely at his odd eyes, the right one bright blue and round and the left eye a little smaller and less penetrating. Occasionally we met at civic functions. He always made a point of seeking me out. Now and again, if one of us was without a car, we gave the other a lift.

"Inspector Wallis."

"Mrs Shackleton."

"Mrs Compton, this is Detective Inspector Wallis. Inspector, Mrs Compton. She and I had just come to the theatre and went up to have a word with Beryl Lister, Selina Fellini's dresser."

Mrs Compton looked upset but I knew she had also decided that it would be better not to mention our unconventional way into the theatre. "Thank heavens Mrs Shackleton had the presence of mind to act so quickly. I hope poor Beryl won't suffer lasting damage."

Harry was listening. We could be sure to rely on him not to complicate matters by mentioning the Empire and underground passages, especially since he had kept quiet about Jarrod's comings and goings.

Inspector Wallis spoke to Harry. "Will you please take Sergeant Ashworth to the dressing room where Mrs Lister was working. Mrs Compton, I'd be obliged if you would accompany the sergeant and show him where you found Mrs Lister. And I'm sure I don't need to tell you to hold hankies to your nose and mouth and not strike a match."

Mrs Compton shot a look at me that was rather severe. The woman had a nerve. As if I would say more than necessary, as if I would involve her precious son without evidence.

The inspector waited until the door to the stairs closed behind them. "A word, Mrs Shackleton, please."

Leather-covered benches ran along two sides of the room. We seated ourselves on the nearest one, keeping a decent amount of space between us.

He took out his notebook. "Yesterday you went into Brownlaws chemist on Boar Lane. What were you doing there?"

That explained why Ernest Brownlaw had been so elusive. He had reported having been asked to test the cigar for poison.

I considered describing my purchase of rose-scented soap flakes, but that was not what he wanted to know. And I thought Ernest Brownlaw was my friend. He might at least have alerted me that he intended to tell tales about the cigar.

"I took in a cigar for analysis."

"To be analysed for . . .?"

"For cyanide." He would know that, of course. Ernest Brownlaw had reported the fact.

"Why was that?"

"Did Mr Brownlaw find something, is that why you're here?"

He smiled. "I'll ask the questions. A brief account if you please."

"Billy Moffatt died yesterday morning. One of the last things he did was to light a cigar. Later, he was found by some of the school's senior boys in a collapsed state."

I gave him a brief account of Billy's admission to Castleberg infirmary, and his death.

"Please don't make me ask every question. You are aware that you need to tell me where Mr Moffatt was found . . ."

"Oh, didn't I say? By Giggleswick School chapel."

". . . who found him, what made you pick up a cigar butt and by what convoluted process did you suspect it might contain cyanide?"

There was nothing for it but to tell him the truth. He would want names, and in particular one name. It was a curse that I knew so little about chemistry. Had I been a science whiz, I might have pretended I was the one who managed to enter the school lab and carry out an analysis. I loved that idea and could imagine myself doing it, with potions and smoke.

"I persuaded one of the boys to help me by conducting a test, and it came up positive. The responsibility is mine."

"That is helpful but too brief. I shall have to ask you to come to headquarters and give me a full statement. I need the name of the boy concerned."

"What if I say no?"

"Then I shall talk to the headmaster and find out from him."

"At least tell me whether the analysis was positive."

Inspector Wallis thought for a moment. "Would I be here if he was wrong?"

"Mr Brownlaw told me something about the type of cigar. That was all. He said he would let me know the results and naturally I would have come to you."

He sighed. "Naturally. And naturally I believe you. The name? If I need to speak to the boy I shall do so discreetly."

"Alex McGregor."

He had not answered my question. Had Ernest Brownlaw found traces of poison? He was a good chemist but a poor friend. He must have struggled with his conscience and the demands of the Poisons and Pharmacy Act. Now I might be on a charge of interfering with evidence.

That would explain why, when the police received Harry's emergency call from the theatre where Billy had performed, Inspect Wallis decided that the City Varieties merited his visit.

"I am keeping an open mind, Mrs Shackleton. Now what else do you have to tell me, assuming that you wish to avoid being charged with obstructing the course of justice?"

"Nothing else regarding Billy's death. Mr Brockett will be going to Giggleswick Hospital when they have the death certificate. I expect I may be asked to attend the inquest. When do you want my statement?"

His tone softened. "Now that you've told me, tomorrow will be soon enough." He glanced at my shoes, which were unusually dusty. Damn the man. He missed nothing.

"Tell me about finding Miss Lister."

"Just that she was slumped over the dressing table, and there was the smell of gas."

"I'll go up in a moment. Do you know her well?"

"Not well, but I don't believe she would have been so careless as to let the flame die in the gas fire. When I was in the dressing room last night, she made a point of turning off the fire."

"Are you saying someone deliberately tried to kill her?"

"Yes."

"Why?"

"I don't know. If she doesn't recover, this will be the fourth death in the company in a matter of eighteen months."

He raised an eyebrow. "So that's why you're here?"

At that moment, the sergeant and Mrs Compton returned from the dressing room.

Wallis waited for his sergeant to speak.

"No sign of anyone else up there, sir. I opened the window. Harry the doorkeeper has gone to fetch the wind machine. He'll have it hooked up to disperse the gas."

"Any note?"

"No note, sir, not unless there's one about the lady's person."

Mrs Compton glared at the two men. "A note? A note? Do you imagine Beryl would begin hemming a dress and then think to herself, I won't finish sewing this costume. I've taken against the colour. I'll just gas myself instead."

Inspector and sergeant pretended deafness.

It was my turn to be helpful. "What about the cup on the dressing table? Was it tea, and was it still warm? If Beryl had taken a tipple that might explain her dropping off, or not being her usual alert self."

The sergeant frowned. "What cup? I didn't see a cup."

"There was one. Did you see it, Mrs Compton?"

She had not. "I was busy looking at poor Beryl, and that dreadful dress she was mending. It's the wrong sort of red for Selina."

"Then someone has moved it. There was definitely a cup there."

"Go up and find Harry, Ashworth. Search the building. I want to know who else is here, and nobody must leave."

He pulled out his police whistle, went to the stage door, signalling for the beat bobby, before picking up the telephone.

Mrs Compton whispered, "You'll look very silly if you imagined the cup."

"I didn't. Earlier you asked me my occupation, well I'm not a solicitor, or a travel agent, I am an enquiry agent or if you prefer, a private detective. And when the inspector is off the phone, tell him I've gone upstairs to see whether someone tipped the contents of that cup into one of the vases or the plant pot because whoever moved it wouldn't have run along a corridor carrying half a cup of tea."

No interloper was discovered in the theatre, perhaps because there were too many ways in and out: the main doors, actors' alley entrance, the scenery dock doors. Every person in the theatre was with someone else and had been nowhere near the dressing rooms.

Mrs Compton and I were allowed to leave by the stage door, with Inspector Wallis's warning ringing in my ears that I must report to headquarters in the morning, to make a statement.

"Poor Beryl," Mrs Compton murmured. "She has devoted the best part of her life to Selina Fellini. More fool her."

"I wonder how long Jarrod had been in his cellar hideaway when we arrived and disturbed him?"

"Don't you dare point a finger at my son, Mrs Shackleton. We talked to him for a quarter of an hour at least. It couldn't possibly have been Jarrod. He would not do such a thing, my Jarrod."

But was he still her Jarrod?

CHAPTER
TWENTY-NINE

The Other Jarrod

A subdued silence prevailed as I drove Mrs Compton back to her house. I must have been mad to go underground with her, but if I hadn't we would not have found our way into the Varieties and Beryl surely would have died. Perhaps our adventure gave Beryl a chance of life. Neither of us had mentioned Jarrod to the inspector, and nor had Harry. Now I wondered whether that had been a mistake. I felt sure that Inspector Wallis knew we were holding back.

I brought the car to a stop outside her gate, expecting her to get out.

She did not.

"Will you come in with me?"

"No thank you. I'd best be off." I chose not to mention that tomorrow I would need to call at police headquarters and give a statement that may well lead me into trouble and Alex McGregor to being disciplined, if not expelled.

"I should like you to come in because that's Jarrod's motorcycle in the back garden and I want you to be absolutely clear in your mind that he would not have attempted to gas Beryl Lister."

"Very well, and if it's any consolation I believe you are right about the timing." Since I had come to find Jarrod, I should follow through and find out what he did know about the other deaths. And in spite of my reassurance to Mrs Compton, there was still the niggling possibility that a powder in her tea and slow release of gas could be the work of the charming Jarrod. If I were a murderer, I would make sure to be charming on the outside.

We walked to the gate. "Jarrod likes Beryl. They've known each other since some youthful theatrical performance when they were at school. Beryl was bridesmaid when he married the Fellini girl."

This seemed an odd way for her to refer to Selina but I expect that's how she thought of her during the courtship: the Fellini girl, whom Jarrod might grow out of.

"Jarrod has a soft spot for Beryl. He used to encourage her to strike out. She had that same dreadful elementary education as Selina but her father paid for a great deal of additional tuition. She speaks French, she designs dresses. Her parents had great hopes for her. She wastes her talents designing for Selina and doing up her buttons."

She took out her door key, and then turned to me. "He is not always as you saw him earlier. He can sometimes turn nasty. I'm just warning you."

Which one of us would he turn on, me or his mother?

Slowly, she turned the key, opened the door and called in a desperately cheerful voice, "Jarrod! I'm home!"

Silence.

Together we looked in each of the downstairs rooms.

Mrs Compton left me in the kitchen and went upstairs.

She came back down. "Will you come with me into the cellar?"

At that moment, I could not face another cellar. "Didn't you say he went in the shed last time he was here?"

"Yes, he did."

The cellar was reached from the kitchen. She called down. No answer.

She opened the back door. Putting on a smiling face, she approached the shed and tapped on the door. I stayed a few steps behind as she called, "Are you in there, Jarrod?"

There was a crashing sound. The door was flung open but Jarrod held onto it so tightly that his knuckles turned white. He looked puzzled, and afraid. "What do you want? What's she doing here?"

"Jarrod, please, your manners!"

He slammed the door shut. That glower of mistrust, almost hatred, turned me cold.

Slowly, we walked back to the house. "He never used to be like this, Mrs Shackleton. It's just these past months that he's changed and it comes and goes. In the old days, I'm sure people went to war and came back and got on with things. That's the impression I always had. And Jarrod was so much better, for so long."

"Has he been seen by anyone recently, a doctor?"

"He avoids them. And to tell you the truth, I think the doctors in Bridlington, good as they are, don't know what to make of him."

"Have you talked to him about it?"

"I've tried, and so has Selina. We think flashes come back to him and everything goes misty in his brain."

It was then that I remembered someone I hadn't thought of for a long time. During my first professional case, when I went to Bridgestead, I met Dr Grainger. He was one of those clever men pioneering talking cures for returned officers. He went to work at the Maudsley Hospital. Last I heard, he was still there.

"I can suggest a doctor who might be able to help. If he can't, then he'll almost certainly recommend a colleague, someone who might give a diagnosis."

"Would this doctor come to the house?"

"That's unlikely. He is based at the Maudsley. You would need to take Jarrod to London."

"I've heard about that place. I've heard some terrible things about it too."

"Dr Grainger is trustworthy. He wouldn't suggest any treatment that would be dangerous."

"None of them do. It's only afterwards they find out something they've done is harmful and irreversible."

"That's true up to a point, but we have such good doctors. There's been massive progress in all sorts of areas."

"I'm not saying there hasn't."

"What else do you think you might do? Do you have a doctor that you do trust?"

"I don't know what to do. There's no one nearby that I know of."

"Then it may be worth considering."

"How would I get him to London? You saw him. He won't come in the house."

"Tell Selina that Jarrod is here. She might persuade him."

"I suppose it's worth a try. Will you telephone her?"

"No! Mrs Compton, you and Selina need to act together, for all of your sakes."

She flung her knitted coat on the kitchen chair. "Beryl put a great deal of effort into knitting this for me. I was wrong to dislike the poor girl in the beginning. I wish he'd married her instead of Selina. But of course Selina was all smiles and sparkle. Beryl was the sensible one. She's too loyal and kind for her own good."

"Will you telephone Selina?"

"I suppose so. When Harry came back up to the dressing room with me, he said he would let Mr Brockett know that Beryl had gone in the ambulance, so I expect Selina will already know that she will have to dress herself tonight."

"And now she needs to know that Jarrod is here and that he is ill, ill in his mind."

"Yes, yes, I know. You're right."

She went into the hall and picked up the telephone. "Let us see if Miss Fellini deigns to speak. Of course she may still be sleeping, or gargling to protect that throat of hers."

I followed her into the hall. "Mrs Compton, if you don't mention Dr Grainger at the Maudsley to Selina, I will. Your son is suffering. If he isn't treated he is likely to be committed to a secure institution and spend his days under sedation. There'll be no writing songs and stories if that happens."

Mrs Compton took a deep breath. I saw by the narrowing of her eyes and the twitch of her mouth that Selina had answered the telephone herself. "Selina, it's me. Have you heard about Beryl?"

Mrs Compton raised her eyes at me. "She hasn't heard." She spoke again into the mouthpiece, giving an account of what had happened. "I hope and pray that Mrs Shackleton and I got to Beryl in time. I have Mrs Shackleton with me, and Jarrod is here. That is my reason for telephoning." She paused, listening. "He is no better, he is worse. Mrs Shackleton has an idea about a London doctor who may be able to help him." There was a pause. "Then I won't say more on the telephone. Come over and see for yourself, *if* you can spare the time. I can't make medical arrangements. I'm only his mother."

She hung up the receiver.

"So Selina is coming?"

"She's on her way, and believe it or not she needs to tell her brother. She always has to bring that family of hers into whatever is going on."

"If you will let me use the telephone, I will try to contact Dr Grainger and see what he says. If it's a yes, perhaps we could book the de Havilland again."

"Is that absolutely necessary?"

Afterwards, I realised that she was shilly-shallying about the need for a London doctor, but at that moment I simply thought her misgivings were to do with hiring an aeroplane. "Can you imagine Jarrod being comfortable in a railway carriage on a four-hour journey to King's Cross? There's also the small matter of how soon it will take for the police to want to interview him. If he's not here, they can't."

"Why should they want to interview him?"

"Think about it."

She did, and quickly. The implications sank in. Billy Moffatt had died under unexplained circumstances, and Jarrod had reason to be jealous. Beryl was in hospital, fighting for her life. Jarrod had found his way into the theatre unannounced. Her eyes widened, her hand went to her mouth. "No!"

"So I may use the telephone?"

She nodded.

It took some time for me to be connected to a nurse who knew Dr Grainger's whereabouts, and an even longer time for him to telephone back to me. I told him about Jarrod, without mentioning his name for prying operators to hear. Yet he needed to know his symptoms.

Mrs Compton took over the conversation. I could see how much it pained her to describe the changes in her son, his increasing aggression and the sudden outbursts of anger. During the moments when she was silent and listening, her look changed. She became more hopeful. She said that she was sure Jarrod could be brought to London very soon. On the pad by the

314

telephone, she made a note of an address and telephone numbers.

"He wants to see Jarrod. He didn't seem at all surprised by the symptoms. There is a doctor visiting from America, Harvey Cushing. He wants Jarrod to meet him. He says not everything can be put down to the war. Sometimes there are other factors that are overlooked because we are too ready to say some condition is due to shell shock or bullet wounds."

We heard the motorcycle engine. Mrs Compton went to the window. "It's Marco Fellini." She watched, and then waved. "He's bringing his cycle onto the path. I'll let him in."

Marco was the brother I had met at Selina's party, the one who played the accordion and sang "Has Anybody Seen My Gal?". Perhaps the whole family had fine voices. I imagined them growing up in the back-to-back house on Grimston Street, creating concerts in the kitchen, singing duets as they squeezed by each other on the stairs.

His voice carried along the hall. "Mrs Compton, Selina telephoned me at work."

"Thank you for coming, Marco. You're like the cavalry riding over the hill to relieve the besieged."

She led Marco into the drawing room. Whatever he did for the family business, he did not need overalls. He was dressed in a smart dark grey suit, white shirt and red tie. He flashed a broad smile. "Kate, hello."

"Hello, Marco." Mrs Compton looked from him to me. "We met at Selina's party." I went to sit in the chair by the window, watching the exchange between the two of them.

"Where's Jarrod?" Marco asked.

Mrs Compton lit a cigarette. "He's in the shed."

"You could let him stay there till he chooses to come out."

"Marco, if you'd seen how tired he looked you wouldn't say that. There's no air in the shed and it gets so warm on a day like this. Try and bring him out."

"What would he do if he comes out?"

I felt sorry for Mrs Compton. She clearly wanted to tuck her little boy up in bed and give him a cup of Ovaltine.

I reminded her. "He came here because he wanted to type a manuscript, with some songs for Selina."

Marco showed interest. "That might bring him out. Where's he going to do this typing?"

"In what was his father's study, upstairs."

"Right. I'll see what I can do." He paused by the door. "Selina seems to think he might be in trouble."

"I'm not sure."

"If he's in trouble, we could take him to Napoli. If he's in big trouble, we could take him soon."

What did they suspect that might necessitate Jarrod being shipped out of the country?

Mrs Compton walked Marco into the hall. She beckoned me to follow.

After Marco had gone through the kitchen door, we watched through the dining room window. "Be ready to duck back. I don't want Jarrod to think we are spying on him."

316

Marco was at the shed door.

"So this is the family you believe might want to murder Jarrod."

"Oh, not Marco, it's the others."

"Why are you so confident that Marco will be able to persuade Jarrod inside?"

"They served together, Jarrod, Billy and Marco." She sighed. "How is it that some men came back unscathed?"

"No one came through unscathed, Mrs Compton, not them, and not us."

Selina arrived in a taxi. She stood in the hall and spoke from there. "I've brought vinegar and brown paper."

Mrs Compton stayed in the drawing room. "It'll take more than vinegar and brown paper to mend his head."

Marco came down the stairs, and tried to usher his sister into the room. She put her head round the door. "I can't come in here, Mother. It's a smoke room. I'm going up to see Jarrod."

Marco would have been an asset at the League of Nations. "Let Jarrod sleep, I'll see to the vinegar and brown paper when he wakes. Look at the beautiful day. Nothing seems so bad when you sit outside."

So there we were, moments later, on the paved area outside the dining room window, seated around a wrought-iron table. A red admiral landed on the hollyhocks. Bees buzzed around the buddleia. Selina wanted to know more about our morning, and details of how we found Beryl.

She and Marco listened as Mrs Compton and I gave her an account of events.

"I'm devastated about Beryl. She's been so selfless and kind and my best friend. I telephoned to the infirmary. They wouldn't say anything, but at least that means she's still alive." Selina slumped a little in the chair. "How did Jarrod seem, when you first saw him?"

Mrs Compton was quick to put a good gloss on our coming across Jarrod in the cellar. "He was calm enough and he certainly would not have harmed Beryl, never in a million years."

Selina bit her lip. "No, of course he wouldn't. It's just that when I told Trotter about Beryl, after you rang me, he immediately asked where was Jarrod when Beryl was found. I'll give him an earful when I see him. He shouldn't have said that on the telephone, linking Jarrod's name to such an . . . accident." She gave me a meaningful look on the word accident.

"Something stank and it wasn't just gas," Mrs Compton said. "But you are being sensitive. Trotter would never suspect Jarrod."

"I suppose not. He had intended to go to Giggleswick, to make arrangements for Billy, but it's too soon apparently. He said he will go to the infirmary and try and see Beryl."

Mrs Compton had brought out the sherry. Selina and Marco declined. She poured a glass for me and one for herself, making her own a double. "Trotter's a good man. He looks after his people."

Selina smiled. "Yes he does. That's why we like to work with him. In these days of sackings and wage cuts

318

he never terminates a contract. He prides himself on that."

Marco was silent. He was listening for any noise from within. We all were. Eventually, Marco asked, "How did you persuade Jarrod to leave the cellar?"

Mrs Compton looked at me. "It was Mrs Shackleton's idea. She suggested that Jarrod might want to type up his manuscript, with songs for Selina."

"He's writing a moving picture for me," Selina said, "but the whole piece is too English for America."

"Not necessarily." Mrs Compton took out a cigarette, and then changed her mind. "Jarrod has been writing to Rodney about it. Rodney says there'll be sound added to talking pictures this year."

Marco smiled. "Jarrod loves his pictures."

There was a long pause, the kind where someone should have offered to make a pot of tea. No one did, thanks to the sherry.

When would they come round to the difficult topic of what to do about Jarrod?

A window opened upstairs.

Around the garden table, the quality of the silence changed. A crow came to rest on the apple tree.

Marco stood.

Selina looked at him.

He shook his head. "Give him time. He thinks he has failed you, but he just needs time."

"What will you do?"

"I'll take him to see Buster Keaton in *The General*. He's seen it before. He might fall asleep."

Selina took the Oxford Pencil Box from her bag, the one that contained the needle and, presumably, morphine. "You may need this when you come back."

He nodded. "And the vinegar and brown paper. I'll tell him you brought it."

When they had gone, Selina decided she would have a sherry after all. "What sort of men are these London doctors, Kate?"

"Tops in their field. Grainger worked with officers who came back badly disturbed. He achieved good outcomes with his talking cures. I don't know Harvey Cushing. He is American and highly regarded. He's a neurosurgeon."

"A neurosurgeon?" She closed her eyes but that did not stop the tears. "I won't let anyone cut holes in Jarrod's head."

Mrs Compton took a deep breath with the result that she suddenly looked brittle enough to break. Her next sip of sherry went down the wrong way.

I waited until Mrs Compton's choking fit ended. "If you take him to the Maudsley, at least you'll elicit sound opinions. That's half the battle. When you don't know, you feel so helpless."

Selina stood. "Give me the number for the airmen. I'll speak to them myself and see how soon they're available. If they're not, there'll be someone else can take us."

I took out my notebook where I still had the aviators' card, and handed it to her.

"When will you arrange to go?" Mrs Compton asked.

"As soon as possible. It's likely that after tonight's performance I'll feel a sore throat coming on." She stood to go to the telephone. "Mother, if I'm in London, will you visit Beryl when it's allowed?"

CHAPTER
THIRTY

Theories

When I returned from Gledhow Lodge, Mrs Sugden was in the front garden, dead-heading the roses. She continued clipping until I stepped onto the path.

"That was a long visit. I thought you must have moved in with Mrs Compton."

"It felt a bit like that." I looked round. "Where's Harriet?"

Mrs Sugden put the secateurs in her apron pocket. "She's round with Miss Merton and they're getting on so well you'd think they'd known each other in a past life. Harriet will be kept busy for a few more hours yet, and again tomorrow until after the garden party."

"That's a great relief."

"Mr Sykes is in the office, writing up his notes."

"Will you come through then? I expect we all have something to report."

Moments later, we were seated around the dining table, comparing notes. I listened to Mrs Sugden's accounts of meeting Mrs Lloyd, the ventriloquist's widow, and her granddaughter Lorna. Sykes attempted not to be too superior in having interviewed both Alf Packer the tram driver and Sandy Sechrest.

They were shocked to hear about Beryl Lister being taken to hospital. "Will she live?" Mrs Sugden asked.

"I hope so. We may have found her in time. I suspect she may have been drugged so as to be unaware of the gassing. I gave a vase to Inspector Wallis where I think the remains of a cup of tea or coffee had been poured. Whoever it was knew their way about the theatre."

"You don't think it was attempted suicide?" Sykes asked.

"Definitely not." I turned to my housekeeper. "There is something about Beryl Lister that reminds me of you, Mrs Sugden. She would be no more likely to give in to life and turn on the gas than you would."

I also told them about Inspector Wallis asking me for a statement, thanks to Ernest Brownlaw having contacted him about my request that he test the found cigar. "He asked me to go in tomorrow morning. I do believe that he just wants me to stew overnight."

"Inspector Wallis gave no hint as to what the chemist found?" Mrs Sugden asked.

Sykes answered for me. "Of course he wouldn't."

It was time to move on and discuss what we did know rather than what yet remained a mystery.

Sykes had already supplied Mrs Sugden with a list of names gleaned from Sandy Sechrest. While they waited for my return, Mrs Sugden had taken the time to write each suspect's name on a separate piece of paper. She had snipped the white margins from yesterday's newspaper into neat oblongs. On each piece of paper she block-printed the name of a suspect in indelible pencil, dipping the pencil lead in an egg cup of water so as not to turn her tongue blue. She divided the names into two: dancers and performers.

These names formed two circles on the table, one exclusively reserved for the Daisy Chain troupe of twelve dancers. The names of the two dancers who left the troupe after the incident of the falling sandbag at the Sunderland Empire were underlined. Mrs Sugden placed them in the centre of the dancers' circle.

Jenny Crawford Tilly O'Hara

We considered the dancers first.

Mrs Sugden revealed her theory. "I'm wondering if the two chorus girls who hopped it after Sunderland conspired to kill Floyd Lloyd."

Sykes perked up. "They would have been agile enough to scale the heights. But why would they want to kill the old ventriloquist?"

"By his widow's accounts he was the best kind of absent husband, being mostly absent. He was a kind granddad. He saw himself as an uncle to the younger performers in his troupe."

"That's true," I said, wondering where Mrs Sugden's thoughts led her. "Miss Fellini thought of him as an uncle figure, someone she could confide in."

When Mrs Sugden began by saying, "Far be it from me to cast aspersions or speak ill of the dead . . ." it was clear that aspersions would follow.

She continued. "We all know about men who like to be seen as uncles to young lasses. How do we know he wasn't a dirty old man? And if he was, his target would be chorus girls. Jenny Crawford and Tilly O'Hara might have had enough and put an end to him."

"That would be a bit drastic." Sykes shook his head. "We're into flimsy speculation. Miss Fellini saw him as an uncle as well, let's not forget."

Mrs Sugden sometimes adopted rather formal speech, to attempt to make Sykes respect her views. "I know whereof I speak, so listen to me. There's a lot of that kind of thing about. When I was fifteen, I was taken up by a magician to be his lovely assistant. He was too fond of searching me for missing playing cards and turtle doves. It didn't stop until I beat him round the head with his wand."

Sykes took a moment to gather his thoughts for a comeback. "But even you wouldn't have killed someone for . . . that kind of thing."

"Don't be so sure." Spending time talking to newspapermen had left its mark on Mrs Sugden. She resorted to sporting metaphors. "Floyd Lloyd wouldn't queer his pitch by making a play for Selina. He might try his luck with the chorus girls." Mrs Sugden held up her hands. "I'm pointing no fingers, I'm just saying."

For some wee while longer, we considered the dancers. None of us had much of value to say because we knew so little about them. They all lodged together in a large house in Chapeltown, and they stuck together too. From the conversations at the party, I had picked up that the most senior dancer was their choreographer who also acted as chaperone to the younger ones. How good a chaperone she was I did not know. Her "minding" did not preclude two of the dancers wearing little gold boxes of cocaine on chains at their throat. Perhaps we may be missing something important, such as an evil and bored dancer with a penchant for murder. But our discussions led nowhere. It was time to move on. "Apart from the Daisy Chain Dancing Troupe, what about everybody else?"

We turned our attention to Mrs Sugden's second circle of names. She explained her method. "In this circle we have the people that Miss Sechrest the memory woman told Mr Sykes had the opportunity to push Douglas Dougan under the tram."

Sandy Sechrest, memory woman
Floyd Lloyd, ventriloquist (d.)
Dougie (dogs) Dougan (d.)
Billy Moffatt, comedian (d.)
Maurice Montague, master of music
Pip Potter, strongman
Charles de Beauvoir, singer
Powolski twins, acrobats
Selina Fellini
Beryl Lister
Trotter Brockett

Sykes looked at me as being able to query Mrs Sugden's logic without the least suggestion of offence.

"Why is Mr Dougan included as a suspect in his own death?" I asked in as mild a fashion as possible.

Naturally, Mrs Sugden's logic was impeccable. "His name is included in my circle in case he wasn't pushed or shoved. He may have decided to top himself, with no

326

thought for the poor tram driver or his own dogs. 'Accidental death', the coroner said, remember? And if it was not 'accidental' then it might just as easily have been suicide as murder."

"I see. Well, that is a possibility, but since two more fatalities followed, Floyd Lloyd and Billy Moffatt, and now an attack on Beryl Lister, perhaps we might simplify our task by removing the dead from our list of suspects, just for the time being."

Mrs Sugden duly removed Douglas Dougan, Floyd Lloyd and Billy Moffatt. "Just as you like." She set them carefully aside, not ready to discard them altogether. "Floyd Lloyd and Billy Moffatt might have killed Douglas between them and Billy killed Floyd to keep him quiet."

Sykes never liked to stay silent for long. "It's good to keep an open mind but it's helpful to narrow the field, at least in the beginning. We can widen the scope of our enquiry if necessary. After what Mrs Shackleton has just told us about Beryl Lister's accident, shouldn't we be looking for one person — someone who is still alive?"

I kicked him under the table. It is very annoying that he finds these subtle ways of reminding Mrs Sugden that she is new to the field of investigation. Fortunately, Mrs Sugden was concentrating too hard on her own ideas to take in the snide edge of his remark.

Something had been niggling away and now I knew what it was. "Beryl Lister is Selina Fellini's oldest friend. They were at school together. If it hadn't been for the generosity of Beryl's parents, Selina would not have had singing and dancing lessons. She would have gone into the ice cream business, married young and produced a brood of young workers. Beryl tried to protect Selina from what she called 'hangers-on' who exploited her good nature. It had crossed my mind that someone else — perhaps even Beryl herself — was getting rid of those hangers-on. Now I'm not sure what to make of it. Certainly Beryl was no hanger-on but an essential part of Selina's success."

Mrs Sugden brightened up at this thought. "Miss Lister could have turned the gas on herself, to divert attention from what she'd been up to. She must have felt under-appreciated and right fed up."

Sykes consulted his notebook. "Miss Sechrest also used the term 'hangers-on'. She dislikes them, too. That's how she regarded Dougan, Lloyd and perhaps Billy Moffatt. Also, my tram driver dreams of a figure dressed in black. We always assume that if someone pushed Dougan it would have been a man. It could equally have been a woman."

I went back over Selina's suspicions. "Miss Fellini's real reason for calling on me was not to do with organising a flight. Anyone could have done that. She thought something bad would happen to yet another of her friends. She was right. First Billy dies, and then there's an attempt to gas Beryl. Whoever is responsible is wasting no time. Just suppose Selina is right, and someone is picking off her friends?"

We looked again at the list of names.

I saw that Mrs Sugden had cut out extra little oblongs of paper. "Mrs Sugden, will you please add a name, Jarrod Compton, Selina's husband."

328

She dipped the point of her pencil in the egg cup of water that had now turned blue. She printed Jarrod's name and placed it in the centre of the circle. "It's always the husband. He's done away with everyone close to her so that she gives up on her career and dons an apron."

"We can't rule him out. There's something seriously wrong with the poor man. He can be charming and polite and suddenly turn nasty. Part of him is aware of this and he tries to hide away. If it is Jarrod, it's not because he wants Selina back in the kitchen and bedroom. He's written a sort of musical play for her. He left the manuscript on her dressing table yesterday. His mother thinks it might be taken up in California and made into a moving picture."

Mrs Sugden was reluctant to give up on a theory. "He'll want to put on the performance in a church hall with her as the star and himself as master of ceremonies."

That was a possibility. "He is mentally unwell." I described his behaviour and how Selina had called on her brother for backup.

Looking at the names set out in a circle made me think of some Ouija game. Would we in a moment join hands and find ourselves dragged against our will to say snap on the guilty party?

Having eliminated the dead and added the maimed Jarrod, we now had nine names in the circle, with the Powolski twins boosting the number to ten.

Sandy Sechrest, memory woman
Maurice Montague, master of music

Pip Potter, strongman
Charles de Beauvoir, singer
Powolski twins, acrobats
Selina Fellini
Beryl Lister
Trotter Brockett
Jarrod Compton

"I think we should eliminate Maurice Montague. He wants shut of the whole business and has another job, though I'm not to say anything yet."

Mrs Sugden thought about the suggestion for a moment and then, acting as monitor of the strips of paper, removed Maurice.

Sykes nodded agreement. "Only it could be worth interviewing Maurice Montague again. Miss Sechrest saw him, Jarrod Compton and Billy Moffatt chatting to each other in the garden on the night of the party."

I made a note. "That's worth checking. I'll see if I can catch up with Mr Montague and ask him. Now, why don't we each pick a name?"

Having just entered Jarrod, I did not want to sway Mrs Sugden and Sykes towards him without having considered the others. "Let us leave Jarrod out of it for now, and come back to him."

Mrs Sugden agreed. "And it doesn't matter who we pick, but we have to come up with a reason."

Well why not? That's how close we were to finding out anything at all. "I'll pick Pip Potter. He is strong enough to push Mr Dougan under a tram and to drop a sandbag on Mr Lloyd accurately from a great height."

Sykes looked solemn. "Don't joke about it. Poor Alfie the tram driver dreams he saw a man in black push Douglas Dougan onto the tram tracks. Pip Potter could easily have donned a black cloak over his leopard skin."

Mrs Sugden intervened. "Well you can't pick him. He's Mrs Shackleton's choice."

"I am not choosing him. I know nothing about the man, but I don't believe a strongman would resort to those methods." Sykes picked up the Charles de Beauvoir slip of paper.

"Why him?" I asked.

"Because he's French and he's a phony charmer."

"Oh, you mean Rosie liked him."

Mrs Sugden waited for silence. "You two aren't taking this seriously." She picked up Sandy Sechrest's name.

We waited for an explanation. She waited to be asked.

Sykes remained silent. It was up to me to prompt. "Go on, then, Mrs Sugden, tell us why."

"She wears black. She could have been the figure the tram driver saw and she is in a permanent state of mourning." She broke her own rule of one suspect and chose another name. "This is my second choice, Trotter Brockett."

Sykes objected. "As their manager, he's hardly likely to do away with his performers."

"He was the one who put the kibosh on the plan that half a dozen performers might go on the wireless and do a variety show." She made a row of our suspects, in alphabetical order of surname.

Trotter Brockett
Charles de Beauvoir
Pip Potter
Sandy Sechrest

"Mr Trotter told Floyd Lloyd that taking part in a wireless programme wasn't practical because of the touring, and their contracts didn't permit."

Sykes came to Brockett's defence. "Well perhaps it wasn't practical. If the performers are touring the country, they may not be able to pop back to a recording studio every week."

I picked up my pen. "Tell us a little more about the visit to Mrs Lloyd. From what you say she was quite forthcoming, and knew a bit about her husband's work."

Mrs Sugden gave an account of Mrs Lloyd and her granddaughter folding and packing stockings, and of their house, the colour of the curtains, and the buns Mrs Lloyd brought back from the bakers. "But do you know who had the most to say?"

"Go on," I encouraged.

"That little dummy, Manny Piccolo. He's a bonny little chap with plump cheeks and bright eyes. The granddaughter, Lorna, she has the workings of him off to a T."

Mr Sykes intervened. "So it wasn't actually the dummy having the most to say, it was Lorna."

"That's what you might think, but he was so lifelike, and with his own voice, as if he really knew something."

"Anything important?" I asked.

"There you have me. The grandmother was a little unnerved by it. She made the child take it upstairs."

There was silence around the table as we pondered the quandary of how best to interview a ventriloquist's dummy.

Sykes tapped his fingers on the table. "So the child knows something. Either she doesn't want to say outright, or she is unaware of the significance of what she knows."

"It could be nothing," Mrs Sugden conceded. "But she's an odd girl. If you met her, you'd think she was lacking in some department but when she sits that dummy on her lap, it's all change at the terminus."

A little spark of possibility lit the proceedings. "I'll follow this up, Mrs Sugden. Perhaps we can arrange some sort of private audition with young Miss Lloyd."

We agreed to make a second choice of suspect. This time, I picked up Jarrod Compton's name. "I don't have strong reasons such as knowing he was in the right place at the right time. But he is the one who seems to come and go at will, and have a knack for not being seen. All the victims, if it was murder in each case, were close to Selina. He would be a saint not to be jealous and he is unstable. I hope he may be taken for treatment before Inspector Wallis gets around to arresting him."

The lack of questions or discussion from my two assistants gave me a sinking feeling in the pit of my stomach. I wanted them to argue against Jarrod Compton. They did not.

The thing nearest to an objection came from Sykes. He considered the list. "Sandy Sechrest didn't mention Jarrod Compton, and I'm thinking of her as a little bit of an oracle." Very reluctantly, Sykes picked up Sandy Sechrest's name. "She dresses in black. She dislikes hangers-on. Her intelligence makes her remote and unemotional. Miss Sechrest has a great deal of sympathy for Miss Fellini and might consider that she was doing her a favour by ridding her of needy courtiers."

Something was troubling me and it was not just that Inspector Wallis had demanded my attendance. "Billy is different from Douglas Dougan and Floyd Lloyd. They were clinging on in the entertainment business. They may not have survived in the theatre without Selina's patronage. Billy was a star. Not quite in Selina's league, but up there all the same."

We thought about it for a moment. Sykes said, "Is there any possibility that Billy Moffatt wasn't the intended victim?"

"I hadn't thought of that." Perhaps because Jarrod was one of my suspects, and that in spite of her denial it seemed probable that Selina was having an affair with Billy. "But how could we know that?"

Mrs Sugden came in sharply. "This play that Mr Brockett planned, was Billy to be part of that?"

"He was."

It had stopped me in my tracks to think that Billy might have smoked a cigar intended for someone else.

Mrs Sugden looked at her carefully written names. "Well I'm sorry but I can't pick anyone else, other than the two dancers and Mr Brockett. You've all seen the show. I haven't seen them in action, otherwise I might have developed a feeling for which performer could be guilty."

"Here's something else to add to the mix relating to Jarrod Compton." Sykes opened his notebook again. "When Mr Trotter Brockett was entertaining us in the bar before the show, he said something about a musical play. I made a note afterwards of anything pertinent in his prattling. Here it is. *Secret — a musical show specially written for Miss F.* Now might the written material the husband put on her dressing table be the play script for Trotter Brockett's musical show? He and Jarrod Compton have cooked up the plan together."

"I ought to be able to check on that with my new friend, Mrs Compton, Jarrod's mother. She told me that Jarrod was writing a moving picture. Her younger son produces pictures in California and I believe it is intended for him. But I don't see why it shouldn't be a London stage show as well. Don't leave me out of any information while I make a telephone call."

"Just a minute!" Sykes called me back. "Why would a singer be making a moving picture?"

"Not many people know this but apparently the moving picture people will soon be able to add sound to their productions."

Leaving them with this astounding piece of information, I went into the hall and picked up the telephone. Mrs Compton had said she would go to the theatre, grill Harry again, and find out whether Trotter Brockett had the latest news on Beryl.

Harry answered the stage door telephone. When I asked to speak to Mrs Compton, he went to find her.

After a wait of several minutes, she picked up. It was best to come straight to the point.

"Sorry to interrupt you, Mrs Compton, but will you please find out if the musical show that Trotter Brockett plans for Selina to tour is the same show that Jarrod wrote and put on her dressing table yesterday."

There was a pause in which I could hear her thinking of several questions. Fortunately she did not ask them. "Very well."

"And telephone me, no matter how late?"

"I will."

"If I'm not here, will you please leave a message with Mrs Sugden?"

"Where will you be?" There was a note of urgency in her voice, making me wonder what fresh horrors she might expect.

"Probably here, but just in case." She did not need to know that Inspector Wallis had demanded a statement from me. "Oh, and just one more thing. Why would Mr Brockett want to keep his plan for Selina's new show secret?"

"Commercial confidentiality," she snapped back. There was a pause when I thought she had gone but I soon realised that she must have been thinking of answering in a way that would make sense to me but not to whoever might be listening. "The only other reason would be that if there were not parts for certain persons then the principal may express a reluctance to step up without them."

"Thank you."

She ended the call with a "Must dash."

When I went back into the dining room, my companions were staring somewhat glumly at the names on the table. I reported the conversation.

"Mrs Compton, Jarrod's mother, says that she'll let me know whether Jarrod's play script is the same as Trotter Brockett mentioned. What she said last is interesting, too. She believes that Selina may not do the play if there aren't parts for her friends." I sat down again. "Her friends are important to her."

Mrs Sugden looked disbelieving. "That's the kind of thing a kid would say. Anyroad, there won't be many of her friends left at this rate."

Sykes looked again at his notebook. "You picked Jarrod Compton and he's a good choice, being the spouse, but you mentioned he lives in Bridlington. Do we know whether Compton might have been in Sunderland and York on the fateful days?"

"I don't know, but he owns a motorcycle so he's capable of travelling about."

"What kind?" Sykes asked.

I had started him off again. He would like to own a motorcycle but won't bear the extravagance because he has the 1913 Jowett motorcar. "It's a Scott Flying Squirrel."

Sykes let out a breath of envy. Such a motorcycle would be out of his price range, unless we achieved some wondrous reward for catching a gang of international diamond thieves.

For several moments we talked in circles. Sykes volunteered to make a pot of tea, just for the diversion of moving about. Mrs Sugden rearranged her list of names and once more studied her circle of dancers.

The telephone rang.

I went to answer, expecting that it would be Mrs Compton. As I picked up the receiver, I suddenly hoped it might be my mother. I would tell her that I was on a case but that if I did manage to come for Sunday dinner, I would be bringing Harriet.

The call was for Sykes, from one of his insurance companies. I called him into the hall and closed the dining room door behind me so that Mrs Sugden and I could go on talking without disturbing him.

Moments later, when Sykes came back, he looked upset. "I did a man a good turn today and it may be that it's repaid me."

"What do you mean?"

"Alf, the tram driver I went to see, he was off work because he can't get over having knocked a man down and killed him. When one of his mates at the depot made a joke about how he was promoted for killing someone, that was the last drop of rain in his bucket of woe."

Mrs Sugden tutted. "People can be so mean. They just don't think."

"I took Alf to Jorvik Insurance Company on Goodramgate because I knew that the manager there was on the lookout for a good chap. Alf won't hear any trams along there. He'll have hours in a day when he'll be too caught up in new work to think about the

338

accident. Well it seems he got on with my contact and he might be having a fresh start soon. Of course he had to talk about why he needed a change. I hope he'll get out of the habit of going on and on about the past."

Sykes must be going soft in his middle age. There was a time when he would have said that the man needed to pull up his socks and grow a thicker skin. "In what way might you have done yourself a good turn?" I asked.

"You shouldn't tell lies. It only complicates things. I told a kind lie to Alf. I said that Douglas Dougan had a fatal disease and not long to live. Well he only communicated that confidential fact — or confidential non-fact — to the manager. Now my manager friend tells me there was an insurance policy claim on Mr Dougan's life and there'd been no mention of a fatal disease on the application form."

Mrs Sugden obviously didn't get the point and for a moment neither did I. She said, "Well, there wouldn't be, would there?"

"No, because I invented the fatal disease. Now I have to either own up to telling a porky or pretend I was misinformed."

Sykes prides himself on his insurance work and I could see that he was seriously upset by this turn of events. He gave a groaning sigh. "I can't admit to making it up. That would be me chucking my integrity and probity out of a high window."

"You could say you were misinformed," I suggested.

"He wants me to look into it."

"Well then look into it. Selina was close to him. I could ask her. Who knows, the story of Douglas Dougan's fatal disease may turn out to be true. Stranger things have happened."

Not liking to be in the wrong, Sykes forced himself to look a little more cheerful. "Yes you're right. He doesn't know I made it up. This gives me another job. I'll do it gratis as a gesture of goodwill."

Mrs Sugden had forgotten her lists of suspects for the moment. She has recently taken on our bookkeeping and accounts. "Be careful about doing anything gratis. He might wonder why and smell a rat. Besides, it's not the manager's money, it's the insurance company's. They expect to pay a professional for his time and expertise."

Sykes agreed. "You're right, Mrs Sugden. I'll have to approach this carefully."

Mrs Sugden, momentarily flabbergasted at Sykes telling her she was right about something, was suddenly lost for words.

So were we all.

It was up to me to rally the troops.

"We all have tricky situations to deal with. You need to tread carefully regarding your insurance work. I have to give a statement to Inspector Wallis about the cigar. I could curse Ernest Brownlaw for not being straight with me."

"He has to comply with regulations and the law," Mr Sykes said. "He could lose his reputation and his licence."

"A nod or a wink would have done."

340

Mrs Sugden chose this moment to re-enter the conversation. "Manny Piccolo is good at nodding and winking. What do you think to the idea of me being the one to try and persuade the grandma to let Lorna and little Manny Piccolo make an appearance for us?"

"That's a very good idea, Mrs Sugden. And I'll see whether Maurice Montague might have any more information for us about his chat with Jarrod Compton and Billy Moffatt."

Sensing that both Sykes and I felt in need of encouragement, Mrs Sugden decided to look on the bright side. "Perhaps it isn't such a bad thing that Inspector Wallis wants to talk to you, Mrs Shackleton. He's the one who brought you the rubber plant. I'd say he has a soft spot for you."

"I sincerely hope not."

"If we find ourselves in a pickle we can call on the police. We have our work cut out with this case. There are just the three of us to investigate two deaths from the past, one from yesterday and a poor gassed woman who might be dead before the day is out."

Sykes blew out his cheeks and drummed his fingers on the table, a sure sign of irritation. "If Wallis is involved, we won't be able to make a move without him looking over our shoulder. He'll snuffle up everything we've learned and take credit."

Mrs Sugden did not like this idea one little bit. She is keen to make sure that the books balance and we stay well in the black. "If the police solve everything, will we still be paid?"

"Good question, Mrs Sugden. Be sure to deposit that cheque tomorrow."

I had earned it by walking through ghostly tunnels today.

When the telephone rang again, Mrs Sugden was making tea and buttering bread. Harriet had set off for the fish and chip shop to buy our supper. I picked up, expecting to hear Mrs Compton, but I was wrong.

"Hello, Mrs Shackleton. Trotter Brockett here."

"Hello, Mr Brockett."

"First of all, thank you for being such an all round brick. Selina might have gone to pieces without you."

"How is Selina?"

"Bearing up, missing Beryl terribly of course and the dratted infirmary won't give any information."

"I'm sorry to hear that. They do have their procedures and it's still quite soon. Perhaps by tomorrow . . .?"

"I certainly hope so. But my reason for telephoning at such a late hour, for which I apologise, is something Bunny asked me."

"Bunny?"

"Sorry. Mrs Compton. She tells me you were asking about Selina's future plans."

"That's right." I deliberately answered briefly, not knowing how Mrs Compton had phrased her question about whether the script Jarrod had delivered, in his inimitable fashion, and the show that Brockett had in mind were one and the same.

There was an amused edge to Brockett's voice. "I don't know what Jarrod has come up with this time. He writes perfect songs for her, but as to constructing a show, he doesn't have the know-how."

"I see, I just wondered."

"Of course you wondered. You wanted to see the full picture, and no doubt you have your own concerns over Jarrod, as we all do."

"So that wouldn't be the show you have in mind for her?"

"No, but what makes you ask?"

"Well, you did say to me that Selina needed good people around her and I love what she does and the shows you put on, so naturally I'm curious."

"Glad to hear it, Mrs Shackleton, and it would be a delight to have you with us for my star."

"Well thank you for telling me. I hope you'll hear news of Beryl soon."

There must be a good reason why the infirmary was withholding information about a patient. Someone was responsible for imposing that silence. I had a good inkling who that someone might be.

CHAPTER
THIRTY-ONE

Inspector Wallis

On Friday morning, on my way to the town centre, I stopped at the infirmary. Roundabout me, girls and women wore bright summer frocks in honour of the summer day. My dress and jacket was grey, piped with white. It could not be mistaken for mourning but with Billy dead and Beryl in I knew not what state, it seemed more appropriate than the tulip print dress I had taken out first thing this morning.

The board in the vestibule listed the patients' numbers. Next to each number, a single word described their condition. Not knowing a patient number for Beryl, I enquired from the porter behind the desk, giving her name and that she was brought in yesterday.

He consulted a list. His finger paused over a name that I could not see, and then he looked up. "Sorry, I have no information about that patient."

There was no point in my saying that yes he did, or his finger would not have stopped at her name. "Might you at least tell me whether she is alive? I was the person who found her."

344

"I'm sorry, madam. I have no information about that patient. If you tell me your name, I will let it be known you were asking about her."

Let it be known to whom, I wondered. "My name is Mrs Catherine Shackleton."

"Thank you."

"So, when might there be information?"

"I'm sorry, madam, that I can't say. Come and enquire later today, or tomorrow."

That was as much as I would get from him. The silence surrounding Beryl Lister's condition must be Inspector Wallis's doing. The only explanation I could think of was that he must suspect foul play, or self-harm. Poor Beryl. I prayed that she had recovered. Selina must be half mad with anxiety at not knowing. Perhaps I might pick up some hint at CID headquarters when I had gone through the humiliation of giving my statement regarding the episode of the poisoned, or not poisoned, cigar.

Inspector G. T. Wallis of Leeds CID is based in the Town Hall. On waking this morning I had made up my mind to avoid him and give the briefest possible statement to his sergeant or a constable. By the time I had climbed the broad staircase, I knew that if I wanted information about Beryl, he was the man to see. I knocked on his door.

"Come in!"

He must have been gazing out of the window because that's where he was standing, perhaps waiting for inspiration.

He gave a smile that reminded me of a short length of curled knicker elastic in the sewing box. "Take a seat, Mrs Shackleton."

I sat down. He sat down. I expected him to call for a constable, but he did not. Surely the great man was not going to write down my statement himself?

"I appreciated your quick thinking and speedy action in the Varieties yesterday."

"How is Mrs Lister?"

"Ah, so you weren't given information when you called at the infirmary just now."

"No."

It is a waste of time to dislike people. They are as they are and nothing can be done about it. Still, here was a person I disliked. In spite of Mrs Sugden's assertions to the contrary, I believed the feeling was mutual. At present, having his titbit of information about the cigar, he was in the ascendancy.

"What I tell you will be in confidence, Mrs Shackleton."

"Very well."

"Beryl Lister is under guard in a private room in the infirmary. As soon as she is able to talk to us she will be interviewed."

This was typical of him, to treat a patient as a suspect or criminal. At that moment, I didn't dislike him, I loathed him.

"How is she? Is she making a recovery?"

"I understand that the prognosis is good."

"Then why can't she speak?"

"Oh, she can speak, but she won't. Nor will she eat or drink."

"But that's terrible. What's gone wrong with the nursing that she is in such a state?"

"The nursing is exemplary. Thank you for your professional interest."

The man was not just annoying. He was totally exasperating. I decided to follow Beryl Lister's example and say nothing. I waited.

He waited.

I waited.

Eyeing up the big glass ashtray, I wondered whether anyone had been tempted to hit him with it and to watch the tab ends cascade over his slightly pointed head.

He gave in. "She has spoken only to ask if she may see Miss Selina Fellini."

"Then let her see Selina."

"She will see no one until she has given a statement."

"Or starved to death. I thought we had come beyond such treatment of prisoners?"

"She is not a prisoner."

"Oh, excuse me. That is what it sounds like."

He clasped his hands and leaned back in his chair. "We are protecting her for her own safety. Either she tried to commit suicide, or someone else is responsible for attempted murder. Even you must understand why she must not speak to anyone else before she gives a statement."

"Then she is afraid, and weak. What good will come of treating her like a criminal when someone attempted to kill her?"

347

"We cannot rule out the possibility of charging her with attempted suicide. She knows that."

"But that's ridiculous. Nobody sits down with a cup of tea to hem a dress and then turns on the gas."

He nodded. "I am inclined to agree with you, not least because you were the one who spotted the cup of tea when you removed Mrs Lister from the room. You were correct in guessing that the tea was disposed of in the glass vase. It had been laced with a powerful sedative that she might have tasted had the tea not been so sweet."

"So there is no question of suicide. Someone came in, disposed of the tea and removed the cup."

"People intent on taking their own life have been known to enlist assistance in that act."

"So what do you intend to do, and why are you confiding in me?"

"I am considering allowing Miss Fellini to visit Mrs Lister, but on one condition."

"And what is that condition?"

"I want you to accompany Miss Fellini, and tell me what passes between them."

I looked beyond him through the high window. The sky was grey with city smoke. "That would be a betrayal of trust."

"Yes, and it might help us find a murderer, or an accomplice in the act of attempted suicide."

"I came in here expecting to give you a statement about the cigar."

"Ah yes, the cigar." He lit a cigarette. "Tell me about the cigar. Don't hurry. Mrs Lister has only been

348

refusing food and drink for about sixteen hours. No harm will come to her. Yet. I suppose there is always a possibility that the guilty party might bribe a hospital nurse or porter to find out what room she is in, and to look for an opportune moment to pay a visit. It has been known. But do tell me about the cigar."

"You don't want to know, do you? Yesterday you asked me for a statement."

He picked up a smooth shiny pebble that doubled as a paperweight. "Orders came from on high to make the day of the eclipse as great a success as possible. There is justifiable pride and celebration of the orderly way in which the public conducted themselves." He straightened the papers on his desk and looked down at the first page. "Ten thousand people arrived by train. There were two thousand five hundred cars and one hundred and fifteen coaches. Eleven thousand two hundred and forty people paid for admission to viewing areas. There was not a single spot of trouble, no arrests. It was an entirely good-natured and good-humoured affair, policed by just one hundred constables. The towns and villages are now back to normal, having prospered from the event. It is an example of everything that is good about this country."

He waited. I said nothing, but a sinking feeling in my stomach told me where this was leading.

He continued. "This is not just a triumph for the country. It shows the world what we in Yorkshire can achieve. The Astronomer Royal, the national press, newsreel people, the broadcasters, members of Parliament. The prime minister himself said that it was the most magnificent and moving spectacle he has ever seen. That is the story."

"That is true, but it was somewhat overshadowed for me by Billy Moffatt's death."

"Quite. I understand." He picked up another piece of paper. "I have the post mortem results on Mr Moffatt." He looked at the paper. "There was evidence of narcotics in his blood but not sufficient to have caused death. In layman's terms, it was believed that he had consistently taken narcotics over a very long period, probably since his return from the Front. Finally that habit caught up with him. You might say he was a casualty of war."

We sat in silence for a moment.

I had come here dreading making a statement regarding the cigar, and my suspicion that Billy had been poisoned. It seemed so unlikely and also unprovable. Now, here was Inspector Wallis telling me that he did not want me to make my statement because it would take the gloss off a successful day in the British calendar for 1927.

He should not have done that.

I do not care about glossy days on the calendar of history if that gloss hides the truth of a dastardly deed.

"Inspector Wallis, I have reason to believe that Billy Moffatt was poisoned and that the method of poisoning was a cigar injected with cyanide. I do not know how he came by the cigar, but I do have a witness who conducted a test and came up with a positive result, as I told you yesterday."

"I see." He sighed. "Tell me again, who is this witness?"

"His name is Alex McGregor, head boy of Giggleswick School. I persuaded him to go into the school lab and conduct a test."

"It won't stand up."

"Perhaps Alex McGregor's evidence would not but Mr Brownlaw's would. You have not told me what Ernest Brownlaw's analysis revealed."

"You realise that young Mr McGregor could be expelled?"

"You'd see to that, would you?"

"Of course not. I have no jurisdiction in that area. The time for calling in Scotland Yard without charge to the local force has passed. Inspector Huddleston is a man whom we all regard highly but he has no experience in handling a murder enquiry, particularly one where there is no evidence and the post mortem points to a contrary finding."

"So if Billy Moffatt was murdered, the perpetrator will go unpunished?"

"I couldn't comment on a hypothetical situation. Since Mr Moffatt was such an imbiber of substances, it is possible that there was something in the cigar — put there by himself."

"That is not a hypothetical situation, Inspector. Can you comment on Ernest Brownlaw's findings?"

"We have our own scientists who conduct such tests. Mr Brownlaw merely did his duty in reporting your request."

"Then what can you do, Inspector?"

"I can try and discover what transpired yesterday in the dressing room at the City Varieties. Information about that may well link to the sad death of William Moffatt."

"So do you want my statement regarding Billy, or not?"

He smiled, slightly. "Of course. I shall have what you've told me typed and ready for your signature, and then I shall file it, for possible future reference. Now, what do you say to my suggestion that you and Miss Fellini visit Beryl Lister?"

CHAPTER
THIRTY-TWO

The Flying Remington

Selina would either have gone to her own light and airy house near Roundhay Park, or stayed at Gledhow Lodge to keep an eye on Jarrod. I took the chance that she would have gone to Gledhow.

Mrs Compton answered the door herself. She seemed pleased to see me. "I've given the girl a few days off," she explained. "I don't want her telling tales about Jarrod and his odd ways. I put a note through her door saying I felt a bad head coming on."

I stepped into the hall. Marco was talking on the telephone. Not that I was listening but I heard the words delivery, and ice cream.

From upstairs came the tap tap of a typewriter. "Is that Jarrod?" I asked.

Mrs Compton smiled. "He is busy typing his moving picture script and songs."

Marco finished his telephone call. He began to tell me the story of the Buster Keaton picture they all went to see last night. Mrs Compton, who had not seen the picture but heard the story, hurried his tale along by jumping in with shortcuts until Marco gave up and went into the drawing room.

"He's using that room as an office." Mrs Compton led the way into the garden, saying that one of her rose bushes had come into bloom that morning. "It's a hive of activity here today, just like the old days when my Reginald was alive."

We paid homage to the new roses and then sat on the bench under the kitchen window.

"Is Selina here, Mrs Compton?"

"Yes. She stayed the night. She's sleeping. I'll give Selina her due. She's not prepared to give up on Jarrod, though she must realise he would be happier here, in familiar surroundings."

I passed on the information that Beryl had recovered.

"Thank God you've had news. I telephoned the infirmary but of course they hate that. Told me the information would be on the board or in the paper. The man I spoke to didn't have a hospital number for me. It was most frustrating."

"They have Beryl under police watch, until she has made a statement."

"That's good."

"It would be, except that she refuses to speak to anyone but Selina. She won't eat or drink until she sees her."

"Why not?"

"I could make a guess, but I won't. I'm allowed to accompany Selina."

"Then I'll wake her now." She stood, and then paused. "You think Beryl won't speak because she will incriminate someone?"

354

"That is a possibility."

"Jarrod wouldn't have harmed her. He must have been with us in the cellar when the accident happened. And he was here when we got back from the Verts."

"Yes he was." That was true, but of course he would have had time to come back to Gledhow Lodge on his motorcycle. She knew that. "Let us hear what Beryl has to say."

"She might be confused after her ordeal."

"We won't know until we speak to her. Please wake Selina, Mrs Compton. Shall I do a slice of toast and a cup of tea?"

"Yes, if you don't mind."

We went back into the house. In the kitchen, I put a light under the kettle. Fortunately, Mrs Compton possessed a double-sided pop-up toaster so it would not take long to provide Selina with a bite to eat before we left the house.

Marco came in to talk to me, and to continue his praise of Buster Keaton and his scene by scene account of *The General*. He took over supervision of the toaster while I made tea.

"How is Jarrod now?" I asked, when Marco paused for breath.

"When he types, he is calm."

"Is this the script and the songs that he left for Selina at the theatre?"

"I don't know, but Selina thinks it very good."

Mrs Compton came back into the kitchen. "Selina will be down shortly. She's very relieved to hear Beryl wants to see her."

She might be less than delighted when she learned that I was under orders to report back to Inspector Wallis.

Marco put the toast and tea on a tray. "Make way, ladies! Let me give my sister her breakfast."

Thus dismissed, Mrs Compton and I went back into the garden.

We sat down on the bench by the window.

"Did Trotter speak to you about your question?" she asked.

"Yes. He telephoned me after we spoke last night." I avoided telling her that Mr Brockett had shown little enthusiasm for Jarrod's moving picture plan. "He told me about his plan for a stage show, for Selina."

"It sounds tremendously exciting. Did he say much about it?"

"No."

"Keep this under your hat, but it's a lush romantic musical being written by an American composer, Milton Ager. It's to be called *Happy Days*."

"Wouldn't that get in the way of Jarrod's plan to have a moving picture?"

"Not at all! If Selina has a big success in the West End, she will be taken far more seriously by the moving picture men."

At that moment there was a crash, so sudden that it was difficult to know where it came from, until a typewriter came flying through an upstairs window. Fortuitously, the window was open, and we were close enough to the house to be out of the typewriter's trajectory.

356

Jarrod's calm had not lasted. Fortunately the machine landed on a flowerbed, softening its fall but causing destruction to a blazing crowd of marigolds.

Mrs Compton stared at the typewriter, which still held a sheet of paper. "It was my husband's. Jarrod will be very sorry when he's himself again."

I made a move to go back in the house. Mrs Compton put a hand on my arm. "Let Marco and Selina deal with it."

"What about the doctors, did Selina make any further contact?"

"Yes. I'm forgetting what day it is."

"It's Friday."

"Jarrod is to go to London tomorrow, Saturday, with your airmen. Marco will go with him. The plane will set off from Soldiers Field. I don't know where they'll land in London but a car is booked to take Jarrod directly to the Maudsley Hospital."

"What about Selina?"

"Marco persuaded her to keep her engagements, the Saturday matinée and evening performance. She will follow on Sunday."

Sunday loomed a vast distance off. Anything might happen between now and then, or between now and Saturday if Inspector Wallis became suspicious about Jarrod. We walked slowly towards the dead typewriter and looked down at it, nestling among broken stems and petals. It would be too heavy to lift. Mrs Compton said quietly, "Do the police know Jarrod is here?"

"I don't believe so."

"Then it may be better if he were not here."

"I'm inclined to agree, Mrs Compton. Marco and Selina will have their hands full, so shall we pick up the typewriter between us?"

"I don't see that we'll manage."

"If you fetch a tablecloth, we can roll it onto that and pick it up by holding either side of the cloth."

"I'll do that." She went inside.

If the police did come, a dent in the marigolds could be accounted for by an animal having made its bed there. A lame Remington would be less easy to explain.

A medley of voices floated into the garden, deep and calm from Marco, gentle and reassuring from Selina, distraught and angry from Jarrod.

Mrs Compton returned with a damask tablecloth in maroon. We set about recovering the typewriter and between us carried it into the house. As we were about to place it on the kitchen table, Mrs Compton let go, leaving me to bear its weight as she pressed her fingers to her temples. "How will we survive the weekend? And will any doctor be able to help my poor son?"

I unrolled a sheet of paper from the machine. There were five typed verses of a song and under that "THE END".

Marco came to help. After Mrs Compton had brushed petals and soil from the platen and keys, he took the machine from us. Carrying it like some holy relic, he placed it in the cupboard under the stairs.

Mrs Compton covered it with the tablecloth.

"A good typewriter mechanic will have it back in working order in no time," I said, attempting to be encouraging.

Marco said, "Selina is weeping."

"She would!" Mrs Compton went towards the stairs.

"Wait!" I stopped her by the banister. If I were Selina, I would be weeping. "You didn't finish telling me about Jarrod's plans for what he has been typing. We should make sure he doesn't destroy the manuscript."

"I told you my younger son Rodney works in the moving picture business in California. Their plan has been that Jarrod will write, Selina will star, and Rodney will produce and direct."

"What does Selina say?"

"What mothers tell their children. She says, 'Wait and see'." Mrs Compton reached the bottom stair, but turned back. "If Jarrod goes on like this, he'll end up mad or dead or behind bars."

Marco patted her shoulder. "It's all right, we will take him to the Gaumont. That will calm his nerves."

"The Gaumont won't be open."

"It will if I ask. We supply their ice cream. We might see Charlie Chaplin. Last time I went we saw two very interesting little extra pictures describing how to get the best from your hens and another about growing big marrows. Jarrod will be soothed."

I marvelled at his confidence in the therapeutic power of flickering images. Did that really work, or was Marco adding a powder to the ice cream he supplied?

Mrs Compton continued walking up the stairs. Halfway, she stopped. "Why am I climbing the stairs? What use am I to him or her, to anyone?"

Selina emerged from the landing, tying her satin robe. "Is the kettle on?"

Mrs Compton glared at her. "Is that all you can say?"

"What do you expect me to say?" She began to walk down. "If we're going to pass on the stairs, you better say bread and I'll say butter. I don't want more bad things happening."

They passed on the stairs.

"Bloody bread."

"Bloodier butter."

CHAPTER
THIRTY-THREE

The Insurance Question

Jim Sykes had been undertaking investigations for Mr Hector Travis of Jorvick Insurance for several years now. Their relationship was cordial. Mr Travis, lord of all he surveyed in the small, stuffy upstairs office on Goodramgate, brought a file from the army issue green metal cabinet. He sat down and straightened his spectacles, which had a habit of slipping down his nose.

Sykes knew him well enough to be aware that Mr Travis liked the line of least resistance, or any course of action which would not require too much effort on his part. Nevertheless, he was a stickler for detail and correctness. Sykes saw that he was not yet ready to open the file on the insurance claim on Douglas Dougan's life.

"I appreciate your bringing Alfred Packer to my attention. He will suit me very well. His references from the tram company are impeccable."

"I'm glad. He's a good man and needs a change. I'm sure he will learn a lot from you, Mr Travis."

Travis now opened the file and looked down, tracing a nicotine stained finger along the print. "I hardly need to look. Douglas Dougan's case was a big news item locally. I dealt with it myself."

Sykes was good at reading upside down. Mr Travis knew this. Sykes saw that the payment, while not substantial, was a respectable figure, and that the beneficiary was Trotter Brockett.

There was nothing unusual about this. Mr Brockett had a financial interest in his performers. In the event of death preventing a performer from fulfilling his contractual obligations, it was only to be expected that the manager would arrange to be compensated.

When he had glanced through the paperwork, Mr Travis looked up. "Not a word about a pre-existing condition when the policy was taken out. Now if Mr Dougan did indeed have a fatal disease and if such a disease was contracted after the commencement of the policy, then there is nothing to investigate. It should have been reported, of course. If, however, the proposer knew of the condition when the policy was taken out, that is a different matter, even though the disease was not the cause of death."

"Yes, as you say, it bears examination."

"The information you had regarding the condition, was it reliable?"

The answer: No, it was invented by me on the spur of the moment, would not do.

"It came from one of Dougan's fellow performers."

"I see. And did that person indicate the nature of the disease?"

Keep it simple, Sykes told himself. "If so, that was out of my hearing. I will make enquiries and if possible trace Mr Dougan's medical records."

Sykes liked the idea of that. Given that Mr Dougan and his dogs travelled the country, in all likelihood there would be no medical records.

"Thank you, Mr Sykes, and for coming so promptly. I thought at the time there was something not quite right about this death, but of course the coroner's word set a seal on the matter."

They shook hands.

As Sykes descended the rickety wooden staircase, a strange thing happened. Fleetingly, he caught sight of a figure in a black cape at the foot of the stairs, only there was no one there.

He gave himself a little shake. That's what comes of mixing with people who have too much imagination and not enough sense.

CHAPTER
THIRTY-FOUR

Beryl's Story

We were sitting in the Jowett, ready to set off for the infirmary. I waited until Selina had fastened her silk head-scarf, the only brightness about her. She wore a costume of midnight blue and slate grey. "Something puzzles me, Selina."

"What's that?"

"You have both Mr Brockett and Jarrod believing you will do either a play or a moving picture."

"Yes."

"Can you do both?"

"I don't see why not, but not at present."

"Why is that?" I started the motor.

"What would become of everyone else in the company next season? There'd be no place for them in Trotter's play, and certainly not in Jarrod's picture."

"Alternative work?"

"Perhaps."

"And is Jarrod's story for the pictures workable?"

"Why wouldn't it be?"

"No reason."

"Jarrod says we could all move to California, including Reggie. I am never sure whether it is Jarrod or his mania that speaks to me. He even has a singer in mind to be my co-star, and this singer, Al somebody or other, will be singing in a picture before the year is out."

"That'll be exciting. I suppose it could catch on. What would happen to your friends in variety then?"

She sighed. "That's the trouble. I don't know. There's always the end of the pier."

"Would Mr Brockett still be your manager?"

"That's a good question."

A uniformed police constable gave us a nod and opened the door of Beryl's private room in the infirmary.

I closed it behind us. It was a little box of a space and must have been partitioned because it shared only a narrow portion of the tall window.

Beryl lay back on her pillows, eyes closed.

Two spindly chairs had been brought in. Selina took one, near the head of the bed. I sat in the other, watching as Selina took Beryl's hand.

"Nah then, daft lass, what ails thee?"

Beryl opened her eyes. "You took your time." She looked at me. "What's yon doing here?"

"I'm here to tell the police what you need to say to Selina that you won't say to them."

"And will you?"

I indicated the door, and that someone may be listening. "Of course. I'm obliged to."

She looked back to Selina, mouthing. "Will she?"

Selina said, "I'm afraid she must." She shook her head and mouthed, "She better not. I've given her a cheque for two hundred quid."

It was the wrong moment to think this, but I wondered what an American audience would make of Selina in the talking pictures.

Selina helped prop up Beryl. I poured a glass of water.

Beryl took a sip. "I have to talk to you on your own, Selina."

"Someone gave you a cup of tea, Beryl, who was it?"

"Perhaps I gave it to myself, only whatever was in that cup knocked me out."

"Kate's on our side. She's helped me arrange for Jarrod to see a doctor in London."

"Good."

"So who was it?"

"I'm naming no names and then there'll be no telling of tales."

I scribbled a few lines in my notebook and handed it to her: *Was it someone who has a doctor's appointment in London?*

Beryl looked at her fingers on the counterpane as if they belonged to someone else. "I'm not saying." And then she nodded, adding, "Why would a person do that?"

I went to look through the glass in the door. The policeman on duty was not listening. He was talking to one of the nurses. Either he was in dereliction of his duty, or Inspector Wallis trusted me.

"It's all right," I said. "You can speak."

366

Beryl waited until Selina gave her the nod. "Jarrod popped in, wanting to know had you read his script. I told him you had, and that so had I. He wanted it back, to type it. I gave him it. He went off and then he came with a cup of tea."

Selina lowered her head. "Will you eat and drink now you've told me?"

Beryl nodded. "I vaguely remember thinking to myself, that's one for the books."

Selina frowned, and waited.

When Beryl showed no signs of continuing, I asked, "What do you mean, one for the books?"

"Well Jarrod had what he wanted, and off he went to do his typing, and he's never in his life made me a cup of tea, and besides that . . ."

"What?" Selina asked.

Beryl took another sip of water. "I'm trying to think, I'm trying to think what it was that struck me."

Eventually, she said, "I know what it was."

"Go on." Selina leaned forward.

"Am I going home with you?"

"They'll want to make sure you're well enough to leave."

"I'll be well enough when I get out of here."

Selina showed signs of impatience.

I edged closer. "Beryl, you've had an ordeal. Take your time, but what thought came to you after Jarrod brought you the cup of tea?"

She stared at the window, and then closed her eyes for a moment. "Jarrod doesn't know I like two and a half sugars. It's not the kind of thing he takes notice of. The tea was sweet."

"Was that it?"

"No, there was something else." She put down the glass of water. "He didn't have time to make a cup of tea. He went out with that scrunched up script of his and then he came back with a cup and saucer, almost straightaway. Someone must have put the cup in his hand."

We sat, contemplating the white walls and the high window. Here was a case that turned on the crucial point of who made a cup of tea with the correct amount of sugar.

I took a slip of paper from my notebook. "I'm going to write a name on here, fold it over and pass it on. It's my guess regarding who poured the tea, and I want each of you to do the same." With my small silver pencil, I wrote a name, folded the paper, and passed it to Selina.

Beryl glared at me. "Mrs Kelly makes the tea. She takes it round."

"So did Mrs Kelly hand the tea to Jarrod to pass to you?"

Beryl thought for a moment. "No."

"How can you be sure?"

"She's chesty. I would have heard her wheezing, and she would have no reason to come along that corridor because she didn't know I was in."

Selina wrote a name.

Beryl's handwriting was a little shaky, mine block-printed, Selina's a scrawl.

The same name appeared twice.

Selina and I had written, *Trotter Brockett*. Selina said, "I didn't see it until now. It's to do with having me do what he wants. Jarrod would get in the way."

Beryl had written, *Mrs Kelly*.

Beryl shook her head when we showed her Trotter's name. "He doesn't make tea either. Have you ever known him lift a finger in that direction?"

"No he doesn't, but he takes two and a half sugars, same as you, when we can get it."

Selina handed me back the silver pencil.

We called at the Varieties to question Harry, but Harry had slipped out on an errand.

This information came from an elderly woman, tiny and wizened. Selina introduced her as Mrs Kelly.

Moving slowly, Mrs Kelly squeezed out her mop. She paused in her mopping to sit on the stage door bench next to Selina. "How is our Miss Lister?"

Before Selina had time to tell the truth, I said, "We're still waiting to hear. Perhaps there'll be news later today. Did you see her yesterday?"

"No. I didn't see her."

I sat down beside Selina and nudged her to ask Mrs Kelly who she saw yesterday.

"Anybody else come in from our company?" Selina asked.

"I saw young Adam Powolski. He mithers the stage hands about the safety of his high wires. I took tea tray round't offices. Give tea to Mr Waterhouse. He was going over the accounts with Mr Brockett. Miss Green, the cashier, was at her books. Oh, and Mr Harry Laycock was here at his desk."

Selina thanked her.

"You'll give my good wishes to Miss Lister?"

"I will. Mrs Kelly, did you make a cup of tea for my dresser yesterday, for anyone else to give to her?"

"I didn't know she was in. I poured another for Mr Brockett. He's fond of his tea. Came back for a second cup."

We thanked Mrs Kelly, and left the theatre.

Selina looked shaken. "I wrote his name because I didn't want to write Jarrod's name. But your inspector only asked you to find out who gave Beryl the tea, and that was Jarrod. What can we do?"

"Let's see what else we can discover. I want to talk to Maurice Montague. Do you know where he might be?"

"We'll go to Whitelock's," Selina announced. "Some of the chaps will be there."

"Good idea. We just need to keep on picking up little pieces of information until we can complete the jigsaw."

"We've barely enough to know what the picture is," Selina said, "much less complete a jigsaw. Even if we did, who might we convince besides ourselves? You saw Mrs Kelly. She is hard of hearing and with poor eyesight. She's kept on out of charity. Sometimes she doesn't remember what she did yesterday."

"I believe she knows what happens to her cups of tea. Brockett added something. When he saw Jarrod coming out of the dressing room with his script, he cleverly passed the tea to him."

"But why?"

370

"Which side would Beryl come down on if she had to advise you between taking up Brockett's stage show and Jarrod's picture script?"

"Well Jarrod's, naturally, but I could do both."

"Brockett won't see it that way."

CHAPTER
THIRTY-FIVE

Whitelock's

From Swan Street, we turned into Briggate.

I had never been to Whitelock's. It is a very old public house and has a reputation for attracting Bohemians, actors and journalists as well as local businessmen. "This is a good idea, Selina."

"I do have them occasionally."

"Let's hope Maurice Montague is there, and anyone else from the company who might have something to say."

"Of course I should warn you, ladies aren't allowed to go to the bar or sit in the men's area. I'll enlist the help of a waiter, or we could shout across the pub until we're ejected."

"Let's hope they will join us, wherever we are allowed to sit."

One could easily miss Turk's Head Yard, but Selina did not. Recognising Selina, the doorman escorted us to the ladies' area and waited until we were seated.

It was still early and there was a table free beside ours.

"Are any of the chaps from the Verts in?" Selina asked.

"I'll go take a look, Miss Fellini. Would you want them to join you?"

"I would indeed."

"Don't you mind the smoke floating across?" I asked.

"There's less smoke this end. Besides, for Jarrod, I'd risk my voice."

I looked about the place, glad of having come into this hidden citadel of chops and ale. It was a cosy spot, dimly lit but with a soft glow of warmth from the coloured leaded light windows and the gently glowing lamps.

The waiter came over, pad and pencil in hand. Selina consulted me and recommended steak and kidney pie and stout which she proceeded to order in a very definite manner. Heads did not turn but she drew many sidelong glances.

Moments later, master of music Maurice Montague, strongman Pip Potter and the suave Charles de Beauvoir came in single file towards us, each carrying a plate of food and a tankard.

With Selina, Maurice and I sitting on the bench and Charles and Pip Potter taking chairs, we fitted ourselves around one table.

"Thank you for joining us, gentlemen." Selina smiled winningly at the three men. "I hope you will be able to help. My friend Kate here is conducting an enquiry into the three deaths that we have suffered as a company and into the outrage of someone attempting to gas Beryl."

All three looked distinctly uncomfortable.

It was my turn. "First of all, my sympathies to all of you at such an upsetting time. I'm sorry for interrupting your dinner."

Simultaneously, they each put a forkful of food into their mouths, as if hoping I would direct my attention to the person who wasn't chewing.

I asked Maurice about the night of the party. "You were one of the last people to talk to Billy before we left for Giggleswick. This sounds an odd question, but do you remember what you talked about, you and Billy and Jarrod?"

"It was about future plans," Maurice said, giving me a meaningful stare to indicate that he had not yet revealed his own future plans to work in the Grand Pygmalion department store.

"What kind of plans?" Selina asked.

The waiter brought drinks for me and Selina.

"Why, you'll know this, Miss Fellini, but Billy talked of a stage show and Mr Compton about his plans for a moving picture. I thought there might be a bit of hard feeling as the moving picture plans didn't seem to include Billy. But there was no needle between them."

Selina had reached for her glass. She put it down again.

The strongman spoke next. "How did Billy die, Miss Fellini?"

She was unable to speak.

I answered for her. "We don't yet know. Natural causes I think."

"There! I told them so. They were linking it with the accidents to Dougie and Floyd." He uttered a derisory grunt. "I know a dozen ways to kill a man. None of them includes a tramcar or a sandbag."

374

Charles de Beauvoir shook his head sadly. "*Non*. Poor Billy. I liked him. I liked Dougie and Floyd too. As for your good companion Beryl, I am most fond of her. How is she?"

Selina simply shook her head.

Charles reached for Selina's hand. "You suspect foul play. I am a lover, not a fighter. I hate no man. I love all women."

Selina pushed his hand away. "Cut out your nonsense, Charles." She looked from one to another of them. "Were any of you in the theatre at all yesterday afternoon or early evening, even for the shortest time?"

Maurice put up his hand like a boy in a classroom. "I called into the theatre, an hour before the performance, just to make sure my instruments were in order. Beryl had already been taken to the infirmary by then. After that I came out for a quick pint."

The waiter brought our pies. I cut into the pie and realised that I was hungry. "Maurice, is there anything else you can tell us, about the other accidents, Dougie's or Floyd's?"

"No. My work is cut out for me. I care for twenty-nine instruments. There is always something to go wrong, some nasty railway worker intent on criminal damage, some nifty temporary stage hand with an eye on my ukulele. I don't have time to pay attention to other people."

"Let's go back to the night of the party. You seemed to be enjoying yourself there. Think carefully. Did you see anyone give Billy a cigar?"

"I did not."

Escorted by the doorman, she came up behind him like an avenging angel in her sweeping black dress. "That is not correct, Maurice. I saw you."

Maurice spluttered into his beer. He turned his head although he did not need to. Sandy Sechrest's voice was as distinctive as her appearance.

"Me? You saw me?" Maurice's voice came out like the squeak of an out of tune violin.

"Yes. You were under the trees and you handed Billy a cigar. He put it in his top pocket."

"Oh that, that cigar. I didn't want it. No use developing a taste for something you can't afford."

"Can't afford or won't afford," Pip Potter murmured. "He only smokes the Somebody Else's Fag brand."

The waiter approached and pulled out a chair for Sandy. Pip Potter and Charles de Beauvoir shuffled up to make room. Sandy sat down.

"Are you ready to order, madam?" the waiter asked.

Sandy ignored him. "I stayed silent too long. I should have known that when a former policeman asks a pointed question, there is a point to it."

Selina raised a finger to the waiter. "She'll have what we're having."

The waiter departed.

We all looked at Maurice. "I was staying under your roof, Selina. I wouldn't bring in a Woodbine, much less a cigar. Not after all the . . . I was going to say fuss, but you don't fuss, you just don't like smoke, do you?"

"It's not me that objects, Maurice. It's my throat. Now, where did you get that cigar?"

376

"I'm an unfortunate man. My luck has been bad, very bad. I thought Mr Brockett was tired of me and impatient. The writing was on the wall. But at the party he was kind. He said, anyone can have a bad patch, and he gave me the cigar." His eyes widened. "Is that what killed Billy?"

Slowly, Maurice looked from Selina, to me, to Sandy. Without anyone uttering another word, it dawned on the unfortunate man that he was Trotter Brockett's intended victim. His face grew pale. He pushed away his plate, rose from the table, and hurried towards the door.

He turned. "He won't find anyone else who plays twenty-nine and more instruments as well as I do."

The doorman bowed him out.

Remembering Mrs Sugden's warnings about the fragility of underappreciated performers, I turned to the strongman, who had fortunately finished eating. "Would you mind going after him, Mr Potter? He might do something desperate."

Pip Potter did not hesitate.

Selina smiled at Monsieur de Beauvoir. "Charles, be a darling and go after them. Pip will be able to pull Maurice from the river but he won't know how to talk to him."

He came to his feet on the instant, and bowed. "Now I understand Mr Trotter's reputation. He terminates no contracts, or not in the usual ways."

Sandy took the chair vacated by Pip Potter, sat erect and looked from Selina to me, waiting for one of us to ask the right question.

One always feels rather dense in the company of a person who knows both the answers and, often more difficult, the right questions. We now knew the answer to who killed Douglas Dougan, Floyd Lloyd and Billy Moffatt, and who almost killed Beryl; or thought we did. How would we prove that Trotter Brockett had done anything other than take good care of his performers?

I gave in first. "What is the question, Miss Sechrest?"

"How does everyone know where they were at the moment the armistice came into being?"

Selina answered. "Because of the time, the eleventh hour of the eleventh day of the eleventh month."

"But how did they know the precise moment? Not everyone has a clock."

My thoughts went back to that day. "A boom was sounded from the Town Hall."

"Correct, Mrs Shackleton."

"And all the church bells rang."

"Correct, Miss Fellini. Do you know where you were at that moment?"

"I do. I was with my mother-in-law. We both cried."

"Where were you, Mrs Shackleton?"

"I was walking in the little wood behind my house, picking up fallen twigs for kindling."

In the fashion of some professor with dim students, Miss Sechrest was giving us a hint as to what question we should ask. "What might be the connection to the Sunderland Empire and Douglas Dougan's death?"

Selina and I looked from one to the other. The tram driver might have known the exact moment of Mr

Dougan's death, because of his timetable. Anyone on the tram who looked at a watch would know.

Selina had another answer. "The dogs howled. All three of Dougie's dogs howled so loudly they were heard in the auditorium. Brandy, Biscuit and Snap."

It was a brilliant stroke of deduction from Miss Sechrest. Unfortunately, a year had gone by and anyone might change the history of where he or she was at that fateful moment when the three performing dogs told the world that they had lost their master.

The waiter approached. "Excuse me, ladies, but the gentlemen who were with you, they all left without paying their bills."

CHAPTER
THIRTY-SIX

A Confab in Park Square

Heads turned to look at Selina in her midnight blue and slate, the dramatically black-clad Sandy Sechrest and me in my grey with white piping as we walked up to Park Square on this day of bright summer frocks. Had there been a greater physical resemblance between us, people might have taken we three for undertaker's daughters. We sat on the grass in a spot of our own where we would not be overheard.

The Town Hall, abode of Inspector Wallis, was a few moments' walk away. "I'll have to tell him, Selina. Just try and keep Jarrod out of sight for now."

Selina nodded. "Marco will keep him safe. With a bit of luck, we'll have him on the aeroplane before he can be questioned."

"That might look suspicious."

"I don't care how it looks. You saw him, Kate, Jarrod is ill." She twisted the strand of hair that had escaped from her chignon. "We could be lucky. Harry or someone else might have seen Mrs Kelly give the tea to Trotter. Someone might have noticed him slip something in it."

That seemed highly unlikely but I did not want to dash her hopes.

Sandy brushed grass from her skirt. "I think we all know who it was, and why."

Selina stared at her. "The who, yes, but it's so hard to believe. He has always been such a thoughtful and caring manager."

"Selina, you see the good in people. I deal in facts. Mr Brockett no longer finds us profitable. You are the one who draws the crowds. You are the one who hesitates to leave her friends behind. He wants you to play London theatres and to tour musical plays. We are the drag, we support acts."

"That would be so callous."

Callous seemed to me too generous a word for a man with at least three murders to his name.

Sandy spoke quietly. "You are his shining star, Selina. The rest of us are the dim planets that only come into view when a watcher has stared at the night sky for a long time."

While I listened to the two of them, I wondered how might the urbane and confident Mr Brockett be shown up for what he had done. A plan, somewhat half-baked but nevertheless a plan, began to form in my mind.

"Does the arrangement for Jarrod to go to London tomorrow still stand?"

"Yes. Charlie and Joe will bring the aeroplane to Soldiers Field at around one o'clock."

"Will you assemble everyone at your house, Selina, at eleven-thirty on Saturday morning? Say you have invited them for a late breakfast or an early lunch."

"The promise of food would bring them in, but why?"

"Mr Brockett has no idea that we suspect him. We can surprise him, take him off-guard."

Sandy Sechrest looked doubtful but said nothing.

"I'd better go see Inspector Wallis. Wish me luck."

They walked with me to the Town Hall. We parted at the steps. "I'll talk to you both before the day is out, and it will be up to you to prime the others."

As I climbed the steps towards the offices of Leeds CID, I wondered what gave me the courage to speak with such confidence when I had only the merest inkling of how to proceed. And I could be wrong.

CHAPTER
THIRTY-SEVEN

Little Manny Piccolo Speaks

Whoever designed Selina's house had done a magnificent job. At 11.30 on Saturday, the great room was filled with sunlight. The doors to the veranda stood open. The large table was spread with cold cuts of meat, bread and butter, cheese and hard-boiled eggs. A large tea urn had been rustled up. The performers had arrived in good time, all looking their best.

Inspector Wallis came last. He and Sergeant Ashworth made themselves unobtrusive beyond the grand piano.

Selina welcomed them all. "We have our last performances in Leeds this afternoon and this evening. I know some of you will be catching the milk train to go home until Monday, so I wanted to put on a bit of a treat as a thank you for being such a great bunch and also to welcome back Beryl, after her ordeal."

Beryl smiled at the round of applause and calls of well wishing.

The stand-in comic who had taken Billy Moffatt's place spoke up. "Our tour ain't over yet, Miss Fellini, so thank you."

Adam Powolski whispered in my ear. "People do not like that he takes some of Billy's catchphrases and turns them for himself."

The inspector caught my eye. I went over to him as the performers began to help themselves to food. "What are you up to? You said Jarrod Compton would be here."

"He will, Inspector."

People perched on the sofas and chairs to eat, and wandered out onto the balcony. Mr Brockett preferred to be at the table. I joined him there.

He was his usual beatific self. "This is my Selina for you, largesse, feeding the multitude."

"She's very kind."

"Too kind for her own good. There'll be no changing her ways but when she is with an elite set of actors for a showcase of her own, things will be different."

"I'm sure they will."

Beryl, still pale but much recovered, took charge of the tea urn. She brought a cup for me and for Brockett. "Here you are, Mrs Shackleton, tea no sugar. Here you are, Trotter, tea with two and a half sugars. We always remember that because we take the same, don't we?"

"We do indeed, Beryl. Thank you."

Selina once more stepped up and stood in front of the piano. She clapped her hands. "I shall leave this announcement to Mrs Shackleton."

Maurice Montague, master of music, stepped up. He opened the piano and gave me a few introductory chords.

I took a deep breath. To perform in front of performers is rather daunting.

"Ladies and gentlemen, some of you may wonder whether Miss Fellini had another reason for inviting you here today, other than this being near the closing point of a very successful tour of northern theatres. You have Huddersfield, you have Halifax and then it will be time to disperse. There has been unease among you during the past year because of the unfortunate incidents concerning fellow performers. So much so that some of you have decided on a new course of action in the wake of this tour. Now is the time for your announcements."

Sandy Sechrest stood, looked around the company, and said, "For some time I have been assisting, by correspondence, Professor Meier at the University of Bern. He is conducting research into memory. I am to join his faculty in September. I will be taking up residence in Bern immediately after we close our show in Halifax."

There were congratulations, applause and cheers.

Sandy urged Maurice to his feet. He glanced about the room. "I know what you think of me. I'm a moaner, I'm a scrounger, but think on this, how would you like to cart about twenty-nine instruments, on and off trains, being thought nothing of a musician because you can play every one of them and more? Jack of all trades. Ha ha. Well I've had enough. I will finish out Huddersfield and Halifax but in the daytime you will find me playing the piano on the music floor of the Grand Pygmalion department store on Boar Lane. A proper job with proper hours and the possibility of tuning pianos in the evenings."

He returned to his seat between Charles de Beauvoir and Pip Potter who led the applause.

Babs Powolski jumped to her feet. "It's back to the circus for Adam and me. And don't look for Jake and his pony. Little Mr Pinto Pony does not like that rake stage. Jake now gives rides to children in the park. Sixpence."

Charles glanced suavely to Selina. "I too honour the Yorkshire commitments after which time I shall dance and sing my passage across the Atlantic, though open to offers."

Trotter Brockett came to his feet, looking at his watch. "Well. Well, well, well. Don't forget who makes up the wage packets." He smiled at his dancers. "I'm looking forward to visiting Blackpool and seeing my lovely Daisy Chain dancers, and good luck to Pip Potter as he takes up residence at the end of the pier in Bournemouth."

I interrupted him. "Please don't rush the proceedings. No one will be late for the matinée, Mr Brockett. And I'm pleased to say that you have a new generation of performers up and coming. May I present Miss Lorna Lloyd and her little chum, Manny Piccolo."

Mrs Sugden led the child to a spot where she had her back to the French windows. She sat on a chair that Jim Sykes had placed there earlier. Now Sykes came forward, providing a footstool so that her little legs did not dangle.

She spoke in a clear voice, showing just the slightest nervousness. "You all know Manny Piccolo, and you all knew my granddad, Floyd Lloyd. Well Manny Piccolo came to me and he thinks you might have questions for him. What do you say, Manny Piccolo?"

The doll straightened up and tilted its head. "Happy to be here, Miss Lloyd. I have a nice girlfriend you know. Give us a kiss."

"Not if you have a nice girlfriend, Manny, that wouldn't be right."

"Lots of things isn't right, Miss Lloyd. If things was right, Mr Floyd Lloyd would be sitting where you are now."

"Then why isn't he?"

"Murder, bloody murder!"

After a gasp of surprise, the quiet room became so utterly silent that I could hear the sound of the wind blowing through a beech tree beyond the veranda.

"What do you mean, murder?" Mrs Sugden had stayed close to the child's chair.

"Manny told me, didn't you, Manny?" The dummy nodded his head. Lorna spoke to everyone in the room, looking round at each of them, taking her time like a seasoned performer. It was the dummy who spoke. "Do you have any questions for me? I give advice to the lovelorn. I tell you what to do when a bill comes through the door."

"What do you do when a bill comes through the door?" Lorna asked.

"Chuck it on top of cupboard till you've coal enough to light fire."

There was an uneasy laugh from Maurice and from Pip Potter.

"Who was murdered?" Mrs Sugden asked.

The dummy looked up at Lorna. When his arm was raised in Lorna's direction, she operated him so smoothly that he appeared to act of his own accord. "Granddad Floyd was murdered, and he pleads to accuse." The dummy's hand moved around the room. "He is here."

"This is preposterous." Brockett spoke quietly but everyone heard him. He came towards Lorna. "This is in the worst of taste, Miss Lloyd."

Beryl stood between them. "Give the child a chance on her first public outing." She looked down at Lorna and the dummy. "Mr Manny Piccolo, are you able to tell us who is the murderer?"

The dummy had for the moment lost his voice. Its arm pointed towards Brockett.

"How do you know it is that gentleman?" Mrs Sugden asked.

The dummy's voice was high and clear. "My Floyd Lloyd, he knew too much. Look at what he said, look at what he wrote. Read the note that is tucked in my shirt."

Lorna brought out a sheet of paper from the dummy's breast.

Trotter stepped forward as if to bring an end to proceedings. He snatched at the piece of paper and began to tear it.

I spoke loudly, to make myself heard above the din of sudden conversation and alarmed comments. "Silence, everyone! Mr Brockett. Please stay where you are. We are here for a reason." I took the original note from my satchel.

Mrs Sugden had merged into the background. Following the example of Manny Piccolo, I pointed at her. "My good friend Mrs Sugden paid a visit to Mrs Lloyd and Lorna this week. Mrs Sugden was startled to hear the dummy that Lorna cherishes made an accusation of murder. We agreed that for all his qualities, Manny Piccolo is not a sentient being. Unless Lorna had an extraordinary and macabre imagination, she could not have come up with such a patter for Manny Piccolo.

"I went back with Mrs Sugden and found that Manny had a secret tucked to his breast. Let me read to you. Here's what Floyd Lloyd wrote, perhaps having sensed danger to come.

"He writes, 'I saw Mr Brockett follow Dougie out of the theatre. Mr Brockett told the police he was in my company when Douglas Dougan died. It is true that he was nearby when I was at the box office arranging a complimentary ticket for a friend. After that I did not see him. I cannot prove anything but if something happens to me, it will be because he knows I know. I should have said this to the police at the time: Mr Trotter Brockett was not with me or near me when the three dogs howled at the moment of Douglas Dougan's death.'"

I handed the note to Inspector Wallis.

Brockett was angry now. "This is ridiculous. Who put you up to this, child?"

Mrs Sugden squared up to him. "I think you should sit down."

Sandy Sechrest came to her feet. "Mr Brockett, you gave a cigar to Maurice on the night of the party."

"So I did. What of it? Have you all gone mad?"

Maurice snorted angrily. "I am mad. You intended that for me. You wanted my musical instruments, and you wanted rid of a person you think belongs in the ark. It's all Selina with you now, Selina and Billy it was to have been. Well I had no grudge against Billy. I liked him. I gave him the cigar that killed him because I thought he might want to be cheered up if the possibility of cloud forecast turned out to be wrong."

Before Brockett had time to respond, Selina said calmly, "It was to have been me and Billy in your show, Trotter, but not now. I'm bound for California with my husband, to make a moving picture."

Even the charge of murder had not shocked Trotter Brockett as much as this announcement.

"You can't. That's not possible. It's all arranged. If you go to America, the British public will turn its back on you."

"Oh, I'll be back, to do a show, only not your show, ever . . ."

"Don't say that!"

". . . and perhaps a home-grown moving picture. We shall have to keep up with our American cousins and our German friends. Jarrod and I have a lot to learn about the picture business."

As she spoke his name, Jarrod entered. Everyone turned to see the tall figure in black, with his scarred face and the white silk muffler draped around his neck.

Brockett shouted. "Call the police. Isn't he the one who gave you the cup of tea, Beryl?"

Jarrod spoke calmly. "What makes you say that, Trotter? Ah, of course, you know because you handed it to me."

I glanced at Inspector Wallis. He began to walk slowly across the room, Sergeant Ashworth beside him. Somewhere in the distance, I heard the whirr of an aeroplane.

Selina looked around the room. "Ladies and gentlemen, it was so good of you to come, but none of us want to be late for our matinée."

"You will never work again, any of you!" Brockett was taking steps backward towards the window. He pointed a finger at me. "Viper! You will not work for me!"

"True, Mr Brockett. I wonder who will."

A uniformed policeman put a hand on Brockett's shoulder, preventing him from turning round and running.

Brockett stared at us all in disbelief. "This slander can be cleared up. Anyone will see through this amateur performance."

He took a cigar from his pocket. The defeat in his eyes turned to triumph as he lit the cigar and inhaled deeply.

Nothing happened. He took the cigar out of his mouth, looked at it, returned it to his lips and inhaled again.

Sergeant Ashworth appeared beside him. "Come along, Mr Brockett."

Mrs Sugden came up close to Brockett. "Wrong cigar, Mr Trotter Brockett. That smoke won't deliver you from the justice of a trial." She waved a cigar. "I think this is the one you're looking for. I worked for a magician once. He was a bit of a pest, but he taught me the art of prestidigitation. The cigar you have just lit was an uncontaminated one, given to me by Inspector Wallis."

All the company walked to Soldiers Field to wave Jarrod off on the plane. Marco held his arm and perhaps Jarrod needed that support because the effort of the last few hours had been great. Selina kissed him goodbye. "I'll come and see you tomorrow. I'm having a mass said at the Cathedral. You, me and Reggie, we'll be all right, Jarrod. You'll come through. Have faith."

CHAPTER
THIRTY-EIGHT

Another Visitor

The de Havilland became a tiny speck on the horizon, taking Jarrod Compton to London, to meet the doctors who may be able to help him go on living without needing to hide underground or fasten himself in a garden shed.

Mrs Compton had arrived at Soldiers Field to wave her son goodbye. She and Selina walked back to the house together.

I drove Mrs Lloyd, Lorna and little Manny Piccolo home to Back Barrack Street. Mrs Lloyd let Lorna go into the house first. We exchanged a few words.

"Lorna did very well, Mrs Lloyd."

"She's a good girl with the dummy and I'm glad of that because she doesn't quite fit in with the normal ways of the world."

"I'm sure she will, given time."

"Maybe, maybe not. There's too much of her granddad in her. And it's been recognised."

"Recognised?"

"I went to the broadcasting building, and I got the chap there to listen to Lorna and Manny Piccolo. He's going to give her a little spot of her own on a radio programme for children."

"That's wonderful. Let me know when she is on. I'll urge everyone I know who has a wireless to listen, and those who don't I'll invite round. We can all write letters saying how good she is."

By the time I reached home, Mrs Sugden had been dropped off by Mr Sykes.

She still wore her coat. "I'm off round to see how Miss Merton is managing her garden party and how young Harriet is coping as a server."

"Let's hope she isn't practising jujitsu on the guests."

"Do you want to come?"

"I'll stay here. I'll telephone my mother and make arrangements to see her tomorrow." Some time soon I would also call Mary Jane, but that would be at a moment when I had gathered some reserves of patience. My sister would be wanting Harriet back as soon as Barbara May decided to return to her husband.

I made the call to my mother who was delighted that Harriet and I would come for Sunday dinner.

There is always a great sense of release when a case is over. Inspector Wallis would have the responsibility now, and Selina would be able to pursue her life and career without the shadow of Trotter Brockett.

I poured a glass of sherry and began to catch up with the newspapers. There was a piece quoting Charlie Chaplin's opinion of the plans for talking pictures. They would not catch on. I had not got very far into my pile of newspapers when there was a knock on the door. The mad thought occurred that Trotter Brockett had escaped from custody and come to take revenge. My nerve endings told me to look through the window first but my head ordered courage. I went to the door.

There stood Alex McGregor, giving me a big smile. "Hello! Bet you didn't expect to see me."

"No I didn't, Alex."

He was wearing khaki shorts, an open-neck shirt and a sweater tied by the sleeves around his waist. His bicycle was propped by the front gate.

"You've cycled from Giggleswick?"

"Yes, we're let out on Saturdays for good behaviour."

"Then you better come in." I took him through to the kitchen.

"I've brought lunch." He produced a packet of sandwiches. "It's cheese. Would you like one?"

Not having had the stomach for the fine spread Selina laid on, a doorstep-size cheese sandwich was just what I needed. I supplemented Alex's offerings with fruitcake, and poured him a glass of Dandelion and Burdock.

"I had to come, Mrs Shackleton. I'm burning with curiosity. What happened when you took the cigar to the chemist?"

"Good question. My friendly chemist did not contact me. The police did."

"So I was right!" In his excitement, he spluttered, and then put a hand to his mouth.

"Don't be too excited, Alex. The result was not confirmed or denied."

"How could that be? That is so wrong!"

"Did you have any repercussions at school?"

He chewed and swallowed before answering. "I was called into the head's study."

"What did he say?"

"This is the extraordinary thing. I have no idea what he said, even though I was there for ten minutes saying yes, sir and no, sir. I expected to be hauled over the coals but it was something between a dressing down and a pep talk. It was all 'the day's events', 'reputation', 'prime minister's standing', 'British values', 'need for discretion', 'doing the right thing'. There was no mention of the cigar, just 'that chapter is closed'. I feel so annoyed with myself for not knowing what to say and for not having the spunk to ask him to speak plainly. Only I didn't want to mention your name."

"Having cousins in government, I hear a lot of that kind of talk. If you ever become part of the establishment, I expect it will all make sense."

"Then I'm glad I have a place at Edinburgh to study medicine." He took a drink. "Of course the locksmiths came. My key to the lab doesn't work now."

"Then you'll have to come out more, in the fresh air on your bicycle. It'll do you good."

"And what about justice for Mr Moffatt?"

"There'll be justice. Keep an eye on the newspapers. Before too long there will be a report of a trial of a certain person for the murder of at least one theatre performer and the attempted murder of a theatre dresser. I don't believe we will ever see a whiff of suspicion attaching to Mr Moffatt's death, but if those other charges are proven, he will have a quiet justice."

"There's a moral to this story, Mrs Shackleton."

"Do tell."

"A chap should only ever smoke a pipe and be in charge of his own tobacco."

We talked for an hour or so before Harriet and Mrs Sugden returned, bearing leftovers from the garden party which were demolished in no time.

That was when we decided to go see Buster Keaton in *The General*. Instead of cycling back, Alex would come with us, and afterwards take himself and his bicycle on the train back to Giggleswick.

We sat in the darkness of the Hyde Park Picture House, watching the action packed adventure. Buster Keaton as Johnnie Gray, railway engineer, pursued his train, "The General", stolen by the Yankee army. His movements, his actions, those eyes of his, told us all we needed to know. His sweetheart's expression, her moments of peril and her courage spoke volumes, without the need to hear her voice.

When captions appeared, a child on the row behind read them to her granny. Across the picture house, whispers from fluent readers mingled with the sound of piano music.

We all laughed at Buster Keaton's antics and willed him to succeed, which of course he did.

When we came out into the light, we felt so lifted and in good humour.

"Who won that war between the north and south in America?" Harriet asked.

Alex was about to answer, but Mrs Sugden jumped in first. "Isn't that obvious? It was Buster Keaton."

We discussed the promised arrival of pictures where actors might talk. It would help the people in the audience who couldn't read, but what about those who were hard of hearing? Perhaps Charlie Chaplin was right and it would not catch on.

Alex said, "If life wasn't laid out for me to be a doctor, I'd like to drive a train. That was my first ambition."

Harriet disagreed. "Trains are too noisy, and there's too much smoke."

The pavement was crowded with people leaving the picture house. Harriet and Alex drew ahead of us. "What will you be then, Harriet, if you don't want to drive a train?"

Harriet was quick to answer. "Well, I'd like a job in a picture house. And in my spare time I'll be a detective, like my auntie."

The Eclipse Cocktail

Harry Craddock, famous barman at the Savoy Hotel, created a special cocktail to serve at celebratory events surrounding the eclipse. Grenadine creates the background of burnished sky. Gin and lemon provide a corona of light surrounding the olive that stands in for the sun.
Here is the Kate Shackleton version.

Ingredients
Grenadine
2 measures of sloe gin
1 measure of dry gin
Olive
1 measure of lemon juice, finely strained
Finely grated orange peel

Method
Place the olive in the bottom of the cocktail glass
Cover the olive with grenadine
Pour sloe gin and dry gin into cocktail shaker and
  blend
Slowly and carefully, using the back of a spoon,
  add blended gin to the grenadine

Slowly and carefully, using the back of a spoon,
add lemon juice
Lightly garnish with orange peel

Acknowledgments

The 1927 total eclipse of the sun caught the imagination of public and press and drew hundreds of thousands of people to viewing points across the line of totality. Sir Frank Dyson, Astronomer Royal, set up his observation point in the grounds of Giggleswick School Chapel. There were other observation points, but this was the lucky one. I am grateful to Barbara Gent, keeper of the archives at Giggleswick School, for being so generous with her time, for the guided tours and for letting me see the two scrapbooks created by Thomas Brayshaw. He collected cuttings, photographs, letters and memorabilia. Endearingly, he added a note saying that had he known how much interest there would be, he would have used better quality scrapbooks.

R. A. Marriott gives a detailed and fascinating account of the planning, importance and social background to the eclipse in *1927: A British Eclipse, Journal of the British Astronomical Association Vol. 109 No 3* pp 117–143, 06/1999. His article is available as a pamphlet from The British Astronomical Association.

The fabulous City Varieties Music Hall, Leeds, built in 1865, has survived changes of taste and fashion. I have enjoyed many shows there, and the backstage tour. Thanks to Catherine White for providing information about the building. As far as we know, "The Verts" did not have a staffed stage door, but Leeds Grand Theatre did. As a Winstanley Babe in pantomime at the Grand, I knew that old stage door entrance well. For the purpose of this story, it is transplanted to the Varieties.

Tales of tunnels, and evidence of them, have long been part of the city's story. To those who call mythical the tale of a tunnel between the City Varieties and the old Empire Palace Theatre, here's a quote from *The Man Who Shot Liberty Valance*: "When the legend becomes fact, print the legend."

As well as Peter Riley's and Andrew Loudon's histories of the Varieties, it was a pleasure to read John Major's *My Old Man*, a personal history of music hall. In his *Popular Music in England 1840–1914*, Dave Russell gives a highly readable social history of music hall.

For his patience and assistance with several unfortunate deaths that befall characters in the Kate Shackleton novels, thanks to Barry Strickland-Hodge, Leeds University Visiting Professor of Prescribing Practice.

Thank you to Sandy Sechrest for her bid in the Bouchercon Charity Auction to have a character named after her.

Lynne Strutt found the reference to the Eclipse Cocktail on the website Cocktail 101. Cheers to Viv Cutbill, Sylvia Gill, Michelle Hughes and Patricia McNeil for their assistance in re-creating and sampling the Eclipse Cocktail, and for much else.

Once again, thanks to my agent Judith Murdoch and to Dominic Wakeford and the team at Piatkus.

INSPECTOR FRENCH AND THE BOX OFFICE MURDERS

Freeman Wills Crofts

The suicide of a sales clerk at the box office of a London cinema leaves another girl in fear for her life. Persuaded to seek help from Scotland Yard, Miss Darke confides in Inspector Joseph French about a gambling scam by a mysterious trio of crooks, adding that she believes her friend was murdered. When she fails to turn up the next day, and the police later find her body, French's inquiries reveal that similar girls have also been murdered, all linked by their jobs and by a sinister stranger with a purple scar . . .

A CAST OF VULTURES

Judith Flanders

Usually sharp-witted editor Sam Clair stumbles through her post-launch-party morning with the hangover to end all hangovers. Before the Nurofen has even kicked in, she finds herself entangled in an elaborate saga of missing neighbours, suspected arson and the odd unidentified body. When the grisly news breaks that the fire has claimed a victim, Sam is already in pursuit. Never has comedy been so deadly as Sam faces down a pair from Thugs "R" Us, aided by nothing more than a CID boyfriend, a stalwart Goth assistant and a seemingly endless supply of purple-sprouting broccoli.

THE CIRCUS TRAIN CONSPIRACY

Edward Marston

1860: Following a string of successful performances, the Moscardi Circus is travelling by train to Newcastle for their next show. Amongst the usual railway hubbub, the animals have been loaded, the clowns — now incognito — are aboard, and Mauro Moscardi himself is comfortable in a first-class compartment with a cigar. Yet a collision on the track with a couple of sleepers causes pandemonium: passengers are thrown about, animals escape into the night, and the future of the circus looks uncertain. When the body of a woman is discovered in woodland next to the derailment, Inspector Colbeck is despatched to lend assistance, believing the two incidents might be connected. It is up to Colbeck to put the pieces together to discover the identity of the nameless woman and unmask who is targeting Moscardi's Magnificent Circus.

THE BOWNESS BEQUEST

Rebecca Tope

Winter has arrived in the town of Windermere, and has brought with it the death of Frances Henderson, the best friend of Simmy Brown's mother. Having known the Hendersons all of her life, Simmy must cope with the loss of an important figure from her childhood — as well as surprise at being bequeathed something in Frances's will. Then, when Frances's husband Kit is violently murdered in his home, Simmy must face the fact that this family she was once so close to as a child holds some dark and sinister secrets. How will Simmy react to seeing their son Christopher, her childhood sweetheart, after so long — and could the rumours of Kit's infidelity provide a clue as to who killed him?